"Every man's black inside. You don't believe it, but that's right. It's midnight inside every man any hour of God's day. But a man can make light out of night, and that's why what come out of a man into a woman be white. Natural got nothin to do with color. Now you close your eyes, honey, because you be tired. Don't you fight! Mama Delorme ain't goan put nothing over on you, chile! Just got sumpin I goan to put in your hand. Now—no, don't look, just close your hand over it." I did what she said and felt something square. Felt like glass or plastic.

"You gonna remember everythin when it be time for you t'think on em. Now go to sleep. Shhh . . . go to sleep . . . shhh . . ."

And that's just what I did. Next thing I remember, I was running down those stairs like the devil was after me. I didn't remember what I was running from, but that didn't make no difference; I ran anyway.

# STEPHEN KING
# DAN SIMMONS
# GEORGE R.R. MARTIN

# Dark Visions

### EDITED BY DOUGLAS E. WINTER

**All original stories**

GOLLANCZ HORROR

First published in Great Britain 1989
by Victor Gollancz Ltd
14 Henrietta Street, London WC2E 8QJ

Published in Gollancz Paperbacks July 1990
Second impression October 1991

*British Library Cataloguing in Publication Data*
King, Stephen, *1947-*
Dark visions
1. Horror stories in English. American writers,
1945-
—Anthologies
I. Title   II. Simmons, Dan
III. Martin, George R.R., *1948–*
823'.01'0816[ES]

ISBN 0-575-04711-9

Printed and bound in Great Britain
by Cox & Wyman Ltd, Reading

# Contents

# INTRODUCTION

²**horror** adj: calculated to inspire feelings of dread or horror: BLOODCURDLING [a—story].
> —Webster's New Collegiate Dictionary

In the beginning was the word.

Stories were not written. They were spoken, told, sung, enacted in movement and dance, rendered in rough-hewn sculpture, sketched in sand, stained into the walls of caves. Their subject was remarkably consistent: "In every study of the human individual and human society," writes anthropologist Yi-Fu Tuan, "fear is a theme." Fear, always fear: of the dark, of drought, of disease, of disaster, of death—and of demons, real and imagined, lurking outside and within. Stories were told to exorcise these fears, to caution others of their dangers . . . and sometimes, simply to instill them.

The written word, when it came—around the time of *Gilgamesh*, some four thousand years ago—brought a new dimension to the concept of story: for the first time, the tale could live beyond its teller, surviving intact over great distances . . . and time. The succeeding centuries witnessed an impressive accumulation of stories of fear— in epic poems, sagas and legends, testaments both Old and New, song-cycles, Elizabethan and Jacobean drama, the prose romance—but only the methods of storytelling had changed, not its relentless subject.

There is little historical precedent for labelling stories of fear as a *kind* of fiction until the 1700s. It was then that the modern novel emerged, made popular by what literary history calls the "Gothic." We remember but a handful of its early voices—Beckford, Lewis, Maturin, Radcliffe, Walpole—but the Gothic was the first written entertainment for the middle class, and thus the first true form of popular fiction. Its legacy has sent academics spinning ever since in an effort to explain and make legitimate a fiction whose intent—and, indeed, singular moral function—was to provoke unease.

The Gothic flame burned bright into the early Nineteenth Century. The great romantics—Blake, Byron, Coleridge, Keats, the Shelleys—fell beneath its influence, then influenced in turn the future of fictional fear through a triumvirate of symbolic characters: the vampire, the wanderer, the seeker of forbidden knowledge.

Across the Atlantic, Charles Brockden Brown fathered American literature by daring to write tales of terror in an age when writing for the sake of "mere" entertainment was considered immoral. His better-known heirs—Hawthorne, Melville, and Poe—created the most memorable fiction of the mid-1800s, weaving mystery and imagination in a tapestry stained scarlet with Puritan guilt. And they worked not only at novel length, but in a new form: the short story.

In America, it was Poe; in England, Joseph Sheridan Le Fanu. Writing about (what else?) fear, they created the modern short story. By the close of the Nineteenth

Century, the talented (and supernaturally inclined) hands of Dickens, Hardy, James, and Kipling had rendered the short story into a major literary form—much to the delight of a new and ever-increasing working-class readership, whose first exposure to written fiction came in "penny dreadfuls" and "shilling shockers." These were halcyon years for the fiction of fear—consider but a few of the writers at work in the 1890s: Bierce, Blackwood, the brothers Benson, Conrad, Chambers, Doyle, Haggard, Hodgson, Jacobs, Henry James, M. R. James, Machen, Stevenson, Stoker, Wells, Wilde.

The Great War no doubt dampened the lure of the supernatural; in its wake, it seemed that ghosts no longer walked, but rested with the millions dead. The fiction of fear virtually disappeared but for the occasional dilettante like de la Mare; when it returned in full force in the "weird tales" of Lovecraft and his generation, it offered a vision of the universe as not merely malign but indifferent. With the advent of the motion picture, the word had succumbed to image, and would survive for decades principally in the pages of cheap pulp magazines.

The film studios of Universal and RKO, Toho and Hammer championed the "monster" as the reigning icon of the tale of terror throughout the middle years of the Twentieth Century. And a new kind of monster emerged from the Second World War: Writers like Barden, Bloch, and Thompson—as well as the legendary E. C. Comics—linked the aesthetics of crime fiction with those of the supernatural, creating the tale of unreason or "psychological horror." The symbolic night creatures were giving way to more literal evils, and the 1960s saw

society embrace the potential reality of the darkly supernatural in ways that earlier (and more God-fearing)
generations had not. Writers began to confront tra-
ditional religious systems and beliefs, sparking a surge
in so-called "occult" fiction that saw both Ira Levin and
William Peter Blatty top the bestseller lists.

Then came Stephen King. Like Dickens one hundred
years before, King is a populist, the ideal spokesman for
a democratic art of darkness; his fiction spearheaded an
enthusiasm for the reading and writing of stories of fear
unmatched since the late Nineteenth Century. He has
become the most popular writer in the English language
today, with a predicted 100 million books in print by the
close of this decade. His success is often described as a
"phenomenon," and his ever-increasing sales are
reported with a kind of wide-eyed wonder that nears
disbelief (and occasionally derision), as if his storytelling
were a quirk, a curio, rather than simply the most recent
installment in a literary history that has been shaped and
guided by the tale of terror.

The reaction is particularly bemusing because King
himself is the first to remind his readers that he is
working within a long and honorable tradition. His first
story here, "The Reploids," is an apt example. It is a
virtual pastiche of the ironic, science fictional horror of
the 1950s, a "reploid" of the kind of short story that
King loved to read in his youth. Both its premise and
Hollywood setting signal an homage to Jack Finney,
whose fiction—especially the novels *The Body Snatchers*
and *The Woodrow Wilson Dime*—must be counted among
King's major influences.

"Sneakers," which follows, is more uniquely King, an

unsettling and yet nervously humorous ghost story set in the recording industry. At its heart is our instinctive (and, as King recognizes, no doubt homophobic) distrust of public lavatories; and it is another of King's carefree assaults on the barriers of manners and good taste. (Indeed, "Sneakers" may have been prompted by a conversation about my anthology *Prime Evil*, in which I mentioned the dearth of original stories about haunted houses. "Oh yeah?" King replied. "What about a haunted *shit*house?")

King's final contribution is the novelette "Dedication," which melds his enthusiasm for outrage with his penchant for the ironic. A tale of witchcraft centered on the bizarre relationship between a black hotel maid and the tormented white novelist whose suite she cleans, it was not well met with editors. The reader is thus forewarned: "Dedication" is perhaps Stephen King's least palatable story, and it is certain to prove one of his most controversial works of fiction.

Dan Simmons captured the 1986 World Fantasy Award with his first novel, *The Song of Kali*, a tapestry of real and imaginary terrors set in contemporary Calcutta. The honor helped establish him as one of the handful of major new writers of horror fiction to emerge in the 1980s. Like Clive Barker, with whom he is inevitably compared, he was first a writer of short stories—and, indeed, saw his first publication as a winner of the *Twilight Zone* short story competition. The three Simmons stories here confirm the substantial range of his ambition and craft.

"Metastasis" is as much homage as King's "The Reploids." The story of a man tormented by delusional visions and a messianic impulse, it seems haunted by the specter of Philip K. Dick. Yet "Metastasis" could only have been written by Dan Simmons, its harrowing subject matter cloaked in a narrative style that moves from matter-of-fact reportage to an intense subjectivity with compelling ease. Here, as in *The Song of Kali*, the reader is overcome by the sheer audacity of Simmons's prose—and his obsessively unblinking eye, which does not hesitate to thrust the view into extreme and explicit closeup.

Nevertheless, as demonstrated by the comic relief of his second story, "Vanni Fucci Is Alive and Well and Living in Hell," vivid imagery is not all that Simmons has to offer. This hardbiting satire moves one step beyond *Mad* magazine's "Scenes We'd Like to See" feature to offer a wishful dark fantasy for the television ministries of Jerry Falwell, Oral Roberts, and other heaven-bent hucksters.

In his closing novelette, "Iverson's Pits," we are treated to yet another side of Dan Simmons: the historian. In a story that spans more than one hundred years of Americana, set at one of history's bloodiest playgrounds, Gettysburg, Simmons melds the real horrors of Civil War battlefields with supernatural horrors of a restless and unburied dead. It is a fiction that reminds us that all historians are, at heart, tellers of the tales of terror; for the past is a ghost which haunts each of our daily lives.

★

George R. R. Martin closes this volume with a short novel, "The Skin Trade." Although first (and still) published in the arena of fantasy and science fiction, Martin is known to readers of horror fiction for his novels *Fevre Dream* and *The Armageddon Rag*, and occasional short stories such as those collected in *Songs the Dead Men Sing*. He has served as scriptwriter for the brief revival of the *Twilight Zone* television series and currently is executive story consultant for the CBS-TV series *Beauty and the Beast*.

Those familiar with Martin's roots in science fiction will not be surprised by the rationalist veneer of his forays into the supernatural, or by his enthusiasm for the alien; but they may be taken with his undeniably humanist impulse. Martin's characters are nervously alive, and their stories are spirited with movement and a page-turning sense of adventure—indeed, his fiction is among the least introspective in contemporary horror. And it is also among the most diverse: he is an unmitigated world-builder, his stories rich with history and a striking sense of place.

His entry here, "The Skin Trade," mingles the hard-boiled fiction of private detectives with the lore of lycanthropy; and it features one of the most unlikely, and yet convincing, werewolves in recent memory. In a landscape worthy of Chandler or Hammett, with its rain-swept streets and rundown office buildings, automats and gothic mansions, blood-haunted stockyards and hunters' woods, Martin depicts a cat-and-mouse game whose stakes are violent death and whose players are werewolves and men . . . and other things.

\*

Three writers. Seven stories. A single theme.

Our title calls them night visions. The cover copy will no doubt offer a smattering of the usual catchwords—tales of terror, dark fantasy, supernatural horror—labels designed for mass consumption, labels as self-limiting as "mystery" or "romance" or "science fiction." In another time, another place, these stories might have been called Gothic, Schauer-Romantik, the stuff of shudder pulps . . .

But Stephen King, Dan Simmons, and George R. R. Martin are writers first; they write a *kind* of fiction only because the publishers and booksellers tell us so. Those who know the history of our literature know that the stories these writers tell have been with us from the very beginning . . . and that they will be with us until the end. As essayist F. Gonzalez-Crussi reminds us: "There are only two themes worth writing or reading about, love and death, *eros* and *thanatos*. And if the pressures of our time, sloth, or inertia, should force us to be compendious, we could do with one theme only . . ."

In a word: Horror.

Douglas E. Winter
Alexandria, Virginia
February 1988

14

# STEPHEN KING

# THE REPLOIDS

No one knew exactly how long it had been going on. Not long. Two days, two weeks; it couldn't have been much longer than that, Cheyney reasoned. Not that it mattered. It was just that people got to watch a little more of the show with the added thrill of knowing the show was real. When the United States—the whole world—found out about the Reploids, it was pretty spectacular. Just as well, maybe. These days, unless it's spectacular, a thing can go on damned near forever. It is neither believed nor disbelieved. It is simply part of the weird Godhead mantra that made up the accelerating flow of events and experience as the century neared its end. It's harder to get peoples' attention. It takes machine-guns in a crowded airport or a live grenade rolled up the aisle of a bus load of nuns stopped at a roadblock in some Central American country overgrown with guns and greenery. The Reploids became national—and international—news on the morning of November 30, 1989, after what happened during the first two chaotic minutes of the *Tonight Show* taping in Beautiful Downtown Burbank, California, the night before.

*

The floor manager watched intently as the red sweep secondhand moved upward toward the twelve. The studio audience clockwatched as intently as the floor manager. When the red sweep second-hand crossed the twelve, it would be five o'clock and taping of the umpty-umptieth *Tonight Show* would commence.

As the red second-hand passed the eight, the audience stirred and muttered with its own peculiar sort of stage fright. After all, they represented *America*, didn't they? Yes!

"Let's have it quiet, people, please," the floor manager said pleasantly, and the audience quieted like obedient children. Doc Severinsen's drummer ran off a fast little riff on his snare and then held his sticks easily between thumbs and fingers, wrists loose, watching the floor manager instead of the clock, as the show-people always did. For crew and performers, the floor manager *was* the clock. When the second-hand passed the ten, the floor manager counted down aloud to *four*, and then held up three fingers, two fingers, one finger . . . and then a clenched fist from which one finger pointed dramatically at the audience. An APPLAUSE sign lit up, but the studio audience was primed to whoop it up; it would have made no difference if it had been written in Sanskrit.

So things started off just as they were supposed to start off: dead on time. This was not so surprising; there were crew members on the *Tonight Show* who, had they been LAPD officers, could have retired with full benefits. The Doc Severinsen band, one of the best show-bands in the world, launched into the familiar theme: *Ta-da-da-Da-da* . . . and the large, rolling voice of Ed

McMahon cried enthusiastically: "From Los Angeles, entertainment capital of the world, it's *The Tonight Show*, live, with Johnny Carson! Tonight, Johnny's guests are actress Cybill Shepherd of *Moonlighting!*" Excited applause from the audience. "Magician Doug Henning!" Even louder applause from the audience. "Pee Wee Herman!" A fresh wave of applause, this time including hoots of joy from Pee Wee's rooting section. "From Germany, the Flying Schnauzers, the world's only canine acrobats!" Increased applause, with a mixture of laughter from the audience. "Not to mention Doc Severinsen, the world's only Flying Bandleader, and his canine band!"

The band members not playing horns obediently barked. The audience laughed harder, applauded harder.

In the control room of Studio C, no one was laughing.

A man in a loud sport-coat with a shock of curly black hair was standing in the wings, idly snapping his fingers and looking across the stage at Ed, but that was all.

The director signaled for Number Two Cam's medium shot on Ed for the umpty-umptieth time, and there was Ed on the ON SCREEN monitors. He barely heard someone mutter, "Where the hell *is* he?" before Ed's rolling tones announced, *also* for the umpty-umptieth time: "And now *heeeere's* JOHNNY!"

Wild applause from the audience.

"Camera Three," the director snapped.

"But there's only that—"

"Camera *Three*, goddammit!"

Camera Three came up on the ON SCREEN monitor, showing every TV director's private nightmare, a dismally empty stage . . . and then someone, some stranger, was striding confidently *into* that empty space, just as if he had every right in the world to be there, filling it with unquestionable presence, charm, and authority. But, whoever he was, he was most definitely *not* Johnny Carson. Nor was it any of the other familiar faces TV and studio audiences had grown used to during Johnny's absences. This man was taller than Johnny, and instead of the familiar silver hair, there was a luxuriant cap of almost Pan-like black curls. The stranger's hair was so black that in places it seemed to glow almost blue, like Superman's hair in the comic-books. The sport-coat he wore was not quite loud enough to put him in the Pleesda-Meetcha-Is-This-The-Missus? car salesman category, but Carson would not have touched it with a twelve-foot pole.

The audience applause continued, but it first seemed to grow slightly bewildered, and then clearly began to thin.

"What the fuck's going on?" someone in the control room asked. The director simply watched, mesmerized.

Instead of the familiar swing of the invisible golf-club, punctuated by a drum-riff and high-spirited hoots of approval from the studio audience, this dark-haired, broad-shouldered, loud-jacketed, unknown gentleman began to move his hands up and down, eyes flicking rhythmically from his moving palms to a spot just above his head—he was miming a juggler with a lot of fragile items in the air, and doing it with the easy grace of the long-time showman. It was only something in his face, something as subtle as a shadow, that told you the objects were eggs or something, and would break if dropped. It was, in fact, very like the way Johnny's eyes followed the invisible ball down the invisible fairway, registering one that had been righteously stroked . . . unless, of course, he chose to vary the act, which he could and did do from time to time, and without even breathing hard.

He made a business of dropping the last egg, or whatever the fragile object was, and his eyes followed it to the floor with exaggerated dismay. Then, for a moment, he froze. Then he glanced toward Cam Three Left . . . toward Doc and the orchestra, in other words.

After repeated viewings of the videotape, Dave Cheyney came to what seemed to him to be an irrefutable conclusion, although many of his colleagues—including his partner—questioned it.

"He was waiting for a sting," Cheyney said. "Look, you can see it on his face. It's as old as burlesque."

His partner, Pete Jacoby, said, "I thought burlesque was where the *girl* with the heroin habit took off her clothes while the *guy* with the heroin habit played the trumpet."

Cheyney gestured at him impatiently. "Think of the lady that used to play the piano in the silent movies, then. Or the one that used to do schmaltz on the organ during the radio soaps."

Jacoby looked at him, wide-eyed. "Did they have those things when you were a kid, daddy?" he asked in a falsetto voice.

"Will you for once be serious?" Cheyney asked him. "Because this is a serious thing we got here, I think."

"What we got here is very simple. We got a nut."

"No," Cheyney said, and hit rewind on the VCR again with one hand while he lit a fresh cigarette with the other. "What we got is a seasoned performer who's mad

21

as hell because the guy on the snare dropped his cue."
He paused thoughtfully and added: "Christ, *Johnny* does
it all the time. And if the guy who was supposed to lay
in the sting dropped his cue, I think he'd look the same
way."

By then it didn't matter. The stranger who wasn't
Johnny Carson had time to recover, to look at a flabber-
gasted Ed McMahon and say, "The moon must be full
tonight, Ed—do you think—" And that was when the
NBC security guards came out and grabbed him.

"Hey! What the fuck do you think you're—"

But by then they had dragged him away.

In the control room of Studio C, there was total
silence. The audience monitors picked up the same
silence. Camera Four was swung toward the audience,
and showed a picture of one hundred and fifty stunned,
silent faces. Camera Two, the one medium-close on Ed
McMahon, showed a man who looked almost cosmically
befuddled.

The director took a package of Winstons from his
breast pocket, took one out, put it in his mouth, took it
out again and reversed it so the filter was facing away
from him, and abruptly bit the cigarette in two. He
threw the filtered half in one direction and spat the
unfiltered half in another.

"Get up a show from the library with Rickles," he
said. "No Joan Rivers. And if I see Totie Fields,
someone's going to get fired." Then he strode away,
head down. He shoved a chair with such violence on his

way out of the control room that it struck the wall, rebounded, nearly fractured the skull of a white-faced intern from USC, and fell on its side.

One of the PA's told the intern in a low voice, "Don't worry; that's just Fred's way of committing honorable *seppuku*."


The man who was not Johnny Carson was taken, bellowing loudly not about his *lawyer* but his *team* of lawyers, to the Burbank Police Station. In Burbank, as in Beverly Hills and Hollywood Heights, there is a wing of the police station which is known simply as "special security functions." This may cover many aspects of the sometimes crazed world of Tinsel-Town law enforcement. The cops don't like it, the cops don't respect it . . . but they ride with it. You don't shit where you eat. Rule One.

"Special security functions" might be the place to which a coke-snorting movie-star whose last picture grossed seventy million dollars might be conveyed; the place to which the battered wife of an extremely powerful film producer might be taken; it was the place to which the man with the dark crop of curls was taken.

The man who showed up in Johnny Carson's place on the stage of Studio C on the afternoon of November 29th identified himsef as Ed Paladin, speaking the name with the air of one who expects everyone who hears it to fall on his or her knees and, perhaps, genuflect. His California driver's license, Blue Cross-Blue Shield card, Amex and Diners' Club cards, also identified him as Edward Paladin.

His trip from Studio C ended, at least temporarily, in a room in the Burbank PD's "special security" area. The room was panelled with tough plastic that almost *did* look like mahogany and furnished with a low, round couch and tasteful chairs. There was a cigarette box on the glass-topped coffee table filled with Dunhills, and the magazines included *Fortune* and *Variety* and *Vogue* and *Billboard* and *GQ*. The wall-to-wall carpet wasn't really ankle-deep but looked it, and there was a Cable-View guide on top of the large-screen TV. There was a bar (now locked), and a very nice neo-Jackson Pollock painting on one of the walls. The walls, however, were of drilled cork, and the mirror above the bar was a little bit too large and a little bit too shiny to be anything but a piece of one-way glass.

The man who called himself Ed Paladin stuck his hands in his just-too-loud sport-coat pockets, looked around disgustedly, and said: "An interrogation room by any other name is still an interrogation room."

Detective 1st Grade Richard Cheyney looked at him calmly for a moment. When he spoke, it was in the soft and polite voice that had earned him the only half-kidding nickname "Detective to the Stars." Part of the reason he spoke this way was because he genuinely liked and respected show people. Part of the reason was because he didn't trust them. Half the time they were lying they didn't know it.

"Could you tell us, please, Mr Paladin, how you got on the set of *The Tonight Show*, and where Johnny Carson is?"

"Who's Johnny Carson?"

Pete Jacoby—who wanted to be Henny Youngman when he grew up, Cheyney often thought—gave Cheyney a momentary dry look every bit as good as a Jack Benny deadpan. Then he looked back at Edward Paladin and said, "Johnny Carson's the guy who used to be Mr Ed. You know, the talking horse? I mean, a lot of people know about Mr Ed, the famous talking horse, but an awful lot of people don't know that he went to Geneva to have a species-change operation and when he came back he was—"

Cheyney often allowed Jacoby his routines (there was really no other word for them, and Cheyney remembered one occasion when Jacoby had gotten a man charged with beating his wife and infant son to death laughing so hard that tears of mirth rather than remorse were rolling down his cheeks as he signed the confession that was going to put the bastard in jail for the rest of his life), but he wasn't going to tonight. He didn't have to *see* the flame under his ass; he could feel it, and it was being turned up. Pete was maybe a little slow on the uptake about some things, and maybe that was why he wasn't going to make Detective 1st for another two or three years . . . if he ever did.

Some ten years ago a really awful thing had happened in a little nothing town called Chowchilla. Two people (they had walked on two legs, anyway, if you could believe the newsfilm) had hijacked a busload of kids, buried them alive, and then had demanded a huge sum of money. Otherwise, they said, those kiddies could just stay where they were and swap baseball trading cards until their air ran out. That one had ended happily, but it could have been a nightmare. And God knew Johnny Carson was no busload of schoolkids, but the case had the same kind of fruitcake appeal: here was that rare event about which both the *Los Angeles Times-Mirror* and *The National Enquirer* would hobnob on their front pages. What Pete didn't understand was that something extremely rare had happened to them: in the world of day-to-day police work, a world where almost everything came in shades of gray, they had suddenly been placed in a situation of stark and simple contrasts: produce within twenty-four hours, thirty-six at the outside, or watch the Feds come in . . . and kiss your ass goodbye.

Things happened so rapidly that even later he wasn't completely sure, but he believed both of them had been going on the unspoken presumption, even then, that Carson had been kidnapped and this guy was part of it.

"We're going to do it by the numbers, Mr Paladin," Cheyney said, and although he was speaking to the man glaring up at him from one of the chairs (he had refused the sofa at once), his eyes flicked briefly to Pete. They had been partners for nearly twelve years, and a glance was all it took.

*No more Comedy Store routines, Pete.*

*Message received.*

"First comes the Miranda Warning," Cheyney said pleasantly. "I am required to inform you that you are in the custody of the Burbank City Police. Although not required to do so immediately, I'll add that a preliminary charge of trespassing—"

"*Trespassing!*" An angry flush burst over Paladin's face.

"—on property both owned and leased by the National

Broadcasting Company has been lodged against you. I am Detective 1st Grade Richard Cheyney. This man with me is my partner, Detective 2nd Grade Peter Jacoby. We'd like to interview you."

"Fucking interrogate me is what you mean."

"I only have one question, as far as interrogation goes," Cheyney said. "Otherwise, I only want to interview you at this time. In other words, I have one question relevant to the charge which has been lodged; the rest deal with other matters."

"Well, what's the fucking question?"

"That wouldn't be going by the numbers," Jacoby said.

Cheyney said: "I am required to tell you that you have the right—"

"To have my lawyer here, you bet," Paladin said. "And I just decided that before I answer a single fucking question, and that includes where I went to lunch today and what I had, he's going to be in here. Albert K. Dellums."

He spoke this name as if it should rock both detectives back on their heels, but Cheyney had never heard of it and could tell by Pete's expression that he hadn't either.

Whatever sort of crazy this Ed Paladin might turn out to be, he was no dullard. He saw the quick glances which passed between the two detectives and read them easily. *You know him?* Cheyney's eyes asked Jacoby's, and Jacoby's replied, *Never heard of him in my life*.

For the first time an expression of perplexity—it was not fear, not yet—crossed Mr Edward Paladin's face.

"Al *Dellums*," he said, raising his voice like some Americans overseas who seem to believe they can make the waiter understand if they only speak loudly enough and slowly enough. "Al Dellums of Dellums, Carthage, Stoneham, and Tayloe. I guess I shouldn't be all that surprised that you haven't heard of him. He's only one of the most important, well-known lawyers in the country." Paladin shot the left cuff of his just-slightly-too-loud sport-coat and glanced at his watch. "If you reach him at home, gentlemen, he'll be pissed. If you have to call his club—and I think this is his club-night—he's going to be pissed like a *bear*."

Cheyney was not impressed by bluster. If you could sell it at a quarter a pound, he never would have had to turn his hand at another day's work. But even a quick peek had been enough to show him that the watch Paladin was wearing was not just a Rolex but a Rolex Midnight Star. It might be an imitation, of course, but his gut told him it was genuine. Part of it was his clear impression that Paladin wasn't trying to *make* an impression—he'd wanted to see what time it was, no more or less than that. And if the watch was the McCoy . . . well, there were cabin-cruisers you could buy for less. What was a man who could afford a Rolex Midnight Star doing mixed up in something weird like this?

Now *he* was the one who must have been showing perplexity clear enough for Paladin to read it, because the man smiled—a humorless skinning-back of the lips from the capped teeth. "The air-conditioning in here's pretty nice," he said, crossing his legs and flicking the crease absently. "You guys want to enjoy it while you can. It's pretty muggy walking a beat out in Watts, even this time of year."

In a harsh and abrupt tone utterly unlike his bright

pitter-patter Comedy Store voice, Jacoby said: "Shut your mouth, jag-off."

Paladin jerked around and stared at him, eyes wide. And again Cheyney would have sworn it had been years since anyone had spoken to this man in that way. Years since anyone would have *dared*.

"What did you say?"

"I said shut your mouth when Detective Cheyney is talking to you. Give me your lawyer's number. I'll see that he is called. In the meantime, I think you need to take a few seconds to pull your head out of your ass and look around and see exactly where you are and exactly how serious the trouble is that you are in. I think you need to reflect on the fact that, while only one charge has been lodged against you, you could be facing enough to put you in the slam well into the next century . . . and you could be facing them before the sun comes up tomorrow morning."

Jacoby smiled. It wasn't his howaya-folks-anyone-here-from-Duluth Comedy Store smile, either. Like Paladin's, it was a brief pull of the lips, no more.

"You're right—the air-conditioning in here isn't half-bad. Also, the TV works and for a wonder the people on it don't look like they're seasick. The coffee's good—perked, not instant. Now, if you want to make another two or three wisecracks, you can wait for your legal talent in a holding cell on the fifth floor. On Five, the only entertainment consists of kids crying for their mommies and winos puking on their sneakers. I don't know who you *think* you are and I don't care, because as far as I'm concerned, you're nobody. I never saw you before in my life, never heard of you before in my life, and if you push me enough I'll widen the crack in your ass for you."

"That's enough," Cheyney said quietly.

"I'll retool it so you could drive a Ryder van up there, *Mister* Paladin—you understand me? Can you grok that?"

Now Paladin's eyes were all but hanging from their sockets on stalks. His mouth was open. Then, without speaking, he removed his wallet from his coat pocket (*some kind of lizard-skin*, Cheyney thought, *two months' salary . . . maybe three*). He found his lawyer's card (the home number was jotted on the back, Cheyney noted—it was most definitely not part of the printed matter on the front) and handed it to Jacoby. His fingers now showed the first observable tremor.

"Pete?"

Jacoby looked at him and Cheyney saw it was no act; Paladin had actually succeeded in pissing his easy-going partner off. No mean feat.

"Make the call yourself."

"Okay." Jacoby left.

Cheyney looked at Paladin and was suddenly amazed to find himself feeling sorry for the man. Before he had looked perplexed; now he looked both stunned and frightened, like a man who wakes from a nightmare only to discover the nightmare is still going on.

"Watch closely," Cheyney said after the door had closed, "and I'll show you one of the mysteries of the West. West LA, that is."

He moved the neo-Pollock and revealed not a safe but a toggle switch. He flicked it, then let the painting slide back into place.

"That's one-way glass," Cheyney said, cocking a thumb at the too-large mirror over the bar.

"I am not terribly surprised to hear that," Paladin said, and Cheyney reflected that, while the man might have some of the shitty egocentric habits of the Veddy Rich and Well-Known in LA, he was also a near-superb actor: only a man as experienced as he was himself could have told how really close Paladin was to the ragged edge of tears.

But not of guilt, that was what was so puzzling, so goddamn—*maddening*.

Of *perplexity*.

He felt that absurd sense of sorrow again, absurd because it presupposed the man's innocence: he did not want to be Edward Paladin's nightmare, did not want to be the heavy in a Kafka novel where suddenly nobody knows where they are, or why they are there.

"I can't do anything about the glass," Cheyney said. He came back and sat down across the coffee table from Paladin, "but I've just killed the sound. So it's you talking to me and vice-versa." He took a pack of Kents from his breast pocket, stuck one in the corner of his mouth, then offered the pack to Paladin. "Smoke?"

Paladin picked up the pack, looked it over, and smiled. "Even my old brand. I haven't smoked one since the night Yul Brynner died, Mr Cheyney. I don't think I want to start again now."

Cheyney put the pack back into his pocket. "Can we talk?" he asked.

Paladin rolled his eyes. "Oh my God, it's Joan Raiford."

"*Who?*"

"Joan Raiford. You know, "I took Elizabeth Taylor to Marine World and when she saw Shamu the Whale she asked me if it came with vegetables?" I repeat, Detective Cheyney: grow up. I have no reason in the world to believe that switch is anything but a dummy. My God, how innocent do you think I am?"

*Joan* Raiford? *Is that what he really said?* *Joan* Raiford?

"What's the matter?" Paladin asked pleasantly. He crossed his legs the other way. "Did you perhaps think you saw a clear path? Me breaking down, maybe saying I'd tell everything, everything, just don't let 'em fry me, copper?"

With all the force of personality he could muster, Cheyney said: "I believe things are very wrong here, Mr Paladin. You've got them wrong and I've got them wrong. When your lawyer gets here, maybe we can sort them out and maybe we can't. Most likely we can't. So listen to me, and for God's sake use your brain. I gave you the Miranda Warning. You said you wanted your lawyer present. If there was a tape turning, I've buggered my own case. Your lawyer would have to say just one word—*enticement*—and you'd walk free, whatever has happened to Carson. And I could go to work as a security guard in one of those flea-bitten little towns down by the border."

"You say that," Paladin said, "but *I'm* no lawyer."

But . . . *Convince me*, his eyes said. *Yeah, let's talk about this, let's see if we can't get together, because you're right, something is weird. So . . . convince me.*

"Is your mother alive?" Cheyney asked abruptly.

"What—yes, but what does that have to—"

"*You talk to me or I'm going to personally take two CHP motorcycle cops and the three of us are going to rape your mother tomorrow!*" Cheyney screamed. "*I'm personally going to take her up the ass! Then we're going to cut off her tits and leave them on the front lawn! So you better talk!*"

Paladin's face was as white as milk: a white so white it is nearly blue.

"*Now* are you convinced?" Cheyney asked softly. "I'm not crazy. I'm not going to rape your mother. But with a statement like that on a reel of tape, you could say you were the guy on the grassy knoll in Dallas and the Burbank police wouldn't produce the tape. I want to *talk* to you, man. What's going *on* here?"

Paladin shook his head dully and said, "I don't know."


In the room behind the one-way glass, Jacoby joined Lieutenant McEachern, Ed McMahon (still looking stunned), and a cluster of technical people at a bank of high-tech equipment. The LAPD chief of police and the mayor were rumored to be racing each other to Burbank.

"He's talking?" Jacoby asked.

"I think he's going to," McEachern said. His eyes had moved toward Jacoby once, quickly, when he came in. Now they were centered only on the window. The men seated on the other side, Cheyney smoking, relaxed, Paladin tense but trying to control it, looked slightly yellowish through the one-way glass. The sound of their voices was clear and undistorted through the overhead speakers—a top-of-the-line Bose in each corner.

Without taking his eyes off the men, McEachern said: "You get his lawyer?"

Jacoby said: "The home number on the card belongs to a cleaning woman named Howlanda Moore."

McEachern flicked him another fast glance.

"Black, from the sound, delta Mississippi at a guess. Kids yelling and fighting in the background. She didn't quite say *I'se gwine whup you if you don't quit!*, but it was close. She's had the number three years. I re-dialed twice."

"Jesus," McEachern said. "Try the office number?"

"Yeah," Jacoby replied. "Got a recording. You think ConTel's a good buy, Loot?"

McEachern flicked his gray eyes in Jacoby's direction again.

"The number on the front of the card is that of a fairly large stock brokerage," Jacoby said quietly. "I looked under lawyers in the Yellow Pages. Found no Albert K. Dellums. Closest is an Albert Dillon, no middle initial. No law firm like the one on the card."

"Jesus please us," McEachern said, and then the door banged open and a little man with the face of a monkey barged in. The mayor had apparently won the race to Burbank.

"What's going on here?" he said to McEachern.

"I don't know," McEachern said.

"All right," Paladin said wearily. "Let's talk about it. I feel, Detective Cheyney, like a man who had just spent two hours or so on some disorienting amusement park ride. Or like someone slipped some LSD into my drink. Since we're not on the record, what was your one interrogatory? Let's start with that."

"All right," Cheyney said. "How did you get into the broadcast complex, and how did you get into Studio C?"

"Those are two questions."

"I apologize."

Paladin smiled faintly.

"I got on the property and into the studio," he said, "the same way I've been getting on the property and into the studio for over twenty years. My pass. Plus the fact that I know every security guard in the place. Shit, I've been there longer than most of them."

"May I see that pass?" Cheyney asked. His voice was quiet, but a large pulse beat in his throat.

Paladin looked at him warily for a moment, then pulled out the lizard-skin wallet again. After a moment of rifling, he tossed a perfectly correct NBC Performer's Pass onto the coffee table.

Correct, that was, in every way but one.

Cheyney crushed out his smoke, picked it up, and looked at it. The pass was laminated. In the corner was the NBC peacock, something only long-timers had on their cards. The face in the photo was the face of Edward Paladin. Height and weight were correct. No space for eye-color, hair-color, or age, of course; when you were dealing with ego. Walk softly, stranger, for here there be tygers.

The only problem with the pass was that it was salmon pink.

NBC Performer's Passes were bright red.

Cheyney had seen something else while Paladin was looking for his pass. "Could you put a one-dollar bill from your wallet on the coffee table there?" he asked softly.

"Why?"

"I'll show you in a moment," Cheyney said. "A five or a ten would do as well."

Paladin studied him, then opened his wallet again. He took back his pass, replaced it, and carefully took out a one-dollar bill. He turned it so it faced Cheyney. Cheyney took his own wallet (a scuffed old Lord Buxton with its seams unravelling; he should replace it but found it easier to think of than to do) from his jacket pocket, and removed a dollar bill of his own. He put it next to Paladin's, and then turned them both around so Paladin could see them right-side-up—so Paladin could study them.

Which Paladin did, silently, for almost a full minute. His face slowly flushed dark red . . . and then the color slipped from it a little at a time. He'd probably meant to bellow *WHAT THE FUCK IS GOING ON HERE?*, Cheyney thought later, but what came out was a breathless little gasp: "—what—"

"I don't know," Cheyney said.

On the right was Cheyney's one, gray-green, not brand-new by any means, but new enough so that it did not yet have that rumpled, limp, shopworn look of a bill which has changed hands many times. Big number 1's at the top corners, smaller 1's at the bottom corners. FEDERAL RESERVE NOTE in small caps between the top 1's and THE UNITED STATES OF AMERICA in larger ones. The letter A in a seal to the left of Washington, along with the assurance that THIS NOTE IS LEGAL TENDER, FOR ALL DEBTS, PUBLIC AND PRIVATE. It was a series 1985 bill, the signature that of James A. Baker III.

Paladin's one was not the same at all.

The 1's in the four corners were the same; THE UNITED STATES OF AMERICA was the same; the assurance that the bill could be used to pay all public and private debts was the same.

But Paladin's one was a bright blue.

Instead of FEDERAL RESERVE NOTE it said CURRENCY OF GOVERNMENT.

Instead of the letter A was the letter F.

But most of all it was the picture of the *man* on the bill that drew Cheyney's attention, just as the picture of the man on Cheyney's bill drew Paladin's.

Cheyney's gray-green one showed George Washington.

Paladin's blue one showed James Madison.

# SNEAKERS

John Tell had been working at Tabori Studios just over a month when he first noticed the sneakers. Tabori Studios was in a building which had once been called Music City but wasn't much anymore.

The sneakers were white, or had been once, when they were new. From the look of them that had been a long time ago. That was all he noticed about them then: just a pair of elderly sneakers under the door of the first stall of the men's room on the third floor. Tell passed them and went into the third and last stall. He came out a few minutes later, washed and dried his hands, combed his hair, and then went back to Studio F, where Paul Janning, the man who had hired him—and just maybe the first friend Tell had ever made—was mixing an album by a heavy metal group called The Dead Beats.

Tell had met Janning, a rock producer of some note, at a party following the premiere of a concert film. They knew some of the same people, and got along. Tell, who normally had problems with ordinary conversation, found he could talk easily and naturally to Paul Janning. Janning asked for his phone number and called him a few days later to ask if he would like to be part of the three-man team mixing The Dead Beats' first album. "I don't know if it's really possible to make a silk purse out of a sow's ear," Janning had said, "but since Atlantic's paying the bills, why not try?"

A week or so after he first saw the sneakers, Tell saw them again. He only registered the fact that they were the same sneakers because they were in the same place: under the door of stall number one in the third floor men's. White—once, anyway—with dirt in the deep creases. He noticed an empty eyelet. Sneakers had laced one of them wrong. *Must not have had your eyes all the way open when you did that, friend*, Tell thought, and went on down to the third stall (which he thought of, in some vague way, as "his" stall).

This time he glanced at the sneakers on the way out and saw something odd: there was a dead fly on one of them.

When he got back to Studio F, Janning was sitting at the board with his head clutched in his hands.

"You okay, Paul?" Tell asked.

"No."

"What's wrong?"

"Me. *I* was wrong."

"What are you talking about?" Tell looked around for Georgie Ronkler and didn't see him anywhere. It didn't surprise him. Janning had periodic fugues and Georgie always left when he saw one coming on. He claimed his karma didn't allow him to deal with strong emotion. "I cry at supermarket openings," Georgie said.

"You *can't* make a silk purse out of a sow's ear," Janning said dully. He gestured at the glass between the mixing room and the performance studio. "At least you can't make one out of pigs like those."

"It's not that bad," said Tell, who knew he spoke only the truth: it was worse. The Dead Beats, comprised of four dull bastards and one dull bitch, were personally repulsive and professionally incompetent.

"Fuck you," Janning said.

"God I hate temperament," Tell said.

Janning looked up at him and giggled. A second later they were both laughing.

The mix ended a week later. Tell asked Janning for a recommendation and a tape.

"Okay, but you know you can't play the tape for anyone until the album comes out," Janning said.

"I know."

"And why you'd ever want to, for *anyone*, is beyond me. These guys make The Dead Kennedys sound like the Beatles."

"Come on, Paul. At least it's over."

He smiled. "Yeah. There's that. And if I ever work in this business again, I'll give you a call."

"That would be great."

They shook hands. Tell left the building which had once been known as Music City, and the thought of the sneakers under the door of stall number one never crossed his mind.

Janning, who had been in the business twenty years, had once told him that when it came to mixing bop (he never called it rock and roll, only bop), you were either shit or

Superman. For the month following the Beats' mixing session, John Tell was shit. He didn't work. He began to get nervous about the rent. Twice he almost called Janning, but something in him thought it would be a mistake.

Then, near the end of May, the music mixer on a film called *Karate Masters of Massacre* died of a massive coronary and Tell got two weeks' work at the Brill Building (which had once been called Tin Pan Alley), finishing the mix. It was mostly library stuff in the public domain—and a few plinking sitars—but it paid the rent. He had no more than walked into his apartment following his last day on the show when the phone rang and Paul Janning was asking him if he had checked *Billboard* lately.

Tell said he hadn't.

"It came on at number seventy-nine." Janning managed to sound simultaneously disgusted, amused, and amazed. "With a *bullet*."

"What did?" But he knew as soon as the question was out of his mouth.

"Diving in the Dirt."

It was the name of a cut on The Dead Beats' *Beat It 'Til It's Dead* album, the only cut which had seemed to Tell and Janning remotely like single material.

"Shit!"

"Agreed, but I think it's gonna go top ten. And that probably means the album'll go top ten. A platinum-covered dog-turd is still a dog-turd, but a ref is still a ref, am I right?"

"You sure are," Tell said, pulling open his desk drawer to make sure his Dead Beats cassette, unplayed since Janning had given it to him on the last day of the mix, was still there.

"So what are you doing?"

"Looking for a job."

"You want to work with me again? Daltrey's new album. Starts in two weeks."

"Christ, yes!"

The money would be good, but it was more than that; following The Dead Beats and two weeks of *Karate Masters of Massacre*, working with Roger Daltrey would be like coming into a warm place on a cold night. The man might turn out to be an utter shit, but at least he could *sing*. And working with Janning again would be good. "Where?"

"Same old stand. Tabori."

"I'm there."

Roger Daltrey could not only sing, he turned out to be a tolerably nice guy. Tell thought the next three or four weeks would be good ones. He had a job, he had a production credit on an album that had popped onto the *Billboard* charts at number forty-one (and "Diving in the Dirt" was up to number seventeen and still climbing), and he felt safe about the rent for the first time since he had come to New York from Pennsylvania four years ago.

It was June, trees were in full leaf, girls were in short skirts, and the world seemed a fine place to be. Tell felt this way on his first day back at work for Paul Janning until approximately 1:45 P.M. Then he walked into the third floor bathroom, saw the same white sneakers under the door of stall one, and all his good feelings suddenly collapsed.

*They are not the same.*

They were, though. That single empty eyelet was the clearest point of identification, but everything else about them was also the same. *Exactly* the same, and that included their positions.

The only difference was that now there were more dead flies around them.

He went slowly into the third stall, "his" stall, lowered his pants, and sat down. He wasn't surprised to find the urge which had brought him there had entirely departed. He only sat there, listening for sounds. Little shifting noises. The rattle of a newspaper. Perhaps a little grunt of effort. Hell, even a fart would do.

There was no sound.

*That's because I'm in here alone*, Tell thought. *Except, that is, for the dead guy in that first stall.*

The outer door banged briskly open. Tell almost screamed.

Someone hummed his way over to the urinals. As he did, an explanation occurred to Tell and he relaxed. It was so simple it was absurd . . . and undoubtedly correct. He glanced at his watch and saw it was 1:47.

*A regular man is a happy man*, his father used to say. Tell's father had been a taciturn man, and that (along with *Clean your hands and then clean your plate*) had been one of his few aphorisms. If regularity really did mean happiness, then Tell supposed he was a happy man. And if you were regular, he supposed that urge came on at about the same time every day . . . at least it did with him. Sneakers was just on the same schedule, that was all, and the sneakers were always under the door of stall one because that was "his" stall just as number three was Tell's.

*If you needed to pass the stalls to get to the urinals, you would have seen that stall empty lots of times, and with different shoes under it lots of other times. And what are the chances a body could stay undiscovered in a business building toilet stall for . . .*

He worked out the time he'd last been there in his mind.

*. . . for nine weeks, give or take?*

No chance at all was the answer to that one. He could believe the janitors weren't too fussy about cleaning the stalls—all those dead flies—but they would have to check on the toilet paper supply every day or two, right? And even if you left those things out, dead people started to smell after a while, right? God knew this wasn't the sweetest-smelling place on earth—and following a visit from the fat guy who worked down the hall at Janus Music it was almost uninhabitable—but surely the stink of a dead body would be *different*.

*How do you know? Did you ever smell a decomposing body?*

No, but he was pretty sure he'd know what it was if he did. Logic was logic and regularity was regularity and that was the end of it. The guy was probably a pencil-pusher from Janus or a writer for Snappy Kards, at the other side of the floor.

*Roses are red and violets are blue!*
*You thought I was dead but that wasn't true!*
*I just deliver my mail at the same time as you!*

*That sucks*, Tell thought, and uttered a wild little laugh. The fellow who had banged the door open, almost startling him into a scream, had progressed to the wash-basins. Now the splashing-lathering sound of him washing his hands stopped briefly. Tell could imagine him listening, wondering who was laughing behind one of the closed stall doors, wondering if it was a joke, a dirty picture, or if the man was just crazy. There were, after all, crazy people in New York. Lots of them. You saw them all the time, talking to themselves and laughing for no appreciable reason . . . the way Tell had just now.

Tell tried to imagine Sneakers also listening and couldn't.

Suddenly he didn't feel like laughing anymore.

Suddenly he just felt like getting out of there.

He didn't want the man at the basin to see him, though. The man would look at him. Just for a moment, but that would be enough to know what he was thinking. People who laughed behind closed toilet stall doors were quite possibly not to be trusted.

*Click-clack* of shoes on the old porcelain tiles. *Whooze* of the door being opened and the *hisshh* of it settling slowly back into place. You could bang it open but the pneumatic elbow-joint kept it from banging shut. That might upset the third-floor receptionist as he sat smoking Camels and reading the latest issue of *Krrang!*

*God, it's so* silent *in here! Why didn't the guy move?*

But there was just the silence, thick and smooth and total, the sort of silence the dead would hear in their coffins if they could still hear, and Tell again became convinced that Sneakers was dead, fuck logic, he was dead and *had* been dead for who knew how long, he was sitting in there and if you opened the door you would see some slumped mossy thing with its hands dangling in the fork of its crotch, you would see—

For a moment he was on the verge of calling, *Hey Sneaks! You all right?*

But what if Sneakers answered, not in a questioning or irritated voice but in a froggy grinding croak? Wasn't there something about waking the dead? About—

Suddenly Tell was up, up fast, flushing the toilet and buttoning his pants, out of the stall, zipping his fly as he headed for the door, aware that in a few seconds he was going to feel silly but not caring. Yet he could not forbear one glance under the first stall as he passed. Dirty white sneakers. And dead flies.

*Weren't any dead flies in my stall. And just how is it that nine weeks have gone by and he still hasn't noticed that he missed one of the eyelets? Or does he just wear them all the time, even to bed?*

Pneumatic elbow or not, Tell hit the door pretty hard coming out. The receptionist, a Camel smoldering between his fingers, was looking at him with the cool curiosity he saved for beings merely mortal (as opposed to such deities in human form as Roger Daltrey).

Tell hurried down the hall to Tabori Studios.


"Paul?"

"What?" Janning answered without looking up from the board. Georgie Ronkler was standing off to one side, watching Janning closely and nibbling a cuticle—cuticles were all he had left to nibble; his fingernails simply did

not exist above the point where they parted company
with live flesh and hot nerve-endings. He was close to
the door. If Janning began to rant, Georgie would slip
through it.

"I think there might be something wrong in—"

Janning groaned. "Something *else?*"

"What do you mean?"

"This drum track is what I mean. It's *badly* botched,
and I don't know what we can do about it." He flicked a
toggle and drums crashed into the studio. "You hear it?"

"The snare, you mean?"

"Of *course* I mean the snare! It stands out a mile from
the rest of the percussion, but it's *married* to it!"

"Yes, but—"

"Jesus bloody *fuck*, I hate shit like this! Forty tracks I
got here, *forty goddamn tracks to record a simple bop tune
and some IDIOT technician*—"

From the tail of his eye Tell saw Georgie disappear
like a cool breeze.

"But look, Paul, if you lower the eq—"

"The eq's got nothing to do with—"

"Shut up and just listen for a minute," Tell said
soothingly—something he could have said to no one else
on the face of the earth—and slid a switch. Janning
stopped ranting and started listening. He asked a question. Tell answered it. Then he asked one Tell *couldn't*
answer, but Janning was able to answer it himself, and
all of a sudden they were looking at a whole new
spectrum of possibilities for a song called "Answer to
You, Answer to Me."

After a while, sensing that the storm had passed,
Georgie Ronkler crept back in.

And Tell forgot what he had meant to say about the sneakers.

He thought about them again the following evening. He was at home, sitting on the toilet in his own bathroom, reading *Everything That Rises Must Converge* while Vivaldi played mildly from the bedroom speakers (although Tell now mixed rock and roll for a living, he only owned four or five rock records, most of them by Creedence Clearwater Revival).

He looked up from his book, somewhat startled. A question of cosmic ludicrousness had suddenly occurred to him: *How long has it been since you took a crap in the evening, John?*

He didn't know, but he thought he might be taking them then quite a bit more frequently in the future. At least one of his habits had changed, it seemed.

Sitting in the living room fifteen minutes later, his book forgotten in his lap, something else occurred to him: he hadn't used the third floor rest room once that day. They had gone across the street for coffee at ten, and he had taken a whizz in the men's room of The Donut Shop while Paul and Georgie sat at the counter, drinking coffee and talking about overdubs. Then, on his lunch hour, he had made a pit-stop at the Brew 'n Burger . . . and another on the first floor late that afternoon when he had gone down to drop off a bunch of mail that he could just as easily stuffed into the mail-slot by the elevators.

Avoiding the third-floor men's? Was that what he'd

been doing today, without even realizing it? You bet your sweatsocks. Avoiding it like a scared kid who goes a block out of his way coming home from school so he won't have to go past the local haunted house. He had been spooked by a pair of dirty sneakers.

Aloud, very clearly, Tell said: "This has got to stop."

But that was Thursday night and something happened on Friday night that changed everything. That was when the door closed between him and Paul Janning.

Tell was a shy man and didn't make friends easily. In high school a quirk of fate had put him up on stage with a guitar in his hands—the last place he ever expected to be. The bassist of a group called The Satin Saturns fell ill with salmonella the day before a well-paying gig. The lead guitarist, who was also in the school band, knew John Tell could play both bass and rhythm. This lead guitarist was big and violent. John Tell was small and breakable. Offered a choice between playing the ill bassist's instrument and having it rammed up his ass to the fifth fret went a long way toward breaking down his horror of playing in front of a large audience.

But by the end of the third song, he was no longer frightened. By the end of the first set he knew he was home. Years after that first gig, Tell heard a story about Bill Wyman, bassist of The Rolling Stones. According to the story, Wyman actually fell asleep during a performance—not in some tiny club, mind you, but a huge hall—and fell from the stage, breaking his collarbone. Tell supposed lots of people either laughed at that story or assumed Wyman had been on something, but Tell guessed it was true. Bassists, he had discovered, are the invisible men of the rock world. There were exceptions—Paul McCartney, for one—but they only proved the rule.

Perhaps because of the job's very lack of glamor, there was a chronic shortage of bass players. When The Satin Saturns broke up a month later (the lead guitarist and the rhythm guitarist had had a fist-fight), Tell joined a band formed by the Saturns' rhythm man (at their first rehearsal he still had a large purple shiner), and his life's course was chosen, as simply and quietly as that.

Playing in the band, not just *at* the party but making the party *happen*—Tell liked that. You were up in front, admired, idolized almost, and yet invisible. Sometimes you had to sing a little back-up, but nobody expected you to make a *speech* or anything. He lived that life, part-time student and full-time band gypsy, for ten years or so. He drifted into session work in New York, began fooling with the boards, and eventually discovered he was a little better—and even more invisible—on the other side of the glass window. During all that time he had made one good friend: Paul Janning. Nor was Georgie Ronkler so different from him, he realized following what happened on that Friday night.

He and Paul were having a drink or two at one of the back tables in McManus's Pub, talking about the mix, the biz, the Mets, whatever, when all of a sudden Janning's right hand was under the table and gently squeezing Tell's crotch.

Tell moved away so violently that the candle in the center of the table fell over and Janning's glass of wine spilled. A waiter came over and righted the candle before it could scorch the tablecloth. Then he left. Tell stared at Janning, his eyes wide and shocked.

"I'm sorry," Janning said, and he *did* look sorry . . . but he also looked unperturbed.

"Jesus *Christ*, Paul!" It was all he could think of to say, and it sounded hopelessly inadequate.

"I thought you were ready, that's all," Janning said. "If I hadn't, I suppose I would have been more subtle. It's just that I've wanted you for quite a while now."

"Ready?" Tell repeated. "Ready? What do you mean? Ready for *what?*"

"To come out. To admit it to yourself and come out."

"I'm not that way," Tell said, but his heart was pounding very fast. Part of it was outrage, part was fear of the implacable certainty he saw in Janning's eyes, most of it was dismay. What Janning had done shut him out. It also shut his mouth, but for the time being that was very much secondary.

"Let's let it go, shall we? Let's just order and make up our minds that it never happened." *Until you want it to*, those implacable eyes added.

*Oh it happened, all right*, Tell wanted to say, but that hand—the one that had been there all his life—was across his mouth. *Don't say what you shouldn't say, this is a job, a good job, you need that Daltrey tape in your portfolio even more than you need the next two weeks' salary. Be careful, John.*

But that wasn't all of it. That was the small of it. The fact was that his mouth closed. It always had. It snapped shut like a bear-trap, a bear-trap with rusty implacable jaws, with all his heart below those interlocked teeth and all his head above. That was the tall of it.

"All right," he said, "it never happened."


Tell slept badly that night, and what sleep he did get was haunted by bad dreams: one of Janning groping him in McManus's was followed by one of the sneakers under the stall door, only in this one Tell opened it and saw Paul Janning sitting there, a corpse with a huge peeling hard-on sticking up from the thatch of his pubic hair like an exclamation point. The mouth of this corpse dropped open with an audible creak. "That's right; I *knew* you were ready," it said on a puff of greenly rotten air, and Tell woke himself up by tumbling onto the floor in a tangle of coverlet. It was four in the morning. The first touches of light were just creeping through the chinks between the buildings outside his window. He dressed and sat smoking one cigarette after another until it was time to go to work.


Around eleven o'clock on that Saturday—they were working six-day weeks to make Daltrey's deadline—Tell went into the third floor bathroom to urinate. He stood just inside the door, rubbing his temples, and then looked around at the stalls.

He couldn't see. The angle was wrong.

*Then never mind! Fuck it! Take your piss and get out of here!*

He walked slowly over to one of the urinals and unzipped.

It took a long time to get going.

On his way out he paused again, head cocked, and then walked slowly around into the stall area just far enough so he could see under the door of the first stall.

The dirty white sneakers were still there. The building which used to be known as Music City was almost completely empty, Saturday morning empty, but the sneakers were still there.

Tell's eyes fixed upon a fly just outside the stall. He watched with an empty sort of avidity as it crawled beneath the stall door and onto one of the sneakers. There it stopped, and simply fell dead. It tumbled into the growing pile around the sneakers. Tell saw with no surprise at all (none that he felt, anyway) that among the flies was a large cockroach, lying on its back like a turtle.

He left in large painless strides, and his progress back to the studios seemed most peculiar; it was as if, instead of walking, the building was flowing past him, around him, like river-rapids around a rock.

*When I get back I'll tell Paul I don't feel well and take the rest of the day off*, he thought, but he wouldn't. Paul had been in an erratic, unpleasant mood all morning, and Tell knew he was part (or maybe all) of the reason why. Might Paul fire him out of spite? A week ago he would have laughed at such an idea. But a week ago he had still believed what he had come to believe in his growing-up: friends were real and ghosts were make-believe. Did he think the sneakers in the men's room belonged to a ghost? Well, as a matter of fact he did. Which, when taken along with the events of the night before, meant he had everything backwards: *friends* were make-believe and *ghosts* were real.

"The prodigal returns," Janning said without looking around as Tell opened the second of the studio's two doors—the one that was called the "dead air" door. "I thought you died in there, Johnny."

"No," Tell said. "Not me."


It *was* a ghost; Tell found out whose a day before the Daltrey mix—and his association with Paul Janning—ended, but before that happened a great many other things did. Except they were all the same thing, just little mile-markers, like the ones on the Pennsylvania Turnpike, announcing John Tell's steady progress toward a nervous breakdown. He knew this was happening, understood why it was happening, and still could not help it from happening. It seemed he was not driving this particular road but being chauffeured.

At first his course of action had seemed clear-cut and simple: avoid that men's room, and avoid all questions about the sneakers. Stop thinking about it.

But he *couldn't* stop thinking about it. It crept up on him at odd moments and pounced like an old grief. He would be sitting home, some stupid game-show on the tube, and think about the flies, or about janitors replacing the toilet paper, and then he would look at the clock and see an hour had passed. Or he would think it was all a malevolent practical joke.

*Paul's in on it, and probably that thin guy from Janus Music I see him talking to every now and then, and probably*

55

*the receptionist, him with his Camels and his dead skeptical eyes. Not George, he couldn't keep it from me even if Paul shouted him into going along, but anyone else is possible. Shit, maybe even Roger Daltrey himself took a turn wearing those sneakers!*

He recognized these thoughts as paranoid fantasies, but the worst thing was that recognition did not lead to dispersion. The thoughts lived their own lives inside his brain. He would tell them to go away, there was no cabal led by Paul Janning out to get him, and his mind would say *Yeah, okay, makes sense to me,* and five hours later— or maybe only twenty minutes—he would see a bunch of them sitting around Desmond's Steak House two blocks downtown: Paul, the receptionist who smoked the Camels, maybe even the fat guy from Snappy Kards, all of them eating shrimp cocktails and drinking. And laughing, of course. Laughing at *him,* while the dirty white sneakers they took turns wearing sat under the table in a crumpled brown bag.

Tell could *see* that brown bag. That was how bad it had gotten.

But the worst was just this: the third-floor men's room had acquired a *pull.* It was as if there was a powerful magnet in there and his pockets were full of iron filings. If someone had *told* him something like that he would have laughed (maybe just inside, if the person making the metaphor seemed very much in earnest), but it was really there, a feeling like a swerve every time he passed the men's on his way to the studios or back to the elevators. It was a terrible feeling, like being pulled toward an open window sixty stories up or watching helplessly, as if from outside yourself, as you raised a pistol to your mouth and sucked the barrel.

He wanted to look again. He realized that one more look was about all it would take to finish him off, but it made no difference. He wanted to look again.

Each time he passed, that mental swerve.

In his dreams he opened that door again and again. Just to get a look.

To get a really *good* look.

He couldn't get it out. That was the worst of it. He understood if he could get it out, pour it into someone else's ear, it would change its shape, perhaps even grow a handle with which he could hold it. Twice he went into bars and managed to strike up conversations with the men next to him. Because bars, he thought, were the places where talk was at its absolute cheapest. Bargain basement rates.

He had no more than opened his mouth on the first occasion when the man he had picked began to sermonize on the subject of the Yankees, Billy Martin, and that asshole George Steinbrunner. Steinbrunner in particular seemed to get under this man's skin. It was impossible to get a word in edgeways and Tell soon gave up trying.

The second time, he managed to work up a fairly casual conversation with a man who looked like a construction worker. They talked about the weather, and baseball (but this man, like Janning, was a Mets fan, and not at all nutty on the subject), progressed to jobs, and so on. Tell was sweating. He felt as if he was doing some heavy piece of manual labor—pushing a wheelbarrow filled with cement up a slight grade, maybe—but he also felt as if he wasn't doing too badly.

The guy who looked like a construction worker was drinking Black Russians. Tell stuck to beer. It felt as if he was sweating it out as fast as he put it in, but after he had bought the guy a couple of drinks and the guy had bought Tell a couple of schooners, he nerved himself to begin.

"You want to hear something really strange?" he said.

"You queer?" the guy who looked like a construction worker asked him before Tell could get any further. He turned on his stool and looked at Tell with amiable curiosity. "I mean, it's nothin' to me whether y'are or not, but I just thought I'd tell you I don't go for that stuff. Have it up front, you know?"

"I'm not queer," Tell said.

"Oh. What's really strange?"

"Huh?"

"You said something was really strange."

"Oh, it really wasn't that strange," Tell said, then glanced at his watch and said it was getting late.

Three days before the end of the mix, Tell left Studio F to urinate. He now used the bathroom on the sixth floor for this purpose. He had first used the one on four, then the one on five, but these were stacked directly above the one on three, and he had begun to feel the owner of the sneakers radiating silently up through the floors, seeming to suck at him. But the men's room on six was on the other side of the building, and that seemed to solve the problem.

He passed the reception desk on his way to the

elevators, blinked, and suddenly he was in the third-floor bathroom with the door *whoozing* softly shut behind him instead of in the elevator car. He had never been so afraid. Part of it was the sneakers, but most of it was knowing he had just dropped three to six seconds of consciousness. For the first time in his life his mind had simply shorted out.

He had no idea how long he might have stood there if the door hadn't suddenly opened behind him, cracking him painfully in the back. It was Paul Janning. "Excuse me, Johnny," he said. "I had no idea you came in here to meditate."

He passed Tell without waiting for a response (he wouldn't have got one in any case, Tell thought later; he was completely incapable of speech, his tongue frozen to the roof of his mouth), and headed for the stalls. Tell was able to walk over to the first urinal and unzip his fly, doing these things only because he thought Paul would really enjoy it if he freaked out. Paul had seemed to take Tell's horrified rejection in stride at the time. But times changed.

Tell flushed the urinal and zipped his fly again (he hadn't even bothered to take his penis, which felt as if it had shrunk to roughly the size of a peanut, from inside his underwear). He started out . . . then stopped. He turned around, took two steps, bent, and looked under the door of the first stall.

The sneakers were there, now surrounded by mounds of dead flies.

So were Paul Janning's Gucci loafers.

What Tell was seeing looked like a double exposure, or one of the hokey ghost effects from the *Topper* TV program. First he would be seeing Paul's loafers through the sneakers; then the sneakers would seem to solidify and he would be seeing them through the loafers, as if Paul were the ghost. Except, even when he was seeing through them, Paul's loafers made little shifts and movements, while the sneakers remained as immobile as always.

Tell left. For the first time in two weeks he felt calm.

The next day he did what he probably should have done at once: he took Georgie Ronkler out to lunch and asked him if he had ever heard anything strange about the building which used to be called Music City. Why he hadn't thought of doing this earlier was a puzzle to him. He only knew that what happened yesterday seemed to have cleared his mind somehow, like a brisk slap or a dashing of cold water. Georgie might not know anything, but he might; he had been working with Paul for at least seven years, and a lot of that work had been done at Music City.

"Oh, the ghost, you mean?" Georgie asked, and laughed. They were in Cartin's, a deli-restaurant on 6th Avenue, and the place was noon-noisy. He bit into his corned beef sandwich, chewed, swallowed, and sipped some of his cream soda through the two straws poked into the bottle. "Who told you 'bout that, Johnny?"

"Some janitor," Tell said. His voice was perfectly calm.

"You sure you didn't see him?" Georgie asked, and winked. This was as close as Georgie could get to teasing.

"Nope." He hadn't. Not really. Just some sneakers. Sneakers and dead flies.

"Yeah, well, everybody used to talk about it," Georgie said, "how the guy's ghost was haunting the place. He got it right up there on the third floor, you know. In the john."

"Yes," Tell said. "That's what I heard. But the janitor wouldn't tell me anymore, or maybe he didn't know anymore. He just laughed and walked away."

"It happened before I started to work with Paul. Paul was the one who told me about it."

"He never saw the ghost himself?" Tell asked, knowing the answer. Yesterday Paul had been *sitting* in it. *Shitting* in it, to be perfectly vulgarly truthful.

"No, he used to laugh about it." Georgie put his sandwich down. "You know how he can be sometimes. Just a little m-mean." If forced to say something even slightly negative about someone, Georgie developed a mild stutter.

"I know. But never mind Paul; who was this ghost? What happened to him?"

"Oh, he was just some dope pusher," Georgie said. "This was back in 1972 or '73, I guess. Before the slump."

Tell nodded. From 1975 until 1980 or so, the rock industry lay becalmed in the horse latitudes. Kids spent their money on video games instead of records. For perhaps the fiftieth time since 1955, the pundits announced the death of rock and roll. And, as on other occasions, it proved to be a lively corpse. Video games topped out; MTV checked in; a fresh wave of stars arrived from England; Bruce Springsteen suddenly

61

became all the things the newsmagazines had said he was ten years before.

"Before the slump, record company execs used to deliver coke backstage in their briefcases before big shows," Georgie said. "I was concert-mixing back then, and I saw it happen. There was one guy—I don't want to say his n-name because he's dead, dead since 1978, but you'd know it—who used to get a jar of olives from his label before every gig. The jar would come wrapped up in pretty paper with bows and ribbon and everything. Only instead of water, the olives came packed in cocaine. He used to put them in his drinks. Called them b-b-blast-off martinis."

"I bet they were, too," Tell murmured.

"Well, back then everybody thought coke was a good clean high. It didn't hook you like heroin or f-fuck you over so you couldn't work. And this building, man, this building was a regular snowstorm. Pills and pot and hash too, but mainly it was cocaine. It was the big fashion drug. And this guy—"

"What was his name?"

Georgie shrugged and worked on his sandwich. "I don't know. But he was like one of the deli delivery boys you see going up and down in the elevators with coffee and doughnuts and b-bagels. Only instead of delivering coffee-and, this guy delivered dope. You'd see him— this is what I heard, anyway—two or three times a week, riding all the way up and then working his way down. He'd have a topcoat slung over his arm and an alligator-skin briefcase in that hand. He kept the overcoat over his arm even when it was hot. That was so people wouldn't see the cuff. But I guess sometimes they did a-a-anyway."

"The *what?*"

"C-C-*Cuff*" Georgie said, spraying out bits of bread and corned beef and immediately going crimson. "Gee, Johnny, I'm sorry."

"No problem. You want another cream soda?"

"Yes, thanks," Georgie said gratefully.

Tell signalled the waitress.

"So he was a delivery-boy," he said, mostly to put Georgie at his ease again—Georgie was still patting his lips with his napkin.

"That's right." The fresh cream soda arrived and Georgie drank some. "When he got off the elevator on the eighth floor, that briefcase chained to his wrist would be full of dope. When he got off it on the ground floor again, it would be full of money."

"Best trick since lead into gold," Tell said.

"Huh?"

"Nothing. Go on."

"Not much to tell. One day he only made it down to the third floor. He made his deliveries, went into the men's room, and someone o-offed him."

"Shot him?" Tell asked, thinking dubiously of silencers—in the movies they made a sound very like that of the pneumatic elbow-joint on the men's room door.

"What I heard," Georgie said, "was that someone opened the door of the stall where he was s-sitting and stuck a pencil in his eye."

For just a moment Tell saw it as vividly as he had seen the crumpled bag under the conspirators' restaurant table: a yellow Eberhard Faber #2, sharpened to an exquisite black point, sliding forward through the air and then shearing into the startled black well of pupil. He winced.

Georgie nodded. "It's probably not true. I mean, not *that* part. Probably someone just, you know, stuck him."

"Yes."

"But whoever it was sure had something sharp with him, all right," Georgie said.

"He did?"

"Yes. Because the briefcase was gone."

Tell looked at Georgie. He could see this, too.

"When the cops came and took the guy off the toilet, they found his left hand in the b-bowl."

"Oh," Tell said.

Georgie looked down at his plate. There was still half a sandwich on it. "I guess maybe I'm f-f-full," he said, and smiled uneasily.

On their way back to the studio, Tell asked, "So the guy's ghost is supposed to haunt . . . what, that bathroom?" And suddenly he laughed, because gruesome as the story had been, there was something comic in the idea of a ghost haunting a men's room.

Georgie smiled. "You know people. At first that was what they said. When I was first working with Paul, guys would tell me they'd *seen* him in there. Not *all* of him, just his sneakers under the stall door."

"Just his sneakers."

"Yeah. That's how you'd know they were making it

up, or imagining it, because you only heard it from guys who knew him when he was alive. From guys who knew he wore sneakers."

Tell, who had been an eleven-year-old kid living in rural Pennsylvania when the murder happened, nodded. They had arrived at the building. As they walked up the hall toward the elevators, Georgie said, "But you know how fast the turnover is in this business. Here today and gone tomorrow. I doubt if there's anybody working here who was working there then, except maybe for a few j-janitors, and none of them would have bought from the guy."

"And he was probably one of those guys who you never even noticed if you didn't buy from him."

"Yeah. Unless you were a c-cop. So you hardly ever hear the story anymore, and no one ever says they *see* the guy."

They were at the elevators.

"Georgie, why do you stick with Paul?"

Although Georgie lowered his head and the tips of his ears turned a bright red, he did not sound really surprised at this abrupt shift in direction. "He takes care of me."

*Do you sleep with him, Georgie?* Something else he couldn't say. Wouldn't, even if he could. Because Georgie would tell him.

Tell, who could barely bring himself to talk to strangers and never made friends (except maybe for today), suddenly hugged Georgie Ronkler. Georgie hugged him back. Then they stepped away from each other, and the elevator came, and the mix continued, and the following evening, at six-fifteen, after the wrap and Janning's curt goodbye (he left with Georgie trailing behind him), Tell stepped into the third-floor men's room to get a look at the owner of the white sneakers.

Talking with Georgie, he had remembered what he had forgotten. Something so simple you learned it in the first grade. Telling was only half. *Showing* was the other half.

There was no lapse in consciousness this time, nor any sensation of fear . . . only that slow steady deep drumming in his chest. All his senses had been heightened. He smelled chlorine, the pink disinfectant cakes in the urinals, old farts. He could see minute cracks in the paint on the wall, and chips on the pipes. He could hear the hollow click of his heels as he walked toward the first stall.

The sneakers were now almost buried in the corpses of dead flies.

*There were only one or two at first. Because there was no need for them to die until the sneakers were there, and they weren't there until I saw them.*

"Why me?" he asked clearly in the stillness.

The sneakers didn't move and no voice answered.

"I didn't *know* you, I never *met* you, I don't even take the kind of stuff you sold. So why me?"

One of the sneakers twitched. There was a papery rustle of dead flies. Then the sneaker—it was the mislaced one—settled back.

Tell pushed the stall door open. One hinge shrieked in properly gothic fashion. And there it was. *Mystery guest, sign in please*, Tell thought.

The mystery guest sat on the john with one hand dangling limply in his crotch. He was much as Tell had seen him in his dreams, with this difference: there was only the single hand. The other arm ended in a dusty maroon stump to which several more flies had adhered. It was only now that Tell realized he had never noticed Sneaker's pants (and didn't you always notice the way lowered pants bunched up over the shoes if you happened to glance under a bathroom stall? something helplessly comic, or just defenseless, or one on account of the other?). He hadn't because they were up, belt buckled, fly zipped. They were bell-bottoms. Tell tried to remember when bells had gone out of fashion and couldn't.

Above the bells Sneakers wore a blue chambray workshirt with an appliqued peace symbol on each flap pocket. He had parted his hair on the right. Tell could see dead flies in the part. From the hook on the back of the door hung the topcoat of which Georgie had told him. There were dead flies on its slumped shoulders.

There was a grating sound not entirely unlike the one the hinge had made. It was the tendons in the dead man's neck, Tell realized. Sneakers was raising his head. Now he looked at him, and Tell saw with no sense of surprise whatever that, except for the two inches of pencil protruding from the socket of the right eye, it was the same face that looked out of the shaving mirror at him every day. Sneakers was him and he was Sneakers.

"I *knew* you were ready," he told himself in the hoarse toneless voice of a man who has not used his vocal cords in a long time.

"I'm not," Tell said. "Go away,"

"This is where you're supposed to be," Tell told Tell, and the Tell in the stall doorway saw circles of white powder around the nostrils of the Tell sitting on the john. He had been using as well as pushing, all right. He had come in here for a short snort, someone had opened the stall door, and stuck a pencil in his eye. But who committed murder by pencil? Maybe only someone who committed the crime on . . .

"Oh, call it impulse," Sneakers said in his hoarse and toneless voice.

And Tell—the Tell standing in the stall doorway— understood a great many things all at once. This had been no premeditated murder, as Georgie had seemed to think. The killer hadn't looked under the stall, and Sneakers hadn't flipped the latch. Or maybe . . .

"It was broken," the thing finished in its toneless husk of a voice.

Broken. Yes. The killer had been holding a pencil in one hand, probably not as a weapon but only because sometimes you wanted something to hold, a cigarette, a bunch of keys, a pen or pencil to fiddle with. Tell thought maybe the pencil had been in Sneakers's eye even before either of them knew the killer was going to put it there. Then, probably because the killer had also been a customer who knew what was in the briefcase, he had closed the door again, left the building, got . . . well, got *something* . . .

"He went to a hardware store five blocks over and bought a hacksaw," Sneakers said in his toneless voice, and Tell suddenly realized it wasn't *his* face anymore; it was the face of a man who looked about thirty, and vaguely Indian. Tell's hair was gingery-blonde, and so had this man's been at first, but now it was a coarse and shineless black.

"Sure," Tell said. "He got it in a bag and came back, didn't he? If somebody had already found you, there'd be a big crowd around the door. That's the way he'd figure. Maybe cops already, too. If no one looked excited, he'd go on in and get the briefcase."

"He tried to cut the chain first," the harsh voice said. "When that didn't work, he cut off my hand."

They looked at each other. Tell suddenly realized he could see the toilet seat and the dirty white tiles of the back wall behind the corpse . . . the corpse that was, finally, becoming a ghost.

"You know now?" it asked Tell. "Why it was you?"

"Yes. You had to tell someone."

"Telling is shit," the ghost said, and then smiled a smile of such sunken malevolence that Tell was struck by horror. "The only things that matter are showing . . . and eating. Eating would have been better."

It was gone.

Tell looked down and saw the flies were gone, too.

He needed to go to the bathroom. Suddenly he needed to go to the bathroom very badly.

He went into the stall, closed the door, lowered his pants, and sat down. He went home that night whistling. A regular man is a happy man, his father used to say.

Tell supposed that was true.

# DEDICATION

1

Around the corner from the doormen, the limos, the
taxis, and the revolving doors at the entrance to Le
Palais, one of New York's oldest and grandest hotels,
there was another door—this one small, unmarked, and
unremarked.

Martha Rosewall approached it one morning at quarter
of seven, her plain blue canvas tote-bag in one hand, a
smile on her face. The tote was usual. The smile was
not. She was not unhappy in her work—being the Chief
Housekeeper of floors Ten through Twelve of Le Palais
might not seem like much to some, but to a woman who
had worn dresses made out of flour-sacks as a girl in
Babylon, Alabama, it seemed a great deal. It was just
that, on any ordinary morning, a person arrives at work
with an ordinary expression on one's face—which is to
say, an expression that says *most of me is still in bed* and
not much more.

Things had not been ordinary for Martha since she
arrived home from work yesterday at three-thirty and
found the package her son had sent from Ohio. The
long-expected had finally come. She had slept little last
night—she had to keep getting up and checking to make
sure it was real, and still there. Finally she had slept
with it under her pillow, like a bridesmaid with a piece
of wedding cake.

She used her key and went down three steps to a long hallway painted flat green and lined with Dandux laundry carts. They were piled high with freshly washed and ironed bed-linen. The hallway was filled with its clean smell, a smell that Martha always associated, in some vague way, with the smell of freshly baked bread.

There was the faint sound of Muzak from the lobby, but Martha no longer heard it, anymore than she heard the hum of the service elevators or the rattle of china in the kitchen.

Halfway down the hall was a door marked CHIEFS OF HOUSEKEEPING. She went in, hung her coat, and passed through the big room where the Chiefs— there were eleven of them—took their coffee-breaks, worked out problems of supply and demand, and tried to keep up with the endless paperwork.

Beyond this room with its huge desk, wall-length bulletin board, and perpetually overflowing ashtrays was a dressing room. Its walls were plain green cinderblock. There were benches, lockers, and two long steel rods festooned with the kind of coat-hangers you can't steal.

The door to the bathroom opened. Delores Williams and a plume of warm steam came out. Delores, fresh from the shower, was wrapped in a Le Palais towel and just stripping a Le Palais shower cap from her head. She took one look at Martha's bright face and came to her with her arms out. "It came!" she cried. "You got it!"

Martha didn't know she was going to cry until the tears came. She hugged Delores and put her face against Delores's warm wet neck.

"That's all right, honey," Delores said. "You let it out. You go on and let it all out."

"It's just that I'm so proud of him," she said. "It's just that I'm so *proud*."

"Of course you are," Delores said, and when Martha finally stopped crying, Delores said she wanted to see it. "But you can hold it," she added, laughing. "I ain't gonna drip on it—I don't want to be talkin' through a hole in my throat."

So, with the reverence reserved for an object of great holiness (which, to Martha Rosewall, it was), she removed her son's first novel from the blue canvas tote. She had wrapped it carefully in tissue paper and put it under her brown nylon uniform. She now carefully removed the tissue so that Delores could view the artifact.

Delores looked carefully at the cover, which showed three Marines, one with a bandage wrapped around his head, charging up a hill with their guns firing. BLAZE OF GLORY, printed in fiery red-orange letters, was the title. And below the picture was this: *A Novel by Peter Rosewall.*

"All right—now show me what's *really* important, Martha!" Delores said.

And, without contradicting her, Martha turned to the dedication page where Delores read: '*This book is dedicated to my mother, MARTHA ROSEWALL. Mom, I couldn't have done it without you.*" And below the printed dedication this was added in a thin and sloping backhand script: "*I really couldn't have done it without you! I love you, Pete.*"

"Why, isn't that just the sweetest thing?" Delores asked, feeling tears start in her own eyes.

"It's more than sweet," Martha said. She re-wrapped

the book in the tissue paper. "It's true." She smiled, and in that smile Delores saw something more than love. She saw triumph.

2

Martha and Delores worked from seven to three. After work they frequently stopped in Patisserie, the hotel's coffee shop. More infrequently they went into Le Cinq, the little pocket bar just off the lobby, for a drink— usually a Singapore Sling for Delores, always a Pink Lady for Martha. After work on the day Martha had shown Delores her son's book, Delores led Martha into the cozy darkness of Le Cinq, got her comfortably situated in one of the booths, and left her there with a bowl of goldfish crackers in front of her while she spoke briefly to Ray, who was tending bar that afternoon. Ray grinned, nodded, and made a circle with thumb and forefinger. Delores came back to the booth and slid in. Martha looked at her with some suspician.

"What was *that* about?"

"You'll see," Delores said. Five minutes later Ray came over with a silver ice-bucket on a stand and placed it beside them. In it was a bottle of Perrier-Jouet champagne and two chilled glasses.

"Here, now!" Martha said in a voice that was half-alarmed, half-laughing. She looked at Delores, startled.

"Hush," Delores said, and to her credit, Martha did.

Ray uncorked the bottle, placed the cork beside Delores, and poured a little into her glass. Delores waved at it and winked at Ray.

"Enjoy, ladies," Ray said, and then blew a little kiss at Martha. "And congratulate your boy for me, m'dear." He walked away before Martha, who was still stunned, could say anything.

Delores poured both glasses full and raised hers. After a moment Martha did the same. The glasses clinked gently. "Here's to your son's first book," Delores said, and they drank. Delores tipped the rim of her glass against Martha's a second time. "And to your son," she said. They drank again, and Delores touched their glasses together yet a third time before Martha could set hers down. "And to a mother's love," she said.

"Amen," Martha said, and although her mouth smiled, her eyes did not—not quite. On each of the first two toasts she had taken a discreet sip of champagne. This time she drained the glass.

3

Delores had gotten the bottle of champagne so that she and her best friend could celebrate Peter Rosewall's breakthrough in the style it seemed to deserve, but that was not the only reason. She was curious about what Martha had said—*It's more than sweet, it's true.* Even more, she was curious about that expression of triumph.

She waited until Martha had gotten through her third glass of champagne and then she said, "What did you mean about the dedication, Martha?"

"What?"

"When you said it wasn't just sweet, it was true?"

Martha looked at her so long without speaking that

Delores thought she was not going to answer at all. Then she uttered a laugh so bitter it was shocking—at least to Delores it was. She'd had no idea that cheerful little Martha Rosewall could be so bitter, in spite of the hard life she had led. But that note of triumph was there, too, an unsettling counterpoint.

"His book is going to be a best-seller," Martha said. "I believe that. Pete says it is, and he says the critics are going to love it. He says those two things hardly ever happen together but they are going to happen for him. And I believe it, too. Because that's what happened with *him*."

"Who?"

"Pete's father," Martha said, looking at her calmly.

"But—" Delores didn't know what to say. She suddenly regretted buying the champagne. She had wanted to celebrate and perhaps hear a secret. She didn't know exactly what secret she had expected to hear, but the disclosure that Martha's beloved Pete wasn't Johnny Rosewall's son hadn't been it. Not that Johnny Rosewall had been much of a catch from what Martha said, but all the same . . .

She cleared her throat and said, "If Johnny wasn't Pete's father, hon—"

Martha's face twisted with a short of fastidious disgust at the mention of her late husband's name.

"He was Pete's *biological* father," she said. "Only have to look at his nose and the shape of his eyes to see *that*. Just wasn't his *natural* father. Any more of that, honey? It do go down smooth." Now that she was tiddly—just this side of being drunk, in fact—the South had begun to resurface in Martha's voice like a child creeping out of its hiding place.

Delores poured what bubbly was left into Martha's glass. Martha held it up by the stem, looking at the way the champagne turned the subdued afternoon light in Le Cinq to gold. Then she drank a little, set the glass down, and laughed that bitter, jagged laugh again.

"You don't know what I'm talking about, do you?"

Delores admitted she did not, but didn't add that she was no longer sure she wanted to hear—and in truth there was a part of her that still did want to hear.

"Well, I'm going to tell you," Martha said. "You probably won't believe me, and you probably won't want to know me anymore if you do, but after all these years I have to tell someone—now more'n ever—now that he's broken through. God knows I can't tell *him*—him least of all. But then—lucky sons never knew how much mothers love them, or the sacrifices they make, or the dedication they show, do they?"

Delores only shook her head, afraid to say anything, and Martha began to speak.

4

There was no need for Martha to go over the basic facts. The two women had worked together at Le Palais for eleven years and had been close friends for most of that time.

Martha knew about the drinking problem Delores' husband had had, and how Delores had finally laid down the law: take the cure or I'm leaving you. Harvey

Williams had fallen off the wagon more than once after that but Delores had been able to recognize honest effort when she saw it. She had stuck with him and her man had finally made it back to sobriety.

Martha knew the great sorrow of Delores's life—the first child who had fallen from a stair-landing in the apartment building where they had lived, the child who had lingered four days in intensive care and who had finally died. There had been other children, four of them, the eldest now the head pediatrics nurse in a Cleveland hospital, but no child could take the place of the one who had been lost.

By the same token, Delores knew about Johnny Rosewall and all the problems he had not been able to surmount—had not wanted to surmount. The drink, the drugs, the outside women. Martha had been new in New York, naive, and had married him two months pregnant. Even then, Martha had told her, she had had an idea of what Johnny Rosewall was—Johnny with his black Trans-Am (financed at 24%) and his tu-tone airtip shoes.

That first child she had lost in the third month. Another five months or so and she had about decided to leave Johnny—there had been too many late nights, too many weak excuses, too many black eyes. Johnny, she said, fell in love with his fists when he was drunk.

"He always looked good," she told Delores once, "but a shitheel in J. Press slacks is still a shitheel."

Then she discovered she was pregnant again. When she told Johnny, he hit her in the stomach with the handle of a broom to try and make her miscarry. His explanation was that they just couldn't afford a rug-rat and they would fire her at Le Palais, where she had a job as a housemaid, as soon as they found out she was pregnant.

Two nights later Johnny and two friends tried to stick up a liquor store on lower 49th Street. The proprietor had a shotgun under the counter. He brought it out. Johnny Rosewall was packing a nickel-plated .32, a hockshop special. He pointed it at the proprietor, pulled the trigger, and the pistol blew up. One of the fragments of the barrel entered Johnny Rosewall's brain through his right eye and killed him instantly.

What Delores knew of Martha's past came down to this: her friend was well-shut of a bad man. She had worked on at Le Palais until her seventh month; she had gotten an assurance from Mrs Proulx, then head of housekeeping, that she could have her old job back later on if she still wanted it; she had borne a seven-pound boy whom she had named Peter; and Peter had, in the fullness of time, written a novel called *Blaze of Glory* which everyone—including the Book-of-the-Month Club and Universal Pictures—thought destined for the best-seller lists.

All this she had heard, but Delores did not hear about Mama Delorme or Peter Jeffries, the man Martha called her Peter's "natural father," until that afternoon in Le Cinq, with glasses of champagne before them and the advance copy of Pete's novel in the plain blue canvas tote by Martha's feet.

## 5

"We were living in Harlem, of course," Martha said to Delores. She was looking down at her champagne glass, twirling it between her fingers. "On Stanton Street, which crosses 119th up by Station Park. I've been back since. It's worse than it was—a lot worse—but it was no beauty spot even then, in 1959.

"There was a woman who lived at the Station Park end of Stanton Street, everyone just called her Mama Delorme, and everyone swore she was a *bruja* woman. I didn't believe in anything like that myself, and once I asked 'Tavia Kinsolving, who lived in the same building as me and Johnny, how people could go on believing such trash in a day when space satellites went whizzing around the earth and there was a cure for just about every disease under the sun. She was an educated woman—had been to Julliard—and was only living in Harlem because she had her mother and three younger brothers to support. I thought she would agree with me but she only laughed and shook her head.

"'Are you telling me you believe in *bruja*?' I asked her.

"'No, I don't believe in *bruja*,' she said, "but I believe in *her*, Martha. She is different. Maybe for every thousand—or ten thousand—or million—women who claim to be witchy, there's one who really is. If so, Mama Delorme is that woman.'"

"I just laughed. People who don't need *bruja* can afford to laugh at it, I reckon, the same way that people who don't need prayer can afford to laugh at *that*. In those days I still thought I could straighten Johnny out, and make a man of him—if you can dig *that*."

Delores nodded. She could dig it.

"Then I had the miscarriage. Johnny was the main reason I had it, I guess, although I didn't like to admit that even to myself back then. He was beating on me all the time, and drinking all the time. He'd take the money I gave him and then he'd take more out of my purse. When I told him I wanted him to quit hooking from my bag he'd get all woundy-faced and claim he hadn't done any such thing. That was if he was sober. If he was drunk he'd just laugh.

"I wrote my momma down in Babylon—it hurt me to write that letter, and it shamed me, and I cried 'most all the time I was writing it—but I had to know what she thought. She wrote back and told me to get out of it, to go right away before he put me in the hospital or even worse. My older sister, Kissy, went that one better—she sent me a Greyhound bus ticket with two words written on the envelope in pink Crayon—GO NOW,"

Martha smiled sadly and took another small sip of her champagne.

"Well, I didn't go. I liked to think I had too much dignity. I suppose it was nothing but stupid pride. Either way, it turned out the same. I stayed. Then I got pregnant again—only I didn't know I was pregnant. I wasn't even sicking up in the morning . . . but then, I never did with the first one, either."

"You didn't go to this Mama Delorme because you were pregnant?" Delores asked. She'd made the assumption that Martha must have gone to the *bruja* woman and asked her to get rid of the bun in her oven.

"No," Martha said. "I went to her because 'Tavia Kinsolving told me Mama Delorme could tell me what the stuff was I found in Johnny's coat pocket. White powder in a little glass bottle."

"Oh-oh," Delores said.

Martha smiled again. "You want to know how bad things can get?" she asked. "Probably you don't, but I'll tell you anyway. Bad is when your man drinks and don't have no steady job. *Really* bad is when he drinks, don't have no job, and beats on you. But real deep-dish bad is when you find a little glass bottle with a spoon on it in your husband's coat pocket—where your hand was so you could maybe find a dollar to buy toilet paper down at the corner market—and you just hope like hell it's coke and not skag."

"You took it to Mama Delorme?"

Martha laughed pityingly.

"The whole *bottle*? No sir, no ma'am, no *way*, I wasn't getting much fun out of life, but I didn't want to *die*. If he'd come home from wherever he was at and found that two-gram bottle gone out of his pocket, he would have plowed me like a pea-field. What I did was take a little of it in a handkerchief. Then I went to 'Tavia and 'Tavia told me to go to Mama Delorme and I went."

"What was she like?"

Martha shook her head, unable to tell her friend exactly what Mama Delorme had been like, or how strange that half-hour in the woman's third floor apartment had been, and how she had nearly run down the crazily leaning stairs to the street, afraid that the woman was following her. The apartment had been dark and smelly, full of the smell of candles and old wallpaper and cinnamon and soured sachet. There had been a picture of Jesus on one wall, Nicodemus on another.

"Very strange," Martha said finally. "She might have been seventy, or ninety, or a hundred and ten. There was a pink-white scar that went up the side of her nose and her forehead and right into her hair. Looked a little like a lightning bolt. It had pulled down her right eye in a kind of droop that looked like a wink. She was sitting in a rocking chair and she had knitting in her lap. I came in and she said, 'I have three things to tell you, little lady. The first is that you don't believe in me. The second is the bottle you found in your husband's coat is full of White Angel heroin. The third is you're three weeks with a boy child you'll name after his natural father.'"

6

"Later on, when I could think straight again, I told myself that as far as those first two things went, she hadn't done anything that a good stage magician couldn't do—one of those mentalist fellows that wear the white turbans. She had maybe gotten a call from 'Tavia Kinsolving telling her I was coming. It could have been as simple as that, but how it got done don't matter. What matters is that a woman interested in being known as a *bruja* woman finds ways to *look* like a *bruja* woman. You see what I mean?"

"Ye-ess—" Delores said doubtfully.

"And as far as her telling me that I was pregnant— well, I'd maybe had a little feeling that I was, sort of a shine on the idea, but even if I was, that didn't make it any more than a lucky guess on her part, or . . . my mother used to be damned good at knowing when a woman had caught pregnant, sometimes before the woman knew, sometimes before she had any *business* being pregnant, if you see what I mean."

Delores laughed and nodded.

"She said it was their smell—their smell changed, and sometimes you could pick up that new smell as soon as a day after she had caught, if your nose was keen."

Delores was nodding. She had heard of such things, certainly.

"But, fact is, none of those things mattered, because I knew *she* knew—she knew all three of those things she'd told me, and she hadn't come by her knowing in any slinky way. To be with her was to believe in *bruja*—her *bruja*, anyway. But it didn't go away, that feeling, the way a dream goes away when you wake up, or the way your belief in a good faker goes away when you're out of his spell."

"What did you do?"

"Well, there was a chair with a saggy old cane seat near the door and I guess that was lucky for me, because when she said what she did, what I was looking at kind of grayed over and my knees came unbolted. I was going to sit down no matter what, but if the chair hadn't been there I would have sat on the floor.

"She just sat there, waiting for me to get myself back together, and went on knitting. It was like she had seen it all a hundred times before. I suppose she had.

"When my heart finally began to slow down I opened

my mouth and what came out was, 'I'm going to leave my husband.'

"'No,' she came back right away, 'he is gonna leave *you*. You're gonna see him out, is all. Stay around. There be a little money. You gonna think he hoit the baby but he din't be doin it.'

"'How,' I said, but that was all I *could* say, it seemed like. 'How . . . how . . . how . . .,' like that. Even now, twenty-six years later, I can smell those old burned candles and kerosene from the kitchen and that old sour smell of dried wallpaper, like old cheese. I can see her, small and frail in this old blue dress with little polka-dots which had once been white but were the yellowy color of old newspapers by then. She was so *little*, but there was such a feeling of power that came from her, like a bright, bright light—"

Martha drained the last of her champagne and set her glass down on the table with a little click.

"Well, it don't do any good to go on and on about it," she said. "If you'd been there you would have felt it. But there ain't anyway I can describe it if you wasn't.

"'How I do anythin or why you married that country piece of shit in the first place ain't neither of them important now,' she said. 'What's important now is you got to find the child's natural father.'

"'What do you mean?' I asked. '*Johnny's* the child's natural father.' Anyone listening would have thought she was as much as saying I'd been screwing around on my man, but it never even occurred to me to be mad at her. I was just too confused.

"She kind of snorted and flapped her hand at me, like

85

she was saying *Pshaw*. 'Ain't nothin natural about *dat* man.'

"Then she leaned a little closer and I started to feel a little scared. There was so much *knowing* in her, and it felt like not all that knowing was nice.

"'Any chile a woman get, the man shoot it out'n his pecker, girl,' she said. 'You know *dat*, don't you?'

"I didn't know any such thing but I felt my head going up 'n down just the same, as if she'd reached across the room with hands I couldn't see and nodded it for me.

"'That's right,' she said, nodding her ownself, 'and that's the way God made it. It's like a seesaw, ain't it? Sho! A man shoots cheerun out'n his pecker, so them cheerun mostly his. But it's a woman who carries em and bears em and has the raising of em, so them cheerun mostly hers. That's the way God planned it. But this man put the chile in your belly ain't gonna be no natural father to it—he wouldn't be no natural father to it even if he was gonna be round, because he was never meant to be yours in the first place. So tell me, girl: who is the chile's natural father?' And she kind of leaned toward me.

"All I could do was shake my head and tell her I didn't know what she was talking about. But I think that maybe part of me—a part of me way back in that part of your mind that only gets a real chance to think in your dreams—I think that part did. Maybe I'm only making that up because of all I know now, but I don't think so. I think that for just a moment or two his name fluttered there in my head—Peter Jefferies.

"I said, 'Please—you're scaring me—I don't know

what it is you want me to say—I don't know anything about natural fathers or unnatural fathers or anything like that—I don't even know if I'm pregnant!'

"Well, she sat back for a minute, and then she smiled. Her smile was like sunshine, and it eased me. 'I didn't mean to scare you, honey,' she said. 'That wasn't none of what I had in my mind at all. I'll just brew us a cup of tea, and that is gonna put you at your ease. It's just that I got the sight, and sometime it be strong. I'll make us tea. You'll like it. It's special to me.'

"I wanted to tell her I didn't want any tea, but it seemed like I couldn't. Seemed like too much of an effort to open my mouth, and all the strength had gone out of my legs.

"She had a greasy little kitchen place that was almost as dark as a cave and I sat there in the chair by the door—same one I fell into when she hit me with those things coming in—and watched her spoon loose tea into an old chipped china pot and put a kettle on the gas fire.

"I sat there thinking I didn't want none of anything that was special to her, nor nothing that came out of that greasy little kitchen neither. I was thinking I'd take just a little sip to be mannerly and then get out of there as fast as I could go and never come back.

"But then she brought over two little china cups just as clean as snow and a tray with sugar and cream and fresh-baked bread rolls. She poured it and it smelled good and hot and strong. It kind of waked me up and before I knew it I'd drunk two cups and eaten one of the bread-rolls, too.

"She drank a cup and ate a roll and we got talking along on more natural subjects—who we knew on the street, where I came from, where I liked to shop, and all like that. Then I looked at my watch and seen over an hour and a half had gone by. I started to get up and a dizzy feeling ran through me and I plopped right back in my chair again."

Delores was looking at her, eyes round.

"'You doped me,' I said, and I was scared, but the scared part of me was way down inside.

"'Girl, I don't mean nothin but a help to you,' she said, 'but you don't want to give up what I need to know and I know damn well you ain't gonna do what you need to do even once you do. So I fixed both things. You are gonna have a little nap here, but before you do you are gonna tell me the name of your babe's natural father.'

"And, sitting there in that chair with its saggy cane bottom and hearing all of Harlem outside, I seen Peter Jefferies as clear as I'm seeing you now, Delores. He was just as white as I am black, just as tall as I am short, just as educated as I am ignorant. We was as different as two people could be except for one thing—we both come from Alabama, me from Babylon down in the toolies by the Florida state line, him from Birmingham. He didn't even know I was alive—I was just the nigger woman who cleaned the suite where he always stayed on the eleventh floor of this hotel. And as for me, I only thought of him to stay out of his way because I heard him talk and seen him operate and I knew well enough what sort of man he was. It wasn't just that he wouldn't use a glass a black person had used before him without it had been washed twice; I seen plenty of that and it don't cross my eyes anymore. It was that he was nothing but a pure-dyed son of a bitch. You know what? He was like Johnny in a lot of ways, or the way Johnny would have been if he'd been smart and had an education and if God had thought to give Johnny a great big slug of talent inside of him instead of just a nose for poontang.

"I thought nothing of him but to steer clear of him, nothing at all. But when she leaned over me, that old black *bruja* woman with the smell of cinnamon that seemed to come right out of the holes in her skin, it was his name that came out with never a pause. 'Peter Jeffries,' I said. 'Peter Jeffries, the man who stays in 1163 when he ain't writing his books down there in Alabama. He's the natural father. But he's white!'

"She leaned closer and said, 'No he ain't, honey. Every man's black inside. You don't believe it, but that's right. It's midnight inside every man any hour of God's day. But a man can make light out of night, and that's why what come out of a man into a woman be white. Natural got nothin to do with color. Now you close your eyes, honey, because you be tired. Now! Say! Now! Don't you fight! Mama Delorme ain't goan put nothin over on you, chile! Just got sumpin I goan to put in your hand. Now—no, don't look, just close your hand over it.' I did what she said and felt something square. Felt like glass or plastic.

"'You gonna remember everythin when it be time for you t'think on em. Now go to sleep. Shhh . . . go to sleep . . . . shhh . . . .'

"And that's just what I did," Martha said. "Next thing I remember, I was running down those stairs like the devil was after me. I didn't remember what I was running from, but that didn't make no difference; I ran

89

anyway. And I never went back there except one more time, and I didn't see her when I did."

7

She paused and they both looked around like women freshly awakened from a shared dream. They saw that Le Cinq had begun to fill up—it was almost five o'clock and executives were drifting in for their after-work drink or three.

Although neither wanted to say so out loud, both wanted suddenly to be somewhere else. They were no longer wearing their uniforms but neither felt she belonged among these men in their suits, their briefcases, their talk of stocks, bonds, debentures, and politics.

"I've got a casserole and a six-pack of beer at my place," Martha said, suddenly timid. "I could warm up the one and cool down the other . . . if you want to hear the rest."

"Honey, I think I *got* to hear the rest," Delores said, and laughed a little nervously.

"And I think I've got to tell it," Martha replied, but she did not laugh. Or even smile.

"Just let me call Harve."

"You do that," Martha said, and while Delores used the telephone, Martha checked in her bag once more just to make sure the precious book was still there.

## 8

The casserole—as much of it as the two of them could use, anyway—was eaten, and they had each had a beer. Martha asked Delores again if she was sure she wanted to hear the rest. Delores said she did.

"Because some of it ain't very nice. I got to be up front with you about that. Some of it's worse'n the sort of magazines the single men leave behind em when they check out."

Delores knew the sort of magazines she meant, but could not imagine her trim, clean little friend in connection with any of the things pictured in them. She told Martha again that she wanted to hear, and after getting them each a fresh beer, Martha began to speak again.

## 9

"I was back home before I woke up all the way, and because I couldn't remember hardly any of what had gone on at Mama Delorme's, I decided the best thing was to forget all about it—to put it behind me. But one thing I knew I best not forget was the little twist of powder I'd taken from the bottle I found in Johnny's sport-coat. It was still in my dress pocket, wrapped up in a twist of tissue paper. I was pretty sure she'd never even looked at it, and all I wanted to do was get rid of it—maybe I didn't make a business of going through Johnny's pockets, but he surely made a business of going through mine, 'case I was holding back a dollar or two he might want.

"So I made a move to grab it and that was the first I knew that I already had something curled up tight in my hand, the way a kid keeps the money his momma gave him for the movies on Saturday afternoon until he gets a chance to spend it. I took it out and looked at it and that was the first I was completely sure I'd seen her, although I still couldn't remember what words might have passed between us.

"It was a little square plastic box with a top you could see through and open. There wasn't nothing in it but an old dried-up mushroom—except after hearing what 'Tavia had said about that woman, I thought maybe it might be a toadstool instead of a mushroom, and probably one that would give you the night-gripes so bad that you'd wish it had just killed you outright like some of em do.

"I decided to flush it right down the commode along with whatever that powder was he'd been sniffing up his nose, but when it came right down to it, I couldn't. Felt like she was right there in the room with me, telling me not to do it. I was scairt to look up in the little square of mirror in case I might see her.

"Well, there wasn't no in-the-apartment commode, like what's right here if we want it—and with beer bein so full of vitamin P as it is and the champagne to boot, I guess we will—it was down at the end of the hall, one bathroom for the second and third floors. Well, one of the little Parker kids from downstairs started whamming on the door and then kicking it, not giving me no chance to think or get my willpower together.

"So I stuffed that little plastic box back in my dress pocket and I took it back to the apartment and I ended up putting it in one of the kitchen cabinets, way in the back. Where I forgot all about it."

10

She stopped for a moment, drumming her fingers restlessly on the table and then said, "I guess I ought to tell you a little more about Peter Jefferies. He was in World War II and he wrote books about it. Novels. My Pete's book is about Viet Nam and his time there; Peter Jefferies's were about what he always called Big Two when he was drunk and partying up with his friends. He wrote the first one while he was still in the service, and it was published in 1946. It was called *Blaze of Heaven*."

Delores looked at her for a long time without speaking and then said, "Is that so? Is that really so?"

"Yes. Maybe you see where I'm going now. Maybe you get a little more what I mean about natural fathers. *Blaze of Heaven: Blaze of Glory*."

"But if your Pete had read this Mr Jefferies's book, isn't it possible that—"

"Course it's *possible*," Martha said, making that *pshaw* gesture again, "but that ain't what *happened*. I ain't going to try and convince you of that, though. You'll either be convinced when I get done or you won't. I just wanted to tell you about the man, a little."

"Then go ahead," Delores said.

"I saw him pretty often from 1957 when I started working at Le Palais right through until 1968 or so, when he got in trouble with his heart and liver. The way the man drank and carried on, I was only surprised he didn't get in trouble with himself earlier on. He was only in half a dozen times in 1969, and I remember how bad he looked—he was never fat, but he'd lost enough weight by then so he wasn't no more than a stuffed string. Went right on drinking, though, yellow face or not. I'd hear him coughing and puking in the bathroom and sometimes crying with the pain and I'd think, 'Well, that's it; that's all; he's got to see what he's doing to himself; he'll quit now.' But he never.

"In 1970 he was only in twice. He had a man with him that he leaned on and who took care of him. He was still drinking, even though I knew he wasn't supposed to.

"The last time he came was in February of 1971. It was a different man he had with him—I guess the first one must have got disgusted and just quit the job. Man was in a wheelchair by then. When I come in to clean and looked in the bathroom, I seen what was hung up to dry on the shower-curtain rail. Man was in continence pants by then, too. He'd been a handsome man, but he wasn't handsome no more. He looked just . . . just *raddled*. Do you know what I'm talkin bout?"

Delores shuddered a little and nodded. She knew. She had seen such creatures at some of the AA meetings she had attended with Harvey, human ships wrecked up on the rocks which border the sea of alcohol.

"He always stayed in 1163, one of those corner suites with the view that looks toward the Chrysler Building, and I always used to do for him. After a while, it got so's he would even call me by name, but that was just my name-tag and his memory. I don't believe he ever once really *saw* me. Until 1960 he always left two dollars on top of the television when he checked out. Then, until '64, it was three. Then, until the end, it was five. Those were good tips for those days, but he wasn't really tipping me; he was following a custom. Custom's important for people like him. He tipped the way he'd hold the door open for a lady. The way he prob'ly used to put his teeth under his pillow when he was small. Only I was the Cleanin Fairy instead of the Tooth Fairy.

"He'd come in to talk to his publishers or sometimes movie or TV people, and he'd call up his friends—some of them were in publishing, too, or were other writers— and then there'd be a party. Always a party. Most I just knew about by the messes I had to clean up the next day—dozens of empty whiskey bottles, mostly Jack Daniel's, millions of cigarette butts, wet towels in the sinks and the tub, left-over room service everywhere— once I found a whole platter of jumbo shrimp turned down into the toilet-bowl. There were glass rings on everything, and people snoring on the sofa and the floors, likely as not. That was mostly. But sometimes those parties were still going on when I started to clean at 10:30 in the morning. Mostly those were just . . . what do men call them? . . . bull-sessions. Talking and drinking. And always it was the war, the war, the war. Who they knew in the war. How they got to the war. Who they served under, who served under them in the war. Things they had seen in the war. How men had been killed in the war. Sometimes—not too often—it would be high-stakes poker instead of just talking about the war. Five or six men sitting around one of the glass-topped tables with their shirts open and their ties pulled way down, the table heaped with more money than a woman like me will make in a lifetime.

"But mostly it was the war.

"For men who seemed like they loved it s'much, they sure-God puked a lot when they talked about it."

11

Delores said she was surprised the management hadn't kicked the man out, famous writer or not—they were fairly stiff about such goings-ons now and had been even worse in years gone by, or so she had heard.

"No, no, no," Martha said, smiling a little. "You got the wrong impression. You thinking the man and his friends carried on like one of those rock-groups that like to tear up hotel suites and throw sofas out the windows. Peter Jefferies was *quality*. He wasn't no ordinary grunt in World War II, like my Pete was in his; he'd been to West Point, went in a Lieutenant and came out a Major. He came from an old Southern family. He could tie his tie four different ways and he knew how to bend over a lady's hand when he kissed it.

"He was *quality*."

Martha's smile took on a little twist as she spoke the word; the twist had a look both bitter and derisive.

"He and his friends sometimes got a little loud, I guess, but they rarely got rowdy—there's a difference, although it's hard to explain—and they *never* got out of control. If there was a complaint from the neighboring room—because it was a corner suite he stayed in, there was only the one—and someone from the front desk had to call Mr Jefferies's room and ask him and his guests to tone it down a little, why, they always did. You understand?"

"Yes," Delores said.

"And that's not all. A quality hotel can work *for* people like Mr Jefferies. It can protect them. They can go right on partying and having a good time with their booze and their cards or maybe their drugs."

"Was he—"

"I don't know. He had plenty at the end, God knows, but they were all the kind with prescription labels on them. I'm just saying that quality calls to quality. He'd been coming there a long time, and you may think it was important that he was a big famous author, but that's only because you haven't been here as long as I have. It was important to them, but what was more important was that he'd been coming there a long time, and even more important that his father, who was a big landowner down in Alabama, had come here before him. The people who ran the hotel back then were people who believed in tradition. Oh, I know the ones who run it now say they believe in the same thing, and maybe they even do when it suits them, but in those days they *really* believed in it. When they knew Mr Jefferies was coming up to New York on the Southern Flyer from Birmingham, you'd see the room right next to that corner suite sort of empty out, unless the hotel was full right up to the scuppers. They never charged him for the empty room next door; they were just trying to spare him the embarrassment of having to tell his pals to keep it down if they could."

Delores shook her head slowly. "That's amazing."

"You don't believe it, honey?"

"I believe it," she said, "but it's still amazing."

That bitter, derisive smile resurfaced. "Ain't nothing too much for *quality* . . . or didn't used to be. Hell, even I recognized that he was quality, in spite of the way that he might tell a Rastus the Coon joke to his friends while I was right there emptying ashtrays or just in the next room with the door open, making a bed. Oh, he hated blacks, all right, but it wasn't just us—he hated just about everyone the same. When it came to hate, the man was an equal opportunity employer. When John Kennedy died, Jefferies happened to be in the city and he threw a party. All of his friends were there, and it went on into the next day. I could barely stand to be in there, the things they were saying—about how things would be perfect if only someone would get that brother of his who wouldn't be happy until every decent white kid in the country was fucking while the Beatles played on the TV and the stereo and the fucking jigaboos were running wild through the streets with a TV under each arm.

"It got so bad that I knew I was going to scream at him. I just kept telling myself to be quiet and do my job and get out as fast as I could; I kept telling myself to remember the man was my Pete's natural father if I couldn't remember anything else; I kept telling myself that Pete was only three years old and I needed this job and I would lose it if I couldn't keep my mouth shut.

"Then one of em said, 'And after we get Bobby, let's go get that fucking candy-ass younger brother!' and one of the others said, 'Then we'll get all the male children and *really* have a party!'

"'That's right!' Mr Jefferies said. 'And when we've

got the last head up on the castle wall we're going to have a party so big I'm going to hire Madison Fucking Square Garden!'

"I had to leave then. I had a headache and belly-cramps from trying so hard to keep my mouth shut. I left the room half-cleaned, which is something I never did before or have done since, but sometimes being black has its advantages; he didn't even know I was gone. Wasn't none of them knew I was gone."

That bitter derisive smile was on her lips again.

12

"I don't see how you can call a man like that quality," Delores said, "or call him the natural father of your unborn child, whatever the circumstances might have been. To me he sounds like he wasn't no more than a beast."

"No—he wasn't a beast. He was a man. In some ways—in *most* ways—he was a bad man, but a man he was. And he did have that something that I mean by *quality*. It come across in his books, too, only even clearer."

"You read one?"

"Honey, I read them *all*," Martha said. "He'd only written three by the time I went to Mama Delorme's with that white powder in late 1959, but I'd read two of them. In time I got caught up, because he wrote even slower than I read." She grinned. "And that's pretty slow, you better believe it."

Delores looked doubtfully toward Martha's bookcase.

There were books there by Alice Walker, Rita Mae Brown, *Yellowback Radio Broke Down* by Ishmael Reed, a couple by Kurt Vonnegut—but the three shelves were pretty dominated by paperback romances and Agatha Christie mystery stories.

"Stories about war don't hardly seem like your pick an' glory, Martha, if you know what I mean."

"Of couse I know," Martha said. She got up and brought them each a fresh beer. "And I'll tell you an ironical thing, Delores Williams: if he'd been a nice man, I never would have read them at all, not even one of them. And I'll tell you another ironical thing: if he'd been a nice man, I don't think they would have been as good as they were."

"Oh, I don't believe *that*."

"Ain't asking you to! All I'm doing is saying what happened to me and what *I* believe. Now do you want me to go on?"

"Yes, of couse I do," Delores said.

"Well, it didn't take me until 1963 and the Kennedy assassination to figure out what kind of man he was. I knew that by the summer of '58. By then I'd seen what a low opinion he had of the human race in general—not his friends, he would've died for them, I have no doubt, but everyone else. Everyone was out looking for a buck to stroke, he used to say—I heard him use that phrase again and again. Stroking the buck, stroking the buck, everyone was stroking the buck. It seemed like him and his friends thought stroking the buck was a real bad thing, unless they were playing poker and had a whole mess of em stacked up in front of them. Seemed to me like then they stroked them, all right. Seemed to me like then they stroked them *plenty*, him included.

"He talked ugly and laughed at people who were trying to do good or improve the world, he hated the blacks and the Jews—which he always called the god-damn sheenies—and he thought we ought to go in there and clobber the Russians or the Cubans or whoever there was going.

"I listened to it all and started to wonder how come all the critics and book-reviewers could say he'd written great books. One of them had even won a National Book Award prize, and there was talk right up to the time he died about giving him a Pulitzer Prize. They never did, though, and I bet that frosted his balls plenty.

"Finally I decided I would just have to see for myself how everybody could be so wrong as to mistake a garbage-eater like him for someone with heart. I went down to the Public Library and got his first book, *Blaze of Heaven*.

"I expected it would turn out to be something like the Emperor's new clothes, everyone lying each other up because no one wanted to be the first to admit he'd made a mistake, but it wasn't like that at all. The book was about these five men and what happened to them in the war, and what happened to their wives and girlfriends back home. When I saw on the jacket it was about the war, I kind of rolled my eyes, thinking it would be like all those boring stories they told each other."

"It wasn't?"

"I read the first ten or twenty pages and thought, 'This ain't so good. It ain't as bad as I thought it'd be, but nothing's happening.' Then I read another thirty pages and I kind of . . . well, I kind of lost myself. Next time I looked up it was almost midnight and I was two hundred pages into that book. I thought to myself, 'You got to go to bed, Martha. You got to go right now, because five-thirty comes early. But I read another thirty pages in spite of how heavy my eyes were getting, and it was quarter to one before I finally got up to brush my teeth."

Martha stopped, looking off toward the darkened window and all the miles of night outside it, her eyes hazed with remembering, her lips pressed together in a light frown. She shook her head a little.

"I didn't know how a man who was so boring when you had to listen to him could write so you didn't never want to close the book he wrote, nor ever see it end, either. How he could make up characters so real you could cry over them when they died—and when Norah got hit and killed by a taxi-cab near the end of *Blaze of Heaven*, I *did* cry. I didn't know how a man who could be so nasty and sour could make you care so much. That book was full of pain and bad things, but it was full of sweetness, too . . . and love . . ."

She laughed.

"I can't explain it like I want to," she said. "I'm not a critic."

"You've explained very well," Delores said.

Martha looked pleased but disbelieving.

"There was a fella worked at the hotel back then named Billy Beck, a nice young man who was majoring in English at Fordham when he wasn't on the door. He and I used to talk sometimes—"

"Was he colored?"

"God, no!" Martha laughed. "Wasn't no black doormen at Le Palais until 1965. Black porters and bellboys and car-park valets, but no black doormen. Wasn't considered right. Quality people like Mr Jefferies wouldn't have liked it.

"Anyway, I asked Billy how the man's books could be so wonderful when he was such a booger in person. Billy asked me if I knew the one about the fat disc jockey with the thin voice, and I said I didn't know what he was talking about. Then he said he didn't know the answer to my question, but he told me something a prof of his had said about Thomas Wolfe. This prof said that some writers—and Wolfe was one of them—were no shakes at all until they sat down to a desk and took up pens in their hands. He said that a pen to fellows like that was like a telephone booth is to Clark Kent. He said that Thomas Wolfe was like a . . ." She hesitated, then smiled. "That he was like a divine wind-chime. He said a wind-chime isn't nothing on its own, but when the wind blows through it, it makes a lovely noise.

"I think Peter Jefferies was a wind chime like that. He *was* quality, he had been raised quality and he *was*, but the quality in him wasn't nothing he could take credit for. It was like God banked it for him and he just spent it."

Martha smiled again.

"I'll tell you something," she said. "After I'd read a couple of his books, I started to feel sorry for him."

"*Sorry?*"

"Because his books were pretty and he was ugly. The way he was and the way my Johnny was, they weren't so much different. But Johnny was luckier, in a way, because he couldn't ever have been any more than what he was. Mr Jefferies—his books were like dreams he had. Like he picked up his pen and dreamed of all the parts of the world he didn't, or couldn't let himself, believe in."

She got up, went to the fridge, and came back to the table with two more beers.

Delores laughed and said she'd pass. "Harvey will smell it on my breath," she said. "He doesn't say anything right out, but he gets uneasy."

"You better take it," Martha said, "this is where the water gets murky." And after looking carefully in her friend's eyes, Delores took it.

13

"One other thing about the man," Martha said. "He wasn't a sexy man. At least not the way you usually think about a man being sexy."

"You mean he was a—"

"No, he wasn't a fag, or a homo, or a gay, or whatever it is right to call them these days. He wasn't sexy for men, but he wasn't much sexy for women, either. There were two, maybe three times in all the years I did for him when I seen cigarette butts with lipstick on them in the bedroom ashtrays when I cleaned up. Those times there was the smell of perfume in the suite, and on one of them I found a Coty eyeliner pencil in the bathroom— it had rolled up under the mirror where you could hardly see it.

"I reckon he'd had call-girls come in and do him, but two or three times in all those years isn't much, is it?"

"It sure isn't," Delores said, thinking of all the panties she had pulled out from under beds, all the condoms she had seen floating in unflushed toilets, all the false eyelashes she had found on and under pillows.

"I think he was sexy for himself," Martha said. "That's what I think. Just for himself. I changed a lot of sheets with stiff patches on them, if you know what I mean."

Delores nodded.

"And there'd always be a little jar of cold cream in the bathroom, or sometimes on the table by his bed. I think he used it when he pulled off. To keep from getting chapped skin."

The two women looked at each other and suddenly began giggling hysterically.

"You sure he wasn't no ass-bandit, honey?" Delores asked finally.

"I said cold cream, not Vaseline," Martha said, and that did it; for the next five minutes the two women laughed until they cried. Delores spilled her bottle of beer and it ran foaming across the table and then they laughed at *that*.

14

But nothing was really funny, and Delores knew it. And when Martha went on, she simply listened, hardly believing what she was hearing.

"It was maybe a week after that time at Mama

Delorme's, or maybe it was two," Martha said. "I don't remember. Been a long time since it all happened. By then I was pretty sure I was pregnant—I wasn't throwing up or nothing, but there's a *feeling* to it. It don't come from places you'd think. It's like your gums and your toenails and the bridge of your nose figure out what's going on before the rest of you. Or you want something like chop suey at three in the afternoon and you say, 'Whoa, now! What's *this*?' But you know what it is.

"I was in the bedroom of his suite. He'd gone out for one of his publishers' meetings. The bed was a double, messed up on both sides, but that didn't mean nothing; he was just a restless sleeper. Sometimes when I came in the groundsheet would be pulled right out from underneath the mattress.

"Well, I stripped off the coverlet and the two blankets underneath—he was thin-blooded and always slept under all he could—and then I started to strip the top sheet off backwards, and I seen it right away. It was his spunk, mostly dried on there.

"I stood there looking at it for . . . oh, I don't know how long. It was like I was hypnotized. I seen him, lying there all by himself after his friends had gone home, lying there smelling nothing but the smoke they'd left behind and his own sweat, I seen him lying there on his back and taking himself by the hand and thinking about something and jacking himself off. I seen that as clear as I see you now, Delores; the only thing I didn't see is what he was thinking about, what sort of pictures he was making in his head to get himself off . . . and considering the way he talked and the way he was when he wasn't writing his books, I'm just as glad I didn't. I might never sleep again if I did."

Delores was looking at her, frozen, saying nothing.

"Next thing I know, this . . . this feeling came over me." She paused, thinking. "This *compulsion* came over me. It was like wanting chop suey at three in the afternoon, or ice cream and pickles at two in the morning, or . . . what did you want, Delores?"

"Rind bacon," Delores said through lips so numb she could hardly feel them. "Harvey went out and couldn't find me any, but he brought back a bag of those pork rinds and I just *gobbled* them."

Martha was nodding.

15

When Delores came back from the bathroom she was at first not able to look at Martha. When she finally made herself, she saw that Martha was looking at her with a warm kindness and concern that nearly broke her heart. With no idea of what she was going to do, she went around the table and hugged her friend. Twenty minutes ago they had laughed madly together; now Martha burst into wild tears. After a few moments of holding back Delores joined her, and when she kissed Martha on the cheek and told her to go on, their tears mingled.

## 16

"I worked the rest of that day in kind of a daze. It was like I was hypnotized. People talked to me, and I answered them, but it was like I was hearing them though a glass wall and speaking back to them the same way. *I'm hypnotized, all right*, I remember thinking. *She hypnotized me. That old woman. Gave me one of those post-hypnotic suggestions, like when a stage hypnotist says, 'Someone says the word Chiclets to you, you're gonna get down on all fours and bark like a dog,' and the guy who was hypnotized does it even if no one says Chiclets to him for the next ten years. She put something in that tea and then told me to do that. That nasty thing.*

"I seen why she would, too—an old woman superstitious enough to believe in stump-water cures, and how you could witch a man into love by putting a little drop of blood from your period onto the heel of his foot while he was sleeping, and cross-tie walkers, and God alone knows what else . . . if a woman like that with a bee in her bonnet about natural fathers could do hypnotism, hypnotizing a woman like me into . . . well, into doing what I did . . . might be just what she would do. Because she would *believe* it. And I had named him to her, hadn't I? Yes indeed.

"It never occurred to me then that I hadn't remembered hardly anything at all about going to Mama Delorme's until after I did what I did in Mr Jefferies's bedroom. It did that night, though.

"I got through the day all right. I mean, I didn't cry

or scream or carry on or anything like that. My sister Kissy acted worse the time she was drawing water from the old well round dusk and a bat flew up out of it and got caught in her hair. There was just that feeling that I was behind a wall of glass, and I figured if that was all, I could get along with it.

"Then, when I got home, I all at once got thirsty. I was thirstier then ever in my life—felt like a sandstorm was going on in my throat. I started to drink water. It seemed like I just couldn't drink enough. And I started to spit. I just spit and spit and spit. Then I started to feel sick to my stomach. I ran down to the bathroom and looked at myself in the mirror and I run out my tongue, and for just a second or two it looked like it was all *white*, like it was still all coated with his . . . you know.

"Then I vomited. I vomited and vomited until my legs wouldn't hold me up and I fell down on my knees in front of the toilet bowl. I was crying and begging God to please forgive me, to let me stop puking before I lost the baby, if I really did have one. And then I thought of myself standing there in his bedroom, scraping his squirt off the sheet and eating it, just doing it and not even thinking about what I was doing—I tell you I could *see* myself doing it, Delores, as if I was looking at myself in a movie. And then I vomited again, and it felt like my stomach had turned itself right inside out.

"Mrs Parker heard me and came to the door and asked if I was all right. That helped me get hold of myself a little, and by the time Johnny came in that night, I was over the worst of it. He was drunk, spoiling for a fight. When I wouldn't give him one he hit me in the eye anyway and walked out. I was almost glad he hit me, because it gave me something else to think about.

"The next day when I went into Mr Jefferies's suite he was sitting in the parlor, still in his pajamas, scribbling away on one of his yellow legal pads. He always travelled with a bunch of them, held together with a big red rubber band, right up until the end. When he come to Le Palais that last time and I didn't see them, I knew he'd made up his mind to die. I wasn't sorry, neither."

Martha looked toward the kitchen window with an expression which held nothing of mercy or forgiveness; as it was a cold look, a look which reports an utter absence of the heart.

"When I come in the next day and seen him there I was relieved, because it meant I could put off the cleaning. He didn't like the housekeepers around when he was working, and he might not want the room made up until Yvonne came on at three.

"I said, 'I'll come back later, Mr Jefferies.'

"'Do it now,' he said. 'Just keep quiet while you do. I've got a bitch of a headache and a hell of a good idea. The combination of the two is killing me.'

"Any other time he would have told me to come back, I swear it. It seemed like I could almost hear that old black mama laughing.

"I went into the bathroom and started tidying that up, taking out the used towels and putting up fresh ones, replacing the soap with a new bar, putting fresh matches out, and all the time I'm thinking, *But you can't hypnotize someone who doesn't want to be hypnotized, old woman. Whatever it was you put in the tea that day, whatever it was*

*you told me to do or how many times you told me to do it, I*
*am wise to you. I am wise to you and I am shut of you.*

"I went into the bedroom and I looked at the bed. I
expected it would look to me like a closet does to a kid
who's scared of the boogeyman, but I saw it was just a
bed. I knew I wasn't going to do anything, and it was a
relief. So I stripped it and there was another of those
sticky patches, still drying, as if he'd woke up maybe
around 9:30, an hour or so before, and just took care of
himself.

"I seen it and waited to see if I was going to feel
anything about it. I didn't. It was just the leftovers of a
man with a letter and no mailbox to put it in, like you
and I have seen a hundred times before. And that old
woman was no more a *bruja* woman than I was. I might
be pregnant or I might not be, but if I was, it was
Johnny's child. He was the only man I'd ever lain with,
and I could eat this man's spunk until it came out of my
ears and it wouldn't change a thing.

"It was a cloudy day, but at the second I thought that,
the sun came out like God had put his final amen on the
subject. I don't recall ever feeling so relieved. I stood
there thanking God everything was all right, and while I
did it I scraped all of his stuff off the sheet I could get
and ate it.

"It was like I was standing outside myself and watching again. And a part of me was saying, *You're crazy to*
*be doing that, girl, but you're even crazier to be doing it with*
*him right there in the next room; he could get up any second*
*and come in here to use the bathroom and see you eating his*
*spend off that sheet. Rugs as thick as they are in this place,*
*you'd never hear him coming. And that would be the end of*

111

*your job at Le Palais—or any other big hotel in New York,
most likely. A girl caught doing a thing like that would never
work in this city again as a chambermaid, at least not in any
half-decent hotel.*

"But it didn't make any difference; I went right on
until I was done—or at least until some part of me was
satisfied—and then I just stood there a minute, looking
down at the sheet in my hands. I could see the wet place,
but now it was only wet because my tongue had been on
it. That other was gone. I couldn't hear nothing at all
from the other room, and it come to me that he was
behind me, standing in the doorway, looking at me. I
knew how he would look. Used to be a travelling show
that came to Babylon every August when I was a girl,
and they had a man with it—I guess he was a man—that
geeked out back of the side show. He'd be down a hole
and some fella would give a spiel about how he was the
missing link and then throw a chicken down and the
geek'd bite the head off it. Once my oldest brother—
Bradford, who died in a car accident in Biloxi about
twenty years ago—went to see that man. My father said
he'd be sorry, but he didn't forbid Brad, because Brad
was nineteen then, a man. He went, and all the time he
was gone me and Kissy meant to ask him what it was
like, but when we saw the expression on his face we
never. We knew better, you know?"

Delores nodded.

"And I knew that Mr Jefferies was standing there, *had*
been standing there all the while, and when I turned
around he'd look just like Brad after Brad seen the geek
bite the head off that chicken.

"I turned around, still holding that sheet in my hands,

but he wasn't there. It had just been my guilty heart seeing him in the eye of my mind. I walked to the door and looked out and seen he was still in the parlor, writing on his yellow pad faster than ever. So I went ahead and changed the bed and freshened the room just like always, but it was like somebody else was doing it. That feeling that I was behind a glass wall was back, stronger than ever.

"I took care of the used towels and linens using the bedroom door like you're supposed to—first thing I ever learned back in 1957 when I came to work here is you don't ever, *ever* take the linen out to the hall through the sitting room of a suite—and then I came back in to where he was. I meant to tell him I'd do the parlor later, when he wasn't working. But when I saw him—saw the way he was acting—I was so surprised that I stopped right there in the doorway, looking at him.

"He was walking around the room so fast that his yellow silk pajamas were whipping around his legs. He had his hands in his hair and he was twirling it every which way. He looked like one of those brainy mathematicians in the old *Saturday Evening Post* cartoons. His eyes were all wild, like he'd had a bad shock. First thing I thought was that he'd seen what I did after all and it had . . . you know . . . made him feel . . ."

"Made him feel so sick it almost drove him crazy?"

Martha nodded.

"Turned out it didn't have anything to do with me. At least *he* didn't think so. That was the only time he talked to me, other than to ask me if I'd get some more stationery or another pillow or change the setting on the air conditioner. He talked to me because he *had* to.

Something had happened to him—something very big—and he had to talk to somebody or go crazy, I guess.

"'My head is splitting,' he said.

"'I'm sorry to hear that, Mr Jefferies,' I said. 'I can get you some aspirin if—'

"'No,' he said. 'That's not it. It's this idea. It's like I went fishing for trout and hooked a marlin instead. I write books for a living. Made-up stories.'

"'Yes sir, Mr Jefferies,' I said, 'I have read two of them and thought they were fine.'

"'*Did* you,' he said, looking at me as if maybe I'd gone crazy. 'Well, that's very kind of you to say, anyway. I woke up this morning and I had an idea.'

"*Yes sir,* I was thinking to myself, *you had an idea, all right, and whatever it was came out all over the sheet. Only it ain't there no more, so you don't have to worry.* And I almost laughed out loud. Only, Delores, I don't think he would have noticed if I had.

"'I ordered up some breakfast,' he said, and pointed at the room service trolley by the door, 'and as I ate it I thought about this little idea. I thought it might make a short story. There's this magazine, you know . . . *The New Yorker* . . . well, never mind.' He wasn't going to explain *The New Yorker* magazine to a darkie spear-chucker like me, you know."

Delores laughed.

"'But by the time I'd finished breakfast,' he went on, 'it began to seem more like it might be a novelette. And then I started to work on it . . . rough out some ideas . . . and now . . .' He gave out this shrill little laugh. 'I don't think I've had an idea this good in ten years. Maybe never. Do you think it would be possible for twin brothers—fraternal, not identical—to end up fighting on opposite sides during World War II?'

"'Well, maybe not in the *Pacific*,' I said. Another time I don't think I would have had nerve enough to speak to him at all, Delores—I would have just stood there and gawped. But I still felt like I was under glass, or like I'd had a bit of nitrous oxide at the dentist's and wasn't quite out from under it yet.

"He laughed like it was the funniest thing he'd ever heard and said, 'No, not there—in the ETO. And they'd come face to face during the Battle of the Bulge.'

"'Well, I guess that could be—' I started, but by then he was walking around the parlor again, fast, running his hands through his hair and making it look wilder and wilder.

"'I know it sounds like Orpheum Circuit melodrama,' he said, 'some silly piece of claptrap like *Armadale*, but the concept of twins . . . and it could be explained rationally . . . I see just how . . .' He whirled on me. 'Would it have dramatic impact?'

"'Yes, sir, everyone likes stories about brothers that don't know they're brothers, especially if they're twins,' I said.

"'Sure they do,' he said. 'And I'll tell you something else—' Then he stopped and I saw the queerest expression come over his face. It was queer, but I could read it letter-perfect. It was like he was waking up to do something foolish, like a man suddenly realizing he's spread his face with shaving cream and then taken his electric razor to it. He was talking to a nigger hotel maid about what was maybe the best idea he'd ever had—a nigger hotel maid whose idea of a good story was probably *The Edge of Night* or *Search for Tomorrow*. He'd forgot me saying I'd read two of his books—"

"Or thought it was just a lie to flatter him and get a bigger tip," Delores murmured.

"Yeah, or maybe that. Anyway, that expression said he'd just realized who he was talking to, that was all.

"'I think I'm going to extend my stay,' he said. 'Tell them at the desk, would you?' He spun around to start walking again and his leg hit the room service cart. 'And get this out of here, would you?'

"'Would you want me to come back later and—' I started.

"'Yes, yes, yes,' he says, 'come back later and do whatever you like. Just be a good girl and take the cart and go.'

"I did just that, and I was never so relieved in my life as when the parlor door shut behind me. I wheeled the room service trolley over to the side of the wall. He'd had juice and scrambled eggs and bacon. I started to walk away and then I seen there was a mushroom on his plate, too, pushed aside with the last of the eggs and a little bit of bacon. I looked at it and it was like a light went on in my head. I remembered the mushroom *she'd* given me—old Mama Delorme—in the little plastic box. Remembered it for the first time since that day. I remembered taking it home, and finding it in my dress pocket, and where I'd put it. The one on his plate looked just the same—old and wrinkled and sort of dried up, like it might be a toadstool instead of a mushroom, and one that would make you powerful sick.

She looked at Delores steadily.

"He'd eaten part of it. More than half of it, I'd say."

## 17

"Mr Buckley was on the desk that day and I told him Mr Jefferies was thinking of extending his stay. Mr Buckley said he didn't think that would present a problem even though Mr Jefferies had been planning to check out the very next day.

"Then I went down to the room service kitchen and talked with Bedelia Aaronson—she died just last year, God rest her sweet soul—and asked her if she'd seen anyone out of the ordinary around that morning. Bedelia asked who did I mean and I said I didn't really know. She said 'Why you asking, Marty?' and I told her I'd rather not say. She said there hadn't been nobody, not even the man from the food service who was trying to date up the girl who was short-ordering then.

"I started away and she said, 'Unless you mean that old Negro lady, the one that got lost looking for the john.'

"I turned back and asked her what old Negro lady that was.

"'Well,' Bedelia said, 'I imagine she came in off the street, looking for the rest room. Happens once or twice a day. They're afraid to ask directions because the hotel people are just as apt to point them at the door as at the can. She probably came downstairs, turned left instead of right, ended up here, and . . .' She stopped and got a look at me. 'Are you all right, Martha? You look like you're going to faint!'

"'I'm not going to faint,' I said. 'What was she doing?'

"'Just wandering around, looking at the breakfast trolleys like she didn't know where she was,' she said. 'Poor old thing! She was eighty if she was a day. Looked like a strong gust of wind would blow her right up into the sky like a kite . . . Martha, you come over here and sit down. You look like the picture of Dorian Gray in that movie.'

"'What did she look like?'

"'I *told* you what she looked like. She looked like an old woman. The only thing I remember is that she had the most awful scar—it ran all the way up her nose and her forehead and into her hair. It—'

"But I didn't hear any more because that was when I *did* faint, right into a big bowl of chef's salad she was making for lunch."

18

"They let me go home early and I no more got there when I started feeling like I wanted to spit again, and drink a lot of water, and probably end up down in that john again, sicking my guts out. But I just sat there by the window, looking out into the street, and gave myself a talking-to.

"What she'd done to me wasn't just hypnosis—I knew that. It was more powerful than that. I still wasn't sure if I believed in any such thing as witchcraft, but she'd done *something* to me, all right, and whatever it was, I was just going to have to ride with it. I couldn't quit my job, not with a man that wasn't turning out to be worth a damn and a baby most likely on the way. I couldn't even request to be switched to a different floor. A year or two before I could have, but I knew there was talk about making me Assistant Chief Housekeeper for Ten to Twelve, and that meant a raise in pay. More'n that, it meant they'd most likely take me back at the same job after I had the baby.

"My mother had a saying: *What can't be cured must be endured.* I thought about going back to see that old black mama and asking her to take it off, but I knew somehow she wouldn't—she'd made up her mind it was best for me, what she was doing, and one thing I've learned as I've made my way through this world, Delores, is that the only time you can never change someone's mind is when they've got it in their head that they're doing you a help.

"I sat there thinking all those things and looking out at the street, all the people coming and going, and I kind of dozed off. Couldn't have been for much more than fifteen minutes, but when I woke up again I knew something else. That old woman wanted me to eat his stuff, and I couldn't do that if he went back to Birmingham. So she got into the room service kitchen and put that mushroom on his tray and he ate part of it and it gave him that idea. Turned out to be a book, in case you're interested—*Boys in the Mist*, it was called. It was about just what he told me that day, twin brothers, one of them an American soldier and the other a German one, that meet at the Battle of the Bulge. The critics didn't like it as well as *Blaze of Heaven*, but the people who go out and buy books surely must have liked it, because it was the biggest seller he ever had."

She paused and added, "I read that in his obituary."

## 19

"He stayed another week. Every day when I went in he'd be bent over the desk in the parlor, writing away on one of his yellow pads, still wearing his pajamas. I'd ask him if he wanted me to come back later and he'd tell me to go ahead and make up the bedroom but be quiet about it. Never looking up from his writing while he talked. Each day I went in telling myself that this time I wasn't going to do it, and each day I went ahead and did it just the same. It wasn't like fighting a—what do you call it?—a compulsion. It was more like blinking for a minute and finding out you'd already done it. Or were *doing* it. He never came in, and the come was always on the sheet, still partly wet, like he woke up at exactly the same time every morning and pulled off at exactly the same time. I had no doubt then and no doubt now that was exactly what he did. He had my morning-sickness and I had his night-sweats.

"It was at night I'd really start thinking about what I was doing, and I'd start to spit and drink water and then I'd go down to the bathroom and throw up once or twice. Mrs Parker got so concerned that I finally told her it was because I was pregnant, only she wasn't to tell Johnny because I wasn't sure how he'd take it.

"Johnny Rosewall was one self-centered son of a bitch, but I think even he would have known something was wrong with me if he hadn't had things of his own to think about—him and a couple of his no-good friends were planning a liquor store holdup. He didn't even have much time to knock me around. I knew by then I'd have to leave him, but I just didn't have the strength to do it. I was still living behind that glass wall, it felt like.

"Then I let myself into 1163 one morning and Mr Jefferies was gone. He'd packed his bags and headed back to Alabama to work on his book and think about his war. Oh, Delores, I can't tell you how happy I felt! I felt the way Lazarus must have felt when he found out he was going to have a second turn at the bat. All at once it seemed like everything might turn out all right after all, like in a story—I would tell Johnny about the baby and he would straighten up, throw out his dope, and get a regular job. He'd be a proper husband to me and a good father to his son—I was already sure it was going to be a boy.

"I went into the bedroom of Mr Jefferies's suite and seen the bedclothes all messed up like they always were when he was there, the blankets kicked off the end and the sheet all tangled up in a ball. I walked over there feeling like I was in a dream again and pulled the sheet back. I was thinking, *Well, all right, if I have to . . . but it's for the last time.*

"But it turned out the last time had already happened. There wasn't no mark of him on that sheet. And since I've told you all this, I might as well tell you the truth about something else: part of me was almost disappointed.

"It was over. Whatever spell that old *bruja* woman had put on me—and on the writer, too—it was over. *That's good enough*, I thought. *I'm gonna have the baby and he's gonna have the book, and we're shut of it. And I don't care anything about natural fathers as long as Johnny will be a good father to my little chap."*

20

"I told him that same night," she said, and then added dryly: "He wasn't too pleased about the idea of becoming a daddy, as I think I've told you."

"He hit you with a broom and tried to make you drop it," Delores said.

"Yes. Hit me more than once. Hit me about five times and then stood over me where I lay crying in the corner and yelled, 'What are you, crazy, woman? We ain't having no *kid*! We ain't having no goddamn *kid*! I think you out your mind!' Then he turned around and walked out.

"I laid there for awhile, thinking of the first miscarriage and scared to death the pains would start any minute, and I'd be on my way to having another one. I thought of my momma writing that I ought to get away from him before he put me in the hospital, and of Kissy sending me that Greyhound ticket with GO NOW written on the folder. And when I was sure that I wasn't going to miscarry the baby, I got up to pack a bag and get the hell out of there—right away, before he could come back. But I was no more than opening the closet door when I thought of Mama Delorme again. I remembered telling her I was going to leave Johnny, and what she said to me: 'No—he's going to leave *you*. You're going to see him out, is all. Stay around. There be a little money. You gonna think he hoit the baby but he din't be doin it.'

"It was like she was right there, telling me what to look for and what to do. I went into the closet, all right, but it wasn't my own clothes I wanted anymore. I started going through his, and I found a couple of things in that same damned sport-coat where I'd found the bottle of White Angel. That coat was his favorite, and I guess it really said everything anyone needed to know about Johnny Rosewall. It was a bright purple niggery-looking thing. I hated it. Wasn't no bottle of dope I found this time. Was a straight-razor in one pocket and the cheap gun he'd bought someplace for the liquor store holdup him and his friends had planned in the other. I took the gun out and looked at it, and that same feeling came over me that came over me those times in the bedroom of Mr Jefferies's suite—like I was doing something just after I woke up from a heavy sleep.

"I walked into the kitchen with the gun in my hand and set it down on the little bit of counter I had beside the stove. Then I opened the overhead cupboard and felt around in back of the spices and the box of tea. At first I couldn't find what she'd given me and this awful stifling panic came over me—I was scared the way you get scared in dreams. Then my hand happened on that plastic box and I drew it down.

"I opened it and took out the mushroom. It was a repulsive thing, too heavy for its size, and *warm*, Delores. It was like holding a lump of flesh that hasn't quite died. That thing I did over and over again in Mr Jefferies's bedroom? That nasty thing? I tell you right now I'd do it again two hundred times over before I'd pick up that mushroom one more time.

"I held it in my right hand and I picked up that cheap little .32 in my left. And then I squeezed my right hand as hard as I could, and I felt the mushroom squelch in my fist, and it sounded . . . well, I know it's almost impossible to believe . . . but it sounded like it screamed. Do you believe that could be?"

Slowly, Delores shook her head. She did not, in fact, know if she believed it or not, but she was absolutely sure of one thing: she did not *want* to believe it.

"Well, I don't believe it, either. But that's what it sounded like. And one other thing you won't believe, but I do, because I saw it: it bled. That mushroom bled. I saw a little stream of blood come out of my fist and splash onto the gun. But the blood disappeared as soon as it hit the barrel.

"After a while there were just drops, and then nothing. I opened my hand, expecting it would be full of blood, but there was just that mushroom, all smashed up, with the shapes of my fingers mashed into it. Wasn't no blood on the mushroom, in my hand, on his gun, nor any-where. And I started to think I'd done nothing but somehow dreamed it all, and then it twitched in my hand and for just a second there it didn't look like a mushroom at all—it looked like a little tiny penis that was still alive. I thought of the blood coming out of my fist when I squeezed it and I thought of her saying 'Any chile a woman get, the man shoot it out'n his pecker, girl.' It twitched again—I tell you I *saw* it do, Delores—and I screamed and threw it in the trash. Then I heard Johnny coming back up the stairs and I grabbed up his gun and took it back into the bedroom and put it back into his coat pocket. Then I climbed into bed with all my clothes on, even my shoes, and pulled the blanket up to my chin. He come in and I seen he was drunk or stoned or both, and that he meant trouble. He had a rug-beater in one hand. I don't know where he got it from, but I knew what he meant to do with it.

"'Ain't gonna be no baby, woman,' he said. 'You get on over here.'

"'No,' I says, 'there ain't going to be no baby. Put that thing away. You don't need it. You already took care of the baby, you worthless piece of shit.'

"I knew it was a risk, calling him that; it might make him mad enough to come back and land on me again, but I thought maybe it would make him believe me . . . and it did. Instead of coming over and beating me up, this big goony stoned grin spread over his face. I tell you, I never hated him so much as I did then.

"'It's gone?' he said.

"'It's gone, all right,' I said.

"'Where?' he said.

"'I got rid of the mess down the hall in the bathroom,' I said, 'where do you think?'

"He come over then and he tried to kiss me, for Jesus's sake. *Kiss* me! I turned my face away and he went upside my head, but not hard.

"'You're gonna see I know best,' he says. 'There'll be time enough for kids later on.'

"Then he went out again. Two nights later him and his friends tried to pull that liquor store job and his gun blew up in his face and killed him."

"You think you witched that gun, don't you?" Delores said.

"No," Martha said calmly, "I think *she* did. She just used me. She saw I wouldn't help myself, and so she *made* me help myself."

"But you think the gun was witched."

"No," Martha said again, and then smiled a cold and unsettling smile of absolute surety. "I don't *think* it was; I *know* it was."

21

"That's really the end," Martha said, shrugging. "Johnny died and I had Pete. Wasn't until I got too pregnant to work that I found out just how many friends I had. If I'd known, I think I would have left him sooner."

"That's not really the end, though, is it?" Delores asked.

"Well, there *are* two more things," she said. "Little things." But she did not look, Delores thought, as though they were so little to her.

"I went back to Mama Delorme's about four months after Pete was born. I didn't want to but I did. I had twenty dollars in an envelope. I couldn't afford it but I knew, somehow, that it belonged to her. It was dark. Stairs seemed even narrower than before, and the higher I climbed the more I could smell her and the smells of her place. Burned candles and dried wallpaper and the cinnamony smell of her tea.

"That feeling came over me for the last time—that

feeling of doing something in a dream. I got up to the door and knocked. There was no answer, so I knocked again. There was still no answer, so I knelt down to slip the envelope under the door. And her voice come from *right on the other side*, as if she was knelt down, too. I was never so scared in my life as I was when that papery old voice came drifting out of the crack under that door—it was like hearing a voice coming out of a closed grave.

"'He goan be a fine boy,' she said. 'Goan be just like he father. Like he *natural* father.'

"'I brought you something,' I said. I could barely hear my own voice.

"'Slip it under here, dearie,' she whispered. I slipped the envelope halfway under and she pulled it the rest of the way. I heard her tear it open and I waited. I just waited.

"'It's enough,' she whispered. 'You go on out of here, dearie, and don't you ever come back to Mama Delorme's again, you hear?'

"I got up and ran out of there just as fast as I could."

22

Martha got up, went over to the bookcase, and came back a moment or two later with a hardcover. Delores was immediately struck by the similarity between the artwork on this jacket and the artwork on the jacket of Peter Rosewall's book. This one was *Blaze of Heaven* by Peter Jefferies, and the cover showed a pair of GI's charging an enemy pillbox. One of them had a grenade in his hand; the other was firing an M-1.

Martha rummaged in her blue canvas tote-bag, brought out her son's book, removed the tissue paper in which it was wrapped, and laid it tenderly next to the Jefferies book. *Blaze of Heaven; Blaze of Glory*. Side by side, the points of comparison were inescapable.

"This was the other thing," Martha said.

"Yes," Delores said doubtfully. "They *do* look similar. But I still think it's possible—"

"No," Martha said. "That's not what I mean."

She picked up the Jefferies novel. She looked at it reflectively for a moment and then looked at Delores. "I bought this about a year after my son was born," she said. "It was still in print, although the bookstore had to special order it from the publisher. When Mr Jefferies was in on one of his visits, I got up my courage and asked if he would sign it for me. I thought he might be put out by me asking, but I think he was actually a little flattered. Look here."

She turned to the dedication page of *Blaze of Heaven*.

Delores read what was printed there and felt an eerie doubling in her mind. *This book is dedicated to my mother, ALTHEA DIXMONT JEFFERIES, the finest woman I have ever known.* And below that Jefferies had written in black fountain-pen ink that was now fading, "For Martha Rosewall, who cleans up my leavings and never complains." Below this he had signed his name and jotted *August, '60*.

The wording of the penned dedication struck her first as contemptuous . . . then as eerie. But before she had a chance to think about it, Martha had opened her son's book, *Blaze of Glory*, to the dedication page and placed it beside the Jefferies book. Once again Delores read the printed matter: *This book is dedicated to my mother, MARTHA ROSEWALL. Mom, I couldn't have done it without you.* Below that he had written in a pen which looked like a fine-line Flair: *I really couldn't have done it without you! I love you, Pete.*

But she didn't really read this; she only looked at it. Her eyes went back and forth, back and forth, between the dedication page which had been inscribed in August of 1960 and the one which had been inscribed in April of 1985.

"You see?" Martha asked softly.

Delores nodded. She saw.

The thin and sloping backhand script was exactly the same in both books, and the same was almost true of the signatures themselves.

Only the dates and the last names differed.

DAN SIMMONS

# METASTASIS

On the day Louis Steig received a call from his sister saying that their mother had collapsed and been admitted to a Denver hospital with a diagnosis of cancer, he promptly jumped into his Camaro, headed for Denver at high speed, hit a patch of black ice on the Boulder Turnpike, flipped his car seven times, and ended up in a coma from a fractured skull and a severe concussion. He was unconscious for nine days. When he awoke he was told that a minute sliver of bone had actually penetrated the left frontal lobe of his brain. He remained hospitalized for eighteen more days—not even in the same hospital as his mother—and when he left it was with a headache worse than anything he had ever imagined, blurred vision, word from the doctors that there was a serious chance that some brain damage had been suffered, and news from his sister that their mother's cancer was terminal and in its final stages.

The worst had not yet begun.

It was three more days before Louis was able to visit his mother. His headaches remained and his vision retained a slightly blurred quality—as with a television channel poorly tuned—but the bouts of blinding pain and uncontrolled vomiting had passed. His sister Lee drove and his fiancée Debbie accompanied him on the twenty mile ride from Boulder to Denver General Hospital.

"She sleeps most of the time but it's mostly the drugs," said Lee. "They keep her heavily sedated. She probably won't recognize you even if she is awake."

"I understand," said Louis.

"The doctors say that she must have felt the lump . . . understood what the pain meant . . . for at least a year. If she had only . . . It would have meant losing her breast even then, probably both of them, but they might have been able to . . ." Lee took a deep breath. "I was with her all morning. I just can't . . . can't go back up there again today, Louis. I hope you understand."

"Yes," said Louis.

"Do you want me to go in with you?" asked Debbie.

"No," said Louis.

Louis sat holding his mother's hand for almost an hour. It seemed to him that the sleeping woman on the bed was a stranger. Even through the slight blurring of his sight, he knew that she looked twenty years older than the person he had known; her skin was gray and sallow, her hands were heavily veined and bruised from IVs, her arms lacked any muscle tone, and her body under the hospital gown looked shrunken and concave. A bad smell surrounded her. Louis stayed thirty minutes beyond the end of visiting hours and left only when his headaches threatened to return in full force. His mother remained asleep. Louis squeezed the rough hand, kissed her on the forehead, and rose to go.

He was almost out of the room when he glanced at the mirror and saw movement. His mother continued to sleep but someone was sitting in the chair Louis had just vacated. He wheeled around.

The chair was empty.

Louis's headache flared like the thrust of a heated wire behind his left eye. He turned back to the mirror, moving his head slowly so as not to exacerbate the pain and vertigo. The image in the mirror was more clear than his vision had been for days.

Something was sitting in the chair he had just vacated.

Louis blinked and moved closer to the wall mirror, squinting slightly to resolve the image. The figure on the chair was somewhat misty, slightly diffuse against a more focused background, but there was no denying the reality and solidity of it. At first Louis thought it was a child—the form was small and frail, the size of an emaciated ten-year-old—but then he leaned closer to the mirror, squinted through the haze of his headache, and all thoughts of children fled.

The small figure leaning over his mother had a large, shaven head perched on a thin neck and even thinner body. Its skin was white—not flesh white but paper white, fish-belly white—and the arms were skin and tendon wrapped tightly around long bone. The hands were pale and enormous, fingers at least six inches long, and as Louis watched they unfolded and hovered over his mother's bedclothes. As Louis squinted he realized that the figure's head was not shaven but simply hairless—he could see veins through the translucent flesh—and the skull was disturbingly broad, brachycephalic, and so out of proportion with the body that the sight of it made him think of photographs of embryos and fetuses. As if in response to this thought, the thing's head began to oscillate slowly as if the long, thin neck could no longer support its weight. Louis thought of a snake closing on its prey.

Louis could do nothing but stare at the image of pale flesh, sharp bone and bruise-colored shadows. He thought fleetingly of concentration camp inmates shuffling to the wire, of week-dead corpses floating to the surface like inflatable things made of rotted white rubber. This was worse.

It had no ears. A rimmed ragged hole with reddened flanges of flesh opened directly into the misshapen skull. The eyes were bruised holes, sunken blue-black sockets in which someone had set two yellowed marbles as a joke. There were no eyelids. The eyes were obviously blind, clouded with yellow cataracts so thick that Louis could see layers of striated mucus. Yet they darted to and fro purposefully, a predator's darting, lurking glare, as the great head moved closer to his mother's sleeping form. In its own way, Louis realized, the thing could see.

Louis whirled around, opened his mouth to shout, took two steps toward the bed and the suddenly empty chair, stopped with fists clenched, mouth still straining with his silent scream, and turned back to the mirror.

The thing had no mouth as such, no lips, but under the long, thin nose the bones of cheeks and jaw seemed to flow forward under white flesh to form a funnel, a long tapered snout of muscle and cartilage which ended in a perfectly round opening which pulsed slightly as pale-pink sphincter muscles around the inner rim expanded and contracted with the creature's breath or pulse. Louis staggered and grasped the back of an empty chair, closing his eyes, weak with waves of headache pain and sudden nausea. He was sure that nothing could be more obscene than what he had just seen.

Louis opened his eyes and realized that he was wrong.

The thing had slowly, almost lovingly, pulled down the thin blanket and topsheet which covered Louis's mother. Now it lowered its misshapen head over his mother's chest until the opening of that obscene proboscis was scant inches away from the faded blue-flower print of her hospital gown. Something appeared in the flesh-rimmed opening, something gray-green, segmented, and moist. Small, fleshy antennae tested the air. The great, white head bent lower, cartilage and muscle contracted, and a five-inch slug was slowly extruded, wiggling slightly as it hung above Louis's mother.

Louis threw his head back in a scream that finally could be heard, tried to turn, tried to remove his hands from their deathgrip on the back of the empty chair, tried to look away from the mirror. And could not.

Under the slug's polyps of antennae was a face that was all mouth, the feeding orifice of some deep sea parasite. It pulsed as the moist slug fell softly onto his mother's chest, coiled, writhed, and burrowed quickly away from the light. Into his mother. The thing left no mark, no trail, not even a hole in the hospital gown. Louis could see the slightest ripple of flesh as the slug disappeared under the pale flesh of his mother's chest.

The white head of the child-thing pulled back, the yellow eyes stared directly at Louis through the mirror, and then the face lowered to his mother's flesh again. A second slug appeared, dropped, burrowed. A third.

Louis screamed again, found freedom from paralysis, turned, ran to the bed and the apparently empty chair, thrashed the air, kicked the chair into a distant corner, and ripped the sheet and blanket and gown away from his mother.

Two nurses and an attendant came running as they heard Louis's screams. They burst into the room to find him crouched over his mother's naked form, his nails clawing at her scarred and shrunken chest where the surgeons had recently removed both breasts. After a moment of shocked immobility, one nurse and the attendant seized and held Louis while the other nurse filled a syringe with a strong tranquilizer. But before she could administer it, Louis looked in the mirror, pointed to a space near the opposite side of the bed, screamed a final time, and fainted.

"It's perfectly natural," said Lee the next day after their second trip to the Boulder Clinic. "A perfectly understandable reaction."

"Yes," said Louis. He stood in his pajamas and watched her fold back the top sheet on his bed.

"Dr Kirby says that injuries to that part of the brain can cause strange emotional reactions," said Debbie from her place by the window. "Sort of like whatshisname . . . Reagan's press secretary who was shot years ago, only temporary, of course."

"Yeah," said Louis, lying back, settling his head into

the tall stack of pillows. There was a mirror on the wall opposite. His gaze never left it.

"Mom was awake for a while this morning," said Lee. "*Really* awake. I told her you'd been in to see her. She doesn't . . . doesn't remember your visit, of course. She wants to see you."

"Maybe tomorrow," said Louis. The mirror showed the reversed images of the three of them. Just the three of them. Sunlight fell in a yellow band across Debbie's red hair and Lee's arm. The pillowcases behind Louis's head were very white.

"Tomorrow," agreed Lee. "Or maybe the day after. Right now you need to take some of the medication Dr Kirby gave you and get some sleep. We can go visit Mom together when you feel better."

"Tomorrow," said Louis, and he closed his eyes.

He stayed in bed for six days, rising only to go to the bathroom or to change channels on his portable TV. The headaches were constant but manageable. He saw nothing unusual in the mirror. On the seventh day he rose about ten A.M., showered slowly, dressed in his camel slacks, white shirt, and blue blazer, and was prepared to tell Lee that he was ready to visit the hospital when his sister came into the room red-eyed.

"They just called," she said. "Mother died about twenty minutes ago."

The funeral home was about two blocks from where his mother had lived, where Louis had grown up after they had moved from Des Moines when he was ten, just east of the Capitol Hill area where old brick homes were becoming rundown rentals and where Hispanic street gangs had claimed the night.

According to his mother's wishes there would be a "visitation" this night where Denver friends could pay their respects before the casket was flown back to Des Moines the next day for the funeral Mass at St Mary's and final interment at the small city cemetery where Louis's father was buried. Louis thought that the open casket was an archaic act of barbarism. He stayed as far away from it as he could, greeting people at the door, catching glimpses only of his mother's nose, folded hands, or rouged cheeks.

About sixty people showed up during the two-hour ordeal, most of them in their early seventies—his mother's age—people from the block whom he hadn't seen in fifteen years or new friends she had met through Bingo or the Senior Citizens Center. Several of Louis's Boulder friends showed up, including two members of his Colorado Mountain Club hiking group and two colleagues from the physics labs at CU. Debbie stayed by his side the entire time, watching his pale, sweaty face and occasionally squeezing his hand when she saw the pain from the headache wash across him.

The visitation period was almost over when suddenly he could no longer stand it. "Do you have a compact?" he asked Debbie.

"A what?"

"A compact," he said. "You know, one of those little make-up things with a mirror."

Debbie shook her head. "Louis, have you *ever* seen me with something like that?" She rummaged in her purse. "Wait a minute. I have this little hand mirror that I use to check my . . ."

"Give it here," said Louis. He raised the small plastic-backed rectangle, turning toward the doorway to get a better view behind him.

About a dozen mourners remained, talking softly in the dim light and flower-scented stillness. Someone in the hallway beyond the doorway laughed and then lowered his voice. Lee stood near the casket, her black dress swallowing light, speaking quietly to old Mrs Narmoth from across the alley.

There were twenty or thirty other small figures in the room, moving like pale shadows between rows of folding chairs and dark-suited mourners. They moved slowly, carefully, seeming to balance their oversized heads in a delicate dance. Each of the child-sized forms awaited its turn to approach the casket and then moved forward, its pale body and bald head emitting its own soft penumbra of greenish-grayish glow. Each thing paused by the casket briefly and then lowered its head slowly, almost reverently.

Gasping in air, his hand shaking so badly the mirror image blurred and vibrated, Louis was reminded of lines of celebrants at his First Communion . . . and of animals at a trough.

"Louis, what is it?" asked Debbie.

He shook off her hand, turned and ran toward the casket, shouldering past mourners, feeling cold churnings in his belly as he wondering if he was passing *through* the white things.

"What?" asked Lee, her face a mask of concern as she took his arm.

Louis shook her away and looked into the casket. Only the top half of the lid was raised. His mother lay there in her best blue dress, the make-up seeming to return some fullness to her ravaged face, her old rosary laced through her folded fingers. The cushioned lining under her was silk and beige and looked very soft. Louis raised the mirror. His only reaction then was slowly to lift his left hand and to grasp the rim of the casket very tightly, as if it were the railing of a ship in rough seas and he were in imminent danger of plunging overboard.

There were several hundred of the slug-things in the coffin, flowing over everything inside it, filling it to the brim. They were more white than green or gray now and much, much larger, some as thick through the body as Louis's forearm. Many were more than a foot long. The antennae tendrils had contracted and widened into tiny yellow eyes and the lamprey mouths were recognizably tapered now.

As Louis watched, one of the pale, child-sized figures to his right approached the casket, laid long white fingers not six inches from Louis's hand, and lowered its face as if to drink.

Louis watched as the thing ingested four of the long, pale slugs, the creature's entire face contracting and expanding almost erotically to absorb the soft mass of its meal. The yellow eyes did not blink. Others approached the casket and joined in the communion. Louis lowered the angle of the mirror and watched two more slugs flow effortlessly out of his mother, sliding through blue material into the churning mass of their fellows. Louis moved the mirror, looked behind him, seeing the half-dozen pale forms standing there, waiting patiently for him to move. Their bodies were pale and sexless blurs. Their fingers were very long and very sharp. Their eyes were hungry.

Louis did not scream. He did not run. Very carefully he palmed the mirror, released his death grip on the edge of the casket, and walked slowly, carefully, away from there. Away from the casket. Away from Lee and Debbie's distantly heard cries and questions. Away from the funeral home.

He was hours and miles away, in a strange section of dark warehouses and factories, when he stopped in the mercury-arc circle of a streetlight, held the mirror high, swiveled 360 degrees to ascertain that nothing and no one was in sight, and then huddled at the base of the streetlight to hug his knees, rock, and croon.

"I think they're cancer vampires," Louis told the psychiatrist. Between the wooden shutters on the doctor's windows, Louis caught a glimpse of the rocky slabs that were the Flatirons. "They lay these tumor-slugs that hatch and change inside people. What we call tumors are really eggs. Then the cancer vampires take them back into themselves."

The psychiatrist nodded, tamped down his pipe, and lighted another match. "Do you wish to tell me more . . . ah . . . details . . . about these images you have?" He puffed his pipe alight.

Louis started to shake his head and then stopped suddenly as headache pain rippled through him. "I've thought it all out in the last few weeks," he said. "I mean, go back more than a hundred years and give me the name of one famous person who died of cancer. Go ahead."

The doctor drew on his pipe. His desk was in front of the shuttered windows and his face was in shadow, only occasionally illuminated when he turned as he relit his pipe. "I can't think of one right now," the doctor said, "but there must be many."

"*Exactly*," said Louis in a more excited tone than he had meant to use. "I mean, today we *expect* people to die of cancer. One in six. Or maybe it's one in four. I mean, I didn't know *anyone* who died in Viet Nam, but *everybody* knows somebody—usually somebody in our family—who's died of cancer. Just think of all the movie stars and politicians. I mean, it's everywhere. It's the plague of the Twentieth Century."

The doctor nodded and kept any patronizing tones out of his voice. "I see your point," he said. "But just because modern diagnostic methods did not exist before this does not mean people did not die of cancer in previous centuries. Besides, research has shown that modern technology, pollutants, food additives and so forth have increased the risk of encountering carcinogens which . . ."

"Yeah," laughed Louis, "carcinogens. That's what I used to believe in. But, Jesus, Doc, have you ever read over the AMA's and American Cancer Society's official lists of carcinogens? I mean it's everything you eat, breathe, wear, touch, and do to have fun. I mean it's *everything*. That's the same as just saying that they don't know. Believe me, I've been reading all of that crap, they don't even know what makes a tumor start growing."

The doctor steepled his fingers. "But you believe that you do, Mr Steig?"

Louis took one of his mirrors from his shirt pocket and moved his head in quick half-circles. The room seemed empty. "Cancer vampires," he said. "I don't know how long they've been around. Maybe something we did this century allowed them to come through some . . . some gate or something. I don't know."

"From another dimension?" the doctor asked in conversational tones. His pipe tobacco smelled vaguely of pine woods on a summer day.

"Maybe," shrugged Louis. "I don't know. But they're here and they're busy feeding . . . and multiplying . . ."

"Why do you think that you are the only one who has been allowed to see them?" asked the doctor brightly.

Louis felt himself growing angry. "Goddammit, I don't *know* that I'm the only one who can see them. I just know that something happened after my accident . . ."

"Would it not be . . . equally probable," suggested the doctor, "that the injury to your skull has caused some *very* realistic hallucinations? You admit that your sight has been somewhat affected." He removed his pipe, frowned at it, and fumbled for his matches.

Louis gripped the arms of his chair, feeling the anger in him rise and fall on the waves of his headache. "I've been back to the Clinic," he said. "They can't find any sign of permanent damage. My vision's a little funny— but that's just because I can see *more* now. I mean, more colors and things. It's like I can see radio waves almost."

"Let us assume that you do have the power to see these . . . cancer vampires," said the doctor. The tobacco glowed on his third inhalation. The room smelled of sunwarmed pine needles. "Does this mean that you also have the power to *control* them?"

Louis ran his hand across his brow, trying to rub away the pain. "I don't know."

"I'm sorry, Mr Steig. I couldn't hear . . ."

"I don't know!" shouted Louis. "I haven't tried to *touch* one. I mean, I don't know if . . . I'm afraid that it might . . . Look, so far the things . . . the cancer vampires—they've ignored me, but . . ."

"If you can see them," said the doctor, "doesn't it follow that they can see you?"

Louis rose and went to the window, tugging open the shutters so the room was filled with late afternoon light. "I think they see what they want to see," said Louis, staring at the foothills beyond the city, playing with his hand mirror. "Maybe we're just blurs to them. They find us easily enough when it's time to lay their eggs."

The doctor squinted in the sudden brightness but removed his pipe and smiled. "You talk about eggs," he said, "but what you described sounded more like feeding behavior. Does this discrepancy and the fact that the . . . vision . . . first occurred when your mother was dying suggest any deeper meanings to you? We all search for ways to control things we have no power over— things we find too difficult to accept. Especially when one's mother is involved."

"Look," sighed Louis, "I don't need this Freudian crap. I agreed to come here today because Deb's been on my case for weeks but . . ." Louis stopped and raised his mirror, and stared.

The doctor glanced up as he scraped at his pipe bowl. His mouth was slightly open, showing white teeth, healthy gums, and a hint of tongue slightly curled in concentration. From beneath that tongue came first the fleshy antennae and then the green-gray body of a tumor slug, this one no more than a few centimeters long. It moved higher along the psychiatrist's jaw, sliding in and out of the muscles and skin of the man's cheek as effortlessly as a maggot moving in a compost heap. Deeper in the shadows of the doctor's mouth, something larger stirred.

"It can't hurt to talk about it," said the doctor. "After all, that's what I'm here for."

Louis nodded, pocketed his mirror, and walked straight to the door without looking back.

Louis found that it was easy to buy mirrors cheaply. They were available, framed and unframed, at used furniture outlets, junk-shops, discount antique dealers, hardware stores, glass shops and even in people's stacks of junk sitting on the curb awaiting pickup. It took Louis less than a week to fill his small apartment with mirrors.

His bedroom was the best protected. Besides the twenty-three mirrors of various sizes on the walls, the ceiling had been completely covered with mirrors. He had put them up himself, pressing them firmly into the glue, feeling slightly more secure with each reflective square he set in place.

Louis was lying on his bed on a Saturday afternoon in May, staring at the reflections of himself, thinking about a conversation he had just had with his sister Lee, when Debbie called. She wanted to come over. He suggested that they meet on the Pearl Street Mall instead.

There were three passengers and two of *them* on the bus. One had been in the rear seat when Louis boarded, another came through the closed doors when the bus stopped for a red light. The first time he had seen one of the cancer vampires pass through a solid object, Louis had been faintly relieved, as if something so insubstantial could not be a serious threat. He no longer felt that way. They did not float through walls in the delicate, effortless glide of a ghost; Louis watched while the hairless head and sharp shoulders of this thing struggled to penetrate the closed doors of the bus, wiggling like someone passing through a thick sheet of cellophane. Or like some vicious newborn predator chewing its way through its own amniotic sac.

Louis pulled down another of the small mirrors attached by wires to the brim of his Panama hat and watched while the second cancer vampire joined the first and the two closed on the old lady sitting with her shopping bags two rows behind him. She sat stiffly upright, hands on her lap, staring straight ahead, not even blinking, as one of the cancer vampires raised its ridged funnel of a mouth to her throat, the motion as intimate and gentle as a lover's opening kiss. For the first time Louis noticed that the rim of the thing's proboscis was lined with a circle of blue cartilage which looked as sharp as razor blades. He caught a glimpse of gray-green flowing into the folds of the old lady's neck. The second cancer vampire lowered its ponderous head to her belly, a tired child preparing to rest on its mother's lap.

Louis stood, pulled the cord, and got off five blocks before his stop.

Few places in America, Louis thought, showed off health and wealth better than the three outdoor blocks of Boulder's Pearl Street Mall. A pine-scented breeze blew down from the foothills less than a quarter of a mile to the west as shoppers browsed, tourists strolled, and the locals lounged. The average person in sight was under thirty-five, tanned and fit, and wealthy enough to dress in the most casual pre-washed, pre-faded, pre-wrinkled clothes. Young men dressed only in brief trunks and sweat jogged down the mall, occasionally glancing down at their watches or their own bodies. The young women in sight were almost unanimously thin and braless, laughing with beautifully capped teeth, sitting on grassy knolls or benches with their legs spread manfully in poses out of *Vogue*. Healthy looking teenagers with spikes of hair dyed unhealthy colors licked at their two-dollar Dove bars and three-dollar Hagen Dasz cones. The spring sunlight on the brick walkways and flower beds promised an endless summer.

"Look," said Louis as he and Debbie sat near Freddy's hot dog stand and watched the crowds flow past, "my view of things right now is just too goddamn ugly to accept. Maybe *everybody* could see this shit if they wanted to, but they just refuse to." He lowered two of his mirrors and swiveled. He had tried mirrored sunglasses but that had not worked; only the full mirror-reversal allowed him to see. There were six mirrors clipped to his hat, more in his pockets.

"Oh, Louis," said Debbie. "I just don't understand . . ."

"I'm serious," snapped Louis. "We're like the people who lived in the villages of Dachau or Auschwitz. We see the fences, watch the trainloads of loaded cattle cars go by everyday, smell the smoke of the ovens . . . and *pretend it isn't happening*. We let these things take everybody, as long as it isn't us. *There*! See that heavyset man near the bookstore?"

"Yes?" Debbie was near tears.

"Wait," said Louis. He brought out his larger pocket mirror and turned at an angle. The man was wearing tan slacks and a loose Hawaiian shirt that did not hide his fat. He sipped at a drink in a red styrofoam cup and stood reading a folded copy of the *Boulder Daily Camera*. Four child-sized blurs clustered around him. One closed long fingers around the man's throat and pulled himself up across the man's arm and belly.

"Wait," repeated Louis and moved away from Debbie, scuttling sideways to keep the group framed in the mirror. The three cancer vampires did not look up as Louis came within arm's length; the fourth slid its long cone of a mouth toward the man's face.

"Wait!" screamed Louis and struck out, head averted, seeing his fist pass through the pale back of the clinging thing. There was the faintest of gelatinous givings and a chill numbed the bones of his fist and arm. Louis stared at his mirror.

All four of the cancer vampires' heads snapped around, blind yellow eyes fixed on Louis. He sobbed and struck again, feeling his fist pass through the thing with no effect and bounce weakly off the fat man's chest. Two of the white blurs swiveled slowly toward Louis.

"Hey, goddamnit!" shouted the fat man and struck at Louis's arm.

The mirror flew out of Louis's left hand and shattered on the brick pavement. "Oh, Jesus," whispered Louis, backing away. "Oh Jesus." He turned and ran, snapping down a mirror on his hat as he did so, seeing nothing but the dancing, vibrating frame. He grabbed Debbie by the wrist and tugged her to her feet. "Run!"

They ran.

Louis awoke sometime after two A.M., feeling disoriented and drugged. He felt for Debbie, remembered that he had gone back to his own apartment after they had made love. He lay in the dark, wondering what had awakened him.

His nightlight had burned out.

Louis felt a flush of cold fear, cursed, and rolled over to turn on the table lamp next to his bed. He blinked in the sudden glare, seeing blurred reflections of himself blink back from the ceiling, walls, and door.

Other things also moved in the room.

A pale face with yellow eyes pushed its way through the door and mirror. Fingers followed, finding a hold on the doorframe, pulling the body through like a climber mastering an overhang. Another face rose to the right of Louis's bed with the violent suddenness of someone stepping out of one's closet in the middle of the night, extracted its arm, and reached for the blanket bunched at the foot of Louis's bed.

"Ah," panted Louis and rolled off the bed. Except for the closet there was only the single door, closed and locked. He glanced up at the ceiling mirrors in time to see the first white shape release itself from the wood and glass and stand between the door and him. As he stared upward at his own reflection, at himself dressed in pajamas and lying on his back on the tan carpet, he watched wide-eyed as something white rippled and rose through the carpet not three feet from where he lay: a broad curve of dead grub flesh followed by a second white oval, the back and head of the thing floating up through the floor like a swimmer rising to his knees in three feet of water. The eye sockets were close enough for Louis to touch; all he had to do was extend his arm. The scent of old carrion came to him from the thing's sharp circle of a mouth.

Louis rolled sideways and back, scrambled to his feet, used a heavy chair by his bed to smash the window glass and threw the chair behind him. The rope ladder tied to the base of his bed had been left behind by a paranoid ex-roommate of Louis's who had refused to live on a third floor without a fire escape.

Louis looked up, saw white hands converging, threw the knotted rope out the window and followed it, bruising knuckles and knees against the brick wall as he clambered down.

He looked up repeatedly but there were no mirrors in

the cold spring darkness and he had no idea if anything was following.

They used Debbie's car to leave, driving west up the canyon into the mountains. Louis was wearing an old pair of jeans, green sweatshirt, and paint-spattered sneakers he had left at Debbie's after helping to paint her new apartment in January. She owned only a single portable mirror—an eighteen by twenty-four inch glass set into an antique frame above the fireplace—and Louis had ripped it off the wall and brought it along, checking every inch of the car before allowing her to enter it.

"Where are we going?" she asked as they turned south out of Nederland on the Peak to Peak Highway. The Continental Divide glowed in weak moonlight to their right. Their headlights picked out black walls of pine and stretches of snow as the narrow road wound up and around.

"Lee's cabin," said Louis. "West on the old Rollins Pass road."

"I know the cabin," said Debbie. "Will Lee be there?"

"She's still in Des Moines," he said. He blinked rapidly. "She called just before you did this afternoon. She found a . . . lump. She saw a doctor there but is going to fly back to get the biopsy."

"Louis, I . . ." began Debbie.

"Turn here," said Louis.

They drove the last two miles in silence.

The cabin had a small generator to power lights and the refrigerator but Louis preferred not to spend time filling it and priming it in the darkness out back. He asked Debbie to stay in the car while he took the mirror inside, lit two of the large candles Lee kept on the mantle, and walked through the three small rooms of the cabin with the mirror reflecting the flickering candle flame and his own pale face and staring eyes. By the time he waved Debbie inside, he had a fire going in the fireplace and the sleeper sofa in the main room was pulled out.

In the dancing light from the fireplace and candles, Debbie's hair looked impossibly red. Her eyes were tired.

"It's only a few hours until morning," said Louis. "I'll go into Nederland when we wake up and get some supplies."

Debbie touched his arm. "Louis, can you tell me what's going on?"

"Wait, wait," he said, staring into the dark corners. "There's one more thing. Undress."

"Louis . . ."

"*Undress!*" Louis was already tugging off his shirt and pants. When they were both out of their clothes, Louis propped the mirror on a chair and had them stand in front of it, turning slowly. Finally satisfied, he dropped to his knees and looked up at Debbie. She stood very still, the firelight rising and falling on her white breasts and the soft V of red pubic hair. The freckles on her shoulders and upper chest seemed to glow.

"Oh, God," said Louis and buried his face in his hands. "God, Deb, you must think I'm absolutely crazy."

She crouched next to him and ran her fingers down his back. "I don't know what's going on, Louis," she whispered, "but I know that I love you."

"I'll tell you . . ." began Louis, feeling the terrible pressure in his chest threaten to expand into sobs.

"In the morning," whispered Debbie and kissed him softly.

They made love slowly, seriously, time and their senses slowed and oddly amplified by the late hour, strange place, and fading sense of danger. Just when both of them felt the urgency quickening, Louis whispered, "Wait a second," and lay on one side, running his hand and then his mouth under the folds of her breasts, up, licking the nipples back into hardness, then kissing the curve of her belly and opening her thighs with his hand, sliding his face and body lower.

Louis closed his eyes and imagined a kitten lapping milk. He tasted the salt sweetness of sea while Debbie softened and opened herself further to him. His palms stroked the tensed smoothness of her inner thighs while her breathing came more quickly, punctuated by soft, sharp gasps of pleasure.

There was a sudden hissing behind them. The light flared and wavered.

Louis turned, sliding off the foot of the bed onto one knee, aware of the pounding of his heart and the extra vulnerability his nakedness and excitement forced on him. He looked and gasped a laugh.

"What?" whispered Debbie, not moving.

"It's just the candle I set on the floor," he whispered back. "It's drowning in its own melted wax. I'll blow it out."

He leaned over and did so, pausing as he moved back to the foot of the bed to take in a single, voyeuristic glance in the mirror propped on the chair.

Firelight played across the two lovers framed there, Louis's flushed face and Debbie's white thighs, both glistening slightly from perspiration and the moisture of their lovemaking. Seen from this angle the dancing light illuminated the copper tangle of her pubic hair and roseate ovals of moist labia with a soft clarity too purely sensuous to be pornographic. Louis felt the tides of love and sexual excitement swell in him.

He caught the movement in the mirror out of the corner of his eye a second before he would have lowered his head again. A glimmer of slick gray-green between pale pink lips. No more than a few centimeters long. Undeterred by the dim light, the twin polyps of antennae emerged slowly, twisting and turning slightly as if to taste the air.

"I didn't know you had an interest in oncology," said Dr Phil Collins. He grinned at Louis across his cluttered desk. "I thought you rarely came out of the physics lab up at the University."

Louis stared at his old classmate. He was much too tired for banter. He had not slept for 52 hours and his eyes felt like they were lined with sand and broken glass. "I need to see the radiation treatment part of chemotherapy," he said.

Collins tapped manicured nails against the edge of his desk. "Louis, we can't just give guided tours of our therapy sessions every time someone gets an interest in the process."

Louis forced his voice to stay even. "Look, Phil, my mother died of cancer a few weeks ago. My sister just underwent a biopsy that showed malignancy. My fiancée checked into Boulder Community a few hours ago with a case of cervical cancer that they're pretty sure also involved her uterus. Now will you let me watch the procedure or not?"

"Jesus," said Collins. He glanced at his watch. "Come on, Louis, you can make the rounds with me. Mr Taylor is scheduled to receive his treatment in about twenty minutes."

The man was forty-seven but looked thirty years older. His eyes were sunken and bruised. His skin had a yellowish cast under the fluorescent lights. His hair had fallen out and Louis could make out small pools of blood under the skin.

They stood behind a lead-lined shield and watched through thick ports. "The medication is a very important part of it," said Collins. "It both augments and complements the radiation treatment."

"And the radiation kills the cancer?" asked Louis.

"Sometimes," said Collins. "Unfortunately it kills healthy cells as well as the ones which have run amok."

Louis nodded and raised his hand mirror. When the device was activated he made a small, involuntary sound. A brilliant burst of violet light filled the room, centering on the tip of the X-ray machine. Louis realized that the glow was similar to that of the bug-zapper devices he had seen in yards at night, the light sliding beyond visible frequencies in a maddening way. But this was a thousand times brighter.

The tumor slugs came out. They slid out of Mr Taylor's skull, antennae thrashing madly, attracted by the brilliant light. They leaped the ten inches to the lens of the device, sliding on slick metal, some falling to the floor and then moving back up onto the table and through the man's body again to reemerge from the skull seconds later only to leap again.

Those that reached the source of the X-rays fell dead to the floor. The others retreated into the darkness of flesh when the X-ray light died.

". . . hope that helps give you some idea of the therapy involved," Collins was saying. "It's a frustrating field because we're not quite sure of why everything works the way it does, but we're making strides all of the time."

Louis blinked. Mr Taylor was gone. The violet glow of the X-rays was gone. "Yes," he said. "I think that helps a lot."

Two nights later, Louis sat next to his sleeping sister in the semi-darkness of her hospital room. The other bed was empty. Louis had sneaked in during the middle of the night and the only sound was the hiss of the ventilation system and the occasional squeak of a rubber-soled shoe in the corridor. Louis reached out a gloved hand and touched Lee's wrist just below the green hospital identity bracelet. "I thought it'd be easy, kiddo," he whispered. "Remember the movies we watched when we were little? James Arness in *The Thing*? Figure out what kills it and rig it up." Louis felt the nausea sweep over him again and he lowered his head, breathing in harsh gulps. A minute later he straightened again, moving to wipe the cold sweat off his brow but frowning when the leather of the thick glove contacted his skin. He held Lee's wrist again. "Life ain't so easy, kiddo. I worked nights in Mac's high energy lab at the University. It was easy to irradiate things with that X-ray laser toy Mac cobbled together to show the sophomores the effects of ionizing radiation."

Lee stirred, moaned slightly in her sleep. Somewhere a soft chime sounded three times and was silenced. Louis heard two of the floor nurses chatting softly as they walked to the staff lounge for their two A.M. break. Louis left his gloved hand just next to her wrist, not quite touching.

"Jesus, Lee," he whispered. "I can see the whole damn spectrum below 100 angstroms. So can *they*. I banked on the cancer vampires being drawn to the stuff I'd irradiated just like the tumor slugs were. I came here last night—to the wards—to check on it. They *do* come, kiddo, but it doesn't kill them. They flock around the irradiated stuff like moths to a flame, but it doesn't kill them. Even the tumor slugs need high dosages if you're going to get them all. I mean, I started in the millirem dosages—like the radiation therapy they use here—and found that it just didn't get enough of them. To be sure, I had to get in the region of 300 to 400 roentgens. I mean, we're talking Chernobyl here, kiddo."

Louis quit talking and walked quickly to the bathroom, lowering his head to the toilet to vomit as quietly as possible. Afterward he washed his face as best he could with the thick gloves on and returned to Lee's bedside. She was frowning slightly in her drugged sleep. Louis remembered the times he had crept into her bedroom as a child to frighten her awake with garter snakes or squirt guns or spiders. "Fuck it," he said and removed his gloves.

His hands glowed like five-fingered, blue-white suns. As Louis watched in the mirrors snapped down on his hat brim, the light filled the room like cold fire. "It won't hurt, kiddo," he whispered as he unsnapped the first two buttons on Lee's pajama tops. Her breasts were small, hardly larger than when he had peeked in on her emerging from the shower when she was fifteen. He smiled as he remembered the whipping he had received for that, and then he laid his right hand on her left breast.

For a second nothing happened. Then the tumor slugs came out, antennae rising like pulpy periscopes from Lee's flesh, their gray-green color bleached by the brilliance of Louis's glowing hand.

They slid into him through his palm, his wrist, the back of his hand. Louis gasped as he felt them slither through his flesh, the sensation faint but nauseating, like having a wire inserted in one's veins while under a local anaesthetic.

Louis counted six . . . eight of the things sliding from Lee's breast into the blue-white flaring of his hand and arm. He held his palm flat for a full minute after the last slug entered, resisting the temptation to scream or pull his hand away as he saw the muscles of his forearm writhe as one of the things flowed upward, swimming through his flesh.

As an extra precaution, Louis moved his palm across Lee's chest, throat, and belly, feeling her stir in her sleep, fighting the sedatives in an unsuccessful battle to awaken. There was one more slug—hardly more than a centimeter long—which rose from the taut skin just below her sternum, but it flared and withered before coming in contact with his blue-white flesh, curling like a dried leaf too close to a hot fire.

Louis rose and removed his thick layers of clothes, watching in the wide mirror opposite Lee's bed. His entire body fluoresced, the brilliance fading from white to blue-white to violet and then sliding away into frequencies even he could not see. Again he thought of the bug-lights one saw near patios and the blind-spot sense of frustration the eye conveyed as it strained at the fringes of perception. The mirrors hanging from the brim of his hat caught and scattered the light.

Louis folded his clothes neatly, laid them on the chair near Lee, kissed her softly on the cheek, and walked from room to room, the brilliance from his body leaping ahead of him, filling the corridors with blue-white shadows and pinwheels of impossible colors.

There was no one at the nurse's station. The tile floor felt cool beneath Louis's bare feet as he went from room to room, laying on his hands. Some of the patients slept on. Some watched him with wide eyes but neither moved nor cried out. Louis wondered at this but glanced down without his mirrors and realized that for the first time he could see the brilliance of his heavily irradiated flesh and bone with his own eyes. His body was a pulsing star in human form. Louis could easily hear the radio waves as a buzzing, crackling sound, like a great forest fire still some miles away.

The tumor slugs flowed from their victims and into Louis. Not everyone on this floor had cancer, but in most rooms he had only to enter to see the frenzied response of green-gray or grub-white worms straining to get at him. Louis took them all. He felt his body swallow the things, sensed the maddened turmoil within. Only once more did he have to stop to vomit. His bowels shifted and roiled, but there was so much motion in him now that Louis ignored it.

In Debbie's room, Louis pulled the sheet off her sleeping form, pulled up the short gown, and laid his cheek to the soft bulge of her belly. The tumor slugs flowed into his face and throat; he drank them in willingly.

Louis rose, left his sleeping lover, and walked to the long, open ward where the majority of cancer patients lay waiting for death.

The cancer vampires followed him. They flowed through walls and floors to follow him. He led them to the main ward, a blazing blue-white pied piper leading a chorus of dead children.

There were at least a score of them by the time he stopped in the center of the ward, but he did not let them approach until he had gone from bed to bed, accepting the last of the tumor slugs into himself, seeing with his surreal vision as the eggs inside these victims hatched prematurely to give up their writhing treasure. Louis made sure the tumor slugs were with him before he moved to the center of the room, raised his arms, and let the cancer vampires come closer.

Louis felt heavy, twice his normal weight, pregnant with death. He glanced at his blazing limbs and belly and saw the very surface of himself alive with the motion of maggots feeding on his light.

Louis raised his arms wider, pulled his head far back, closed his eyes, and let the cancer vampires feed.

The things were voracious, drawn by the X-ray beacon of Louis's flesh and the silent beckoning of their larval offspring. They shouldered and shoved each other aside in their eagerness to feed. Louis grimaced as he felt a dozen sharp piercings, felt himself almost lifted off the floor by nightmare energies suddenly made tangible. He looked once, saw the terrible curve of the top of a dead-child's head as the thing buried its face to the temples in Louis's chest, and then he closed his eyes until they were done.

Louis staggered, gripped the metal footboard of a bed to keep from falling. The score of cancer vampires in the room had finished feeding but Louis could feel his own body still weighted with slugs. He watched.

The child-thing nearest to him seemed bloated, its body as distended as a white spider bursting with eggs. Through its translucent flesh, Louis could see glowing tumor slugs shifting frantically like electric silverfish.

Even through his nausea and pain, Louis smiled. Whatever the reproductive-feeding cycle of these things had been, Louis now felt sure that he had disrupted it with the irradiated meal he had offered the tumor slugs.

The cancer vampire in front of him staggered, leaned

far forward, and looked even more spiderish as its impossibly long fingers stretched to keep it from falling.

A blue-white gash appeared along the thing's side and belly. Two bloated, thrashing slugs appeared in a rush of violet energy. The cancer vampire arched its back and raised its feeding mouth in a scream that was audible to Louis as someone scraping their teeth down ten feet of blackboard.

The slugs ripped free of the vampire's shredded belly, dumping themselves on the floor and writhing in a bath of ultraviolet blood, steaming and shriveling there like true slugs Louis had once seen sprinkled with salt. The cancer vampire spasmed, clutched at its gaping, eviscerated belly, and then thrashed several times and died, its bony limbs and long fingers slowly closing up like the legs of a crushed spider.

There were screams, human and otherwise, but Louis paid no attention as he watched the death throes of the two dozen spectral forms in the room. His vision had altered permanently now and the beds and their human occupants were mere shadows in a great space blazing in ultraviolet and infrared but dominated by the blue-white corona which was his own body. He vomited once more, doubling over to retch up blood and two dying, glowing slugs, but this was a minor inconvenience as long as his strength held out and at that second he felt that it would last forever.

Louis looked down, through the floor, through *five* floors, seeing the hospital as levels of clear plastic interlaced with webs of energy from electrical wiring, lights, machines, and organisms. Many organisms. The healthy ones glowed a soft orange but he could see the pale yellow infections, the grayish corruptions, and the throbbing black pools of incipient death.

Rising, Louis stepped over the drying corpses of cancer vampires and the acid-pools which had been thrashing slugs seconds before. Although he already could see beyond, he opened wide doors and stepped out onto the terrace. The night air was cool.

Drawn by the extraordinary light, they waited. Hundreds of yellow eyes turned upwards to stare from blue-black pits set in dead faces. Mouths pulsed. Hundreds more of the things converged as Louis watched.

Louis raised his own eyes, seeing more stars than anyone had ever seen as the night sky throbbed with uncountable X-ray sources and infinite tendrils of unnamed colors. He looked down to where they continued to gather, by the thousands now, their pale faces glowing like candles in a procession. Louis prayed for a single miracle. He prayed that he could feed them all. "Tonight, Death," he whispered, the sound too soft for even him to hear, "you shall die."

Louis stepped to the railing, raised his arms, and went down to join those who waited.

# VANNI FUCCI IS ALIVE AND WELL AND LIVING IN HELL

On his last day on earth, Brother Freddy rose early, showered, shaved his chins, sprayed his hair, put on his television make-up, dressed in his trademark three-piece white suit with white shoes, pink shirt, and black string tie, and went down to his office to have his pre-Hallelujah Breakfast Club breakfast with Sister Donna Lou, Sister Betty Jo, Brother Billy Bob, and George.

The four munched on sweet rolls and sipped coffee as the slate-gray sky began to lighten beyond the thirty-foot wall of bulletproof, heavily tinted glass. Clusters of tall, brick buildings comprising the campus of Brother Freddy's Hallelujah Bible College and Graduate School of Christian Economics seemed to solidify out of the pre-dawn Alabama gloom. Far to the east, just visible above the pecan groves, rose the artificial mountain of the Mount Sinai Mad Mouse Ride in the Bible Land section of Brother Freddy's Born Again Family Amusement Complex and Christian Convention Center. Much closer, the great dish of a Holy Beamer, one of six huge satellite dishes on the grounds of Brother Freddy's Bible Broadcast Center, sliced a black arc from the cloud-laden sky. Brother Freddy glanced at the rain-sullen weather and smiled. It did not matter what the real world beyond his office window offered. The large "bay window" on the homey set of the Hallelujah Breakfast Club was actually a $38,000 rear-projection television screen which played the same fifty-two minute tape of a glorious May sunrise each morning. On Brother Freddy's Hallelujah Breakfast Club it was always spring.

"What's the line-up like?" asked Brother Freddy as he took a sip of his coffee, his little finger lifted delicately, the pinky ring gleaming in the light of the overhead spots. It was eight minutes until air time.

"First half hour you got the usual lead-in from Brother Beau, your opening talk and Prayer Partner plea, six-and-a-half minutes of the Hallelujah Breakfast Club Choir doing "We're On the Brink of a Miracle" and a medley of off-Broadway Christian hits, and then your Breakfast Guests come on," said Brother Billy Bob Grimes, the floor director.

"Who we got today?" asked Brother Freddy.

Brother Billy Bob read from his clipboard. "You've got Matt, Mark, and Luke the Miracle Triplet Evangelists, Bubba Deeters who says he wants to tell the story again how the Lord told him to throw himself on a grenade in 'Nam, Brother Frank Flinsey who's pushing his new book *After the Final Days*, and Dale Evans."

Brother Freddy frowned slightly. "I thought we were going to have Pat Boone today," he said softly. "I like Pat."

Brother Billy Bob blushed and made a notation on his thick sheath of forms. "Yessir," he said. "Pat wanted to be here today but he did Swaggart's show last night, he has a personal appearance with Paul and Jan at the Bakersfield Revival this afternoon, and he has to be up at tomorrow's Senate hearing testifying about those

Satanic messages you can hear on CDs when you aim the laser between the grooves."

Brother Freddy sighed. It was four minutes until air time. "All right," he said. "But try to get him for next Monday. I like Pat. Donna Lou? How're we doing with the Lord's work these days, little lady?"

Sister Donna Lou Patterson adjusted her glasses. As comptroller of Brother Freddy's vast conglomerate of tax-exempt religious organizations, corporations, ministries, colleges, missions, amusement parks and the chain of Brother Freddy's Motels for the Born Again, Donna Lou was dressed appropriately in a beige business suit, the seriousness of which was lightened only by a rhinestone Hallelujah Breakfast Club pin which matched the rhinestones on her glasses. "Projected earnings for this fiscal year are just under $187 million, up three per cent from last year," she said. "Ministry assets stand at $214 million with outstanding debts of $63 million, give or take .3 million depending upon Brother Carlisle's decision on replacing the Gulfstream with a new Lear."

Brother Freddy nodded and turned toward Sister Betty Jo. There were three minutes left until air time. "How'd we do yesterday, Sister?"

"Twenty-seven broadcast share Arbitron, twenty-five point five Nielsen," said the thin woman dressed in white. "Three new cable outlets; two in Texas, one in Montana. Current cable reaches 3.37 million homes, up .6 per cent from last month. The mail room handled 17,385 pieces yesterday, making a total of 86,217 for the week. Ninety-six per cent of the envelopes yesterday included donations. Thirty-nine per cent requested your Intercession Prayer. Total envelope volume handled this year is 3,585,220, with an approximate 2.5 million additional pieces projected by the end of the fiscal year."

Brother Freddy smiled and turned his gaze on George Cohen, legal counsel for Brother Freddy's Born Again Ministries. "George?" Two minutes remained until air time.

The thin man in the dark suit unhurriedly cleared his throat. "The IRS continues to make threatening noises but they don't have a leg to stand on. Since all of the ministry affiliates are under the Born Again Ministries exemption, you don't have to file a thing. The Huntsville papers have reported that your daughter's house has been assessed at one million five and they know that it and your son's ranch were built with a three million dollar loan from the ministry, but they're just guessing when it comes to salaries. Even if they found out . . . which they won't . . . your official annual salary from the Board comes to only $92,300, a third of which you tithe back to the ministry. Of course, your wife, daughter, son-in-law, and seven other family members receive considerably more liberal incomes from the ministry but I don't think . . ."

"Thank you, George," interrupted Brother Freddy. He stood, stretched and walked to the color monitor attached to the computer terminal on his desk. "Sister Betty Jo, you said there were several thousand requests for the Personal Intercession Prayer?"

"Yes, Brother," said the woman in white, laying her small hand on the console next to her chair.

Brother Freddy smiled at George Cohen. "I told these folks I'd personally pray over their letters if they'd send in a love offering," he said. "Might as well do it now.

I've got thirty seconds before Brother Beau goes into his intro. Betty Jo?"

The woman tapped a button and smiled as the list of thousands of names flashed by on the color monitor. After each name was a code relating to the category of problem for which intercession was requested according to the checklist provided on the Love Offering form: H-health, MP-marital problems, $-money problems, SG-spiritual guidance, FS-forgiveness of sins, and so on. There were twenty-seven categories. Any one of Brother Freddy's two hundred mail room operators could code more than four hundred intercession requests a day while simultaneously sorting the letter contents into stacks of cash and checks while cueing computers to provide the appropriate reply letter.

"Dear Lord," intoned Brother Freddy, "please hear our prayers for the receipt of Thy mercy for these requests which are made in Jesus's name . . ." The list of names and codes flashed past in a blur until the suddenly blank screen held only a flashing cursor. "Amen."

Brother Freddy turned on his heel and led the suddenly scurrying-to-keep-up retinue on the thirty yard walk to the Hallelujah Breakfast Club studio just as the program's opening graphics and triumphant music filled the sixty-two monitors in the Broadcast Headquarters' corridors, offices, and board rooms.

Brother Freddy knew there was a problem eighteen minutes into the program when he introduced Dale

Evans only to watch a tall, dark-skinned man with long, black hair walk onto the set. Brother Freddy knew at once that the man was a foreigner; the stranger's long hair was curled in ringlets which fell to his shoulders, he wore an expensive three-piece suit which looked to be made of silk, his immaculately polished shoes were of soft Italian leather, his starched collar and cuffs dazzled with their whiteness, and gold cufflinks gleamed in the studio lights. Brother Freddy knew that some mistake had been made; his born again guests—despite their personal wealth—went in for polyester blends, pastel shirts, and South Carolina haircuts if for no other reason than to stay in touch with their video faithful.

Brother Freddy glanced down at his notes and then looked helplessly at the floor director. Brother Billy Bob shrugged with a depth of confusion that Brother Freddy felt but could not show while the red eye of the camera glowed.

The Hallelujah Breakfast Club prided itself on being live in three time zones. Brother Freddy smiled at the advancing intruder and wished they had gone with the tape-delayed programs his competitors preferred. Brother Freddy usually prided himself on the fact that he wore no earphone to hear the booth director's instructions and comments, trusting instead on Brother Billy Bob's hand signals and his own well-honed sense of media timing. Now, as Brother Freddy rose to his feet to shake hands with the swarthy stranger, he wished that he had an earphone to learn what was going on. He wished that they had a commercial to cut to. He wished that *somebody* would tell him what was happening.

"Good morning," Brother Freddy said affably, retrieving his hand from the foreigner's firm grip. "Welcome to the Hallelujah Breakfast Club." He glanced toward Brother Billy Bob, who was muttering urgently into his bead microphone. Camera Three dollied in for a close-up of the swarthy stranger. Camera Two remained fixed on the long divan crowded with the Miracle Triplets, Bubba Deeters, and Frank Flinsey grinning mechanically from beneath his military-trimmed mustache. The floor monitors showed the medium close-up of Brother Freddy's florid, politely smiling, and only slightly perspiring face.

"Thank you, I've been looking forward to this for some time," said the stranger as he sat in the velour guest chair next to Brother Freddy's desk. There was a hint of Italian accent in the man's deep voice even though the English was precisely correct.

Brother Freddy sat, smile still fixed, and glanced toward Billy Bob. The floor director shrugged and made the hand signal for "carry on."

"I'm sorry." said Brother Freddy, "I guess I've mixed up the introductions. I also guess you're not my dear friend, Dale Evans." Brother Freddy paused and looked into the stranger's brown eyes, surprised at the anger and intensity he saw there, praying that this was only a scheduling mix-up and not some political terrorist or Pentecostal crazy who had gotten past Security. Brother Freddy was acutely aware that the signal was being telecast live to more than three million homes.

"No, I am not Dale Evans," agreed the stranger. "My name is Vanni Fucci." Again the hint of an Italian accent. Brother Freddy noted that the name had been pronounced VAH-nee FOO-tchee. Brother Freddy had nothing against Italians; growing up in Greenville, Alabama, he had known very few of them. As an adult he had learned not to call them wops. He presumed most Italians were Catholic, therefore not Christians, and therefore of little interest to him or his ministry. But now this particular Italian was a bit of a problem.

"Mr Fucci," smiled Brother Freddy, "why don't you tell our viewers where you're from?"

Vanni Fucci turned his intense gaze toward the camera. "I was born in Pistoia," he said, "but for the last seven hundred years I have lived in Hell."

Brother Freddy's smile froze but did not falter. He glanced left at Billy Bob. The floor director was frantically making the signal of a star over his left breast. At first Brother Freddy thought it was some obscure religious symbol but then he realized that the man meant that Security . . . or the real police . . . had been called. Behind the wall of lights and cameras a live studio audience of almost three hundred people had ceased their usual background murmur of whispers and shiftings and stifled sneezes. The auditorium was dead silent.

"Ah," said Brother Freddy and chuckled softly. "Ah. I see your point, Mr Fucci. In a sense all of us who were sinners have spent our time in Hell. It's only through the mercy of Jesus that we can avoid that as our ultimate address. When did you finally accept Christ as your Saviour?"

Vanni Fucci smiled, showing very white teeth against dark skin. "I never did," he said. "In my day, one was not—as you Fundamentalists put it—'saved.' We were baptized into the Church as children. But I made a slight mistake as a young man and your so-called Saviour saw fit to condemn me to an eternity of inhuman punishment in the Seventh Bolgia of the Eighth Circle of Hell."

"Uh-huh," said Brother Freddy. He swiveled around and gestured toward Camera One to dolly in closer for an extreme close-up on him. He waited until he could see only his own face on the floor monitor and said, "Well, we're having an enjoyable conversation here with our guest, Mr Vanni Fucci, but I'm afraid we're going to have to take a break for a minute while we show you that tape I promised you of Brother Beau and I dedicating the new Holy Beamer we installed last week in Amarillo. Beau?" Below the frame of the close-up, out of sight of the viewing audience, Brother Freddy drew his right hand repeatedly across his throat. On the floor, Billy Bob nodded, turned toward the booth, and spoke rapidly into his microphone.

"No," said Vanni Fucci, "let us go on with our conversation."

The floor monitors showed a long shot of the entire set. The Miracle Triplets sat staring, the bottoms of their little shoes looking like exclamation marks. The Reverend Bubba Deeters raised his right arm as if he was going to scratch his head, glanced at the steel hook that was the reminder of the Lord's Will during his Viet Nam days, and lowered his arm to the divan. Frank Flinsey, a media pro, was staring in astonishment at the three cameras where no lights glowed and then back at the monitors which definitely showed a picture. Brother Freddy was frozen with his hand still raised to his throat. Only Vanni Fucci seemed unruffled.

"Do you think," said the Italian guest, "that if Dale

had passed away before Trigger, Roy would have had *her* stuffed and mounted in the living room?"

"Ah?" managed Brother Freddy. He had heard very old men make similar sounds in their sleep.

"Just a thought," continued Vanni Fucci. "Would you rather I go on about my own situation?"

Brother Freddy nodded. Out of the corner of his eye he saw three uniformed Security men trying to get on stage. Someone seemed to have lowered an invisible Plexiglas wall around the edge of the set.

"It actually has not been seven hundred years that I have been in Hell," said Vanni Fucci, "only six hundred and ninety. But you know how slowly time passes in such a situation. Like in a dentist's office."

"Yes," said Brother Freddy. The word was a little better than a squeak.

"And did you know that one condemned soul from each Bolgia is allowed one visit back to the mortal world during our eternity of punishment? Much like your American custom of one phone call allotted to the arrested man."

"No," said Brother Freddy and cleared his throat. "No."

"Yes," said Vanni Fucci. "I think the idea is that the visit sharpens our torments by reminding us of the pleasures we once knew. Something like that. Actually, we are only allowed to return for fifteen minutes, so the pleasures sampled could not be too extensive, could they?"

"No," said Brother Freddy, pleased that his voice was stronger. The single syllable sounded wise and slightly amused, mildly patronizing. He was deciding which

Biblical verse he would use when it was time to regain control of the conversation.

"That's neither here nor there," said Vanni Fucci. "The point is that all of the condemned souls in the Seventh Bolgia of the Eighth Circle voted unanimously for me to come here, on your show." Vanni Fucci leaned forward, his cuffs shooting perfectly so that gold cuff-links caught the light. "Do you know what a Bolgia is, Brother Freddy?"

"Ah . . . no," said Brother Freddy, derailed slightly from his line of thought. He had decided on a verse but it seemed inappropriate at right this instant. "Or rather . . . yes," he said. "A Bolgia is that duchess or countess or whatever who used to poison people in the Middle Ages."

Vanni Fucci leaned back and sighed. "No," he said, "you're thinking of the Borgias. A Bolgia is a word in my native language which means both 'ditch' and 'pouch.' The Eighth Circle of Hell has ten such Bolgias filled with shit and sinners."

The silent audience was silent no longer. Even the cameramen gasped. Brother Freddy glanced at the monitors and closed his eyes as he realized that his very own Hallelujah Breakfast Club, the top-rated Christian program in the world except for the occasional Billy Graham Crusade, would be the first program in TBN and CBN history to allow the word "shit" to go out over the airwaves. He imagined what the Ministry Board of Trustees would say. The fact that seven of the eleven Board members were also members of his own family did not make the image any more pleasant.

"Now listen here . . ." Brother Freddy began sternly.

"Have you read the *Comedy?*" asked Vanni Fucci.

There was something more than anger and intensity in the man's eyes. Brother Freddy decided he was dealing with an escaped mental patient.

"Comedy?" said Brother Freddy, wondering if the man were some sort of deranged standup comic and all of this a publicity stunt. On the floor, the cameramen had swung the heavy cameras around and were peering in the lenses. The monitors showed a steady shot framing only Vanni Fucci and Brother Freddy. Brother Billy Bob was running from camera to camera, occasionally tripping over a cable or coming to the end of his mike cord and jerking to a stop like a crazed Dachshund on a short leash.

"He called it his *Comedy*," said Vanni Fucci. "Later generations of sycophants added the *Divine*." He frowned at Brother Freddy, an impatient teacher waiting for a slow child to respond.

"I'm sorry . . . I don't . . ." began Brother Freddy. One of the cameramen was disassembling his camera. None of the remaining cameras was aimed at the set. The picture held steady.

"Alighieri?" prompted Vanni Fucci. "A dirty little Florentine who lusted after an eight-year-old girl? Wrote one readable thing in his entire miserable life?" He turned toward the guests on the divan. "Come on, come on, don't any of you read?"

The five Christians on the couch seemed to shrink back.

"Dante!" shouted the handsome foreigner. "Dante Alighieri. What's the deal here, gentlemen? To join the Fundamentalists Club you have to park your brains at the door and stuff your skull with hominy and grits, is that it? Dante!"

"Just one minute . . ." said Brother Freddy, rising.

"Who do you think you . . ." began Frank Flinsey, standing.

"What do you think you're . . ." said Bubba Deeters, getting to his feet and brandishing his hook.

"Hey! Hey! Hey!" cried the Miracle Triplets, struggling to get their feet to the floor.

"SIT DOWN." It was not a human voice. At least not an unamplified human voice. Brother Freddy had made the mistake once on an outdoor Crusade of standing in front of a bank of thirty huge speakers when the soundman tested them at full volume. This was a little like that. Only worse. Brother Billy Bob and others with headphones on ripped them off and fell to their knees. Several overhead spots shattered. The audience leaned backward like a single three-hundred-headed organism, whimpered once, and adopted a silence unbroken even by the sound of breathing. Brother Freddy and the guests on the divan sat down.

"Alighieri did it," said Vanni Fucci in soft, conversational tones. "The man was a mental midget with the imagination of a moth, but he did it *because no one before him did it*."

"Did what?" asked Brother Freddy, staring in fascinated horror at the madman in the crushed velour chair next to his desk.

"Created Hell," said Vanni Fucci.

"Nonsense!" cried Reverend Frank Flinsey, author of fourteen books about the end of the world. "The Lord God Jehovah created Hell as He did everything else."

"Oh?" said Vanni Fucci. "Where does it say so in that grab-bag of tribal stories and jingoist posturings you call a Bible?"

Brother Freddy thought that it was quite possible that he was going to have a heart attack right there on the Brother Freddy's Hallelujah Breakfast Club hour going live into three million three hundred thousand American homes. But even while his heart fibrillated and his red face grew redder, his mind raced to come up with the appropriate Scriptural verse.

"Let me tell you about an experiment performed in 1982," said Vanni Fucci, "at the University of Paris-South. A group of quantum physicists headed by Alain Aspect tested the behavior of two photons flying in opposite directions from a light source. The test confirmed an underlying theory of quantum mechanics—namely, that a measurement made on one photon has an instantaneous effect on the nature of another photon. *Photons*, gentlemen, traveling at the speed of *light*. Obviously no information could be transmitted faster than the speed of light itself, but the *act* of defining the nature of one photon *instantaneously* changed the nature of the other photon. The conclusion drawn from this is obvious, is it not?"

"Ah?" said Brother Freddy.

"Ah?" said the five guests on the divan.

"Precisely," said Vanni Fucci. "It confirms in the physical world what we in Hell have known for some time. *Reality* is shaped by the first great mind which focuses on measuring it. New concepts create new laws and the universe abides. Newton *created* universal gravity and the cosmos rearranged itself accordingly. Einstein defined space/time and the universe retrofitted itself to agree. And Dante Alighieri—that neurotic little whimshit—created the first comprehensive map of hell and Hell came into existence to appease the public perception."

"That's ridiculous," managed Brother Freddy, forgetting the cameras, forgetting the audience, forgetting everything but the monstrous illogic—not to mention blasphemy—of what this crazy Italian had just said. "If that was . . . true," cried Brother Freddy, "then the world . . . things . . . everything would be changing all the time."

"Precisely," smiled Vanni Fucci. His teeth looked small and white and very sharp.

"Then . . . well . . . Hell wouldn't be the same either," said Brother Freddy. "Dante wrote a long time ago. Three or four hundred years, at least . . ."

"He died in 1321," said Vanni Fucci.

"Yeah . . . well . . . so . . ." concluded Brother Freddy.

Vanni Fucci shook his head. "You understand nothing. When an idea is strong enough, large enough, *comprehensive* enough to redefine the universe, it has tremendous staying power. It lasts until an equally powerful paradigm is formulated . . . and accepted by the popular imagination . . . to replace it. For instance, your Old Testament God lasted thousands of years before it . . . He . . . was actively redefined by a much more civilized if somewhat schizophrenic New Testament deity. Even the newer and weaker version has lasted fifteen hundred years or so before being on the verge of being sneezed out of existence by the allergy of modern science."

Brother Freddy was certain he was going to have a stroke.

"But who has bothered to redefine Hell?" Vanni Fucci asked rhetorically. "The Germans came close in this century, but their visionaries were snuffed out before the new concept could take root in the mass mind. So we remain. Hell persists. Our eternal torments drag on with no more reason for existence than could be offered for your little toe or vermiform appendix."

Brother Freddy realized that he might be dealing with a demon here. After almost forty years of preaching about demons, teaching about demons, finding the spiritual footprints of demons in everything from rock music to FCC legislation, warning against demons being in the schools and kids' games and in the symbols on breakfast cereal boxes, and generally making a fair-sized fortune by being one of the nation's foremost experts on demons, Brother Freddy found it a bit disconcerting to be sitting three feet from someone who might very well be possessed by a demon if not actually *be* one. The closest he could recall to coming to one before this was when he was around the Reverend Jim Bakker's wife Tammy Faye when her "shoppin' demons were hoppin'" back before the couple's unfortunate publicity.

Brother Freddy clutched the Bible in his left hand and raised his right hand in a powerfully curved claw over Vanni Fucci's head. "I abjure thee, Satan!" he cried. "And all of the powers and dominions and servants of Satan . . . BE GONE from this place of God! In the name of JE-SUS I *command* thee! In the name of JE-SUS I *command* thee!"

"Oh, shut up," said Vanni Fucci. He glanced at his gold wristwatch. "Look, let me get to the important part of all this. I don't have too much time."

As the Italian began to speak, Brother Freddy kept his pose with the raised hand and clutched Bible. After a minute his arm got tired and he lowered his hand. He did not release the Bible.

"My crime was political," said Vanni Fucci, "even though that Short Eyes Florentine put me in the Bolgia reserved for thieves. Yes, yes, I *know* you don't know what I'm talking about. In those days the political battles between we Blacks and the dogspittle Whites were of great importance—a third of Dante's damned *Inferno* is filled with it—but I realize that today no one even knows what the parties were, any more than people seven hundred years from now will remember the Republicans or Democrats.

"In 1293 two friends and I stole the treasure of San Jacopo in the Duomo of San Zeno to help our political cause. The Duomo was a church. The treasure included a chalice. But I didn't go to Dante's Hell just because of one little robbery about as common then as knocking over a convenience store today. *No.* I have prime billing in the Seventh Bolgia of the Eighth Circle because I was a Black and because Dante was a White and the unfairness of it all *pisses me off.*"

Brother Freddy closed his eyes.

Vanni Fucci said, "You'd think an eternity of wallowing in a trench of *merde* and hot embers would be enough revenge for the sickest S-M deity, but that's not the half

183

of it." Vanni Fucci swiveled toward the Breakfast Club guests on the divan. "I admit it. I have a temper. When I get mad I give God the fig."

Frank Flinsey, Reverend Deeters, and the Miracle Triplets looked blankly at Vanni Fucci.

"The fig," repeated the Italian. He clenched his fist, ran his thumb out between his first and index fingers, and thrust it rapidly back and forth. Based on the mass intake of breath from the crowd, the symbol must have been clear enough. Vanni Fucci swiveled back toward Brother Freddy. "And then, of course, when I do that, every thief within a hundred yards—which is everyone *in* that goddamned Bolgia, of course—turns into reptiles . . ."

"Reptiles?" croaked Brother Freddy.

"*Chelidrids, jaculi, phareans, cenchriads,* and *two-headed amphisbands,* that sort of thing," confirmed Vanni Fucci. "Alighieri got *that* right. And then, of course, every one of these damned snakes attacks *me.* Naturally I burst into flame and scatter into a heap of smoking ashes and charred bone . . ."

Brother Freddy nodded attentively. Out of the corner of his eye he could see Sisters Donna Lou and Betty Jo helping the three Security men use a chair as a battering ram against the invisible barrier that kept them off the set. The barrier held.

"I mean," said Vanni Fucci, leaning closer, "it's not pleasant . . ."

Brother Freddy decided that when all of this was over he would take a little vacation at his religious retreat in the Bahamas.

"And being *Hell,*" continued Vanni Fucci, "the

pieces, my pieces, don't die, they just reassemble—
which is the most painful part, let me tell you—and
then, when I'm back together, the *unfairness* of it all gets
me so pissed off that . . . well, you can guess . . ."

"The fig?" guessed Brother Freddy and clapped a
hand over his own mouth.

Vanni Fucci nodded dolorously, "Both hands," he
said, "And off we go again." He looked directly into
Camera One. "But that's not the worst part."

"No?" said Brother Freddy.

"No?" echoed the five Breakfast Club guests.

"Hell is a lot like a theme park," said Vanni Fucci.
"The management is always trying to improve the attrac-
tions, add a more effective touch to the entertainment.
And can you guess what the Big Warden in the Sky has
provided the last ten years or so to add to our torment?"
The Italian's voice had climbed the scale as his anger
visibly grew.

Brother Freddy and the Breakfast guests vigorously
shook their heads.

"BROTHER FREDDY'S HALLELUJAH BREAK-
FAST CLUB!" screamed Vanni Fucci, rising to his feet.
"EIGHT TIMES A GODDAMNED DAY. 90-INCH
SYLVANIA SUPERSCREENS EVERY TWENTY-
FIVE FEET IN BOLGIA SEVEN!"

Brother Freddy pushed back in his chair as Vanni
Fucci's saliva spattered his desk top.

"I MEAN . . ." bellowed Vanni Fucci, his wide,
glaring eyes fixed on something above the catwalks, ". . .
IT'S ONE THING TO SPEND ALL OF ETERNITY
BURNING IN HELL AND BEING RENT LIMB

FROM LIMB EVERY FEW MINUTES BUT THIS
. . . THIS . . ." He raised both arms skyward.

"No!" screamed Brother Freddy.

"No!" cried the Breakfast guests.

"THIS REALLY PISSES ME OFF!" bellowed Vanni
Fucci and gave God the fig. Twice.

Things happened very quickly after that. To get the
full effect, one has to play back the videotape in Extreme
Slow Motion and even then the sequence of events can
be confusing.

Brother Freddy went first. He doubled over the desk
as if an Invisible Force were vigorously practicing the
Heimlich Maneuver on him, opened his mouth to scream
only to find that three rows of long fangs there made that
highly impractical, and then grew scales and a tail faster
than one could say "born again." The metamorphosis
was so fast and the movement afterward was so quick
that no one can say for sure, but most observers agree
that the Reverend Brother Freddy looked a lot like a
cross between a giant bullfrog and an orange python in
the brief second before he—it—leaped across the desk
with one thrash of its powerful tail and lashed itself
around Vanni Fucci from crotch to throat.

Frank Flinsey turned into something altogether different; in less than a second the middle-aged Armageddon
expert evolved into something resembling a six-armed
newt with a jagged tail-stinger straight out of *Aliens*. The
thing used its tail to plow a path through the carpet,
floor, divan, and crushed velour to the hapless Vanni
Fucci, where it joined the Brother Freddy python-thing
in a full-fanged attack. Experts agreed that Flinsey was
probably the *pharean* to Brother Freddy's *chelidrid*.

There was no doubt about Bubba Deeters's transmo-grification: the street preacher who had found God in a foxhole deliquesced like day-old fungi, reformed as a green-striped *amphisband* with a head at each end, and slithered toward Vanni Fucci to get in on the action.

The Miracle Triplets instantly changed into slimy, dart-shaped things which shot through the air, leaving contrails of green mucus, and embedded themselves deep in Vanni Fucci's flesh. Scholars are certain that the Triplets had become what Dante and Lucan had described as *jaculi*, but most viewers of the videotape today merely refer to them as "the snot rockets."

While these creatures threw themselves on Vanni Fucci in a roiling, writhing, snake-biting mass, there was more action on the set and elsewhere.

Brother Billy Bob had put his earphones back on just in time to turn into what a nearby cameraman later described as ". . . a thirteen-foot-long garter snake with leprosy." A second cameraman, since relieved of his duties by the Born Again Ministries, was reported to have said, "I didn't see no change in Billy Bob. All them directors look the same to me."

Sisters Donna Lou and Betty Jo fell to the ground only to slither onto the set a second later as two immense pink worms. Much has been written about the phallic symbolism inherent in this particular set of metamor-phoses, but the irony was lost on the three security guards who emptied their service revolvers into the giant worms and then ran like hell.

The audience was not untouched. Vanni Fucci had said that all thieves within a hundred yards of his blasphemy traditionally were transformed. Out of 319

187

audience members present that morning 226 were unaccounted for the next day. The auditorium was filled with screams as those who stayed human watched their husbands or wives or parents or in-laws or the stranger next to them transform in a flash into snakes, fanged newt-things, legless toads, giant iguanas, four-armed boa constrictors, and the usual assortment of *chelidrids, jaculi, phareans, cenchriads,* and *amphisbands.* A University of Alabama study done a month after the incident showed that most of the thieves-turned-reptiles in the audience had been in sales, but other occupations included—lawyers (8), politicians (3), visiting ministers (31), psychiatrists (1), advertising executives (2), judges (4), medical doctors (4), stock market brokers (12), absentee landlords (7), accountants (3), and a car thief (1) who had ducked into the auditorium to get away from the Alabama Highway Patrol (2).

In less than ten seconds, Vanni Fucci was the center of a mass of scales and fangs representing every reptile-thing in the Bible Broadcast Center auditorium. The Italian struggled to get his hands free to get off another fig.

Brother Freddy sank its bullfrog-python *chelidrid* fangs deep into Vanni Fucci's throat and the blasphemer burst into flame.

The studio filled with a stink of sulphur so strong that thousands of cable subscribers later swore that they could smell it at home.

The entire mass of reptiles exploded into flame along with Vanni Fucci, disappearing with him in a napalmish, orange-green flash that left the vidicon tubes of the RCA computerized color cameras with a 40-second after-image.

The Hallelujah Breakfast Club set was suddenly empty except for the flaming wreckage of the divan, desk, and crushed velour chair. Overhead sprinklers came on and the "bay window" imploded with a shower of sparks and glass. The sunrise did not survive.

Later that night, the *Nightline* video replay drew a sixty-share. On the same show, Dr Carl Sagan went on record with Ted Koppel as saying that the entire event could be attributed to natural causes.

That week Brother Freddy's Hallelujah Breakfast Club Prayer Partners sent in Love Offerings totalling $23,267,894.79.

Except for the occasional Billy Graham Crusade, it set a new weekly record.

# IVERSON'S PITS

As a young boy, I was not afraid of the dark. As an old man, I am wiser. But it was as a boy of ten in that distant summer of 1913 that I was forced to partake of communion with that darkness which now looms so close. I remember the taste of it. Even now, three-quarters of a century later, I am unable to turn over black soil in the garden or to stand alone in the grassy silence of my grandson's backyard after the sun has set without a hint of cold fingers on the back of my neck.

The past is, as they say, dead and buried. But even the most buried things have their connections to the present, gnarled old roots rising to the surface, and I am one of these. Yet there is no one to connect to, no one to tell. My daughter is grown and gone, dead of cancer in 1953. My middle-aged grandson is a product of those Eisenhower years, that period of endless gestation when all the world seemed fat and confident and looking to the future. Paul has taught science at the local high school for twenty-three years and were I to tell him now about the events of that hot first day and night of July, 1913, he would think me mad. Or senile.

My great-grandchildren, a boy and a girl in an age that finds little reason to pay attention to such petty distinctions as gender, could not conceive of a past as ancient and irretrievable as my own childhood before the Great War, much less the blood-and-leather reality of the Civil War era from which I carry my dark message. My great-grandchildren are as colorful and mindless as the guppies Paul keeps in his expensive aquarium, free from the terrors and tides of the ocean of history, smug in their almost total ignorance of everything that came before themselves, Big Macs, and MTV.

So I sit alone on the patio in Paul's backyard (why was it, I try to recall, that we turned our focus away from the front porch attention to the communal streets and sidewalks into the fenced isolation of our own backyards?) and I study the old photograph of a serious ten-year-old in his Boy Scout uniform.

The boy is dressed far too warmly for such a hot summer day—his small form is almost lost under the heavy, woolen Boy Scout tunic, broad-brimmed campaign hat, baggy wool trousers, and awkward puttees laced almost to the knees. He is not smiling—a solemn, miniature doughboy four years before the term doughboy had passed into the common vocabulary. The boy is me, of course, standing in front of Mr Everett's ice wagon on that day in June when I was about to leave on a trip much longer in time and to places much more unimaginably distant than any of us might have dreamed.

I look at the photograph knowing that ice wagons exist now only as fading memories in aging skulls, that the house in the background has long since been torn down to be replaced by an apartment building which in turn was replaced by a shopping mall, that the wool and leather and cotton of the Boy Scout uniform have rotted away, leaving only the brass buttons and the boy himself to be lost somewhere, and that—as Paul would explain— every cell in that unsmiling ten-year-old's body has been replaced several times. For the worse, I suspect. Paul would say that the DNA is the same, and then give an explanation which makes it sound as if the only continuity between me *now* and me *then* is some little parasite-architect, blindly sitting and smirking in each otherwise unrelated cell of the then-me and the now-me.

Cow manure.

I look at that thin face, those thin lips, the eyes narrowed and squinting in the light of a sun seventy-five years younger (and hotter, I *know*, despite the assurances of reason and the verities of Paul's high school science) and I feel the thread of sameness which unites that unsuspecting boy of ten—so confident for one so young, so unafraid—with the old man who has learned to be afraid of the dark.

I wish I could warn him.

The past is dead and buried. But I know now that buried things have a way of rising to the surface when one least expects them to.

In the summer of 1913 the Commonwealth of Pennsylvania made ready for the largest invasion of military veterans the nation had ever seen. Invitations had been sent out from the War Department for a Great Reunion of Civil War veterans to commemorate the fiftieth anniversary of the three-day battle at Gettysburg.

All that spring our Philadelphia newspapers were filled

with details of the anticipated event. Up to 40,000 veterans were expected. By mid-May, the figure had risen to 54,000 and the General Assembly had to vote additional monies to supplement the Army's budget. My mother's cousin Celia wrote from Atlanta to say that the Daughters of the Confederacy and other groups affiliated with the United Confederate Veterans were doing everything in their power to send their old men North for a final invasion.

My father was not a veteran. Before I was born, he had called the trouble with Spain "Mr Hearst's War" and five years after the Gettysburg Reunion he would call the trouble in Europe "Mr Wilson's War." By then I would be in high school, with my classmates chafing to enlist and show the Hun a thing or two, but by then I shared my father's sentiments; I had seen enough of war's legacy.

But in the late spring and early summer of 1913 I would have given anything to join those veterans in Gettysburg, to hear the speeches and see the battle flags and crouch in the Devil's Den and watch those old men re-enact Pickett's Charge one last time.

And then the opportunity arrived.

Since my birthday in February I had been a Boy Scout. The Scouts were a relatively new idea then—the first groups in the United States had been formed only three years earlier—but in the spring of 1913 every boy I knew was either a Boy Scout or waiting to become one.

The Reverend Hodges had formed the first Troop in Chestnut Hill, our little town outside of Philadelphia, now a suburb. The Reverend allowed only boys of good character and strong moral fiber to join: Presbyterian boys. I had sung in the Fourth Avenue Presbyterian Boys' Choir for three years and, in spite of my frailness and total inability to tie a knot, I was allowed to become a Boy Scout three days after my tenth birthday.

My father was not totally pleased. Our Scout uniforms might have been castoffs from the returning Roughriders' army. From hobnailed boots to puttees to campaign hats we were little troopers, drowning in yards of khaki and great draughts of military virtue. The Reverend Hodges had us on the high school football field each Tuesday and Thursday afternoon from four to six and every Saturday morning from seven until ten, practicing close-order drill and applying field dressings to one another until our Troop resembled nothing so much as a band of mummies with swatches of khaki showing through our bandages. On Wednesday evening we met in the church basement to learn Morse Code—what the Reverend called General Service Code—and to practice our semaphore signals.

My father asked me if we were training to fight the Boer War over again. I ignored his irony, sweated into my khaki woolens through those warming weeks of May, and loved every minute of it.

When the Reverend Hodges came by our house in early June to inform my parents that the Commonwealth had requested all Boy Scout Troops in Pennsylvania to send representatives to Gettysburg to help with the Great Reunion, I knew that it had been Divine Intervention which would allow me to join the Reverend, thirteen-year-old Billy Stargill (who would later die in the Argonne), and a pimply-faced overweight boy whose name I cannot recall on the five-day visit to Gettysburg.

195

My father was non committal but my mother agreed at once that it was a unique honor, so on the morning of June 30 I posed in front of Mr Everett's ice wagon for a photograph taken by Dr Lowell, Chestnut Hill's undertaker and official photographer, and at a little after two P.M. on that same day I joined the Reverend and my two comrades-in-arms for the three-hour train ride to Gettysburg.

As a part of the official celebration, we paid the veterans' travel rate of one cent a mile. The train ride cost me $1.21. I had never been to Gettysburg. I had never been away from home overnight.

We arrived late in the afternoon; I was tired, hot, thirsty, and desperately needing to relieve myself since I had been too shy to use the lavatory aboard the train. The small town of Gettysburg was a mass of crowds, confusion, noise, horses, automobiles, and old men whose heavy uniforms smelled of camphor. We stumbled after Reverend Hodges through muddy lanes between buildings draped in flags and bunting. Men outnumbered women ten to one and most of the main streets were a sea of straw boaters and khaki caps. As the Reverend checked in the lobby of the Eagle Hotel for word from his Scouting superiors, I slipped down a side hall and found a public restroom.

Half an hour later we dragged our duffel bags into the back of a small motor carriage for the ride out southwest of town to the Reunion tent city. A dozen boys and their Scoutmasters were crowded into the three benches as the vehicle labored its way through heavy traffic down Franklin Street, past a temporary Red Cross Hospital on the east side of the street and a score of Ambulance Corps wagons parked on the west side, and then right onto a road marked Long Lane and into a sea of tents which seemed to stretch on forever.

It was past seven o'clock and the rich evening light illuminated thousands of canvas pyramids covering hundreds of acres of open farmland. I craned to make out which of the distant hills was Cemetery Ridge, which heap of rocks the Little Round Top. We passed State Policemen on horseback, Army wagons pulled by Army mules, huge heaps of firewood, and clusters of portable field bakeries where the aroma of fresh-baked bread still lingered.

Reverend Hodges turned in his seat. "Afraid we missed the evening chow lines, boys," he said. "But we weren't hungry, were we?"

I shook my head despite the fact my stomach was cramping with hunger. My mother had packed me a dinner of fried chicken and biscuits for the train, but the Reverend had eaten the drumstick and the fat boy had begged the rest. I had been too excited to eat.

We turned right onto East Avenue, a broad dirt road between neat rows of tents. I looked in vain for the Great Tent I had read about—a huge bigtop with room for 13,000 chairs where President Wilson was scheduled to speak in four days, on Friday, the Fourth of July. Now the sun was low and red in the haze to the west, the air thick with dust and the scent of trampled grass and sun-warmed canvas. I was starving and I had dirt in my hair

197

and grit between my teeth. I do not ever remember being happier.

Our Boy Scout Station was at the west end of East Avenue, a hundred yards past a row of portable kitchens set in the middle of the Pennsylvania veterans' tent area. Reverend Hodges showed us to our tents and commanded us to hurry back to the station for our next day's assignments.

I set my duffel on a cot in a tent not far from the latrines. I was slow setting out my bedroll and belongings and when I looked up the fat boy was asleep on another cot and Billy was gone. A train roared by on the Gettysburg and Harrisburg tracks not fifty feet away. Suddenly breathless with the panic of being left behind, I ran back to the Scoutmasters' tent to receive my orders.

Reverend Hodges and Billy were nowhere to be seen but a fat man with a blond mustache, thick spectacles, and an ill-fitting Scoutmaster's uniform snapped, "You there, Scout!"

"Yessir?"

"Have you received your assignment?"

"No, sir."

The fat man grunted and pawed through a stack of yellow cardboard tags lying on a board he was using as a desk. He pulled one from the stack, glanced at it, and tied it to the brass button on my left breast pocket. I craned my neck to read it. Faint blue, type-written letters said: MONTGOMERY, P. D., Capt., 20th N.C. Reg., SECT. 27, SITE 3424, North Carolina Veterans.

"Well, *go*, boy!" snapped the Scoutmaster.

"Yessir," I said and ran toward the tent entrance. I paused. "Sir?"

"What is it?" The Scoutmaster was already tying another ticket on another Scout's blouse.

"Where am I to go, sir?"

The fat man flicked his fingers as if brushing an insect away. "To find the veteran you are assigned to, of course."

I squinted at the ticket. "Captain Montgomery?"

"Yes, yes. If that is what it says."

I took a breath. "Where do I find him, sir?"

The fat man scowled, took four angry steps toward me, and glared at the ticket through his thick glasses. "20th North Carolina . . . Section 27 . . . up *there*." He swept his arm in a gesture that took in the railroad tracks, a distant stream lined with trees, the setting sun, and another tent city on a hill where hundreds of pyramid tents glowed redly in the twilight.

"Pardon me, sir, but what do I do when I find Captain Montgomery?" I asked the Scoutmaster's retreating back.

The man stopped and glowered at me over his shoulder with a thinly veiled disgust that I had never guessed an adult would show toward someone my age. "You do whatever he *wants*, you young fool," snapped the man. "Now *go*."

I turned and ran toward the distant camp of the Confederates.


Lanterns were being lighted as I made my way through long rows of tents. Old men by the hundreds, many in heavy gray uniforms and long whiskers, sat on campstools and cots, benches and wooden stumps, smoking and talking and spitting into the early evening gloom. Twice I lost my way and twice I was given directions in slow, Southern drawls that might as well have been German for all I understood them.

Finally I found the North Carolina contingent sandwiched in between the Alabama and Missouri camps, just a short walk from the West Virginians. In the years since I have found myself wondering why they put the Union-loyal West Virginian veterans in the midst of the rebel encampment.

Section 27 was the last row on the east side of the North Carolina camp and Site 3424 was the last tent in the row. The tent was dark.

"Captain Montgomery?" My voice was little more than a whisper. Hearing no answer from the darkened tent, I ducked my head inside to confirm that the veteran was not home. It was not my fault, I reasoned, that the old gentleman was not here when I called. I would find him in the morning, escort him to the breakfast tent, run the necessary errands for him, help him to find the latrine or his old comrades-in-arms, or whatever. *In the morning*. Right now I thought I would run all the way back to the Boy Scout Station, find Billy and Reverend Hodges, and see if anyone had any cookies in their duffel bags.

"I been waitin' for you, Boy."

I froze. The voice had come from the darkness in the depths of the tent. It was a voice from the South but sharp as cinders and brittle with age. It was a voice that

I imagined the Dead might use to command those still beyond the grave.

"Come in here, Johnny. Step lively!"

I moved into the hot, canvas-scented interior and blinked. For a second my breath would not come.

The old man who lay on the cot was propped on his elbows so that his shoulders looked like sharp wings in the dim light, predatory pinions rising above an otherwise indistinct bundle of gray cloth, gray skin, staring eyes, and faded braid. He was wearing a shapeless hat which had once boasted a brim and crown but which now served only to cast his face into deeper shadow. A beak of a nose jutted into the dim light above wisps of white beard, thin purplish lips, and a few sharp teeth gleaming in a black hole of a mouth. For the first time in my life I realized that a human mouth was really an opening into a skull. The old man's eye sockets were darker pits of shadow beneath brows still black, the cheeks hollowed and knife-edged. Huge, liver-spotted hands, misshapen with age and arthritis, glowed with a preternatural whiteness in the gloom and I saw that while one leg ended in the black gleam of a high boot, the other terminated abruptly below the knee. I could see the rolled trouser leg pulled above pale, scarred skin wrapped tautly around the bone of the stump.

"Goddamnit, boy, did you bring the wagon?"

"Pardon me, sir?" My voice was a cicada's frightened chirp.

"The wagon, goddamnit, Johnny. We need a wagon. You should be knowin' that, boy." The old man sat up, swung his leg and his stump over the edge of the cot, and began fumbling in his loose coat.

"I'm sorry, Captain Montgomery . . . uh . . . you *are* Captain Montgomery, aren't you, sir?"

The old man grunted.

"Well, Captain Montgomery, sir, my name's not Johnny, it's . . ."

"*Goddamnit,* boy!" bellowed the old man. "Would you quit makin' noise and go get the goddamned wagon! We need to get up there to the Pits before that bastard Iverson beats us to it."

I started to reply and then found myself with no wind with which to speak as Captain Montgomery removed a pistol from the folds of his coat. The gun was huge and gray and smelled of oil and I was certain that the crazy old man was going to kill me with it in that instant. I stood there with the wind knocked out of me as certainly as if the old Confederate had struck me in the solar plexus with the barrel of that formidable weapon.

The old man laid the revolver on the cot and reached into the shadows beneath it, pulling out an awkward arrangement of straps, buckles, and mahogany which I recognized as a crude wooden leg. "Come on now, Johnny," he mumbled, bending over to strap the cruel thing in place, "I've waited long enough for you. Go get the wagon, that's a good lad. I'll be ready and waitin' when you get back."

"Yessir," I managed, and turned, and escaped.

I have no rational explanation for my next actions. All I had to do was the natural thing, the thing that every fiber of my frightened body urged me to do—run back to the Boy Scout Station, find Reverend Hodges, inform him that my veteran was a raving madman armed with a pistol, and get a good night's sleep while the grownups sorted things out. But I was not a totally rational creature at this point. (How many ten-year-old boys are, I wonder?) I was tired, hungry, and already homesick after less than seven hours away from home, disoriented in space and time, and—perhaps most pertinent—not used to disobeying orders. And yet I am sure to this day that I would have run the entire way back to the Boy Scout Station and not thought twice about it if my parting glance of the old man had not been of him painfully strapping on that terrible wooden leg. The thought of him standing in the deepening twilight on that awful pegleg, trustingly awaiting a wagon which would never arrive was more than I could bear.

As fate arranged it, there was a wagon and untended team less than a hundred yards from Captain Montgomery's tent. The back of the slat-sided thing was half-filled with blankets, but the driver and deliverers were nowhere in sight. The team was a matched set of grays, aged and swaybacked but docile enough as I grabbed their bridles and clumsily turned them around and tugged them back up the hill with me.

I had never ridden a horse or driven a team. Even in 1913, I was used to riding in automobiles. Chestnut Hill still saw buggies and wagons on the street occasionally, but already they were considered quaint. Mr Everett, our iceman, did not allow boys to ride on his wagon and his horse had the habit of biting any child who came in range.

Gingerly, trying to keep my knuckles away from the

grays' teeth, I led the team up the hill. The thought that I was stealing the wagon never crossed my mind. Captain Montgomery needed a wagon. It was my job to deliver it.

"Good boy, Johnny. Well done." Outside, in the light, the old man was only slightly less formidable. The long gray coat hung in folds and wrinkles and although there was no sight of the pistol, I was sure that it was tucked somewhere close to hand. A heavy canvas bag hung from a strap over his right shoulder. For the first time I noticed a faded insignia on the front of his hat and three small medals on his coat. The ribbons were faded so that I could not make out their colors. The Captain's bare neck reminded me of the thick tangle of ropes dangling into the dark maw of the old well behind our house.

"Come on, Boy. We have to move smartly if we're to beat that son-of-a-bitch Iverson." The old man heaved himself up to the seat with a wide swing of his wooden leg and seized the reins in fists that looked like clusters of gnarled roots. With no hesitation I ran to the left side of the wagon and jumped to the seat beside him.


Gettysburg was filled with lights and activity that last, late evening in June, but the night seemed especially dark and empty as we passed through town on our way north. The house and hotel lights felt so distant to our purpose—whatever that purpose was—that the lights appeared pale and cold to me, the fading glow of fireflies dying in a jar.

In a few minutes we were beyond the last buildings on

the north end of town and turning northwest on what I later learned was Mummasburg Road. Just before we passed behind a dark curtain of trees, I swiveled in my seat and caught a last glimpse of Gettysburg and the Great Reunion Camp beyond it. Where the lights of the city seemed pale and paltry, the flames of the hundreds of campfires and bonfires in the Tent City blazed in the night. I looked at the constellations of fires and realized that there were more old veterans huddling around them that night than there were young men in many nations' armies. I wondered if this is what Cemetery Ridge and Culp's Hill had looked like to the arriving Confederate armies fifty years earlier.

Suddenly I had the chilling thought that fifty years ago Death had given a grand party and 140,000 revelers had arrived in their burial clothes. My father had told me that the soldiers going into battle had often pinned small scraps of paper to their uniforms so that their bodies could be identified after the killing was finished. I glanced to my right as if half-expecting to see a yellowed scrap of paper pinned to the old man's chest, his name, rank, and home town scrawled on it. Then I realized with a start that *I* was wearing the tag.

I looked back at the lights and marveled that fifty years after Death's dark festival, 50,000 of the survivors had returned for a second celebration.

We passed deeper into the forest and I could see no more of the fires of the Reunion Camp. The only light came from the fading glow of the summer sky through limbs above us and the sporadic winking of fireflies along the road.

"You don't remember Iverson, do you, Boy?"

"No, sir."

"Here." He thrust something into my hands. Leaning closer, squinting, I understood that it was an old tintype, cracked at the edges. I was able to make out a pale square of face, shadows which might have been mustaches. Captain Montgomery grabbed it back. "He's not registered at the goddamn reunion," he muttered. "Spent the goddamn day lookin'. Never arrived. Didn't expect him to. Newspaper in Atlanta two years ago said he died. Goddamn lie."

"Oh," I said. The horses' hooves made soft sounds in the dirt of the road. The fields we were passing were as empty as my mind.

"Goddamn lie," said the Captain. "He's goin' be back here. No doubt about it, is there, Johnny?"

"No, sir." We came over the brow of a low hill and the old man slowed the wagon. His pegleg had been making a rhythmic sound as it rattled against the wooden slat where it was braced and as we slowed the tempo changed. We had passed out of the thickest part of the forest but dark farmfields opened out to the left and right between stands of trees and low stone walls. "Damn," he said. "Did you see Forney's house back there, boy?"

"I . . . no, sir. I don't think so." I had no idea if we had passed Forney's house. I had no idea who Forney was. I had no idea what I was doing wandering around the countryside at night with this strange old man. I was amazed to find myself suddenly on the verge of tears.

Captain Montgomery pulled the team to a stop under some trees set back off the right side of the road. He panted and wheezed, struggling to dismount from the driver's seat. "Help me down, Boy. It's time we bivouacked."

I ran around to offer my hand but he used my shoulder as a brace and dropped heavily to the ground. A strange, sour scent came from him and I was reminded of an old, urine-soaked mattress in a shed near the tracks behind our school where Billy said hoboes slept. It was fully dark now. I could make out the Big Dipper above a field across the road. All around us, crickets and tree toads were tuning up for their nightly symphony.

"Bring some of them blankets along, Boy." He had picked up a fallen limb to use as a walking stick as he moved clumsily into the trees. I grabbed some Army blankets from the back of the wagon and followed him.

We crossed a wheat field, passed a thin line of trees, and climbed through a meadow before stopping under a tree where broad leaves stirred to the night breeze. The Captain directed me to lay the blankets out into rough bedrolls and then he lowered himself until he was lying with his back propped against the tree and his wooden leg resting on his remaining ankle. "You hungry, Boy?"

I nodded in the dark. The old man rummaged in the canvas bag and handed me several strips of something I thought was meat but which tasted like heavily salted leather. I chewed on the first piece for almost five minutes before it was soft enough to swallow. Just as my lips and tongue were beginning to throb with thirst, Captain Montgomery handed me a wineskin of water and showed me how to squirt it into my open mouth.

"Good jerky, ain't it, Boy?" he asked.

"Delicious," I answered honestly and worked to bite off another chunk.

"That Iverson was a useless son-of-a-bitch," the Captain said around his own jawful of jerky. It was as if he were picking up the sentence he had begun half an hour earlier back at the wagon. "He would've been a harmless son-of-a-bitch if those dumb bastards in my own 20th North Carolina hadn't elected him camp commander back before the war begun. That made Iverson a colonel sort of automatic like, and by the time we'd fought our way up North, the stupid little bastard was in charge of one of Rodes's whole damn brigades."

The old man paused to work at the jerky with his few remaining teeth and I reflected on the fact that the only other person I had ever heard curse anything like the Captain was Mr Bolton, the old fire chief who used to sit out in front of the firehouse on Third Street and tell stories to the new recruits, apparently oblivious to the uninvited presence of us younger members of the audience. Perhaps, I thought, it had something to do with wearing a uniform.

"His first name was Alfred," said the Captain. The old man's voice was soft, preoccupied, and his southern accent was so thick that the meaning of each word reached me some seconds after the sound of it. It was a bit like lying in bed, already dreaming, and hearing the soft voices of my mother and father coming upstairs through a curtain of sleep. Or like magically understanding a foreign language. I closed my eyes to hear better. "Alfred," said the Captain, "just like his daddy. His daddy'd been a Senator from Georgia, good friend of the President." I could feel the old man's gaze on me. "President Davis. It was Davis, back when he was a senator too, who give young Iverson his first commission.

That was back durin' the trouble with Mexico. Then when the real war come up, Iverson and his daddy got 'em up a regiment. Them days, when a rich goddamn family like the Iversons wanted to play soldiers, they just bought themselves a regiment. Bought the goddamn uniforms and horses and such. Then they got to be officers. Goddamn grown men playin' at toy soldiers, Boy. Only once't the real war begun, *we* was the toy soldiers, Johnny."

I opened my eyes. I could not recall ever having seen so many stars. Above the slope of the meadow, constellations came all the way down to the horizon; others were visible between the dark masses of trees. The Milky Way crossed the sky like a bridge. Or like the pale tracks of an army long since passed by.

"Just goddamned bad luck we got Iverson," said the Captain, "because the brigade was good 'un and the 20th North Carolina was the best goddamn regiment in Ewell's corps." The old man shifted to look at me again. "You wasn't with us yet at Sharpsburg, was you, Johnny?"

I shook my head, feeling a chill go up my back as he again called me by some other boy's name. I wondered where that boy was now.

"No, of course not," said Captain Montgomery. "That was in '62. You was still in school. The regiment was still at Fredericksburg after the campaign. Somebody'd ordered up a dress parade and Nate's band played 'Dixie.' All of the sudden, from acrost the Rappahannock, the Yankee band starts playin' Dixie back at us. Goddamnest thing, Boy. You could hear that music so clear acrost the water it was like two parts of the same band playin'. So our band—all boys from the 20th—they commence to playin' 'Yankee Doodle.' All of us standin' there at parade rest in that cold sunlight, feelin' mighty queer by then, I don't mind tellin' you. Then, when our boys is done with 'Yankee Doodle,' just like they all rehearsed it together, both bands commence playin' 'Home Sweet Home.' Without even thinkin' about it, Perry and ol' Thomas and Jeffrey an' me and the whole line starts singin' along. So did Lieutenant Williams—young Mr Oliver hisself—and before long the whole brigade's singin'—the damn Yankees too—their voices comin' acrost the Rappahannock and joinin' ours like we'd been one big choir that'd gotten busted up by mistake or accident or somethin'. I tell you, Boy, it was sorta like singin' with ghosts. And sorta like we was ghosts our own selves."

I closed my eyes to hear the deep voices singing that sad, sweet song, and I realized suddenly that even grownups—soldiers even—could feel as lonely and homesick as I had felt earlier that evening. Realizing that, I found that all of my own homesickness had fled. I felt that I was where I should be, part of the Captain's army, part of all armies, camping far from home and uncertain what the next day would bring but content to be with my friends. My comrades. The voices were as real and as sad as the soughing of wind through the midsummer leaves.

The Captain cleared his throat and spat. "And then that bastard Iverson kilt us," he said. I heard the sound of buckles as the old man unstrapped his false leg.

I opened my eyes as he pulled his blanket over his shoulders and turned his face away. "Get some sleep,

Boy," came his muffled voice. "We step off at first light come mornin'."

I pulled my own blanket up to my neck and laid my cheek against the dark soil. I listened for the singing but the voices were gone. I went to sleep to the sound of the wind in the leaves sounding like angry whispers in the night.

I awoke once before sunrise when there was just enough false light to allow me to see Captain Montgomery's face a few inches from my own. The old man's hat had slipped off in the night and the top of his head was a relief map of reddened scalp scarred by liver spots, sores, and a few forlorn wisps of white hair. His brow was furrowed as if in fierce concentration, eyebrows two dark eruptions of hair, eyelids lowered but showing a line of white at the bottom. Soft snores whistled out of his broken gourd of a mouth and a thin line of drool moistened his whiskers. His breath was as dry and dead as a draft of air from a cave unsealed after centuries of being forgotten.

I stared at the time-scoured flesh of the old face inches from mine, at the swollen and distorted fingers clutching, childlike, at his blanket, and I realized, with a precise and prescient glimpse at the terrible fate of my own longevity, that age was a curse, a disease, and that all of us unlucky to survive our childhoods were doomed to suffer and perish from it. Perhaps, I thought, it is why young men go willingly to die in wars.

I pulled the blanket across my face.

When I awoke again, just after sunrise, the old man was standing ten paces from the tree and staring toward Gettysburg. Only a white cupola was visible above the trees, its dome and sides painted in gold from the sun. I disentangled myself from the blankets and rose to my feet, marveling at how stiff and clammy and strange I felt. I had never slept out of doors before. Reverend Hodges had promised us a campout but the Troop had been too busy learning close order drill and semaphore. I decided that I might skip the campout part of the agenda. Staggering upright on legs still half asleep, I wondered how Captain Montgomery had strapped on his wooden leg without awakening me.

"Mornin', Boy," he called as I returned from the edge of the woods where I had relieved myself. His gaze never left the cupola visible to the southeast.

We had breakfast while standing there under the tree—more beef jerky and water. I wondered what Billy, the Reverend, and the other Scouts were having down in the tents near the field kitchens. Pancakes, probably. Perhaps with bacon. Certainly with tall glasses of cold milk.

"I was there with Mr Oliver when muster was called on the mornin' of the first," rasped the old man. "1,470 present for duty. 114 was officers. I wasn't among 'em. Still had my sergeant stripes then. Wasn't 'til the second Wilderness that they gave me the bar. Anyway, word had come the night before from A. P. Hill that the Federals was massin' to the south. Probably figurin' to cut us off. Our brigade was the first to turn south to Hill's call.

"We heard firin' as we come down the Heidlersburg

212

Pike, so General Rodes took us through the woods 'til we got to Oak Hill." He turned east, smoothly pivoting on his wooden leg, shielding his eyes from the sun. "Bout there, I reckon, Johnny. Come on." The old man spun around and I rolled the blankets and scurried to follow him back down the hill toward the southeast. Toward the distant cupola.

"We come right down the west side of this ridge then, too, didn't we, Boy? Not so many trees then. Been marchin' since before sunup. Got here sometime after what should've been dinner time. One o'clock, maybe one-thirty. Had hardtack on the hoof. Seems to me that we stopped a while up the hill there so's Rodes could set out some guns. Perry an' me was glad to sit. He wanted to start another letter to our Ma, but I told him there wasn't goin' to be time. There wasn't, either, but I wish to hell I'd let him write the damned thing.

"From where we was, you could see the Yanks comin' up the road from Gettysburg and we knew there'd be a fight that day. Goddamnit, Boy, you can put them blankets down. We ain't goin' to need 'em today."

Startled, I dropped the blankets in the weeds. We had reached the lower end of the meadow and only a low, split rail fence separated us from what I guessed to be the road we had come up the night before. The Captain swung his pegleg over the fence and after we crossed we both paused a minute. I felt the growing heat of the day as a thickness in the air and a slight pounding in my temples. Suddenly there came the sound of band music and cheering from the south, dwindled by distance.

The Captain removed a stained red kerchief from his pocket and mopped at his neck and forehead. "Goddamn idiots," he said. "Celebratin' like it's a county fair. Damned nonsense."

"Yessir," I said automatically, but at that moment I was thrilled with the idea of the Reunion and with the reality of being with a veteran—*my* veteran—walking on the actual ground he had fought on. I realized that someone seeing us from a distance might have mistaken us for *two* soldiers. At that moment I would have traded my Boy Scout khaki for butternut brown or Confederate gray and would have joined the Captain in any cause. At that moment I would have marched against the Eskimoes if it meant being part of an army, setting off at sunrise with one's comrades, preparing for battle, and generally feeling as *alive* as I felt at that instant.

The Captain had heard my "yessir" but he must have noticed something else in my eyes because he leaned forward, rested his weight on the fence, and brought his face close to mine. "Goddamnit, Johnny, don't you fall for such nonsense twice. You think these dumb sons-of-bitches would've come back all this way if they was honest enough to admit they was celebratin' a slaughterhouse?"

I blinked.

The old man grabbed my tunic with his swollen fist. "That's all it is, Boy, don't you see? A goddamn *abattoir* that was built here to grind up *men* and now they're reminiscin' about it and tellin' funny stories about it and weepin' old man tears about what good times we had when we was fed to it." With his free hand he stabbed a finger in the direction of the cupola. "Can't you see it, Boy? The holdin' pens and the delivery chutes and the killin' rooms—only not everybody was so lucky as to have their skull busted open on the first pop, some of us got part of us fed to the grinder and got to lay around and watch the others swell up and bloat in the heat. Goddamn slaughterhouse, Boy, where they kill you and gut you down the middle . . . dump your insides out on the goddamn floor and kick 'em aside to get at the next fool . . . hack the meat off your bones, grind up the bones for fertilizer, then grind up everythin' else you got that ain't prime meat and wrap it in your own guts to sell it to the goddamn public as sausage. Parades. War stories. Reunions. *Sausage*, Boy." Panting slightly, he released me, spat, wiped his whiskers and stared a long minute at the sky. "And we was led into that slaughterhouse by a Judas goat named Iverson, Johnny," he said at last, his voice empty of all emotion. "Never forget that."

The hill continued to slope gently downward as we crossed the empty road and entered a field just to the east of an abandoned farmhouse. Fire had gutted the upper stories years ago and the windows on the first floor were boarded up, but irises still grew tall around the foundation and along the overgrown lane leading to sagging outbuildings. "John Forney's old place," said Captain Montgomery. "He was still here when I come back in '98. Told me then that none of his farmhands'd stay around here after night begun to settle. Because of the Pits."

"Because of what, sir?" I was blinking in the early heat and glare of a day in which the temperatures certainly would reach the mid-nineties. Grasshoppers hopped mindlessly in the dusty grass.

The old man did not seem to hear my question. The cupola was no longer visible because we were too close to the trees, but the Captain's attention was centered on the field which ran downhill less than a quarter of a mile to a thicker line of trees to the southeast. He withdrew the pistol from his coat and my heart pounded as he drew back the hammer until it clicked. "This is a double-action, Boy," he said. "Don't forget that."

We forced our way through a short hedge and began crossing the field at a slow walk. The old man's wooden leg made soft sounds in the soil. Grass and thistles brushed at our legs. "That son-of-a-bitch Iverson never got this far," said the Captain. "Ollie Williams said he heard him give the order up the hill there near where Rodes put his guns out. 'Give 'em hell,' Iverson says, then goes back up to his tree there to sit in the shade an' eat his lunch. Had him some wine too. Had wine every meal when the rest of us was drinkin' water out of the ditch. Nope, Iverson never come down here 'til it was all over and then it was just to say we'd tried to surrender and order a bunch of dead men to stand up and salute the general. Come on, Boy."

We moved slowly across the field. I could make out a stone fence near the treeline now, half-hidden in the dapple of leaf shadow. There seemed to be a jumble of tall grass or vines just this side of the wall.

"They put Daniels' brigade on our right." The Captain's pistol gestured toward the south, the barrel just missing the brim of my hat. "But they didn't come down 'til we was shot all to pieces. Then Daniels' boys run right into the fire of Stone's 149th Pennsylvania . . . them damn sharpshooters what were called the Bogus Bucktails for some damn reason I don't recall now. But we was all alone when we come down this way before Daniels and Ramseur and O'Neal and the rest come along. Iverson sent us off too soon. Ramseur wasn't ready for another half hour and O'Neal's brigade turned back even before they got to the Mummasburg Road back there."

We were half way across the field by then. A thin screen of trees to our left blocked most of the road from sight. The stone wall was less than three hundred yards ahead. I glanced nervously at the cocked pistol. The Captain seemed to have forgotten he was carrying it.

"We come down like this at an angle," he said. "Brigade stretched about halfway acrost the field, sorta slantin' northeast to southwest. The 5th North Carolina was on our left. The 20th was right about here, couple of hundred of us in the first line, and the 23rd and 12th was off to our right there and sorta trailin' back, the right flank of the 12th about halfway to that damned railroad cut down there."

I looked toward the south but could see no railroad tracks. There was only the hot, wide expanse of field which may have once borne crops but which had now gone back to brambles and sawgrass.

The Captain stopped, panting slightly, and rested his weight on his good leg. "What we didn't know, Johnny, was that the Yanks was all set behind that wall there. Thousands of them. Not showin' a goddamn cap or battle flag or rifle barrel. Just hunkerin' down there and waitin'. Waitin' for the animals to come in the door so

217

the slaughter could begin. And Colonel Iverson never even ordered skirmishers out in front of us. I never even *seen* an advance without skirmishers, and there we was walkin' across this field while Iverson sat up on Oak Hill eatin' lunch and havin' another glass of wine."

The Captain raised his pistol and pointed at the treeline. I stepped back, expecting him to fire, but the only noise was the rasp of his voice. "Remember? We got to that point . . .'bout there where them damn vines is growing . . . and the Yanks rise up along that whole quarter mile of wall there and fire right into us. Like they're comin' up out of the ground. No noise at all except the swish of our feet 'n legs in the wheat and grass and then they let loose a volley like to sound like the end of the world. Whole goddamn world disappears in smoke and fire. Even a Yank couldn't miss at that range. More of 'em come out of the trees back up there . . ." The Captain gestured toward our left where the wall angled northwest to meet the road. "That puts us in an enfilade fire that just sweeps through the 5th North Carolina. Like a scythe, Boy. There was wheat in these fields then. But it was just stubble. No place to go. No place to hide. We could've run back the way we come but us North Carolina boys wasn't goin' to start learnin' ourselves how to run this late in the day. So the scythe just come sweepin' into us. Couldn't move forward. That goddamn wall was just a wall of smoke with fire comin' through it there fifty yards away. I seen Lieutenant Colonel Davis of the 5th—Old Bill his boys called him—get his regiment down into that low area there to the south. See about where that line of scrub brush is? Not nearly so big as a ditch, but it give 'em some cover, not much. But us in the 20th and Cap'n Turner's boys in the 23rd didn't have no choice but to lie down here in the open and take it."

The old man advanced slowly for a dozen yards and stopped where the grass grew thicker and greener, joining with tangles of what I realized were grapevines to create a low, green thicket between us and the wall. Suddenly he sat down heavily, thrusting his wooden leg out in front of him and cradling the pistol in his lap. I dropped to my knees in the grass near him, removed my hat, and unbuttoned my tunic. The yellow tag hung loosely from my breast pocket button. It was very hot.

"The Yanks kept pourin' the fire into us," he said. His voice was a hoarse whisper. Sweat ran down his cheeks and neck. "More Federals come out of the woods down there . . . by the railroad gradin' . . . and started enfiladin' Old Bill's boys and our right flank. We couldn't fire back worth horseshit. Lift your head outta the dirt to aim and you caught a Minié ball in the brain. My brother Perry was layin' next to me and I heard the ball that took him in the left eye. Made a sound like someone hammerin' a side of beef with a four-pound hammer. He sort of rose up and flopped back next to me. I was yellin' and cryin', my face all covered with snot and dirt and tears, when all of a sudden I feel Perry tryin' to rise up again. Sort of jerkin', like somebody was pullin' him up with strings. Then again. And again. I'd got a glimpse of the hole in his face where his eye'd been and his brains and bits of the back of his head was still smeared on my right leg, but I could *feel* him jerkin' and pullin', like he was tuggin' at me to go with him somewhere. Later, I seen why. More bullets had been

219

hittin' him in the head and each time it'd snap him back some. When we come back to bury him later, his head looked like a mushmelon someone'd kicked apart. It wasn't unusual, neither. Lot of the boys layin' on the field that day got just torn apart by that Yankee fire. Like a scythe, Boy. Or a meatgrinder."

I sat back in the grass and breathed through my mouth. The vines and black soil gave off a thick, sweet smell that made me feel lightheaded and a little ill. The heat pressed down like thick, wet blankets.

"Some of the boys stood up to run then," said Captain Montgomery, his voice still a hoarse monotone, his eyes focused on nothing. He was holding the cocked pistol in both hands with the barrel pointed in my direction, but I was sure that he had forgotten I was there. "Everybody who stood up got hit. The sound was . . . you could hear the balls hittin' home even over the firin'. The wind was blowin' the smoke back into the woods so there wasn't even any cover you usually got once't the smoke got heavy. I seen Lieutenant Ollie Williams stand up to yell at the boys of the 20th to stay low and he was hit twice while I watched.

"The rest of us was tryin' to form a firin' line in the grass and wheat, but we hadn't got off a full volley before the Yanks come runnin' out, some still firin', some usin' their bayonets. And that's when I seen you and the other two little drummers get kilt, Johnny. When they used them bayonets . . ." The old man paused and looked at me for the first time in several minutes. A cloud of confusion seemed to pass over him. He slowly lowered the pistol, gently released the cocked hammer, and raised a shaking hand to his brow.

Still feeling dizzy and a little sick myself, I asked, "Is that when you lost your . . . uh . . . when you hurt your leg, sir?"

The Captain removed his hat. His few white hairs were stringy with sweat. "What? My leg?" He stared at the wooden peg below his knee as if he had never noticed it before. "My leg. No, Boy, that was later. The Battle of the Crater. The Yankees tunneled under us and blowed us up while we was sleepin'. When I didn't die right away, they shipped me home to Raleigh and made me an honorary Cap'n three days before the war ended. No, that day . . . *here* . . . I got hit at least three times but nothin' serious. A ball took the heel of my right boot off. Another'n knocked my rifle stock all to hell and gave me some splinters in my cheek. A third'n took off a chunk of my left ear, but hell, I could still hear all right. It wasn't 'til I sat down to try to go to sleep that night that I come to find out that another ball'd hit me in the back of the leg, right below the ass, but it'd been goin' so slow it just give me a big bruise there."

We sat there for several minutes in silence. I could hear insects rustling in the grass. Finally the Captain said, "And that son-of-a-bitch Iverson never even come down here until Ramseur's boys finally got around to clearin' the Yankees out. That was later. I was layin' right around here somewhere, squeezed in between Perry and Nate's corpses, covered with so much of their blood an' brains that the goddamn Yanks just stepped over all three of us when they ran out to stick bayonets in our people or drive 'em back to their line as prisoners. I opened my eyes long enough to see ol' Cade Tarleton bein' clubbed along by a bunch of laughin' Yankees.

They had our regimental flag, too, goddamnit. There was no one left alive around it to put up a fight.

"Ramseur, him who the Richmond papers was always callin' the Chevalier Bayard, whatever the hell that meant, was comin' down the hill into the same ambush when Lieutenant Crowder and Lieutenant Dugger run up and warned him. Ramseur was an officer but he wasn't nobody's fool. He crossed the road further east and turned the Yankee's right flank, just swept down the backside of that wall, drivin' 'em back toward the seminary.

"Meanwhile, while the few of us who'd stayed alive was busy crawlin' back towards Forney's house or layin' there bleedin' from our wounds, that son-of-a-bitch Iverson was tellin' General Rodes that he'd seen our regiment put up a white flag and go over to the Yanks. Goddamn lie, Boy. Them who got captured was mostly wounded who got drove off at the point of a bayonet. There wasn't any white flags to be seen that day. Leastways not here. Just bits of white skull and other stuff layin' around.

"Later, while I was still on the field lookin' for a rifle that'd work, Rodes brings Iverson down here to show him where the men had surrendered, and while their horses is pickin' their way over the corpses that used to be the 20th North Carolina, that bastard Iverson . . ." Here the old man's voice broke. He paused a long minute, hawked, spat, and continued. "That *bastard* Iverson sees our rows of dead up here, 700 men from the finest brigade the South ever fielded, layin' shot dead in lines as straight as a dress parade, and Iverson thinks they're still duckin' from fire even though Ramseur had driven the Yanks off, and he stands up in his stirrups, his goddamn sorrel horse almost steppin' on Perry, and he screams, 'Stand up and salute when the general passes, you men! Stand up this instant!' It was Rodes who realized that they was lookin' at dead men."

Captain Montgomery was panting, barely able to get the words out between racking gasps for breath. I was having trouble breathing myself. The sickeningly sweet stench from the weeds and vines and dark soil seemed to use up all of the air. I found myself staring at a cluster of grapes on a nearby vine; the swollen fruit looked like bruised flesh streaked with ruptured veins.

"If I'd had my rifle," said the Captain, "I would have shot the bastard right then." He let out a ragged breath. "Him and Rodes went back up the hill together and I never seen Iverson again. Captain Halsey took command of what was left of the regiment. When the brigade reassembled the next mornin', 362 men stood muster where 1,470 had answered the call the day before. They called Iverson back to Georgia and put him in charge of a home guard unit or somethin'. Word was, President Davis saved him from bein' court-martialed or reprimanded. It was clear none of us would've served under the miserable son-of-a-bitch again. You know how the last page of our 20th North Carolina regimental record reads, Boy?"

"No, sir," I said softly.

The old man closed his eyes. "Initiated at Seven Pines, sacrificed at Gettysburg, and surrendered at Appomattox. Help me get to my feet, Boy. We got to find a place to hide."

"To hide, sir?"

"Goddamn right," said the Captain as I acted as a crutch for him. "We've got to be ready when Iverson comes here today." He raised the heavy pistol as if it explained everything. "We've got to be ready when he comes."

It was mid-morning before we found an adequate place to hide. I trailed along behind the limping old man and while part of my mind was desperate with panic to find a way out of such an insane situation, another part—a larger part—had no trouble accepting the logic of everything. Colonel Alfred Iverson, Jr, would have to return to his field of dishonor this day and we had to hide in order to kill him.

"See where the ground's lower here, Boy? Right about where these damn vines is growin'?"

"Yessir."

"Them's Iverson's Pits. That's what the locals call 'em according to John Forney when I come to visit in '98. You know what they are?"

"No, sir," I lied. Part of me knew very well what they were.

"Night after the battle . . . battle, hell, *slaughter* . . . the few of us left from the regiment and some of Lee's pioneers come up and dug big shallow pits and just rolled our boys in where they lay. Laid 'em in together, still in their battle lines. Nate 'n Perry's shoulders was touchin'. Right where I'd been layin'. You can see where the Pits start here. The ground's lower an' the grass is higher, ain't it?"

"Yessir."

"Forney said the grass was always higher here, crops too, when they growed them. Forney didn't farm this field much. Said the hands didn't like to work here. He told his niggers that there weren't nothing to worry about, that the UCV'd come up and dug up everythin' after the war to take our boys back to Richmond, but that ain't really true."

"Why not, sir?" We were wading slowly through the tangle of undergrowth. Vines wrapped around my ankle and I had to tug to free myself.

"They didn't do much diggin' here," said the Captain. "Bones was so thick and scattered that they jes' took a few of 'em and called it quits. Didn't like diggin' here any more than Forney's niggers liked workin' here. Even in the daytime. Place that's got this much shame and anger in it . . . well, people *feel* it, don't they, Boy?"

"Yessir," I said automatically, although all I felt at that moment was sick and sleepy.

The Captain stopped. "Goddamnit, that house wasn't here before."

Through a break in the stone wall I could see a small house—more of a large shack, actually—made of wood so dark as to be almost black and set back in the shade of the trees. No driveway or wagon lane led to it, but I could see a faint trampling in Forney's field and the forest grass where horses might have passed through the break in the wall to gain access. The old man seemed deeply offended that someone had built a home so close to the field where his beloved 20th North Carolina had fallen. But the house was dark and silent and we moved away from that section of the wall.

The closer we came to the stone fence, the harder it was to walk. The grass grew twice as high as in the fields beyond and the wild grapevines marked a tangled area about the size of the football field where our Troop practiced its close order drill.

In addition to the tangled grass and thick vines there to hamper our progress, there were the holes. Dozens of them, scores of them, pockmarking the field and lying in wait under the matted foliage.

"Goddamn gophers," said Captain Montgomery, but the holes were twice as wide across the opening as any burrow I had seen made by mole or gopher or ground squirrel. There were no heaps of dirt at the opening. Twice the old man stepped into them, the second time ramming his wooden leg in so deeply that we both had to work to dislodge it. Tugging hard at his wool-covered leg, I suddenly had the nightmarish sense that someone or something was pulling at the other end, refusing to let go, trying to suck the old man underground.

The incident must have disconcerted Captain Montgomery as well, because as soon as his leg popped free of the hole he staggered back a few steps and sat down heavily with his back against the stone wall. "This is good enough, Boy," he panted. "We'll wait here."

It was a good place for an ambush. The vines and grass grew waist high there, allowing us glimpses of the field beyond but concealing us as effectively as a duck blind. The wall sheltered our backs.

Captain Montgomery removed his topcoat and canvas bag and commenced to unload, clean, and reload his pistol. I lay on the grass nearby, at first thinking about what was going on back at the Reunion, then wondering about how to get the Captain back there, then wondering what Iverson had looked like, then thinking about home, and finally thinking about nothing at all as I moved in and out of a strange, dream-filled doze.

Not three feet from where I lay was another of the ubiquitous holes, and as I fell into a light slumber I remained faintly aware of the odor rising from that opening: the same sickening sweetness I had smelled earlier, but thicker now, heavier, almost erotic with its undertones of corruption and decay, of dead sea creatures drying in the sun. Many years later, visiting an abandoned meat processing plant in Chicago with a real estate agent acquaintance, I was to encounter a similar smell; it was the stench of a charnel house, disused for years but permeated with the memory of blood.

The day passed in a haze of heat, thick air, and insect noises. I dozed and awoke to watch with the Captain, dozed again. Once I seem to remember eating hard biscuits from his bag and washing them down with the last water from his wineskin, but even that fades into my dreams of that afternoon, for I remember others seated around us, chewing on similar fare and talking in low tones so that the words were indistinguishable but the southern dialect came through clearly. It did not sound strange to me. Once I remember awakening, even though I was sitting up and staring and had thought I was already awake, as the sound of an automobile along the Mummasburg Road shocked me into full consciousness. But the trees at the edge of the field shielded any traffic from view, the sounds faded, and I returned to the drugged doze I had known before.

Sometime late that afternoon I dreamed the one dream I remember clearly.

I was lying in the field, hurt and helpless, the left side of my face in the dirt and my right eye staring unblinkingly at a blue summer sky. An ant walked across my cheek, then another, until a stream of them crossed my cheek and eye, others moving into my nostrils and open mouth. I could not move. I did not blink. I felt them in my mouth, between my teeth, removing bits of morning bacon from between two molars, moving across the soft flesh of my palate, exploring the dark tunnel of my throat. The sensations were not unpleasant.

I was vaguely aware of other things going deeper, of slow movement in the swelling folds of my guts and belly. Small things laid their eggs in the drying corners of my eye.

I could see clearly as a raven circled overhead, spiralling lower, landed nearby, paced to and fro in a wing-folding strut, and hopped closer. It took my eye with a single stab of a beak made huge by proximity. In the darkness which followed I could still sense the light as my body expanded in the heat, a hatchery to thousands now, the loose cloth of my shirt pulled tight as my flesh expanded. I sensed my own internal bacteria, deprived of other foods, digesting my body's decaying fats and rancid pools of blood in a vain effort to survive a few more hours.

I felt my lips wither and dry in the heat, pulling back from my teeth, felt my jaws open wider and wider in a mirthless, silent laugh as ligaments decayed or were chewed away by small predators. I felt lighter as the eggs hatched, the maggots began their frenzied cleansing, my

body turning toward the dark soil as the process acceler-
ated. My mouth opened wide to swallow the waiting
Earth. I tasted the dark communion of dirt. Stalks of
grass grew where my tongue had been. A flower found
rich soil in the humid sepulcher of my skull and sent its
shoot curling upward through the gap which had once
held my eye.

Settling, relaxing, returning to the acid-taste of the
blackness around me, I sensed the others there. Random,
shifting currents of soil sent decaying bits of wool or
flesh or bone in touch with bits of them, fragments
intermingling with the timid eagerness of a lover's first
touch. When all else was lost, mingling with the darkness
and anger, my bones remained, brittle bits of memory,
forgotten, sharp-edged fragments of pain resisting the
inevitable relaxation into painlessness, into nothingness.

And deep in that rotting marrow, lost in the loam-
black acid of forgetfulness, I remembered. And waited.


"Wake up, Boy! It's him. It's Iverson!"

The urgent whisper shocked me up out of sleep. I
looked around groggily, still tasting the dirt from where
I had lain with my lips against the ground.

"Goddamnit, I *knew* he'd come!" whispered the Captain, pointing to our left where a man in a dark coat had
come out of the woods through the gap in the stone wall.

I shook my head. My dream would not release me and
I knuckled my eyes, trying to shake the dimness from
them. Then I realized that the dimness was real. The
daylight had faded into evening while I slept. I wondered

where in God's name the day had gone. The man in the black coat moved through a twilight grayness which seemed to echo the eerie blindness of my dreams. I could make out the man's white shirt and pale face glowing slightly in the gloom as he turned our direction and came closer, clearing a path for himself with short, sharp chops with a cane or walking stick.

"By God, it *is* him," hissed the Captain and raised his pistol with shaking hands. He thumbed the hammer back as I watched in horror.

The man was closer now, no more than twenty-five feet away, and I could see the dark mustaches, black hair, and deepset eyes. It did indeed look like the man whose visage I had glimpsed by starlight in the old tintype.

Captain Montgomery steadied his pistol on his left arm and squinted over the sights. I could hear hisses of breath from the man in the dark suit as he walked closer, whistling an almost inaudible tune. The Captain squeezed the trigger.

"No!" I cried and grabbed the revolver, jerking it down, the hammer falling cruelly on the web of flesh between my thumb and forefinger. It did not fire.

The Captain shoved me away with a violent blow of his left forearm and struggled to raise the weapon again even as I clung to his wrist. "No!" I shouted again. "He's too young! *Look*. He's too young!"

The old man paused then, his arms still straining, but squinting now at the stranger who stood less than a dozen feet away.

It was true. The man was far too young to be Colonel Iverson. The pale, surprised face belonged to a man in his early thirties at most. Captain Montgomery lowered the pistol and raised trembling fingers to his temples. "My God," he whispered. "My God."

"Who's there?" The man's voice was sharp and assured, despite his surprise. "Show yourself."

I helped the Captain up, sure that the mustached stranger had sensed our movement behind the tall grass and vines but had not witnessed our struggles nor seen the gun. The Captain squinted at the younger man even as he straightened his hat and dropped the pistol in the deep pocket of his coat. I could feel the old man trembling as I steadied him upright.

"Oh, a veteran!" called the man and stepped forward with his hand extended, batting away the grasping vines with easy flicks of his walking stick.

We walked the perimeter of the Pits in the fading light, our new guide moving slowly to accommodate the Captain's painful hobble. The man's walking stick served as a pointer while he spoke. "This was the site of a skirmish before the major battles began," he said. "Not many visitors come out here . . . most of the attention is given to more famous areas south and west of here . . . but those of us who live or spend summers around here are aware of some of these lesser-known spots. It's quite interesting how the field is sunken here, isn't it?"

"Yes," whispered the Captain. He watched the ground, never raising his eyes to the young man's face.

The man had introduced himself as Jessup Sheads and said that he lived in the small house we had noticed set back in the trees. The Captain had been lost in his confused reverie so I had introduced both of us to Mr Sheads. Neither man paid notice of my name. The Captain now glanced up at Sheads as if he still could not believe that this was not the man whose name had tormented him for half a century.

Sheads cleared his throat and pointed again at the tangle of thick growth. "As a matter of fact, this area right along here was the site of a minor skirmish before the serious fighting began. The forces of the Confederacy advanced along a broad line here, were slowed briefly by Federal resistance at this wall, but quickly gained the advantage. It was a small Southern victory before the bitter stalemates of the next few days." Sheads paused and smiled at the Captain. "But perhaps you know all this, sir. What unit did you say you have had the honor of serving with?"

The old man's mouth moved feebly before the words could come. "20th North Carolina," he managed at last.

"Of course!" cried Sheads and clapped the Captain on the shoulder. "Part of the glorious brigade whose victory this site commemorates. I would be honored, sir, if you and your young friend would join me in my home to toast the 20th North Carolina regiment before you return to the Reunion Camp. Would this be possible, sir?"

I tugged at the Captain's coat, suddenly desperate to be away from there, lightheaded from hunger and a sudden surge of unreasoning fear, but the old man straightened his back, found his voice, and said clearly, "The boy and me would be honored, sir."

The cottage had been built of tar-black wood. An expensive-looking black horse, still saddled, was tied to the railing of the small porch on the east side of the house. Behind the house, a thicket of trees and a tumble of boulders made access from that direction seem extremely difficult if not impossible.

The house was small inside and showed few signs of being lived in. A tiny entrance foyer led to a parlor where sheets covered two or three pieces of furniture or to the dining room where Sheads led us, a narrow room with a single window, a tall hoosier cluttered with bottles, cans, and a few dirty plates, and a narrow plank table on which burned an old-style kerosene lamp. Behind dusty curtains there was a second, smaller room, in which I caught a glimpse of a mattress on the floor and stacks of books. A steep staircase on the south side of the dining room led up through a hole in the ceiling to what must have been a small attic room, although all I could see when I glanced upward was a square of blackness.

Jessup Sheads propped his heavy walking stick against the table and busied himself at the hoosier, returning with a decanter and three crystal glasses. The lamp hissed and tossed our shadows high on the roughly plastered wall. I glanced toward the window but the twilight had given way to true night and only darkness pressed against the panes.

"Shall we include the boy in our toast?" asked Sheads, pausing, the decanter hovering above the third wine-glass. I had never been allowed to taste wine or any other spirits.

"Yes," said the Captain, staring fixedly at Sheads. The

lamplight shone upward into the Captain's face, emphasizing his sharp cheekbones and turning his bushy, old-man's eyebrows into two great wings of hair above his falcon's beak of a nose. His shadow on the wall was a silhouette from another era.

Sheads finished pouring and we raised our glasses. I stared dubiously at the wine; the red fluid was dull and thick, streaked through with tendrils of black which may or may not have been a trick of the flickering lamp.

"To the 20th North Carolina Regiment," said Sheads and raised his glass. The gesture reminded me of Reverend Hodges lifting the communion cup. The Captain and I raised our glasses and drank.

The taste was a mixture of fruit and copper. It reminded me of the day, months earlier, when a friend of Billy Stargill had split my lip during a schoolyard fight. The inside of my lip had bled for hours. The taste was not dissimilar.

Captain Montgomery lowered his glass and scowled at it. Droplets of wine clotted his white whiskers.

"The wine is a local variety," said Sheads with a cold smile which showed red-stained teeth. "Very local. The arbors are those which we just visited."

I stared at the thickening liquid in my glass. Wine made from grapes grown from the rich soil of Iverson's Pits.

Sheads' loud voice startled me. "Another toast!" He raised his glass. "To the honorable and valiant gentleman who led the 20th North Carolina into battle. To Colonel Alfred Iverson."

Sheads raised the glass to his lips. I stood frozen and staring. Captain Montgomery slammed his glass on the table. The old man's face had gone as blood red as the spilled wine. "I'll be goddamned to hell if I . . ." he spluttered. "I'll . . . *never!*"

The man who had introduced himself as Jessup Sheads drained the last of his wine and smiled. His skin was as white as his shirt front, his hair and long mustaches as black as his coat. "Very well," he said and then raised his voice. "Uncle Alfred?"

Even as Sheads had been drinking, part of my mind had registered the soft sound of footsteps on the stairs behind us. I turned only my head, my hand still frozen with the glass of wine half-raised.

The small figure standing on the lowest step was a man in his mid-eighties, at least, but rather than wearing the wrinkles of age like Captain Montgomery, this old man's skin had become smoother and pinker, almost translucent. I was reminded of a nest of newborn rats I had come across in a neighbor's barn the previous spring—a mass of pale-pink, writhing flesh which I had made the mistake of touching. I did not want to touch Iverson.

The Colonel wore a white beard very much like the one I had seen in portraits of Robert E. Lee, but there was no real resemblance. Where Lee's eyes had been sad and shielded under a brow weighted with sorrow, Iverson glared at us with wide, staring eyes shot through with yellow flecks. He was almost bald and the taut, pink scalp reinforced the effect of something almost infantile about the little man.

Captain Montgomery stared, his mouth open, his breath rasping out in short, labored gasps. He clutched at his own collar as if unable to pull in enough air.

235

Iverson's voice was soft, almost feminine, and edged with the whine of a petulant child. "You all come back sooner or later," he said with a hint of a slight lisp. He sighed deeply. "Is there no end to it?"

"You . . ." managed the Captain. He lifted a long finger to point at Iverson.

"Spare me your outrage," snapped Iverson. "Do you think you are the first to seek me out, the first to try to explain away your own cowardice by slandering me? Samuel and I have grown quite adept at handling trash like you. I only hope that you are the last."

The Captain's hand dropped, disappeared in the folds of his coat. "You goddamned, sonofabitching . . ."

"Silence!" commanded Iverson. The Colonel's wide-eyed gaze darted around the room, passing over me as if I weren't there. The muscles at the corners of the man's mouth twitched and twisted. Again I was reminded of the nest of newborn rats. "Samuel," he shouted, "bring your stick. Show this man the penalty for insolence." Iverson's mad stare returned to Captain Montgomery. "You will salute me before we are finished here."

"I will see you in hell first," said the Captain and pulled the revolver from his coat pocket.

Iverson's nephew moved very fast, lifting the heavy walking stick and slamming it down on the Captain's wrist before the old man could pull back the hammer. I stood frozen, my wine glass still in my hand, as the pistol thudded to the floor. Captain Montgomery bent and reached for it—awkward and slow with his false leg— but Iverson's nephew grabbed him by the collar and flung him backward as effortlessly as an adult would handle a child. The Captain struck the wall, gasped, and slid down it, his false leg gouging splinters from the uneven floorboards as his legs straightened. His face was as gray as his uniform coat.

Iverson's nephew crouched to recover the pistol and set it on the table. Colonel Iverson himself smiled and nodded, his mouth still quivering toward a grin. I had eyes only for the Captain.

The old man lay huddled against the wall, clutching at his own throat, his body arching with spasms as he gasped in one great breath after another, each louder and more ragged than the last. It was obvious that no air was reaching his lungs; his color had gone from red to gray to a terrible dark purple bordering on black. His tongue protruded and saliva flecked his whiskers. The Captain's eyes grew wider and rounder as he realized what was happening to him, but his horrified gaze never left Iverson's face.

I could see the immeasurable frustration in the Captain's eyes as his body betrayed him in these last few seconds of a confrontation he had waited for through half a century of single-minded obsession. The old man drew in two more ragged, racking breaths and then quit breathing. His chin collapsed onto his sunken chest, the gnarled hands relaxed into loose fists, and his eyes lost their fixed focus on Iverson's face.

As if suddenly released from my own paralysis, I let out a cry, dropped the wineglass to the floor, and ran to crouch next to Captain Montgomery. No breath came from his grotesquely opened mouth. The staring eyes already were beginning to glaze with an invisible film. I touched the gnarled old hands—the flesh already seeming to cool and stiffen in death—and felt a terrible constriction in my own chest. It was not grief. Not exactly. I had known the old man too briefly and in too strange a context to feel deep sorrow so soon. But I found it hard to draw a breath as a great emptiness opened in me, a knowledge that sometimes there is no justice, that life was not fair. *It wasn't fair*. I gripped the old man's dead hands and found myself weeping for myself as much as for him.

"Get out of the way." Iverson's nephew thrust me aside and crouched next to the Captain. He shook the old man by his shirtfront, roughly pinched the bruise-colored cheeks, and laid an ear to the veteran's chest.

"Is he dead, Samuel?" asked Iverson. There was no real interest in his voice.

"Yes, Uncle." The nephew stood and nervously tugged at his mustache.

"Yes, yes," said Iverson in his distracted, petulant voice. "It does not matter." He flicked his small, pink hand in a dismissive gesture. "Take him out to be with the others, Samuel."

Iverson's nephew hesitated and then went into the back room to emerge a moment later with a pickaxe, a long-handled shovel, and a lantern. He jerked me to my feet and thrust the shovel and lantern into my hands.

"What about the boy, Uncle?"

Iverson's yellow gaze seemed absorbed with the shadows near the foot of the stairs. He wrung his soft hands. "Whatever you decide, Samuel," he whined. "Whatever you decide."

The nephew lighted the lantern I was holding, grasped the Captain under one arm, and dragged his body toward the door. I noticed that some of the straps holding the old man's leg had come loose; I could not look away from where the wooden peg dangled loosely from the stump of dead flesh and bone.

The nephew dragged the old man's body through the foyer, out the door, and into the night. I stood there—a statue with shovel and hissing lantern—praying that I would be forgotten. Cool, thin fingers fell on the nape of my neck. A soft, insistent voice whispered, "Come along, young man. Do not keep Samuel and me waiting."

Iverson's nephew dug the grave not ten yards from where the Captain and I had lain in hiding all day. Even if it had been daylight, the trees along the road and the grape arbors would have shielded us from view of anyone passing along the Mummasburg Road. No one passed. The night was brutally dark; low clouds occluded the stars and the only illumination was from my lantern and the faintest hint of light from Iverson's cabin a hundred yards behind us.

The black horse tied to the porch railing watched our strange procession leave the house. Captain Montgomery's hat had fallen off near the front step and I awkwardly bent to pick it up. Iverson's soft fingers never left my neck.

The soil in the field was loose and moist and easily excavated. Iverson's nephew was down three feet before twenty minutes had passed. Bits of root, rock, and other things glowed whitely in the heap of dirt illuminated by the lantern's glare.

"That is enough," ordered Iverson. "Get it over with, Samuel."

The nephew paused and looked up at the Colonel. The cold light turned the young man's face into a white mask, glistening with sweat, the whiskers and eyebrows broad strokes of charcoal, as black as the smudge of dirt on his left cheek. After a second to catch his breath, he nodded, set down his shovel, and reached out to roll Captain Montgomery's body into the grave. The old man landed on his back, eyes and mouth still open. His wooden leg had been dragging loosely and now remained behind on the brink of the hole. Iverson's nephew looked at me with hooded eyes, reached for the leg, and tossed it onto the Captain's chest. Without looking down, the nephew retrieved the shovel and quickly began scooping dirt onto the body. *I* watched. I watched the black soil land on my old veteran's cheek and forehead. I watched the dirt cover the staring eyes, first the left and then the right. I watched the open mouth fill with dirt and I felt the constriction in my own throat swell and break loose. Huge, silent sobs shook me.

In less than a minute, the Captain was gone, nothing more than an outline on the floor of the shallow grave.

"Samuel," lisped Iverson.

The nephew paused in his labors and looked at the Colonel.

"What is your advice about . . . the other thing?" Iverson's voice was so soft that it was almost lost beneath the hissing of the lantern and the pounding of pulse in my ears.

The nephew wiped his cheek with the back of his hand, broadening the dark smear there, and nodded slowly. "I think we have to, Uncle. We just cannot afford to . . . we cannot risk it. Not after the Florida thing . . ."

Iverson sighed. "Very well. Do what you must. I will abide by your decision."

The nephew nodded again, let out a breath, and reached for the pickaxe where it lay embedded in the heap of freshly excavated earth. Some part of my mind screamed at me to run, but I was capable only of standing there at the edge of that terrible pit, holding the lantern and breathing in the smell of Samuel's sweat and a deeper, more pervasive stench that seemed to rise out of the pit, the heap of dirt, the surrounding arbors.

"Put the light down, young man," Iverson whispered, inches from my ear. "Put it down carefully." His cool fingers closed more tightly on my neck. I set the lantern down, positioning it with care so that it would not tip over. Iverson's cold grip moved me forward to the very brink of the pit. His nephew stood waist-high in the hole, holding the pickaxe and fixing his dark gaze on me with a look conveying something between regret and anticipation. He shifted the pick handle in his large, white hands. I was about to say "It's all right" when his determined stare changed to wide-eyed surprise.

Samuel's body lurched, steadied, and then lurched again. It was as if he had been standing on a platform which had dropped a foot, then eighteen inches. Where the edges of the grave had come just to his waist, they now rose to his armpits.

Iverson's nephew threw aside the pickaxe and thrust his arms out onto solid ground. But the ground was no longer solid. Colonel Iverson and I stumbled backwards

241

as the earth seemed to vibrate and then flow like a mudslide. The nephew's left hand seized my ankle, his right hand sought a firm grip on thick vines. Iverson's hand remained firm on my neck, choking me.

Suddenly there came the sound of collapsing, sliding dirt, as if the floor of the grave had given way, collapsing through the ceiling of some forgotten mine or cavern, and the nephew threw himself forward, half out of the grave, his chest pressed against the slippery edges of the pit, his fingers releasing my ankle to claw at loam and vines. He reminded me of a mountain climber on a rocky overhang, using only his fingers and the friction of his upper body to defy the pull of gravity.

"Help me." His voice was a whisper, contorted by effort and disbelief.

Colonel Iverson backed away another five steps and I was pulled along.

Samuel was winning the struggle with the collapsing grave. His left hand found the pickaxe where he had buried it in the mound of dirt and he used the handle for leverage, pulling himself upward until his right knee found purchase on the edge of the pit.

The edge collapsed.

Dirt from the three-foot high mound flowed past the handle of the pick, over the nephew's straining arm and shoulder, back into the pit. The earth had been moist but solid where Samuel excavated it; now it flowed like frictionless mud, like water . . . like black wine.

Samuel slid back into the pit, now filled with viscous dirt, with only his face and upraised fingers rising out of the pool of black, shifting soil.

Suddenly there came a sound from all around us as if

many large forms had shifted position under blankets of grass and vines. Leaves stirred. Vines snapped. There was no breeze.

Iverson's nephew opened his mouth to scream and a wave of blackness flowed in between his teeth. His eyes were not human. Without warning, the ground shifted again and the nephew was pulled violently out of sight. He disappeared as quickly and totally as a swimmer pulled down by a shark three times his size.

There came the sound of teeth.

Colonel Iverson whimpered then, making the sound of a small child being made to go to his room without a light. His grip loosened on my neck.

Samuel's face appeared one last time, protruding eyes filmed with dirt. Something had taken most of the flesh from his right cheek. I realized that the sound I now heard was a man trying to scream with his larynx and esophagus half-filled with dirt.

He was pulled under again. Colonel Iverson took another three steps back and released my neck. I grabbed up the lantern and ran.

I heard a shout behind me and I looked over my shoulder just long enough to see Colonel Iverson coming through the break in the fence. He was out of the field, staggering, wheezing, but still coming on.

I ran with the speed of a terrified ten-year-old, the lantern swinging wildly from my right hand, throwing shifting patterns of light on leaves, branches, rocks. I had to have the light with me. There was a single thought in my mind: the Captain's pistol lying where Samuel had laid it on the table.

The saddled horse was pulling at its tether when I reached the house; its eyes were wild, alarmed at me, the swinging lantern, Iverson shouting far behind me, or the sudden terrible stench that drifted from the fields. I ignored the animal and slammed through the doorway, past the foyer, and into the dining room. I stopped, panting, grinning with terror and triumph.

The pistol was gone.

For seconds or minutes I stood in shock, not being able to think at all. Then, still holding the lantern, I looked under the table, in the hoosier, in the tiny back room. The pistol was not there. I started for the door, heard noises on the porch, headed up the stairs, and then paused in indecision.

"Is this . . . what you are after . . . young man?" Iverson stood panting at the entrance to the dining room, his left hand braced against the doorjamb, his right hand raised with the pistol leveled at me. "Slander, all slander," he said and squeezed the trigger.

The Captain had called the pistol a "double action." The hammer clicked back, locked into place, but did not fire. Iverson glanced at it and raised it toward me again. I threw the lantern at his face.

The Colonel batted it aside, breaking the glass. Flames ignited the ancient curtains and shot toward the ceiling, scorching Iverson's right side. He cursed and dropped the revolver. I vaulted over the stair railing, grabbed the kerosene lamp from the table, and threw it into the back room. Bedding and books burst into flame as the lamp oil spread. Dropping on all fours, I scrabbled toward the pistol but Iverson kicked at my head. He was old and slow and I easily rolled aside, but not before the burning curtain fell between me and the weapon. Iverson reached for it, pulled his hand back from the flames, and fled cursing out the front door.

I crouched there a second, panting. Flames shot along cracks in the floorboards, igniting pitch pine and the framework of the tinder-dry house itself. Outside the horse whinnied, either from the smell of smoke or the attempts of the Colonel to gain the saddle. I knew that nothing could stop Iverson from riding south or east, into the woods, toward the town, away from Iverson's Pits.

I reached into the circle of flame, screaming silently as part of my tunic sleeve charred away and blisters erupted on my palm, wrist, and lower arm. I dragged the pistol back, tossing the heated metal from hand to hand. Only later did I wonder why the gunpowder in the cartridges did not explode. Cradling the weapon in my burned hands, I stumbled outside.

Colonel Iverson had mounted but had only one boot in a stirrup. One rein dragged loosely while he tugged violently at the other, trying to turn the panicked horse back toward the forest. Toward the burning house. The mare had backed away from the flames and was intent on running toward the break in the wall. Toward the Pits. Iverson fought it. The result was that the mare spun in circles, the whites of its eyes showing at each revolution.

I stumbled off the porch of the burning cottage and lifted the heavy weapon just as Iverson managed to stop the horse's gyrations and leaned forward to grab the loose rein. With both reins in hand and the mare under control, he kicked hard to ride past me—or ride me down—on his way into the darkness of the trees. It took all of my strength to thumb the hammer back, blisters bursting on my thumb as I did so, and fire. I had not taken time to aim. The bullet ripped through branches ten feet above Iverson. The recoil almost made me drop the gun.

The mare spun back toward the darkness behind it. Iverson forced it around again, urged it forward with violent kicks of his small, black shoes.

My second shot went into the dirt five feet in front of me. Flesh peeled back from my burned thumb as I forced the hammer back the third time, aiming the impossibly heavy weapon between the mare's rolling eyes. I was sobbing so fiercely that I could not see Iverson clearly, but I could clearly hear him curse as his horse refused to approach the flames and source of noise a third time. I wiped at my eyes with my scorched sleeve just as Iverson wheeled the mare away from the light and gave it its head. My third shot went high again, but Iverson's horse galloped into the darkness, not staying on the faint path, jumping the stone wall in a leap which cleared the rocks by two feet.

I ran after them, still sobbing, tripping twice in the darkness but keeping possession of the pistol. By the time I reached the wall, the entire house was ablaze behind me, sparks drifting overhead and curtains of red light dancing across the forest and fields. I jumped to the top of the wall and stood there weaving, gasping for breath, and watching.

Iverson's mount had made it thirty yards or so beyond

the wall before being forced to a halt. It was rearing now, both reins flying free as the white-bearded man on its back clung desperately with both hands in its mane.

The arbors were moving. Tall masses of vines rose as high as the horse's head, vague shapes seeming to move under a shifting surface of leaves. The earth itself was heaving into hummocks and ridges. And holes.

I saw them clearly in the bonfire light. Mole holes. Gopher holes. But as broad across the opening as the trunk of a man. And ribbed inside, lined with ridges of blood-red cartilage. It was like looking down the maw of a snake as its insides pulsed and throbbed expectantly.

Only worse.

If you have seen a lamprey preparing to feed you might know what I mean. The holes had teeth. Rows of teeth. They were ringed with teeth. The earth had opened to show its red-rimmed guts, ringed with sharp white teeth.

The holes moved. The mare danced in panic but the holes shifted like shadows in the broad circle of bare earth which had cleared itself of vines. Around the circumference, dark shapes rose beneath the arbors.

Iverson screamed then. A second later his horse let out a similar noise as a hole closed on its right front leg. I clearly heard the bone snap and sever. The horse went down with Iverson rolling free. There were more snapping noises and the horse lifted its neck to watch with mad, white eyes as the earth closed around its four stumps of legs, shredding the ligament and muscle from bone as easily as someone stripping strands of dark meat from a drumstick.

In twenty seconds there was only the thrashing trunk

of the mare, rolling in the black dirt and black blood in a vain attempt to avoid the shifting lamprey teeth. Then the holes closed on the animal's neck.

Colonel Iverson rose to his knees, then to his feet. The only sounds were the crackling of flames behind me, the rustling of vines, and the high, hysterical panting of Iverson himself. The man was giggling.

In rows five hundred yards long, in lines as straight as a dress parade and as precise as battle lines, the earth trembled and furrowed, folding on itself, vines and grass and black soil rising and falling, rippling like rats moving under a thin blanket. Or like the furling of a flag.

Iverson screamed as the holes opened under him and around him. Somehow he managed to scream a second time as the upper half of his body rolled free across the waiting earth, one hand clawing for leverage in the undulating dirt while the other hand vainly attempted to tuck in the parts of himself which trailed behind.

The holes closed again. There was no screaming now as only the small, pink oval rolled in the dirt, but I will be certain to my dying day that I saw the white beard move as the jaws opened silently, saw the flicker of white and yellow as the eyes blinked.

The holes closed a third time.

I stumbled away from the wall, but not before I had thrown the revolver as far out into the field as I could manage. The burning house had collapsed into itself but the heat was tremendous, far too hot for me to sit so close. My eyebrows were quickly singed away and steam rose from my sweat-soaked clothes, but I stayed as close to the fire as I could for as long as I could.

Close to the light.


I have no memory of the fire brigade that found me or of the men who brought me back to town sometime before dawn.

Wednesday, July 2, was Military Day at the Great Reunion. It rained hard all afternoon but speeches were given in the Great Tent. Sons and grandsons of General Longstreet and General Pickett and General Meade were present on the speakers' platform.

I remember awakening briefly in the hospital tent to the sound of rain on canvas. Someone was explaining to someone that facilities were better there than in the old hospital in town. My arm and hands were swathed in bandages. My brow burned with fever. "Rest easy, lad," said Reverend Hodges, his face heavy with worry. "I've cabled your parents. Your father will be here before nightfall." I nodded and stifled the urge to scream in the interminable seconds before sleep claimed me again. The beating of rain on the tent had sounded like teeth scraping bone.

Thursday, July 3, was Civic Day at the Great Reunion. Survivors of Pickett's brigade and ex-Union troops from the Philadelphia Brigade Association formed two lines and walked fifty feet north and south to the wall on Cemetery Ridge which marked the so-called high water mark of the Confederacy. Both sides lowered battle flags until they crossed above the wall. Then a bearer symbolically lifted the Stars and Stripes above the crossed battleflags. Everyone cheered. Veterans embraced one another.

I remember fragments of the train ride home that morning. I remember my father's arm around me. I remember my mother's face when we arrived at the station in Chestnut Hill.

Friday, July 4, was National Day at the Great Reunion. President Wilson addressed all of the veterans in the Great Tent at 11 A.M. He spoke of healing wounds, forgetting past differences, of forgetting old quarrels. He spoke of valor and courage and glory which the ages would not diminish. When he was finished, they played the National Anthem and an honor guard fired a salute. Then all the old men went home.

I remember parts of my dreams that day. They were the same dreams I have now. Several times I awoke screaming. My mother tried to hold my hand but I wanted nothing to touch me. Nothing at all.

Seventy-five years have passed since my first trip to Gettysburg. I have been back many times. The guides and rangers and librarians there know me by name. Some flatter me with the title historian.

Nine veterans died during the Great Reunion of 1913—five of heart problems, two of heatstroke, and one of pneumonia. The ninth veteran's death certificate lists the cause of death as "old age". One veteran simply disappeared sometime between his registration and the date he was expected back at a home for retired veterans in Raleigh, North Carolina. The name of Captain Powell

D. Montgomery of Raleigh, North Carolina, veteran of the 20th North Carolina Regiment was never added to the list of the nine veterans who died. He had no family and was not missed for some weeks after the Reunion ended.

Jessup Sheads had indeed built the small house southeast of the Forney farm, on the site where the 97th New York regiment had silently waited behind a stone wall for the advance of Colonel Alfred Iverson's men. Sheads designed the small house as a summer home and erected it in the spring of 1893. He never stayed in it. Sheads was described as a short, stout, redheaded man, clean-shaven, with a weakness for wine. It was he who had planted the grape arbors shortly before his death from a heart attack in that same year of 1893. His widow rented the summer house out through agents for the years until the cottage burned in the summer of 1913. No records were kept of the renters.

Colonel Alfred Iverson, Jr, ended the war as a Brigadier General despite being relieved of his command after undisclosed difficulties during the opening skirmishes of the Battle of Gettysburg. After the war, Iverson was engaged in unlucky business ventures in Georgia and then in Florida, leaving both areas under unclear circumstances. In Florida, Iverson was involved in the citrus business with his grand-nephew, Samuel Strahl, an outspoken member of the KKK and a rabid defender of his grand-uncle's name and reputation. It was rumored that Stahl had killed at least two men in illegal duels and he was wanted for questioning in Broward County in relation to the disappearance of a 78-year-old man named Phelps Rawlins. Rawlins had been a veteran of the 20th

North Carolina Regiment. Stahl's wife reported him missing during a month-long hunting trip in the summer of 1913. She lived on in Macon, Georgia, until her death in 1948.

Alfred Iverson, Jr, is listed in different sources as dying in 1911, 1913, or 1915. Historians frequently confused Iverson with his father, the Senator, and although both are supposed to be buried in the family crypt in Atlanta, records at the Oakland Cemetery show that there is only one coffin entombed there.

Many times over the years have I dreamt the dream I remember from that hot afternoon in the grape arbors. Only my field of view in that dream changes—from blue sky and a stone wall under spreading branches to trenches and barbed wire, to rice paddies and monsoon clouds, to frozen mud along a frozen river, to thick, tropical vegetation which swallows light. Recently I have dreamed that I am lying in the ash of a city while snow falls from low clouds. But the fruit and copper taste of the soil remains the same. The silent communion among the casually sacrificed and the forgotten-buried also remains the same. Sometimes I think of the mass graves which have fertilized this century and I weep for my grandson and great-grandchildren.

I have not visited the battlefields in some years. The last time was twenty-five years ago in the quiet spring of 1963, three months before the insanity of that summer's centennial celebration of the battles. The Mummasburg Road had been paved and widened. John Forney's house had not been there for years but I did note a proliferation of iris where the foundation had once stood. The town of Gettysburg is much larger, of course, but zoning restrictions and the historical park have kept new houses from being built in the vicinity.

Many of the trees along the stone wall have died of Dutch elm disease and other blights. Only a few yards of the wall itself remain, the stones having been carried off for fireplaces and patios. The city is clearly visible across the open fields.

No sign of Iverson's Pits remains. No one I spoke to who lives in the area remembers them. The fields there are green when lying fallow and incredibly productive when tilled, but this is true of most of the surrounding Pennsylvania countryside.

Last winter a friend and fellow amateur historian wrote to tell me that a small archaeological team from Penn State University had done a trial dig in the Oak Hill area. He wrote that the dig had yielded a veritable goldmine of relics—bullets, brass buttons, bits of mess kits, canister fragments, five almost intact bayonets, bits of bone—all of the stubborn objects which decaying flesh leaves behind like minor footnotes in time.

And teeth, wrote my friend.

Many, many teeth.

GEORGE R. R. MARTIN

Willie smelled the blood a block away from her apartment.

He hesitated and sniffed at the cool night air again. It was autumn, with the wind off the river and the smell of rain in the air, but the scent, *that* scent, was copper and spice and fire, unmistakable. He knew the smell of human blood.

A jogger bounced past, his orange sweats bright under the light of the full moon. Willie moved deeper into the shadows. What kind of fool ran at this hour of the night? *Asshole*, Willie thought, and the sentiment emerged in a low growl. The man looked around, startled. Willie crept back further into the foliage. After a long moment, the jogger continued up the bicycle path, moving a little faster now.

Taking a chance, Willie moved to the edge of the park, where he could stare down her street from the bushes. Two police cruisers were parked outside her building, lights flashing. What the hell had she gone and done?

When he heard the distant sirens and saw another set of lights approaching, flashing red and blue, Willie felt close to panic. The blood scent was heavy in the air, and set his skull to pounding. It was too much. He turned and ran deep into the park, for once not caring who might see him, anxious only to get away. He ran south, swift and silent, until he was panting for breath, his tongue lolling out of his mouth. He wasn't in shape for this kind of shit. He yearned for the safety of his own apartment, for his La-Z-Boy and a good shot of Prima-teen Mist.

Down near the riverfront, he finally came to a stop, wheezing and trembling, half-drunk with blood and fear. He crouched near a bridge abutment, staring at the headlights of passing cars and listening to the sound of traffic to soothe his ragged nerves.

Finally, when he was feeling a little stronger, he ran down a squirrel. The blood was hot and rich in his mouth, and the flesh made him feel ever so much stronger, but afterwards he got a hairball from all the goddamned fur.

"Willie," Randi Wade said suspiciously, "if this is just some crazy scheme to get into my pants, it's not going to work."

The small man studied his reflection in the antique oval mirror over her couch, tried out several faces until he found a wounded look he seemed to like, then turned back to let her see it. "You'd think that? You'd think that of *me?* I come to you, I need your help, and what do I get, cheap sexual innuendo. You ought to know me better than that, Wade, I mean, Jesus, how long we been friends?"

"Nearly as long as you've been trying to get into my

pants," Randi said. "Face it, Flambeaux, you're a horny little bastard."

Willie deftly changed the subject. "It's very amateur hour, you know, doing business out of your apartment." He sat in one of her red velvet wingback chairs. "I mean, it's a nice place, don't get me wrong, I love this Victorian stuff, can't wait to see the bedroom, but isn't a private eye supposed to have a sleazy little office in the bad part of town? You know, frosted glass on the door, a bottle in the drawer, lots of dust on the filing cabinets . . ."

Randi smiled. "You know what they charge for those sleazy little offices in the bad part of town? I've got a phone machine, I'm listed in the Yellow Pages . . ."

"AAA-Wade Investigations," Willie said sourly. "How do you expect people to find you? Wade, it should be under W, if God had meant everybody to be listed under A, he wouldn't have invented all those other letters." He coughed. "I'm coming down with something," he complained, as if it were her fault. "Are you going to help me, or what?"

"Not until you tell me what this is all about," Randi said, but she'd already decided to do it. She liked Willie, and she owed him. He'd given her work when she needed it, with his friendship thrown into the bargain. Even his constant, futile attempts to jump her bones were somehow endearing, although she'd never admit it to Willie. "You want to hear about my rates?"

"Rates?" Willie sounded pained. "What about friendship? What about old times' sake? What about all the times I bought you lunch?"

"You never bought me lunch," Randi said accusingly.

"Is it my fault you kept turning me down?"

"Taking a bucket of Popeye's extra spicy to an adult motel for a snack and a quickie does not constitute a lunch invitation in my book," Randi said.

Willie had a long, morose face, with broad rubbery features capable of an astonishing variety of expressions. Right now he looked as though someone had just run over his puppy. "It would not have been a quickie," he said with vast wounded dignity. He coughed, and pushed himself back in the chair, looking oddly childlike against the red velvet cushions. "Randi," he said, his voice suddenly gone scared and weary, "this is for real."

She'd first met Willie Flambeaux when his collection agency had come after her for the unpaid bills left by her ex. She'd been out of work, broke, and desperate, and Willie had taken pity on her and given her work at the agency. As much as she'd hated hassling people for money, the job had been a godsend, and she'd stayed long enough to wipe out her debt. Willie's lopsided smile, endless propositions, and mordant intelligence had somehow kept her sane. They'd kept in touch, off and on, even after Randi had left the hounds of hell, as Willie liked to call the collection agency.

All that time, Randi had never heard him sound scared, not even when discoursing on the prospect of imminent death from one of his many grisly and undiagnosed maladies. She sat down on the couch. "Then I'm listening," she said. "What's the problem?"

"You see this morning's *Courier*?" he asked. "The woman that was murdered over on Parkway?"

"I glanced at it." Randi said.

"She was a friend of mine."

260

"Oh, Jesus." Suddenly Randi felt guilty for giving him a hard time. "Willie, I'm so sorry."

"She was just a kid," Willie said. "Twenty-three. You would have liked her. Lots of spunk. Bright too. She'd been in a wheelchair since high school. The night of her senior prom, her date drank too much and got pissed when she wouldn't go all the way. On the way home he floored it and ran head-on into a semi. Really showed her. The boy was killed instantly. Joanie lived through it, but her spine was severed, she was paralyzed from the waist down. She never let it stop her. She went on to college and graduated with honors, had a good job."

"You knew her through all this?"

Willie shook his head. "Nah. Met her about a year ago. She'd been a little overenthusiastic with her credit cards, you know the tune. So I showed up on her doorstep one day, introduced her to Mr Scissors, one thing led to another and we got to be friends. Like you and me, kind of." He looked up into her eyes. "The body was mutilated. Who'd do something like that? Bad enough to kill her, but . . ." Willie was beginning to wheeze. His asthma. He stopped, took a deep breath. "And what the fuck does it mean? *Mutilated*, Jesus, what a nasty word, but mutilated *how*? I mean, are we talking Jack the Ripper here?"

"I don't know. Does it matter?"

"It matters to me." He wet his lips. "I phoned the cops today, tried to get more details. It was a draw. I wouldn't tell them my name and they wouldn't give me any information. I tried the funeral home too. A closed casket wake, then the body is going to be cremated. Sounds to me like something getting covered up."

261

"Like what?" she said.

Willie sighed. "You're going to think this is real weird, but what if . . ." He ran his fingers through his hair. He looked very agitated. "What if Joanie was . . . well, savaged . . . ripped up, maybe even . . . well, partially eaten . . . you know, like by . . . some kind of animal."

Willie was going on, but Randi was no longer listening.

A coldness settled over her. It was old and gray, full of fear, and suddenly she was twelve years old again, standing in the kitchen door listening to her mother make that sound, that terrible high thin wailing sound. The men were still trying to talk to her, to make her understand . . . *some kind of animal*, one of them said. Her mother didn't seem to hear or understand, but Randi did. She'd repeated the words aloud, and all the eyes had gone to her, and one of the cops had said, *Jesus, the kid*, and they'd all stared until her mother had finally gotten up and put her to bed. She began to weep uncontrollably as she tucked in the sheets . . . her mother, not Randi. Randi hadn't cried. Not then, not at the funeral, not ever in all the years since.

"Hey. Hey! Are you okay?" Willie was asking.

"I'm fine," she said sharply.

"Jesus, don't scare me like that, I got problems of my own, you know? You looked like . . . hell, I don't know what you looked like, but I wouldn't want to meet it in a dark alley."

Randi gave him a hard look. "The paper said Joan Sorenson was murdered. An animal attack isn't murder."

"Don't get legal on me, Wade. I don't know, I don't even know that an animal was involved, maybe I'm just nuts, paranoid, you name it. The paper left out the grisly details. The fucking paper left out a lot." Willie was breathing rapidly, twisting around in his chair, his fingers drumming on the arm.

"Willie, I'll do whatever I can, but the police are going to go all out on something like this, I don't know how much I'll be able to add."

"The police," he said in a morose tone. "I don't trust the police." He shook his head. "Randi, if the cops go through her things, my name will come up, you know, on her rolodex and stuff."

"So you're afraid you might be a suspect, is that it?"

"Hell, I don't know, maybe so."

"You have an alibi?"

Willie looked very unhappy. "No. Not really. I mean, not anything you could use in court. I was supposed to . . . to see her that night. Shit, I mean, she might have written my name on her fucking *calendar* for all I know. I just don't want them nosing around, you know?"

"Why not?"

He made a face. "Even us turnip-squeezers have our dirty little secrets. Hell, they might find all those nude photos of you." She didn't laugh. Willie shook his head. "I mean, god, you'd think the cops would have better things to do than go around solving murders—I haven't gotten a parking ticket in over a year. Makes you wonder what the hell this town is coming to." He had begun to wheeze again. "Now I'm getting too worked up again, damn it. It's you, Wade. I'll bet you're wearing crotch-less panties under those jeans, right?" Glaring at her accusingly, Willie pulled a bottle of Primateen Mist from his coat pocket, stuck the plastic snout in his mouth, and gave himself a blast, sucking it down greedily.

"You must be feeling better," Randi said.

"When you said you'd do anything you could to help, did that include taking off all of your clothes?" Willie said hopefully.

"No," Randi said firmly. "But I'll take the case."


River Street was not exactly a prestige address, but Willie liked it just fine. The rich folks up on the bluffs had "river views" from the gables and widows' walks of their old Victorian houses, but Willie had the river itself flowing by just beneath his windows. He had the sound of it, night and day, the slap of water against the pilings, the foghorns when the mists grew thick, the shouts of pleasure-boaters on sunny afternoons. He had moonlight on the black water, and his very own rotting pier to sit on, any midnight when he had a taste for solitude. He had eleven rooms that used to be offices, a men's room (with urinal) *and* a ladies' room (with Tampax dispenser), hardwood floors, lovely old skylights, and if he ever got that loan, he was definitely going to put in a kitchen. He also had an abandoned brewery down on the ground floor, should he ever decide to make his own beer. The drafty red brick building had been built a hundred years ago, which was about how long the flats had been considered the bad part of town. These days what wasn't boarded up was industrial, so Willie didn't have many neighbors, and that was the best part of all.

Parking was no problem either. Willie had a monstrous old lime-green Cadillac, all chrome and fins, that he left by the foot of the pier, two feet from his door. It took him five minutes to undo all his locks. Willie believed in locks, especially on River Street. The brewery was dark and quiet. He locked and bolted the doors behind him and trudged upstairs to his living quarters.

He was more scared than he'd let on to Randi. He'd been upset enough last night, when he'd caught the scent of blood and figured that Joanie had done something really dumb, but when he'd gotten the morning paper and read that she'd been the victim, that she'd been tortured and killed and mutilated . . . *mutilated*, dear god, what the hell did that *mean*, had one of the others . . . no, he couldn't even think about that, it made him sick.

His living room had been the president's office back when the brewery was a going concern. It fronted on the river, and Willie thought it was nicely furnished, all things considered. None of it matched, but that was all right. He'd picked it up piece by piece over the years, the new stuff usually straight repossession deals, the antiques taken in lieu of cash on hopeless and long-overdue debts. Willie nearly always managed to get *something*, even on the accounts that everyone else had written off as a dead loss. If it was something he liked, he paid off the client out of his own pocket, ten or twenty cents on the dollar, and kept the furniture. He got some great bargains that way.

He had just started to boil some water on his hotplate when the phone began to ring.

Willie turned and stared at it, frowning. He was almost

afraid to answer. It could be the police . . . but it could be Randi or some other friend, something totally innocent. Grimacing, he went over and picked it up. "Hello."

"Good evening, William." Willie felt as though someone was running a cold finger up his spine. Jonathan Harmon's voice was rich and mellow; it gave him the creeps. "We've been trying to reach you."

I'll bet you have, Willie thought, but what he said was, "Yeah, well, I been out."

"You've heard about the crippled girl, of course."

"*Joan*," Willie said sharply. "Her name was Joan. Yeah, I heard. All I know is what I read in the paper."

"I own the paper," Jonathan reminded him. "William, some of us are getting together at Blackstone to talk. Zoe and Amy are here right now, and I'm expecting Michael any moment. Steven drove down to pick up Lawrence. He can swing by for you as well, if you're free."

"No," Willie blurted. "I may be cheap, but I'm never free." His laugh was edged with panic.

"William, your life may be at stake."

"Yeah, I'll bet, you sonofabitch. Is that a threat? Let me tell you, I wrote down everything I know, *everything*, and gave copies to a couple of friends of mine." He hadn't, but come to think of it, it sounded like a good idea. "If I wind up like Joanie, they'll make sure those letters get to the police, you hear me?"

He almost expected Jonathan to say, calmly, 'I *own* the police,' but there was only silence and static on the line, then a sigh. "I realize you're upset about Joan—"

"Shut the fuck up about Joanie," Willie interrupted. "You got no right to say jackshit about her, I know how you felt about her. You listen up good, Harmon, if it turns out that you or that twisted kid of yours had anything to do with what happened, I'm going to come up to Blackstone one night and kill you myself, see if I don't. She was a good kid, she . . . she . . ." Suddenly, for the first time since it had happened, his mind was full of her—her face, her laugh, the smell of her when she was hot and bothered, the graceful way her muscles moved when she ran beside him, the noises she made when their bodies joined together. They all came back to him, and Willie felt tears on his face. There was a tightness in his chest as if iron bands were closing around his lungs. Jonathan was saying something, but Willie slammed down the receiver without bothering to listen, then pulled the jack. His water was boiling merrily away on the hotplate. He fumbled in his pocket and gave himself a good belt of his inhaler, then stuck his head in the steam until he could breathe again. The tears dried up, but not the pain.

Afterwards he thought about the things he'd said, the threats he made, and he got so shaky that he went back downstairs to doublecheck all his locks.

Courier Square was far gone in decay. The big department stores had moved to suburban malls, the grandiose old movie palaces had been chopped up into multi-screens or given over to porno, once-fashionable store-fronts now housed palm readers and adult bookstores. If Randi had really wanted a seedy little office in the bad part of town, she could find one on Courier Square.

What little vitality the Square had left came from the newspaper.

The Courier Building was a legacy of another time, when downtown was still the heart of the city and the newspaper its soul. Old Douglas Harmon, who'd liked to tell anyone who'd listen that he was cut from the same cloth as Hearst and Pulitzer, had always viewed journalism as something akin to a religious vocation, and the "gothic deco" edifice he built to house his newspaper looked like the result of some unfortunate mating between the Chrysler Building and some especially grotesque cathedral. Five decades of smog had blackened its granite facade and acid rain had eaten away at the wolfshead gargoyles that snarled down from its walls, but you could still set your watch by the monstrous old presses in the basement and a Harmon still looked down on the city from the publisher's office high atop the Iron Spire. It gave a certain sense of continuity to the square, and the city.

The black marble floors in the lobby were slick and wet when Randi came in out of the rain, wearing a Burberry raincoat a couple sizes too big for her, a souvenir of her final fight with her ex-husband. She'd paid for it, so she was damn well going to wear it. A security guard sat behind the big horseshoe-shaped reception desk, beneath a wall of clocks that once had given the time all over the world. Most were broken now, hands frozen into a chronological cacophony. The lobby was a gloomy place on a dark afternoon like this, full of drafts as cold as the guard's face. Randi took off her hat, shook out her hair, and gave him a nice smile. "I'm here to see Barry Schumacher."

"Editorial. Third floor." The guard barely gave her a glance before he went back to the bondage magazine spread across his lap. Randi grimaced and walked past, heels clicking against the marble.

The elevator was an open grillwork of black iron; it rattled and shook and took forever to deliver her to the city room on the third floor. She found Schumacher alone at his desk, smoking and staring out his window at the rain-slick streets. "Look at that," he said when Randi came up behind him. A streetwalker in a leather minis-kirt was standing under the darkened marquee of the Castle. The rain had soaked her thin white blouse and plastered it to her breasts. "She might as well be topless," Barry said. "Right in front of the Castle too. First theater in the state to show *Gone With the Wind*, you know that? All the big movies used to open there." He grimaced, swung his chair around, ground out his cigarette. "Hell of a thing," he said.

"I cried when Bambi's mother died," Randi said.

"In the Castle?"

She nodded. "My father took me, but he didn't cry. I only saw him cry once, but that was later, much later, and it wasn't a movie that did it."

"Frank was a good man," Schumacher said dutifully. He was pushing retirement age, overweight and balding, but he still dressed impeccably, and Randi remembered a young dandy of a reporter who'd been quite a rake in his day. He'd been a regular in her father's Wednesday night poker game for years. He used to pretend that she was his girlfriend, that he was waiting for her to grow up so they could get married. It always made her giggle. But that had been a different Barry Schumacher; this

269

one looked as if he hadn't laughed since Kennedy was president. "So what can I do for you?" he asked.

"You can tell me everything that got left out of the story on that Parkway murder," she said. She sat down across from him.

Barry hardly reacted. She hadn't seen him much since her father died; each time she did, he seemed grayer and more exhausted, like a man who'd been bled dry of passion, laughter, anger, everything. "What makes you think anything was left out?"

"My father was a cop, remember? I know how this city works. Sometimes the cops ask you to leave something out."

"They ask," Barry agreed. "Them asking and us doing, that's two different things. Once in a while we'll omit a key piece of evidence, to help them weed out fake confessions. You know the routine." He paused to light another cigarette.

"How about this time?"

Barry shrugged. "Hell of a thing. Ugly. But we printed it, didn't we?"

"Your story said the victim was mutilated. What does that mean, exactly?"

"We got a dictionary over by the copyeditors' desk, you want to look it up."

"I don't want to look it up," Randi said, a little too sharply. Barry was being an asshole; she hadn't expected that. "I know what the word means."

"So you are saying we should have printed all the juicy details?" Barry leaned back, took a long drag on his cigarette. "You know what Jack the Ripper did to his last victim? Among other things, he cut off her breasts.

Sliced them up neat as you please, like he was carving white meat off a turkey, and piled the slices on top of each other, beside the bed. He was very tidy, put the nipples on top and everything." He exhaled smoke. "Is that the sort of detail you want? You know how many kids read the *Courier* every day?"

"I don't care what you print in the *Courier*," Randi said. "I just want to know the truth. Am I supposed to infer that Joan Sorenson's breasts were cut off?"

"I didn't say that," Schumacher said.

"No. You didn't say much of anything. Was she killed by some kind of animal?"

That did draw a reaction. Schumacher looked up, his eyes met hers, and for a moment she saw a hint of the friend he had been in those tired eyes behind their wire-rim glasses. "An animal?" he said softly. "Is that what you think? This isn't about Joan Sorenson at all, is it? This is about your father." Barry got up and came around his desk. He put his hands on her shoulders and looked into her eyes. "Randi, honey, let go of it. I loved Frank too, but he's dead, he's been dead for . . . hell, it's almost twenty years now. The coroner said he got killed by some kind of rabid dog, and that's all there is to it."

"There was no trace of rabies, you know that as well as I do. My father emptied his gun. What kind of rabid dog takes six shots from a police .38 and keeps on coming, huh?"

"Maybe he missed," Barry said.

"*He didn't miss!*" Randi said sharply. She turned away from him. "We couldn't even have an open casket, too much of the body had been . . ." Even now, it was hard

271

to say without gagging, but she was a big girl now and she forced it out. ". . . eaten," she finished softly. "No animal was ever found."

"Frank must have put some bullets in it, and after it killed him the damned thing crawled off somewhere and died," Barry said. His voice was not unkind. He turned her around to face him again. "Maybe that's how it was and maybe not. It was a hell of a thing, but it happened eighteen years ago, honey, and it's got nothing to do with Joan Sorenson."

"Then tell me what happened to her," Randi said.

"Look, I'm not supposed to . . ." He hesitated, and the tip of his tongue flicked nervously across his lips. "It was a knife," he said softly. "She was killed with a knife, it's all in the police report, just some psycho with a sharp knife." He sat down on the edge of his desk, and his voice took on its familiar cynicism again. "Some weirdo seen too many of those damn sick holiday movies, you know the sort, *Halloween, Friday the 13th*, they got one for every holiday."

"All right." She could tell from his tone that she wouldn't be getting any more out of him. "Thanks."

He nodded, not looking at her. "I don't know where these rumors come from. All we need, folks thinking there's some kind of wild animal running around, killing people." He patted her shoulder. "Don't be such a stranger, you hear? Come by for dinner some night. Adele is always asking about you."

"Give her my best." She paused at the door. "Barry . . ." He looked up, forced a smile. "When they found the body, there wasn't anything missing?"

He hesitated briefly. "No," he said.

Barry had always been the big loser at her father's poker games. He wasn't a bad player, she recalled her father saying, but his eyes gave him away when he tried to bluff . . . like they gave him away right now.

Barry Schumacher was lying.

The doorbell was broken, so he had to knock. No one answered, but Willie didn't buy that for a minute. "I know you're there, Mrs Juddiker," he shouted through the window. "I could hear the TV a block off. You turned it off when you saw me coming up the walk. Gimme a break, okay?" He knocked again. "Open up, I'm not going away."

Inside, a child started to say something, and was quickly shushed. Willie sighed. He hated this. Why did they always put him through this? He took out a credit card, opened the door, and stepped into a darkened living room, half-expecting a scream. Instead he got shocked silence.

They were gaping at him, the woman and two kids. The shades had been pulled down and the curtains drawn. The woman wore a white terrycloth robe, and she looked even younger than she'd sounded on the phone. "You can't just walk in here," she said.

"I just did," Willie said. When he shut the door, the room was awfully dark. It made him nervous. "Mind if I put on a light?" She didn't say anything, so he did. The furniture was all ratty Salvation Army stuff, except for the gigantic big-screen projection TV in the far corner of the room. The oldest child, a little girl who looked

273

about four, stood in front of it protectively. Willie smiled at her. She didn't smile back.

He turned back to her mother. She looked maybe twenty, maybe younger, dark, maybe ten pounds overweight but still pretty. She had a spray of brown freckles across the bridge of her nose. "Get yourself a chain for the door and use it," Willie told her. "And don't try the no-one's-home game on us hounds of hell, okay?" He sat down in a black vinyl recliner held together by electrical tape. "I'd love a drink. Coke, juice, milk, anything, it's been one of those days." No one moved, no one spoke. "Aw, come on," Willie said, "cut it out. I'm not going to make you sell the kids for medical experiments, I just want to talk about the money you owe, okay?"

"You're going to take the television," the mother said.

Willie glanced at the monstrosity and shuddered. "It's a year old and it weighs a million pounds. How'm I going to move something like that, with my bad back? I've got asthma too." He took the inhaler out of his pocket, showed it to her. "You want to kill me, making me take the damned TV would do the trick."

That seemed to help a little. "Bobby, get him a can of soda," the mother said. The boy ran off. She held the front of her robe closed as she sat down on the couch, and Willie could see that she wasn't wearing anything underneath. He wondered if she had freckles on her breasts too, sometimes they did. "I told you on the phone, we don't have no money. My husband run off. He was out of work anyway, ever since the pack shut down."

"I know," Willie said. The pack was short for meat-packing plant, which is what everyone liked to call the south side slaughterhouse that had been the city's largest employer until it shut its doors two years back. Willie took a notepad out of his pocket, flipped a few pages. "Okay, you bought the thing on time, made two payments, then moved, left no forwarding address. You still owe two-thousand-eight-hundred-sixteen dollars. And thirty-one cents. We'll forget the interest and late charges." Bobby returned and handed him a can of Diet Chocolate Ginger Beer. Willie repressed a shudder and cracked the pop top.

"Go play in the back yard," she said to the children. "Us grown-ups have to talk." She didn't sound very grown-up after they had left, however; Willie was half-afraid she was going to cry. He hated it when they cried. "It was Ed bought the set," she said, her voice trembling. "It wasn't his fault. The card came in the mail."

Willie knew that tune. A credit card comes in the mail, so the next day you run right out and buy the biggest item you can find. "Look, I can see you got plenty of troubles. You tell me where to find Ed, and I'll get the money out of him."

She laughed bitterly. "You don't know Ed. He used to lug around those big sides of beef at the pack, you ought to see the arms on him. You go bother him and he'll just rip your face off and shove it up your asshole, mister."

"What a lovely turn of phrase," Willie said. "I can't wait to make his acquaintance."

"You won't tell him it was me that told you where to find him?" she asked nervously.

"Scout's honor," Willie said. He raised his right hand in a gesture that he thought was vaguely Boy-Scoutish, although the can of Diet Chocolate Ginger Beer spoiled the effect a little.

"Were you a Scout?" she asked.

"No," he admitted. "But there was one troop that used to beat me up regularly when I was young."

That actually got a smile out of her. "It's your funeral. He's living with some slut now, I don't know where. But weekends he tends bar down at Squeaky's."

"I know the place."

"It's not real work," she added thoughtfully. "He don't report it or nothing. That way he still gets the unemployment. You think he ever sends anything over for the kids? No way!"

"How much you figure he owes you?" Willie said.

"Plenty," she said.

Willie got up. "Look, none of my business, but it is my business, if you know what I mean. You want, after I've talked to Ed about this television, I'll see what I can collect for you. Strictly professional, I mean, I'll take a little cut off the top, give the rest to you. It may not be much, but a little bit is better than nothing, right?"

She stared at him, astonished. "You'd do that?"

"Shit, yeah. Why not?" He took out his wallet, found a twenty. "Here," he said. "An advance payment. Ed will pay me back." She looked at him incredulously, but did not refuse the bill. Willie fumbled in the pocket of his coat. "I want you to meet someone," he said. He always carried a few cheap pairs of scissors in the pocket of his coat. He found one and put it in her hand. "Here, this is Mr Scissors. From now on, he's your best friend."

She looked at him like he'd gone insane.

"Introduce Mr Scissors to the next credit card that

comes in the mail," Willie told her, "and then you won't have to deal with assholes like me."

He was opening the door when she caught up to him. "Hey, what did you say your name was?"

"Willie," he told her.

"I'm Betsy." She leaned forward to kiss him on the cheek, and the white robe opened just enough to give him a quick peek at her small breasts. Her chest was lightly freckled, her nipples wide and brown. She closed the robe tight again as she stepped back. "You're no asshole, Willie," she said as she closed the door.

He went down the walk feeling almost human, better than he'd felt since Joanie's death. His Caddy was waiting at the curb, the ragtop up to keep out the off-again on-again rain that had been following him around the city all morning. Willie got in and started her, then glanced into the rearview mirror just as the man in the back seat sat up.

The eyes in the mirror were pale blue. Sometimes, after the spring runoff was over and the river had settled back between its banks, you could find stagnant pools along the shore, backwaters cut off from the flow, foul-smelling places, still and cold, and you wondered how deep they were and whether there was anything living down there in that darkness. Those were the kind of eyes he had, deepset in a dark, hollow-cheeked face and framed by brown hair that fell long and straight to his shoulders.

Willie swiveled around to face him. "What the hell were you doing back there, catching forty winks? Hate to point this out, Steven, but this vehicle is actually one of the few things in the city that the Harmons do not

George R. R. Martin

own. Guess you got confused, huh? Or did you just mistake it for a bench in the park? Tell you what, no hard feelings, I'll drive you to the park, even buy you a newspaper to keep you warm while you finish your little nap."

"Jonathan wants to see you," Steven said, in that flat, chill tone of his. His voice, like his face, was still and dead.

"Yeah, good for him, but maybe I don't want to see Jonathan, you ever think of that?" He was dogmeat, Willie thought; he had to suppress the urge to bolt and run.

"Jonathan wants to see you," Steven repeated, as if Willie hadn't understood. He reached forward. A hand closed on Willie's shoulder. Steven had a woman's fingers, long and delicate, his skin pale and fine. But his palm was crisscrossed by burn scars that lay across the flesh like brands, and his fingertips were bloody and scabbed, the flesh red and raw. The fingers dug into Willie's shoulder with ferocious, inhuman strength. "Drive," he said, and Willie drove.

"I'm sorry," the police receptionist said. "The chief has a full calendar today. I can give you an appointment on Thursday."

"I don't want to see him on Thursday. I want to see him now." Randi hated the cophouse. It was always of full of cops. As far as she was concerned, cops came in three flavors: those who saw an attractive woman they could hit on, those who saw a private investigator and resented her, and the old ones who saw Frank Wade's little girl and felt sorry for her. Types one and two annoyed her; the third kind really pissed her off.

The receptionist pressed her lips together, disapproving. "As I've explained, that simply isn't possible."

"Just tell him I'm here," Randi said. "He'll see me."

"He's with someone at the moment, and I'm quite sure that he doesn't want to be interrupted."

Randi had about had it. The day was pretty well shot, and she'd found out next to nothing. "Why don't I just see for myself?" she said sweetly. She walked briskly around the desk, and pushed through the waist-high wooden gate.

"You can't go in there!" the receptionist squeaked in outrage, but by then Randi was opening the door. Police Chief Joseph Urquhart sat behind an old wooden desk cluttered with files, talking to the coroner. Both of them looked up when the door opened. Urquhart was a tall, powerful man in his early sixties. His hair had thinned considerably, but what remained of it was still red, though his eyebrows had gone completely gray. "What the hell—" he started.

"Sorry to barge in, but Miss Congeniality wouldn't give me the time of day," Randi said as the receptionist came rushing up behind her.

"Young lady this is the police department, and I'm going to throw you out on your ass," Urquhart said gruffly as he stood up and came around the desk, "unless you come over here right now and give your Uncle Joe a big hug."

Smiling, Randi crossed the bearskin rug, wrapped her arms around him, and laid her head against his chest as the chief tried to crush her. The door closed behind them, too loudly. Randi broke the embrace. "I miss you," she said.

"Sure you do," he said, in a faintly chiding tone. "That's why we see so much of you."

Joe Urquhart had been her father's partner for years, back when they were both in uniform. They'd been tight, and the Urquharts had been like an aunt and uncle to her. His older daughter had babysat for her, and Randi had returned the favor for the younger girl. After her father's death, Joe had looked out for them, helped her mother through the funeral and all the legalities, made sure the pension fund got Randi through college. Still, it hadn't been the same, and the families drifted apart, even more so after her mother had finally passed away. These days Randi saw him only once or twice a year, and felt guilty about it. "I'm sorry," she said. "You know I mean to keep in touch, but—"

"There's never enough time, is there?" he said.

The coroner cleared her throat. Sylvia Cooney was a local institution, a big brusque woman of indeterminate age, built like a cement mixer, her iron-gray hair tied in a tight bun at the back of her smooth, square face. She'd been coroner as long as Randi could remember. "Maybe I should excuse myself," she said.

Randi stopped her. "I need to ask you about Joan Sorenson. When will autopsy results be available?"

Cooney's eyes went quickly to the chief, then back to Randi. "Nothing I can tell you," she said. She left the office and closed the door with a soft click behind her.

"That hasn't been released to the public yet," Joe

Urquhart said. He walked back behind his desk, gestured. "Sit down."

Randi settled into a seat, let her gaze wander around the office. One wall was covered by commendations, certificates, and framed photographs. She saw her father there with Joe, both of them looking so achingly young, two grinning kids in uniform standing in front of their black-and-white. A moose head was mounted above the photographs, peering down at her with its glassy eyes. More trophies hung from the other walls. "Do you still hunt?" she asked him.

"Not in years," Urquhart said. "No time. Your Dad used to kid me about it all the time. Always said that if I ever killed anyone on duty, I'd want the head stuffed and mounted. Then one day it happened, and the joke wasn't so funny anymore." He frowned. "What's your interest in Joan Sorenson?"

"Professional," Randi said.

"Little out of your line, isn't it?"

Randi shrugged. "I don't pick my cases."

"You're too good to waste your life snooping around motels," Urquhart said. It was a sore point between them. "It's not too late to join the force."

"No," Randi said. She didn't try to explain; she knew from past experience that there was no way to make him understand. "I went out to the precinct house this morning to look at the report on Sorenson. It's missing from the file; no one knows where it is. I got the names of the cops who were at the scene, but none of them had time to talk to me. Now I'm told the autopsy results aren't being made public either. You mind telling me what's going on?"

Joe glanced out the windows behind him. The panes were wet with rain. "This is a sensitive case," he said. "I don't want the media blowing this thing all out of proportion."

"I'm not the media," Randi said.

Urquhart swiveled back around. "You're not a cop either. That's your choice. Randi, I don't want you involved in this, do you hear?"

"I'm involved whether you like it or not," she said. She didn't give him time to argue. "How did Joan Sorenson die? Was it an animal attack?"

"No," he said. "It was not. And that's the last question I'm going to answer." He sighed. "Randi," he said, "I know how hard you got hit by Frank's death. It was pretty rough on me too, remember? He phoned me for back-up. I didn't get there in time. You think I'll ever forget that?" He shook his head. "Put it behind you. Stop imagining things."

"I'm not imagining anything," Randi snapped. "Most of the time I don't even think about it. This is different."

"Have it your way," Joe said. There was a small stack of files on the corner of the desk near Randi. Urquhart leaned forward and picked them up, tapped them against his blotter to straighten them. "I wish I could help you." He slid open a drawer, put the file folders away. Randi caught a glimpse of the name on the top folder: *Helander*. "I'm sorry," Joe was saying. He started to rise. "Now, if you'll excuse—"

"Are you just rereading the Helander file for old times' sake, or is there some connection to Sorenson?" Randi asked.

Urquhart sat back down. "Shit," he said.

"Or maybe I just imagined that was the name on the file."

Joe looked pained. "We have reason to think the Helander boy might be back in the city."

"Hardly a boy any more," Randi said. "Roy Helander was three years older than me. You're looking at him for Sorenson?"

"We have to, with his history. The state released him two months ago, it turns out. The shrinks said he was cured." Urquhart made a face. "Maybe, maybe not. Anyway, he's just a name. We're looking at a hundred names."

"Where is he?"

"I wouldn't tell you if I knew. He's a bad piece of business, like the rest of his family. I don't like you getting mixed up with his sort, Randi. Your father wouldn't either."

Randi stood up. "My father's dead," she said, "and I'm a big girl now."

Willie parked the car where 13th Street dead-ended, at the foot of the bluffs. Blackstone sat high above the river, surrounded by a ten-foot high wrought iron fence with a row of forbidding spikes along its top. You could drive to the gatehouse easily enough, but you had to go all the way down Central, past downtown, then around on Grandview and Harmon Drive, up and down the hills and all along the bluffs where aging steamboat gothic mansions stood like so many dowagers staring out over the flats and river beyond, remembering better days. It was a long, tiresome drive.

Back before the automobile, it had been even longer and more tiresome. Faced with having to travel to Courier Square on a daily basis, Douglas Harmon made things easy for himself. He built a private cable car: a two-car funicular railway that crept up the gray stone face of the bluffs from the foot of 13th below to Blackstone above.

Internal combustion, limousines, chauffeurs, and paved roads had all conspired to wean the Harmons away from Douglas' folly, making the cable car something of a back door in more recent years, but that suited Willie well enough. Jonathan Harmon always made him feel like he ought to come in by the servant's entrance anyway.

Willie climbed out of the Caddy and stuck his hands in the sagging pockets of his raincoat. He looked up. The incline was precipitous, the rock wet and dark. Steven took his elbow roughly and propelled him forward. The cable car was wooden, badly in need of a whitewash, with bench space for six. Steven pulled the bell cord; the car jerked as they began to ascend. The second car came down to meet them, and they crossed halfway up the bluff. The car shook and Willie spotted rust on the rails. Even here at the gate of Blackstone, things were falling apart.

Near the top of the bluff, they passed through a gap in the wrought iron fence, and the New House came into view, gabled and turreted and covered with Victorian gingerbread. The Harmons had lived there for almost a century, but it was still the New House, and always would be. Behind the house the estate was densely forested, the narrow driveway winding through thick stands of old growth. Where the other founding families had long ago sold off or parceled out their lands to developers, the Harmons had held tight, and Blackstone remained intact, a piece of the forest primeval in the middle of the city.

Against the western sky, Willie glimpsed the broken silhouette of the tower, part of the Old House whose soot-dark stone walls gave Blackstone its name. The house was set well back among the trees, its lawns and courts overgrown, but even when you couldn't see it you knew it was there somehow. The tower was a jagged black presence outlined against the red-stained gray of the western horizon, crooked and forbidding. It had been Douglas Harmon, the journalist and builder of funicular railways, who had erected the New House and closed the Old, immense and gloomy even by Victorian standards, but neither Douglas, his son Thomas, nor his grandson Jonathan had ever found the will to tear it down. Local legend said the Old House was haunted. Willie could just about believe it. Blackstone, like its owner, gave him the creeps.

The cable car shuddered to a stop, and they climbed out onto a wooden deck, its paint weathered and peeling. A pair of wide French doors led into the New House. Jonathan Harmon was waiting for them, leaning on a walking stick, his gaunt figure outlined by the light that spilled through the door. "Hello, William," he said. Harmon was barely past sixty, Willie knew, but long snow-white hair and a body wracked by arthritis made him look much older. "I'm so glad that you could join us," he said.

"Yeah, well, I was in the neighborhood, just thought I'd drop by," Willie said. "Only thing is, I just remembered, I left the windows open in the brewery. I better run home and close them, or my dust bunnies are going to get soaked."

"No," said Jonathan Harmon. "I don't think so."

Willie felt the bands constricting across his chest. He wheezed, found his inhaler, and took two long hits. He figured he'd need it. "Okay, you talked me into it, I'll stay," he told Harmon, "but I damn well better get a drink out of it. My mouth still tastes like Diet Chocolate Ginger Beer.'

"Steven, be a good boy and get our friend William a snifter of Remy Martin, if you'd be so kind. I'll join him. The chill is on my bones." Steven, silent as ever, went inside to do as he was told. Willie made to follow, but Jonathan touched his arm lightly. "A moment," he said. He gestured. "Look."

Willie turned and looked. He wasn't quite so frightened anymore. If Jonathan wanted him dead, Steven would have tried already, and maybe succeeded. Steven was a dreadful mistake by his father's standards, but there was a freakish strength in those scarred hands. No, this was some other kind of deal.

They looked east over the city and the river. Dusk had begun to settle, and the streetlights were coming on down below, strings of luminescent pearls that spread out in all directions as far as the eye could see and leapt across the river on three great bridges. The clouds were gone to the east, and the horizon was a deep cobalt blue. The moon had begun to rise.

"There were no lights out there when the foundations of the Old House were dug," Jonathan Harmon said. "This was all wilderness. A wild river coursing through the forest primeval, and if you stood on high at dusk, it must have seemed as though the blackness went on forever. The water was pure, the air was clean, and the woods were thick with game . . . deer, beaver, bear . . . but no people, or at least no white men. John Harmon and his son James both wrote of seeing Indian campfires from the tower from time to time, but the tribes avoided this place, especially after John had begun to build the Old House."

"Maybe the Indians weren't so dumb after all," Willie said.

Jonathan glanced at Willie, and his mouth twitched. "We built this city out of nothing," he said. "Blood and iron built this city, blood and iron nurtured it and fed its people. The old families knew the power of blood and iron, they knew how to make this city great. The Rochmonts hammered and shaped the metal in smithies and foundries and steel mills, the Anders family moved it on their flatboats and steamers and railroads, and your own people found it and pried it from the earth. You come from iron stock, William Flambeaux, but we Harmons were always blood. We had the stockyards and the slaughterhouse, but long before that, before this city or this nation existed, the Old House was a center of the skin trade. Trappers and hunters would come here every season with furs and skins and beaver pelts to sell the

Harmons, and from here the skins would move down-river. On rafts, at first, and then on flatboats. Steam came later, much later."

"Is there going to be a pop quiz on this?" Willie asked.

"We've fallen a long way," he said, looking pointedly at Willie. "We need to remember how we started. Black iron and red, red blood. You need to remember. Your grandfather had the Flambeaux blood, the old pure strain."

Willie knew when he was being insulted. "And my mother was a Pankowski," he said, "which makes me half-frog, half-polack, and all mongrel. Not that I give a shit. I mean, it's terrific that my great-grandfather owned half the state, but the mines gave out around the turn of the century, the Depression took the rest, my father was a drunk, and I'm in collections, if that's okay with you." He was feeling pissed off and rash by then. "Did you have any particular reason for sending Steven to kidnap me, or was it just a yen to discuss the French and Indian War?"

Jonathan said, "Come. We'll be more comfortable inside, the wind is cold." The words were polite enough, but his tone had lost all faint trace of warmth. He led Willie inside, walking slowly, leaning heavily on the cane. "You must forgive me," he said. "It's the damp. It aggravates the arthritis, inflames my old war wounds." He looked back at Willie. "You were unconscionably rude to hang up on me. Granted, we have our differences, but simple respect for my position—"

"I been having a lot of trouble with my phone lately," Willie said. "Ever since they deregulated, service has turned to shit." Jonathan led him into a small sitting room. There was a fire burning in the hearth; the heat felt good after a long day tromping through the cold and the rain. The furnishings were antique, or maybe just old; Willie wasn't too clear on the difference.

Steven had preceded them. Two brandy snifters, half-full of amber liquid, sat on a low table. Steven squatted by the fire, his tall, lean body folded up like a jackknife. He looked up as they entered and stared at Willie a moment too long, as if he'd suddenly forgotten who he was or what he was doing there. Then his flat blue eyes went back to the fire, and he took no more notice of them or their conversation.

Willie looked around for the most comfortable chair and sat in it. The style reminded him of Randi Wade, but that just made him feel guilty. He picked up his cognac. Willie was couth enough to know that he was supposed to sip but cold and tired and pissed-off enough so that he didn't care. He emptied it in one long swallow, put it down on the floor, and relaxed back into the chair as the heat spread through his chest.

Jonathan, obviously in some pain, lowered himself carefully onto the edge of the couch, his hands closed round the head of his walking stick. Willie found himself staring. Jonathan noticed. "A wolf's head," he said. He moved his hands aside to give Willie a clear view. The firelight reflected off the rich yellow metal. The beast was snarling, snapping.

Its eyes were red. "Garnets?" Willie guessed.

Jonathan smiled the way you might smile at a particularly doltish child. "Rubies," he said, "set in 18 karat gold." His hands, large and heavily-veined, twisted by

289

arthritis, closed round the stick again, hiding the wolf from sight.

"Stupid," Willie said. "There's guys in this city would kill you as soon as look at you for a stick like that."

Jonathan's smile was humorless. "I will not die on account of gold, William." He glanced at the window. The moon was well above the horizon. "A good hunter's moon," he said. He looked back at Willie. "Last night you all but accused me of complicity in the death of the crippled girl." His voice was dangerously soft. "Why would you say such a thing?"

"I can't imagine," Willie said. He felt light-headed. The brandy had rushed right to his mouth. "Maybe the fact that you can't remember her name had something to do with it. Or maybe it was because you always hated Joanie, right from the moment you heard about her. My pathetic little mongrel bitch, I believe that was what you called her. Isn't it funny the way that little turns of phrase stick in the mind? I don't know, maybe it was just me, but somehow I got this impression that you didn't exactly wish her well. I haven't even mentioned Steven yet."

"Please don't," Jonathan said icily. "You've said quite enough. Look at me, William. Tell me what you see."

"You," said Willie. He wasn't in the mood for asshole games, but Jonathan Harmon did things at his own pace.

"An old man," Jonathan corrected. "Perhaps not so old in years alone, but old nonetheless. The arthritis grows worse every year, and there are days when the pain is so bad I can scarcely move. My family is all gone but for Steven, and Steven, let us be frank, is not all that I might have hoped for in a son." He spoke in firm, crisp tones, but Steven did not even look up from the flames. "I'm tired, William. It's true, I did not approve of your crippled girl, or even particularly of you. We live in a time of corruption and degeneracy, when the old truths of blood and iron have been forgotten. Nonetheless, however much I may have loathed your Joan Sorenson and what she represented, I had no taste of her blood. All I want is to live out my last years in peace."

Willie stood up. "Do me a favor and spare me the old sick man act. Yeah, I know all about your arthritis and your war wounds. I also know who you are and what you're capable of. Okay, you didn't kill Joanie. So who did? Him?" He jerked a thumb toward Steven.

"Steven was here with me."

"Maybe he was and maybe he wasn't," Willie said.

"Don't flatter yourself, Flambeaux, you're not important enough for me to lie to you. Even if your suspicion was correct, my son is not capable of such an act. Must I remind you that Steven is crippled as well, in his own way?"

Willie gave Steven a quick glance. "I remember once when I was just a kid, my father had to come see you, and he brought me along. I used to love to ride your little cable car. Him and you went inside to talk, but it was a nice day, so you let me play outside. I found Steven in the woods, playing with some poor sick mutt that had gotten past your fence. He was holding it down with his foot, and pulling off its legs, one by one, just ripping them out with his bare hands like a normal kid might pull petals off a flower. When I walked up behind him, he had two off and was working on the third. There was blood all over his face. He couldn't have been more than eight."

Jonathan Harmon sighed. "My son is . . . disturbed. We both know that, so there is no sense in my denying it. He is also dysfunctional, as you know full well. And whatever residual strength remains is controlled by his medication. He has not had a truly violent episode for years. Have you, Steven?"

Steven Harmon looked back at them. The silence went on too long as he stared, unblinking, at Willie. "No," he finally said.

Jonathan nodded with satisfaction, as if something had been settled. "So you see, William, you do us a great injustice. What you took for a threat was only an offer of protection. I was going to suggest that you move to one of our guest rooms for a time. I've made the same suggestion to Zoe and Amy."

Willie laughed. "I'll bet. Do I have to fuck Steven too, or is that just for the girls?"

Jonathan flushed, but kept his temper. His futile efforts to marry off Steven to one of the Anders sisters was a sore spot. "I regret to say they declined my offer. I hope you will not be so unwise. Blackstone has certain . . . protections . . . but I cannot vouch for your safety beyond these walls."

"Safety?" Willie said. "From what?"

"I do not know, but I can tell you this—in the dark of night, there are things that hunt the hunters."

"Things that hunt the hunters," Willie repeated. "That's good, has a nice beat, but can you dance to it?" He'd had enough. He started for the door. "Thanks but

no thanks. I'll take my chances behind my own walls."
Steven made no move to stop him.

Jonathan Harmon leaned more heavily on his cane. "I
can tell you how she was really killed," he said quietly.

Willie stopped and stared into the old man's eyes.
Then he sat back down.


It was on the south side in a neighborhood that made the
flats look classy, on an elbow of land between the river
and that old canal that ran past the pack. Algae and raw
sewage choked the canal and gave off a smell that drifted
for blocks. The houses were single-story clapboard
affairs, hardly more than shacks. Randi hadn't been
down here since the pack had closed its doors. Every
third house had a sign on the lawn, flapping forlornly in
the wind, advertising a property for sale or for rent, and
at least half of those were dark. Weeds grew waist-high
around the weathered rural mailboxes, and they saw at
least two burned-out lots.

Years had passed, and Randi didn't remember the
number, but it was the last house on the left, she knew,
next to a Sinclair station on the corner. The cabbie
cruised until they found it. The gas station was boarded
up, even the pumps were gone, but the house stood
there much as she recalled. It had a For Rent sign on the
lawn, but she saw a light moving around inside. A
flashlight, maybe? It was gone before she could be sure.

The cabbie offered to wait. "No," she said. "I don't
know how long I'll be." After he was gone, she stood on

the barren lawn for a long time, staring at the front door, before she finally went up the walk.

She'd decided not to knock, but the door opened as she was reaching for the knob. "Can I help you, miss?"

He loomed over her, a big man, thick-bodied but muscular. His face was unfamiliar, but he was no Helander. They'd been a short, wiry family, all with the same limp, dirty blonde hair. This one had hair black as wrought iron, and shaggier than the department usually liked. Five o'clock shadow gave his jaw a distinct blue-black cast. His hands were large, with short blunt fingers. Everything about him said cop.

"I was looking for the people who used to live here."

"The family moved away when the pack closed," he told her. "Why don't you come inside?" He opened the door wider. Randi saw bare floors, dust, and his partner, a beer-bellied black man standing by the door to the kitchen.

"I don't think so," she said.

"I insist," he replied. He showed her a gold badge pinned to the inside of his cheap gray suit.

"Does that mean I'm under arrest?"

He looked taken a back. "No. Of course not. We'd just like to ask you a few questions." He tried to sound friendlier. "I'm Rogoff."

"Homicide," she said.

His eyes narrowed. "How—?"

"You're in charge of the Sorenson investigation," she said. She'd been given his name at the cophouse that morning. "You must not have much of a case if you've got nothing better to do than hang around here waiting for Roy Helander to show."

"We were just leaving. Thought maybe he'd get nostalgic, hole up at the old house, but there's no sign of it." He looked at her hard and frowned. "Mind telling me your name?"

"Why?" she asked. "Is this a bust or a come-on?"

He smiled. "I haven't decided yet."

"I'm Randi Wade." She showed him her license.

"Private detective," he said, his tone carefully neutral. He handed the license back to her. "You working?"

She nodded.

"Interesting. I don't suppose you'd care to tell me the name of your client."

"No."

"I could haul you into court, make you tell the judge. You can get that license lifted, you know. Obstructing an on-going police investigation, withholding evidence."

"Professional privilege," she said.

Rogoff shook his head. "PIs don't have privilege. Not in this state."

"This one does," Randi said. "Attorney-client relationship. I've got a law degree too." She smiled at him sweetly. "Leave my client out of it. I know a few interesting things about Roy Helander I might be willing to share."

Rogoff digested that. "I'm listening."

Randi shook her head. "Not here. You know the automat on Courier Square?" He nodded. "Eight o'clock," she told him. "Come alone. Bring a copy of the coroner's report on Sorenson."

"Most girls want candy or flowers," he said.

"The coroner's report," she repeated firmly. "They still keep the old case records downtown?"

"Yeah," he said. "Basement of the courthouse."

"Good. You can stop by and do a little remedial reading on the way. It was eighteen years ago. Some kids had been turning up missing. One of them was Roy's little sister. There were others—Stanski, Jones, I forget all the names. A cop named Frank Wade was in charge of the investigation. A gold badge, like you. He died."

"You saying there's a connection?"

"You're the cop. You decide." She left him standing in the doorway and walked briskly down the block.

Steven didn't bother to see him down to the foot of the bluffs. Willie rode the little funicular railway alone, morose and lost in thought. His joints ached like nobody's business and his nose was running. Every time he got upset his body fell to pieces, and Jonathan Harmon had certainly upset him. That was probably better than killing him, which he'd half expected when he found Steven in his car, but still . . .

He was driving home along 13th Street when he saw the bar's neon sign on his right. Without thinking, he pulled over and parked. Maybe Harmon was right and maybe Harmon had his ass screwed on backwards, but in any case Willie still had to make a living. He locked up the Caddy and went inside.

It was a slow Tuesday night, and Squeaky's was empty. It was a workingman's tavern. Two pool tables, a shuffleboard machine in back, booths along one wall. Willie took a bar stool. The bartender was an old guy, hard and dry as a stick of wood. He looked mean. Willie considered ordering a banana daquiri, just to see what the guy would say, but one look at that sour, twisted old face cured the impulse, and he asked for a boilermaker instead. "Ed working tonight?" he asked when the bartender brought the drinks.

"Only works weekends," the man said, "but he comes in most nights, plays a little pool."

"I'll wait," Willie said. The shot made his eyes water. He chased it down with a gulp of beer. He saw a pay phone back by the men's room. When the bartender gave him his change, he walked back, put in a quarter, and dialed Randi. She wasn't home; he got her damned machine. Willie hated phone machines. They'd made life a hell of a lot more difficult for collection agents, that was for sure. He waited for the tone, left Randi an obscene message, and hung up.

The men's room had a condom dispenser mounted over the urinals. Willie read the instructions as he took a leak. The condoms were intended for prevention of disease only, of course, even though the one dispensed by the left-hand slot was a French tickler. Maybe he ought to install one of these at home, he thought. He zipped up, flushed, washed his hands.

When he walked back out into the taproom, two new customers stood over the pool table, chalking up cues. Willie looked at the bartender, who nodded. "One of you Ed Juddiker?" Willie asked.

Ed wasn't the biggest—his buddy was as large and pale as Moby Dick—but he was big enough, with a real stupid-mean look on his face. "Yeah?"

"We need to talk about some money you owe." Willie offered him one of his cards.

Ed looked at the hand, but made no effort to take the card. He laughed. "Get lost," he said. He turned back to the pool table. Moby Dick racked up the balls and Ed broke.

That was all right, if that was the way he wanted to play it. Willie sat back on the bar stool and ordered another beer. He'd get his money one way or the other. Sooner or later Ed would have to leave, and then it would be his turn.

Willie still wasn't answering his phone. Randi hung up the pay phone and frowned. He didn't have an answering machine either, not Willie Flambeaux, that would be too sensible. She knew she shouldn't worry. The hounds of hell don't punch time-clocks, as he'd told her more than once. He was probably out running down some dead-beat. She'd try again when she got home. If he still didn't answer, then she'd start to worry.

The automat was almost empty. Her heels made hollow clicks on the old linoleum as she walked back to her booth and sat down. Her coffee had gone cold. She looked idly out the window. The digital clock on the State National Bank said 8:13. Randi decided to give him ten more minutes.

The red vinyl of the booth was old and cracking, but she felt strangely comfortable here, sipping her cold coffee and staring off at the Iron Spire across the square. The automat had been her favorite restaurant when she was a little girl. Every year on her birthday she would demand a movie at the Castle and dinner at the automat, and every year her father would laugh and oblige. She loved to put the nickels in the coin slots and make the windows pop open, and fill her father's cup out of the old brass coffee machine with all its knobs and levers.

Sometimes you could see disembodied hands through the glass, sticking a sandwich or a piece of pie into one of the slots, like something from an old horror movie. You never saw any people working at the automat, just hands; the hands of people who hadn't paid their bills, her father once told her, teasing. That gave her the shivers, but somehow made her annual visits even more delicious, in a creepy kind of way. The truth, when she learned it, was much less interesting. Of course, that was true of most everything in life.

These days, the automat was always empty, which made Randi wonder how the floor could possibly stay so filthy, and you had to put quarters into the coin slots beside the little windows instead of nickels. But the banana cream pie was still the best she'd ever had, and the coffee that came out of those worn brass spigots was better than anything she'd ever brewed at home.

She was thinking of getting a fresh cup when the door opened and Rogoff finally came in out of the rain. He wore a heavy wool coat. His hair was wet. Randi looked out at the clock as he approached the booth. It said 8:17. "You're late," she said.

"I'm a slow reader," he said. He excused himself and went to get some food. Randi watched him as he fed dollar bills into the change machine. He wasn't bad-looking if you liked the type, she decided, but the type was definitely cop.

Rogoff returned with a cup of coffee, the hot beef

sandwich with mashed potatoes, gravy, and overcooked carrots, and a big slice of apple pie.

"The banana cream is better," Randi told him as he slid in opposite her.

"I like apple," he said, shaking out a paper napkin.

"Did you bring the coroner's report?"

"In my pocket." He started cutting up the sandwich. He was very methodical, slicing the whole thing into small bite-sized portions before he took his first taste. "I'm sorry about your father."

"So was I. It was a long time ago. Can I see the report?"

"Maybe. Tell me something I don't already know about Roy Helander."

Randi sat back. "We were kids together. He was older, but he'd been left back a couple of times, till he wound up in my class. He was a bad kid from the wrong side of the tracks and I was a cop's daughter, so we didn't have much in common . . . until his little sister disappeared."

"He was with her," Rogoff said.

"Yes he was. No one disputed that, least of all Roy. He was fifteen, she was eight. They were walking the tracks. They went off together, and Roy came back alone. He had blood on his dungarees and all over his hands. His sister's blood."

Rogoff nodded. "All that's in the file. They found blood on the tracks too."

"Three kids had already vanished. Jessie Helander made four. The way most people looked at it, Roy had always been a little strange. He was solitary, inarticulate, used to hook school and run off to some secret hideout he had in the woods. He liked to play with the younger kids instead of boys his own age. A degenerate from a bad family, a child molester who had actually raped and killed his own sister, that was they said. They gave him all kinds of tests, decided he was deeply disturbed, and sent him away to some kiddie snakepit. He was still a juvenile, after all. Case closed, and the city breathed easier."

"If you don't have any more than that, the coroner's report stays in my pocket," Rogoff said.

"Roy said he didn't do it. He cried and screamed a lot, and his story wasn't coherent, but he stuck to it. He said he was walking along ten feet or so behind his sister, balancing on the rails and listening for a train, when a monster came out of a drainage culvert and attacked her."

"A monster," Rogoff said.

"Some kind of big shaggy dog, that was what Roy said. He was describing a wolf. Everybody knew it."

"There hasn't been a wolf in this part of the country for over a century."

"He described how Jessie screamed as the thing began to rip her apart. He said he grabbed her leg, tried to pull her out of its jaws, which would explain why he had her blood all over him. The wolf turned and looked at him and growled. It had red eyes, burning red eyes, Roy said, and he was real scared, so he let go. By then Jessie was almost certainly dead. It gave him one last snarl and ran off, carrying the body in its jaws." Randi paused, took a sip of coffee. "That was his story. He told it over and over, to his mother, the police, the psychologists, the judge, everyone. No one ever believed him."

"Not even you?"

"Not even me. We all whispered about Roy in school, about what he'd done to his sister and those other kids. We couldn't quite imagine it, but we knew it had to be horrible. The only thing was, my father never quite bought it."

"Why not?"

She shrugged. "Instincts, maybe. He was always talking about how a cop had to go with his instincts. It was his case, he'd spent more time with Roy than anyone else, and something about the way the boy told the story had affected him. But it was nothing that could be proved. The evidence was overwhelming. So Roy was locked up." She watched his eyes as she told him. "A month later, Eileen Stanski vanished. She was six."

Rogoff paused with a forkful of the mashed potatoes, and studied her thoughtfully. "Inconvenient," he said.

"Dad wanted Roy released, but no one supported him. The official line was that the Stanski girl was unconnected to the others. Roy had done four, and some other child molester had done the fifth."

"It's possible."

"It's bullshit," Randi said. "Dad knew it and he said it. That didn't make him any friends in the department, but he didn't care. He could be a very stubborn man. You read the file on his death?"

Rogoff nodded. He looked uncomfortable.

"My father was savaged by an animal. A dog, the coroner said. If you want to believe that, go ahead." This was the hard part. She'd picked at it like an old scab for years, and then she'd tried to forget it, but nothing ever made it easier. "He got a phone call in the middle of the night, some kind of lead about the missing kids. Before he left he phoned Joe Urquhart to ask for back-up."

"Chief Urquhart?"

Randi nodded. "He wasn't chief then. Joe had been his partner when he was still in uniform. He said Dad told him he had a hot tip, but not the details, not even the name of the caller."

"Maybe he didn't know the name."

"He knew. My father wasn't the kind of cop who goes off alone in the middle of the night on an anonymous tip. He drove down to the stockyards by himself. It was waiting for him there. Whatever it was took six rounds and kept coming. It tore out his throat and after he was dead it ate him. What was left by the time Urquhart got there . . . Joe testified that when he first found the body he wasn't even sure it was human."

She told the story in a cool, steady voice, but her stomach was churning. When she finished Rogoff was staring at her. He set down his fork and pushed his plate away. "Suddenly I'm not very hungry anymore."

Randi's smile was humorless. "I love our local press. There was a case a few years ago when a woman was kidnapped by a gang, held for two weeks. She was beaten, tortured, sodomized, raped hundreds of times. When the story broke, the paper said she'd been quote— *assaulted* unquote. It said my father's body had been mutilated. It said the same thing about Joan Sorenson. I've been told her body was intact." She leaned forward, looked hard into his dark brown eyes. "That's a lie."

"Yes," he admitted. He took a sheet of paper from his breast pocket, unfolded it, passed it across to her. "But it's not the way you think."

Randi snatched the coroner's report from his hand, and scanned quickly down the page. The words blurred, refused to register. It wasn't adding up the way it was supposed to.

*Cause of death: exsanguination.*

Somewhere far away, Rogoff was talking. "It's a security building, her apartment's on the fourteenth floor. No balconies, no fire escapes, and the doorman didn't see a thing. The door was locked. It was a cheap spring lock, easy to jimmy, but there was no sign of forced entry."

*The instrument of death was a blade at least twelve inches long, extremely sharp, slender and flexible, perhaps a surgical instrument.*

"Her clothing was all over the apartment, just ripped to hell, in tatters. In her condition, you wouldn't think she'd put up much of a struggle, but it looks like she did. None of the neighbors heard anything, of course. The killer chained her to her bed, naked, and went to work. He worked fast, knew what he was doing, but it still must have taken her a long time to die. The bed was soaked with her blood, through the sheets and mattress, right down to the box spring."

Randi looked back up at him, and the coroner's report slid from her fingers onto the formica table. Rogoff reached over and took her hand.

"Joan Sorenson wasn't devoured by any animal, Miss Wade. She was flayed alive, and left to bleed to death. And the part of her that's missing is her skin."

It was a quarter past midnight when Willie got home. He parked the Caddy by the pier. Ed Juddiker's wallet was on the seat beside him. Willie opened it, took out the money, counted. Seventy-nine bucks. Not much, but it was a start. He'd give half to Betsy this first time, credit the rest to Ed's account. Willie pocketed the money and locked the empty wallet in the glovebox. Ed might need the driver's license. He'd bring it by Squeaky's over the weekend, when Ed was on, and talk to him about a payment schedule.

Willie locked up the car and trudged wearily across the rain-slick cobbles to his front door. The sky above the river was dark and starless. The moon was up by now, he knew, hidden somewhere behind those black cotton clouds. He fumbled for his keys, buried down under his inhaler, his pillbox, a half-dozen pairs of scissors, a handkerchief, and the miscellaneous other junk that made his coat pocket sag. After a long minute, he tried his pants pocket, found them, and started in on his locks. He slid the first key into his double deadbolt.

The door opened slowly, silently.

The pale yellow light from a streetlamp filtered through the brewery's high, dusty windows, patterning the floor with faint squares and twisted lines. The hulks of rusting machines crouched in the dimness like great dark beasts. Willie stood in the doorway, keys in hand, his heart pounding like a triphammer. He put the keys in his pocket, found his Primateen, took a hit. The hiss of the inhaler seemed obscenely loud in the stillness.

He thought of Joanie, of what happened to her.

He could run, he thought. The Cadillac was only a few feet behind him, just a few steps, whatever was waiting in there couldn't possibly be fast enough to get him before he reached the car. Yeah, hit the road, drive all night, he had enough gas to make Chicago, it wouldn't follow him there. Willie took the first step back, then stopped, and giggled nervously. He had a sudden picture of himself sitting behind the wheel of his big lime-green chromeboat, grinding the ignition, grinding and grinding and flooding the engine as something dark and terrible emerged from inside the brewery and crossed the cobblestones behind him. That was silly, it was only in bad horror movies that the ignition didn't turn over, wasn't it? Wasn't it?

Maybe he had just forgotten to lock up when he'd left for work that morning. He'd had a lot on his mind, a full day's work ahead of him and a night of bad dreams behind, maybe he'd just closed the fucking door behind him and forgotten about his locks.

He never forgot about his locks.

But maybe he had, just this once.

Willie thought about changing. Then he remembered Joanie, and put the thought aside. He stood on one leg, pulled off his shoe. Then the other. Water soaked through his socks. He edged forward, took a deep breath, moved into the darkened brewery as silently as he could, pulling the door shut behind him. Nothing moved. Willie reached down into his pocket, pulled out Mr Scissors. It wasn't much, but it was better than bare hands. Hugging the thick shadows along the wall, he crossed the room and began to creep upstairs on stockinged feet.

The streetlight shone through the window at the end of the hall. Willie paused on the steps when his head came up to the level of the second-story landing. He could look up and down the hallway. All the office doors were shut. No light leaking underneath or through the frosted-glass transoms. Whatever waited for him waited in darkness.

He could feel his chest constricting again. In another moment he'd need his inhaler. Suddenly he just wanted to get it over with. He climbed the final steps and crossed the hall in two long strides, threw open the door to his living room, and slammed on the lights.

Randi Wade was sitting in his beanbag chair. She looked up blinking as he hit the lights. "You startled me," she said.

"I startled *you*!" Willie crossed the room and collapsed into his La-Z-Boy. The scissors fell from his sweaty palm and bounced on the hardwood floor. "Jesus H. Christ on a crutch, you almost made me lose control of my personal hygiene. What the hell are you doing here? Did I forget to lock the door?"

Randi smiled. "You locked the door and you locked the door and then you locked the door some more. You're world class when it comes to locking doors, Flambeaux. It took me twenty minutes to get in."

Willie massaged his throbbing temples. "Yeah, well, with all the women who want this body, I got to have some protection, don't I?" He noticed his wet socks, pulled one off, grimaced. "Look at this," he said. "My shoes are out in the street getting rained on, and my feet are soaking. If I get pneumonia, you get the doctor bills, Wade. You could have waited."

"It was raining," she pointed out. "You wouldn't have

wanted me to wait in the rain, Willie. It would have pissed me off, and I'm in a foul mood already."

Something in her voice made Willie stop rubbing his toes to look up at her. The rain had plastered loose strands of light brown hair across her forehead, and her eyes were grim. "You look like a mess," he admitted.

"I tried to make myself presentable, but the mirror in your ladies' room is missing."

"It broke. There's one in the men's room."

"I'm not that kind of girl," Randi said. Her voice was hard and flat. "Willie, your friend Joan wasn't killed by an animal. She was flayed. The killer took her skin."

"I know," Willie said, without thinking.

Her eyes narrowed. They were gray-green, large and pretty, but right now they looked as cold as marbles. "You *know?*" she echoed. Her voice had gone very soft, almost to a whisper, and Willie knew he was in trouble. "You give me some bullshit story and send me running all around town, and you *know?* Do you know what happened to my father too, is that it? It was just your clever little way of getting my attention?"

Willie gaped at her. His second sock was in his hand. He let it drop to the floor. "Hey, Randi, gimme a break, okay? It wasn't like that at all. I just found out a few hours ago, honest. How could I know? I wasn't there, it wasn't in the paper." He was feeling confused and guilty. "What the hell am I supposed to know about your father? I don't know jackshit about your father. All the time you worked for me, you mentioned your family maybe twice."

Her eyes searched his face for signs of deception. Willie tried to give his warmest, most trustworthy smile.

Randi grimaced. "Stop it," she said wearily. "You look like a used car salesman. All right, you didn't know about my father. I'm sorry. I'm a little wrought up right now, and I thought . . ." She paused thoughtfully. "Who told you about Sorenson?"

Willie hesitated. "I can't tell you," he said. "I wish I could, I really do. I can't. You wouldn't believe me anyway." Randi looked very unhappy. Willie kept talking. "Did you find out whether I'm a suspect? The police haven't called."

"They've probably been calling all day. By now they may have an APB out on you. If you won't get a machine, you ought to try coming home occasionally." She frowned. "I talked to Rogoff from Homicide." Willie's heart stopped, but she saw the look on his face and held up a hand. "No, your name wasn't mentioned. By either of us. They'll be calling everyone who knew her, probably, but it's just routine questioning. I don't think they'll be singling you out."

"Good," Willie said. "Well, look, I owe you one, but there's no reason for you to go on with this. I know it's not paying the rent, so—"

"So what?" Randi was looking at him suspiciously. "Are you trying to get rid of me now? After you got me involved in the first place?" She frowned. "Are you holding out on me?"

"I think you've got that reversed," Willie said lightly. Maybe he could joke his way out of it. "You're the one who gets bent out of shape whenever I offer to help you shop for lingerie."

"Cut the shit," Randi said sharply. She was not amused in the least, he could see that. "We're talking about the torture and murder of a girl who was supposed to be a friend of yours. Or has that slipped your mind somehow?"

"No," he said, abashed. Willie was very uncomfortable. He got up and crossed the room, plugged in the hotplate. "Hey, listen, you want a cup of tea? I got Earl Grey, Red Zinger, Morning Thunder—"

"The police think they have a suspect," Randi said.

Willie turned to look at her. "Who?"

"Roy Helander," Randi said.

"Oh, boy," Willie said. He'd been a PFC in Hamburg when the Helander thing went down, but he'd had a subscription to the *Courier* to keep up on the old hometown, and the headlines had made him ill. "Are you sure?"

"No," she said. "They're just rounding up the usual suspects. Roy was a great scapegoat last time, why not use him again? First they have to find him, though. No one's really sure that he's still in the state, let alone the city."

Willie turned away, busied himself with hotplate and kettle. All of a sudden he found it difficult to look Randi in the eye. "You don't think Helander was the one who grabbed those kids."

"Including his own sister? Hell no. Jessie was the last person he'd ever have hurt, she actually *liked* him. Not to mention that he was safely locked away when number five disappeared. I knew Roy Helander. He had bad teeth and he didn't bathe often enough, but that doesn't make him a child molester. He hung out with younger kids because the older ones made fun of him. I don't think he had any friends. He had some kind of secret place in the woods where he'd go to hide when things got too rough, he—"

She stopped suddenly, and Willie turned toward her, a teabag dangling from his fingers. "You thinking what I'm thinking?"

The kettle began to scream.


Randi tossed and turned for over an hour after she got home, but there was no way she could sleep. Every time she closed her eyes she would see her father's face, or imagine poor Joan Sorenson, tied to that bed as the killer came closer, knife in hand. She kept coming back to Roy Helander, to Roy Helander and his secret refuge. In her mind, Roy was still the gawky adolescent she remembered, his blonde hair lank and unwashed, his eyes frightened and confused as they made him tell the story over and over again. She wondered what had become of that secret place of his during all the years he'd been locked up and drugged in the state mental home, and she wondered if maybe sometimes he hadn't dreamt of it as he lay there in his cell. She thought maybe he had. If Roy Helander had indeed come home, Randi figured she knew just where he was.

Knowing about it and finding it were two different things, however. She and Willie had kicked it around without narrowing it down any. Randi tried to remember but it had been so long ago, a whispered conversation in the schoolyard. A secret place in the woods, he'd said, a place where no one ever came that was his and his alone, hidden and full of magic. That could be anything, a cave by the river, a treehouse, even something as simple as a cardboard lean-to. But where were these woods? Outside the city were suburbs and industrial parks and farms, the nearest state forest was forty miles north along the river road. If this secret place was in one of the city parks, you'd think someone would have stumbled on it years ago. Without more to go on, Randi didn't have a prayer of finding it. But her mind worried it like a pit bull with a small child.

Finally her digital alarm clock read 2:13, and Randi gave up on sleep altogether. She got out of bed, turned on the light, and went back to the kitchen. The refrigerator was pretty dismal, but she found a couple of bottles of Pabst. Maybe a beer would help put her to sleep. She opened a bottle and carried it back to bed.

Her bedroom furnishings were a hodge-podge. The carpet was a remnant, the blonde chest-of-drawers was boring and functional, and the four-poster queen-sized bed was a replica, but she did own a few genuine antiques—the massive oak wardrobe, the full-length clawfoot dressing mirror in its ornate wooden frame, and the cedar chest at the foot of the bed. Her mother always used to call it a hope chest. Did little girls still keep hope chests? She didn't think so, at least not around here. Maybe there were still places where hope didn't seem so terribly unrealistic, but this city wasn't one of them.

Randi sat on the floor, put the beer on the carpet, and opened the chest.

Hope chests were where you kept your future, all the little things that were part of the dreams they taught you to dream when you were a child. She hadn't been a child since she was twelve, since the night her mother woke her with that terrible inhuman sound. Her chest was full of memories now.

She took them out, one by one. Yearbooks from high school and college, bundles of love letters from old boyfriends and even that asshole she'd married, her school ring and her wedding ring, her diplomas, the letters she'd won in track and girls' softball, a framed picture of her and her date at the senior prom.

Way, way down at the bottom, buried under all the other layers of her life, was a police .38. Her father's gun, the gun he emptied the night he died. Randi took it out and carefully put it aside. Beneath it was the book, an old three-ring binder with a blue cloth cover. She opened it across her lap.

The yellowed *Courier* story on her father's death was scotchtaped to the first sheet of paper, and Randi stared at that familiar photograph for a long time before she flipped the page. There were other clippings: stories about the missing children that she'd torn furtively from *Courier* back issues in the public library, magazine articles about animal attacks, serial killers, and monsters, all sandwiched between the lined pages she'd filled with her meticulous twelve-year-old's script. The handwriting grew broader and sloppier as she turned the pages; she'd kept up the book for years, until she'd gone away to college and tried to forget. She'd thought she'd done a pretty good job of that, but now, turning the pages, she knew that was a lie. You never forget. She only had to glance at the headlines, and it all came back to her in a sickening rush.

Eileen Stanski, Jessie Helander, Diane Jones, Gregory Corio, Erwin Weiss. None of them had ever been found, not so much as a bone or a piece of clothing. The police said her father's death was accidental, unrelated to the case he was working on. They'd all accepted that, the chief, the mayor, the newspaper, even her mother, who only wanted to get it all behind them and go on with their lives. Barry Schumacher and Joe Urquhart were the last to buy in, but in the end even they came around, and Randi was the only one left. Mere mention of the subject upset her mother so much that she finally stopped talking about it, but she didn't forget. She just asked her questions quietly, kept up her binder, and hid it every night at the bottom of the hope chest.

For all the good it had done.

The last twenty-odd pages in the back of the binder were still blank, the blue lines on the paper faint with age. The pages were stiff as she turned them. When she reached the final page, she hesitated. Maybe it wouldn't be there, she thought. Maybe she had just imagined it. It made no sense anyway. He would have known about her father, yes, but their mail was censored, wasn't it? They'd never let him send such a thing.

Randi turned the last page. It was there, just as she'd known it would be.

She'd been a junior in college when it arrived. She'd put it all behind her. Her father had been dead for seven years, and she hadn't even looked at her binder for three. She was busy with her classes and her sorority and her boyfriends, and sometimes she had bad dreams but mostly it was okay, she'd grown up, she'd gotten real. If she thought about it at all, she thought that maybe the adults had been right all along, it had just been some kind of an animal.

*. . . some kind of animal . . .*

Then one day the letter had come. She'd opened it on the way to class, read it with her friends chattering beside her, laughed and made a joke and stuck it away, all very grown-up. But that night, when her roommate had gone to sleep, she took it out and turned on her tensor to read it again, and felt sick. She was going to throw it away, she remembered. It was just trash, a twisted product of a sick mind.

Instead she'd put it in the binder.

The scotch tape had turned yellow and brittle, but the envelope was still white, with the name of the institution printed neatly in the left-hand corner. Someone had probably smuggled it out for him. The letter itself was scrawled on a sheet of cheap typing paper in block letters. It wasn't signed, but she'd known who it was from.

Randi slid the letter out of the envelope, hesitated for a moment, and opened it.

## IT WAS A WEREWOLF

She looked at it and looked at it and looked at it, and suddenly she didn't feel very grown up any more. When the phone rang she nearly jumped a foot.

Her heart was pounding in her chest. She folded up the letter and stared at the phone, feeling strangely guilty, as if she'd been caught doing something shameful. It was 2:53 in the morning. Who the hell would be calling now? If it was Roy Helander, she thought she might just scream. She let the phone ring.

On the fourth ring, her machine cut in. "This is AAA-Wade Investigations, Randi Wade speaking. I can't talk right now, but you can leave a message at the tone, and I'll get back to you."

The tone sounded. "Uh, hello," said a deep male voice that was definitely not Roy Helander.

Randi put down the binder, snatched up the receiver. "Rogoff? Is that you?"

"Yeah, he said. "Sorry if I woke you. Listen, this isn't by the book and I can't figure out a good excuse for why I'm calling you, except that I thought you ought to know."

Cold fingers crept down Randi's spine. "Know what?"

"We've got another one," he said.

Willie woke in a cold sweat.

*What was that?*

A noise, he thought. Somewhere down the hall.

Or maybe just a dream? Willie sat up in bed and tried to get a grip on himself. The night was full of noises. It could have been a towboat on the river, a car passing by underneath his windows, anything. He still felt sheepish about the way he'd let his fear take over when he found his door open. He was just lucky he hadn't stabbed Randi with those scissors. He couldn't let his imagination eat him alive. He slid back down under the covers, rolled over on his stomach, closed his eyes.

Down the hall, a door opened and closed.

His eyes opened wide. He lay very still, listening.

He'd locked all the locks, he told himself, he'd walked Randi to the door and locked all his locks, the spring-lock, the chain, the double deadbolt, he'd even lowered the police bar. No one could get in once the bar was in place, it could only be lifted from inside, the door was solid steel. And the back door might as well be welded shut, it was so corroded and unmovable. If they broke a window he would have heard the noise, there was no way, no way. He was just dreaming.

The knob on his bedroom door turned slowly, clicked. There was a small metallic rattle as someone pushed at the door. The lock held. The second push was slightly harder, the noise louder.

By then Willie was out of bed. It was a cold night, his jockey shorts and undershirt small protection against the chill, but Willie had other things on his mind. He could see the key still sticking out of the keyhole. An antique key for a hundred-year-old lock. The office keyholes were big enough to peek through. Willie kept the keys inside them, just to plug up the drafts, but he never turned them . . . except tonight. Tonight for some reason he'd turned that key before he went to bed and somehow felt a little more secure when he heard the tumblers click. And now that was all that stood between him and whatever was out there.

He backed up against the window, glanced out at the cobbled alley behind the brewery. The shadows lay thick and black beneath him. He seemed to recall a big green-metal dumpster down below, directly under the window, but it was too dark to make it out.

Something hammered at the door. The room shook.

Willie couldn't breathe. His inhaler was on the dresser

317

across the room, over by the door. He was caught in a giant's fist and it was squeezing all the breath right out of him. He sucked at the air.

The thing outside hit the door again. The wood began to splinter. Solid wood, a hundred years old, but it split like one of your cheap-ass hollow-core modern doors.

Willie was starting to get dizzy. It was going to be real pissed off, he thought giddily, when it finally got in here and found that his asthma had already killed him. Willie peeled off his undershirt, dropped it to the floor, hooked a thumb in the elastic of his shorts.

The door shook and shattered, falling half away from its hinges. The next blow snapped it in two. His head swam from lack of oxygen. Willie forgot all about his shorts and gave himself over to the change.

Bones and flesh and muscles shrieked in the agony of transformation, but the oxygen rushed into his lungs, sweet and cold, and he could breathe again. Relief shuddered through him and he threw back his head and gave it voice. It was a sound to chill the blood, but the dark shape picking its way through the splinters of his door did not hesitate, and neither did Willie. He gathered his feet up under him, and leapt. Glass shattered all around him as he threw himself through the window, and the shards spun outward into the darkness. Willie missed the dumpster, landed on all fours, lost his footing, and slid three feet across the cobbles.

When he looked up, he could see the shape above him, filling his window. Its hands moved, and he caught the terrible glint of silver, and that was all it took. Willie was on his feet again, running down the street faster than he had ever run before.

The cab let her off two houses down. Police barricades had gone up all around the house, a dignified old Victorian manor badly in need of fresh paint. Curious neighbors, heavy coats thrown on over pajamas and bathrobes, lined Grandview, whispering to each other and glancing back at the house. The flashers on the police cars lent a morbid avidity to their faces.

Randi walked past them briskly. A patrolman she didn't know stopped her at the police barrier. "I'm Randi Wade," she told him. "Rogoff asked me to come down."

"Oh," he said. He jerked a thumb back at the house. "He's inside, talking to the sister."

Randi found them in the living room. Rogoff saw her, nodded, waved her off, and went back to his questioning. The other cops looked at her curiously, but no one said anything. The sister was a young-looking forty, slender and dark, with pale skin and a wild mane of black hair that fell half down her back. She sat on the edge of a sectional in a white silk teddy that left little to the imagination, seemingly just as indifferent to the cold air coming through the open door as she was to the lingering glances of the policemen.

One of the cops was taking some fingerprints off a shiny black grand piano in the corner of the room. Randi wandered over as he finished. The top of the piano was covered with framed photographs. One was a summer scene, taken somewhere along the river, two pretty girls in matching bikinis standing on either side of an intense young man. The girls were dappled with moisture, laughing for the photographer, long black hair hanging wetly down across wide smiles. The man, or boy, or whatever he was, was in a swimsuit, but you could tell he was bone dry. He was gaunt and sallow, and his blue eyes stared into the lens with a vacancy that was oddly disturbing. The girls could have been as young as eighteen or as old as twenty. One of then was the woman Rogoff was questioning, but Randi could not have told you which one. Twins. She glanced at the other photos, half-afraid she'd find a picture of Willie. Most of the faces she didn't recognize, but she was still looking them over when Rogoff came up behind her.

"Coroner's upstairs with the body," he said. "You can come up if you've got the stomach."

Randi turned away from the piano and nodded. "You learn anything from the sister?"

"She had a nightmare," he said. He started up the narrow staircase, Randi close behind him. "She says that as far back as she can remember, whenever she had bad dreams, she'd just cross the hall and crawl in bed with Zoe." They reached the landing. Rogoff put his hand on a glass doorknob, then paused. "What she found when she crossed the hall this time is going to keep her in nightmares for years to come."

He opened the door. Randi followed him inside.

The only light was a small bedside lamp, but the police photographer was moving around the room, snapping pictures of the red twisted thing on the bed. The light of his flash made the shadows leap and writhe, and

Randi's stomach writhed with them. The smell of blood was overwhelming. She remembered summers long ago, hot July days when the wind blew from the south and the stink of the slaughterhouse settled over the city. But this was a thousand times worse.

The photographer was moving, flashing, moving, flashing. The world went from gray to red, then back to gray again. The coroner was bent over the corpse, her motions turned jerky and unreal by the strobing of the big flash gun. The white light blazed off the ceiling, and Randi looked up and saw the mirrors there. The dead woman's mouth gaped open, round and wide in a silent scream. He'd cut off her lips with her skin, and the inside of her mouth was no redder than the outside. Her face was gone, nothing left but the glistening wet ropes of muscle and here and there the pale glint of bone, but he'd left her her eyes. Large dark eyes, pretty eyes, sensuous, like her sister's downstairs. They were wide open, staring up in terror at the mirror on the ceiling. She'd been able to see every detail of what was being done to her. What had she found in the eyes of her reflection? Pain, terror, despair? A twin all her life, perhaps she'd found some strange comfort in her mirror image, even as her face and her flesh and her humanity had been cut away from her.

The flash went off again, and Randi caught the glint of metal at wrist and ankle. She closed her eyes for a second, steadied her breathing, and moved to the foot of the bed, where Rogoff was talking to the coroner.

"Same kind of chains?" he asked.

"You got it. And look at this." Coroner Cooney took the unlit cigar out of her mouth and pointed.

The chain looped tightly around the victim's ankle. When the flash went off again, Randi saw the other circles, dark, black lines, scored across the raw flesh and exposed nerves. It made her hurt just to look.

"She struggled," Rogoff suggested. "The chain chafed against her flesh."

"Chafing leaves you raw and bloody," Cooney replied. "What was done to her, you'd never notice chafing. That's a burn, Rogoff, a third-degree burn. Both wrists, both ankles, wherever the metal touched her. Sorenson had the same burn marks. Like the killer heated the chains until they were white hot. Only the metal is cold now. Go on, touch it."

"No thanks," Rogoff said. "I'll take your word for it."

"Wait a minute," Randi said.

The coroner seemed to notice her for the first time. "What's she doing here?" she asked.

"It's a long story," Rogoff replied. "Randi, this is official police business, you'd better keep—"

Randi ignored him. "Joan Sorenson had the same kind of burn marks?" she asked Cooney. "At wrist and ankle, where the chains touched her skin?"

"That's right," Cooney said. "So what?"

"What are you trying to say?" Rogoff asked her.

She looked at him. "Joan Sorenson was a cripple. She had no use of her legs, no sensation at all below the waist. So why bother to chain her ankles?"

Rogoff stared at her for a long moment, then shook his head. He looked over to Cooney. The coroner shrugged. "Yeah. So. An interesting point, but what does it mean?"

She had no answer for them. She looked away, back

at the bed, at the skinned, twisted, mutilated thing that had once been a pretty woman.

The photographer moved to a different angle, pressed his shutter. The flash went off again. The chain glittered in the light. Softly, Randi brushed a fingertip across the metal. She felt no heat. Only the cold, pale touch of silver.

The night was full of sounds and smells.

Willie had run wildly, blindly, a gray shadow streaking down black rain-slick streets, pushing himself harder and faster than he had ever pushed before, paying no attention to where he went, anywhere, nowhere, everywhere, just so it was far away from his apartment and the thing that waited there with death shining bright in its hand. He darted along grimy alleys, under loading docks, bounded over low chain-link fences. There was a cinder-block wall somewhere that almost stopped him, three leaps and he failed to clear it, but on the fourth try he got his front paws over the top, and his back legs kicked and scrabbled and pushed him over. He fell onto damp grass, rolled in the dirt, and then he was up and running again. The streets were almost empty of traffic, but as he streaked across one wide boulevard, a pick-up truck appeared out of nowhere, speeding, and caught him in its lights. The sudden glare startled him; he froze for a long instant in the center of the street, and saw shock and terror on the driver's face. A horn blared as the pick-up began to brake, went into a skid, and fishtailed across the divider.

323

By then Willie was gone.

He was moving through a residential section now, down quiet streets lined by neat two-story houses. Parked cars filled the narrow driveways, realtor's signs flapped in the wind, but the only lights were the streetlamps . . . and sometimes, when the clouds parted for a second, the pale circle of the moon. He caught the scent of dogs from some of the back yards, and from time to time he heard a wild, frenzied barking, and knew that they had smelled him too. Sometimes the barking woke owners and neighbors, and then lights would come on in the silent houses, and doors would open in the back yards, but by then Willie would be blocks away, still running.

Finally, when his legs were aching and his heart was thundering and his tongue lolled redly from his mouth, Willie crossed the railroad tracks, climbed a steep embankment, and came hard up against a ten-foot chain-link fence with barbed wire strung along the top. Beyond the fence was a wide, empty yard and a low brick building, windowless and vast, dark beneath the light of the moon. The smell of old blood was faint but unmistakable, and abruptly Willie knew where he was.

The old slaughterhouse. The pack, they'd called it, bankrupt and abandoned now for almost two years. He'd run a long way. At last he let himself stop and catch his breath. He was panting, and as he dropped to the ground by the fence, he began to shiver, cold despite his ragged coat of fur.

He was still wearing jockey shorts, Willie noticed after he'd rested a moment. He would have laughed, if he'd had the throat for it. He thought of the man in the pick-up and wondered what he'd thought when Willie appeared in his headlights, a gaunt gray specter in a pair of white briefs, with glowing eyes as red as the pits of hell.

Willie twisted himself around and caught the elastic in his jaws. He tore at them, growling low in his throat, and after a brief struggle managed to rip them away. He slung them aside and lowered himself to the damp ground, his legs resting on his paws, his mouth half-open, his eyes wary, watchful. He let himself rest. He could hear distant traffic, a dog barking wildly a half-mile away, could smell rust and mold, the stench of diesel fumes, the cold scent of metal. Under it all was the slaughterhouse smell, faded but not gone, lingering, whispering to him of blood and death. It woke things inside him that were better left sleeping, and Willie could feel the hunger churning in his gut.

He could not ignore it, not wholly, but tonight he had other concerns, fears that were more important than his hunger. Dawn was only a few hours away, and he had nowhere to go. He could not go home, not until he knew it was safe again, until he had taken steps to protect himself. Without keys and clothes and money, the agency was closed to him too. He had to go somewhere, trust someone.

He thought of Blackstone, thought of Jonathan Harmon sitting by his fire, of Steven's dead blue eyes and scarred hands, of the old tower jutting up like a rotten black stake. Jonathan might be able to protect him, Jonathan with his strong walls and his spiked fence and all his talk of blood and iron.

But when he saw Jonathan in his mind's eye, the long white hair, the gold wolf's head cane, the veined arthritic hands twisting and grasping, then the growl rose unbidden in Willie's throat, and he knew Blackstone was not the answer.

Joanie was dead, and he did not know the others well enough, hardly knew all their names, didn't want to know them better.

So, in the end, like it or not, there was only Randi.

Willie got to his feet, weary now, unsteady. The wind shifted, sweeping across the yards and the runs, whispering to him of blood until his nostrils quivered. Willie threw back his head and howled, a long shuddering lonely call that rose and fell and went out through the cold night air until the dogs began to bark for blocks around. Then, once again, he began to run.

Rogoff gave her a lift home. Dawn was just starting to break when he pulled his old black Ford up to the front of her six-flat. As she opened the door, he shifted into neutral and looked over at her. "I'm not going to insist right now," he said, "but it might be that I need to know the name of your client. Sleep on it. Maybe you'll decide to tell me."

"Maybe I can't," Randi said. "Attorney-client privilege, remember?"

Rogoff gave her a tired smile. "When you sent me to the courthouse, I had to look at your file too. You never went to law school."

"No?" She smiled back. "Well, I meant to. Doesn't

that count for something?" She shrugged. "I'll sleep on it, we can talk tomorrow." He got out, closed the door, moved away from the car. Rogoff shifted into drive, but Randi turned back before he could pull away. "Hey, Rogoff, you have a first name?"

"Mike," he said.

"See you tomorrow, Mike."

He nodded and pulled away just as the streetlamps began to go out. Randi walked up the stoop, fumbling for her key.

"*Randi!*"

She stopped, looked around. "Who's there?"

"Willie." The voice was louder this time. "Down here by the garbage cans."

Randi leaned over the stoop and saw him. He was crouched down low, surrounded by trash-bins, shivering in the morning chill. "You're naked," she said.

"Somebody tried to kill me last night. I made it out. My clothes didn't. I've been here an hour, not that I'm complaining mind you, but I think I have pneumonia and my balls are frozen solid. I'll never be able to have children now. Where the fuck have you been?"

"There was another murder. Same m.o."

Willie shook so violently that the garbage cans rattled together. "Jesus," he said, his voice gone weak. "Who?"

"Her name was Zoe Anders."

Willie flinched. "Fuck fuck fuck," he said. He looked back up at Randi. She could see the fear in his eyes, but he asked anyway. "What about Amy?"

"Her sister?" Randi said. He nodded. "In shock, but fine. She had a nightmare." She paused a moment. "So you knew Zoe too. Like Sorenson?"

"No. Not like Joanie." He looked at her wearily. "Can we go in?"

She nodded and opened the door. Willie looked so grateful she thought he was about to lick her hand.

The underwear was her ex-husband's, and it was too big. The pink bathrobe was Randi's, and it was too small. But the coffee was just right, and it was warm in here, and Willie felt bone-tired and nervous but glad to be alive, especially when Randi put the plate down in front of him. She'd scrambled the eggs up with cheddar cheese and onion and done up a rasher of bacon on the side, and it smelled like nirvana. He fell to eagerly.

"I think I've figured out something," she said. She sat down across from him.

"Good," he said. "The eggs, I mean. That is, whatever you figured out, that's good too, but Jesus, I *needed* these eggs. You wouldn't believe how hungry you get—" He stopped suddenly, stared down at the scrambled eggs, and reflected on what an idiot he was, but Randi hadn't noticed. Willie reached for a slice of bacon, bit off the end. "Crisp," he said. "Good."

"I'm going to tell you," Randi said, as if he hadn't spoken at all. "I've got to tell somebody, and you've known me long enough so I don't think you'll have me committed. You may laugh." She scowled at him. "If you laugh, you're back out in the street, minus the boxer shorts and the bathrobe."

"I won't laugh," Willie said. He didn't think he'd

have much difficulty not laughing. He felt rather apprehensive. He stopped eating.

Randi took a deep breath and looked him in the eye. She had very lovely eyes, Willie thought. "I think my father was killed by a werewolf," she said seriously, without blinking.

"Oh, Jesus," Willie said. He didn't laugh. A very large invisible anaconda wrapped itself around his chest and began to squeeze. "I," he said, "I, I, I." Nothing was coming in or out. He pushed back from the table, knocking over the chair, and ran for the bathroom. He locked himself in and turned on the shower full blast, twisting the hot tap all the way around. The bathroom began to fill up with steam. It wasn't nearly as good as a blast from his inhaler, but it did beat suffocating. By the time the steam was really going good, Willie was on his knees, gasping like a man trying to suck an elephant through a straw. Finally he began to breathe again.

He stayed on his knees for a long time, until the spray from the shower had soaked through his robe and his underwear and his face was flushed and red. Then he crawled across the tiled floor, turned off the shower, and got unsteadily to his feet. The mirror above the sink was all fogged up. Willie wiped it off with a towel and peered in at himself. He looked like shit. Wet shit. Hot wet shit. He felt worse. He tried to dry himself off, but the steam and the shower spray had gone everywhere and the towels were as damp as he was. He heard Randi moving around outside, opening and closing drawers. He wanted to go out and face her, but not like this. A man has to have some pride. For a moment he just wanted to be home in bed with his Primateen on the end table, until he remembered that his bedroom had been occupied the last time he'd been there.

"Are you ever coming out?" Randi asked.

"Yeah," Willie said, but it was so weak that he doubted she heard him. He straightened and adjusted the frilly pink robe. Underneath the undershirt looked as though he'd been competing in a wet tee-shirt contest. He sighed, unlocked the door, and exited. The cold air gave him goosepimples.

Randi was seated at the table again. Willie went back to his place. "Sorry," he said. "Asthma attack."

"I noticed," Randi replied. "Stress related, aren't they?"

"Sometimes."

"Finish your eggs," she urged. "They're getting cold."

"Yeah," Willie said, figuring he might as well, since it would give him something to do while he figured out what to tell her. He picked up his fork.

It was like the time he'd grabbed a dirty pot that had been sitting on top of his hotplate since the night before and realized too late that he'd never turned the hotplate off. Willie shrieked and the fork clattered to the table and bounced, once, twice, three times. It landed in front of Randi. He sucked on his fingers. They were already starting to turn red. Randi looked at him very calmly and picked up the fork. She held it, stroked it with her thumb, touched its prongs thoughtfully to her lip. "I brought out the good silver while you were in the bathroom," she said. "Solid sterling. It's been in the family for generations."

His fingers hurt like hell. "Oh, Jesus. You got any butter? Oleo, lard, I don't care, anything will . . ." He stopped when her hand went under the table and came out again holding a gun. From where Willie sat, it looked like a very big gun.

"Pay attention, Willie. Your fingers are the least of your worries. I realize you're in pain, so I'll give you a minute or two to collect your thoughts and try to tell me why I shouldn't blow off your fucking head right here and now." She cocked the hammer with her thumb.

Willie just stared at her. He looked pathetic, like a half-drowned puppy. For one terrible moment Randi thought he was going to have another asthma attack. She felt curiously calm, not angry or afraid or even nervous, but she didn't think she had it in her to shoot a man in the back as he ran for the bathroom, even if he was a werewolf.

Thankfully, Willie spared her that decision. "You don't want to shoot me," he said, with remarkable aplomb under the circumstances. "It's bad manners to shoot your friends. You'll make a hole in the bathrobe."

"I never liked that bathrobe anyway. I hate pink."

"If you're really so hot to kill me, you'd stand a better chance with the fork," Willie said.

"So you admit that you're a werewolf?"

"A lycanthrope," Willie corrected. He sucked at his burnt fingers again and looked at her sideways. "So sue me. It's a medical condition. I got allergies, I got asthma, I got a bad back, and I got lycanthropy, is it my fault? I didn't kill your father. I never killed anyone. I ate half a pit bull once, but can you blame me?" His voice turned querulous. "If you want to shoot me, go ahead and try. Since when do you carry a gun anyway? I thought all that shit about private eyes stuffing heat was strictly television?"

"The phrase is *packing* heat, and it is. I only bring mine out for special occasions. My father was carrying it when he died."

"Didn't do him much good, did it?" Willie said softly.

Randi considered that for a moment. "What would happen if I pulled the trigger?" The gun was getting heavy, but her hand was steady.

"I'd try to change. I don't think I'd make it, but I'd have to try. A couple bullets in the head at this range, while I'm still human, yeah, that'd probably do the job. But you don't want to miss and you *really* don't want to wound me. Once I'm changed, it's a whole different ballgame."

"My father emptied his gun on the night he was killed," Randi said thoughtfully.

Willie studied his hand and winced. "Oh fuck," he said. "I'm getting a blister."

Randi put the gun on the table and went to the kitchen to get him a stick of butter. He accepted it from her gratefully. She glanced toward the window as he treated his burns. "The sun's up," she said, "I thought werewolves only changed at night, during the full moon?"

"Lycanthropes," Willie said. He flexed his fingers, sighed. "That full moon shit was all invented by some screenwriter for Universal, go look at your literature, we change at will, day, night, full moon, new moon, makes no difference. Sometimes I *feel* more like changing during the full moon, some kind of hormonal thing, but more like getting horny than going on the rag, if you know what I mean." He grabbed his coffee. It was cold by now, but that didn't stop Willie from emptying the cup. "I shouldn't be telling you all this, fuck, Randi, I like you, you're a friend, I care about you, you should only forget this whole morning, believe me, it's healthier."

"Why?" she said bluntly. She wasn't about to forget anything. "What's going to happen to me if I don't? Are you going to rip my throat out? Should I forget Joanie Sorenson and Zoe Anders too? How about Roy Helander and all those missing kids? *Am I supposed to forget what happened to my father?*" She stopped for a moment, lowered her voice. "You came to me for help, Willie, and pardon, but you sure as hell look as though you still need it."

Willie looked at her across the table with a morose hangdog expression on his long face. "I don't know whether I want to kiss you or slap you," he finally admitted. "Shit, you're right, you know too much already." He stood up. "I got to get into my own clothes, this wet underwear is giving me pneumonia. Call a cab, we'll go check out my place, talk. You got a coat?"

"Take the Burberry," Randi said. "It's in the closet."

The coat was even bigger on him than it had been on Randi, but it beat the pink bathrobe. He looked almost human as he emerged from the closet, fussing with the belt. Randi was rummaging in the silver drawer. She found a large carving knife, the one her grandfather used to use on Thanksgiving, and slid it through the belt of her jeans. Willie looked at it nervously. "Good idea," he finally said, "but take the gun too."

The cab driver was the quiet type. The drive crosstown passed in awkward silence. Randi paid him while Willie climbed out to check the doors. It was a blustery overcast day, and the river looked gray and choppy as it slapped against the pier.

Willie kicked his front door in a fit of pique, and vanished down the alley. Randi waited by the pier and watched the cab drive off. A few minutes later Willie was back, looking disgusted. "This is ridiculous," he said. "The back door hasn't been opened in years, you'd need a hammer and chisel just to knock through the rust. The loading docks are bolted down and chained with the mother of all padlocks on the chains. And the front door . . . there's a spare set of keys in my car, but even if we got those, the police bar can only be lifted from inside. So how the hell did it get in, I ask you?"

Randi looked at the brewery's weathered brick walls appraisingly. They looked pretty solid to her, and the second floor windows were a good twenty feet off street level. She walked around the side to take a look down the alley. "There's a window broken," she said.

"That was me getting out," Willie said, "not my nocturnal caller getting in."

Randi had already figured out that much from the broken glass all over the cobblestones. "Right now I'm more concerned about how *we're* going to get in." She pointed. "If we move that dumpster a few feet to the left and climb on top, and you climb on my shoulders, I think you might be able to hoist yourself in."

Willie considered that. "What if it's still in there?"

"What?" Randi said.

"Whatever was after me last night. If I hadn't jumped through that window, it'd be me without a skin this morning, and believe me, I'm cold enough as is." He looked at the window, at the dumpster, and back at the window. "Fuck," he said, "we can't stand here all day. But I've got a better idea. Help me roll the dumpster away from the wall a little."

Randi didn't understand, but she did as Willie suggested. They left the dumpster in the center of the alley, directly opposite the broken window. Willie nodded and began unbelting the coat she'd lent him. "Turn around," he told her. "I don't want you freaking out. I've got to get naked and your carnal appetites might get the best of you."

Randi turned around. The temptation to glance over her shoulder was irresistible. She heard the coat fall to the ground. Then she heard something else . . . soft padding steps, like a dog. She turned. He'd circled all the way down to the end of the alley. Her ex-husband's old underwear lay puddled across the cobblestones atop the Burberry coat. Willie came streaking back toward the brewery, building speed. He was, Randi noticed, not a very prepossessing wolf. His fur was a dirty gray-brown color, kind of mangy, his rear looked too large and his legs too thin, and there was something ungainly about the way he ran. He put on a final burst of speed, leapt on top of the dumpster, bounded off the metal lid, and flew through the shattered window, breaking more glass as he went. Randi heard a loud *thump* from inside the bedroom.

She went around to the front. A few moments later, the locks began to unlock, one by one, and Willie opened the heavy steel door. He was wearing his own bathrobe, a red tartan flannel, and his hand was full of keys. "Come on," he said. "No sign of night visitors. I put on some water for tea."

"The fucker must have crawled out of the toilet," Willie said. "I don't see any other way he could have gotten in."

Randi stood in front of what remained of his bedroom door. She studied the shattered wood, ran her finger lightly across one long, jagged splinter, then knelt to look at the floor. "Whatever it was, it was strong. Look at these gouges in the wood, look at how sharp and clean they are. You don't do that with a fist. Claws, maybe. More likely some kind of knife. And take a look at this." She gestured toward the brass doorknob, which lay on the floor amidst a bunch of kindling.

Willie bent to pick it up.

"Don't touch," she said, grabbing his arm. "Just look."

He got down on one knee. At first he didn't notice anything. But when he leaned close, he saw how the brass was scored and scraped.

"Something sharp," Randi said, "and hard." She stood up. "When you first heard the sounds, what direction were they coming from?"

Willie thought for a moment. "It was hard to tell," he said. "Toward the back, I think."

Randi walked back. All along the hall, the doors were closed. She studied the banister at the top of the stairs, then moved on, and began opening and closing doors. "Come here," she said, at the fourth door.

Willie trotted down the hall. Randi had the door ajar. The knob on the hall side was fine; the knob on the inside displayed the same kind of scoring they'd seen on his bedroom door. Willie was aghast. "But this is the *men's room*," he said. "You mean it *did* come out of the toilet? I'll never shit again."

"It came out of this room," Randi said. "I don't know about the toilet." She went in and looked around. There wasn't much to look at. Two toilet stalls, two urinals, two sinks with a long mirror above them and antique brass soap dispensers beside the water taps, a paper towel dispenser, Willie's towels and toiletries. No window. Not even a small frosted-glass window. No window at all.

Down the hall the tea kettle began to whistle. Randi looked thoughtful as they walked back to the living room. "Joan Sorenson died behind a locked door, and the killer got to Zoe Anders without waking her sister right across the hall."

"The fucking thing can come and go as it pleases," Willie said. The idea gave him the creeps. He glanced around nervously as he got out the teabags, but there was nobody there but him and Randi.

"Except it can't," Randi said. "With Sorenson and Anders, there was no damage, no sign of a break-in,

337

nothing but a corpse. But with you, the killer was stopped by something as simple as a locked door."

"Not stopped," Willie said, "just slowed down a little." He repressed a shudder and brought the tea over to his coffee table.

"Did he get the right Anders sister?" she asked.

Willie stood there stupidly for a moment holding the kettle poised over the cups. "What do you mean?"

"You've got identical twins sharing the same house. Let's presume it's a house the killer's never visited before. Somehow he gains entry, and he chains, murders, and flays only *one* of them, without even waking the other." Randi smiled up at him sweetly. "You can't tell them apart by sight, he probably didn't know which room was which, so the question is, did he get the werewolf?"

It was nice to know that she wasn't infallible. "Yes," he said, "and no. They were twins, Randi. Both lycanthropes." She looked honestly surprised. "How did you know?" he asked her.

"Oh, the chains," she said negligently. Her mind was far away, gnawing at the puzzle. "Silver chains. She was burned wherever they'd touched her flesh. And Joan Sorenson was a werewolf too, of course. She was crippled, yes . . . but only as a human, not after her transformation. That's why her legs were chained, to hold her if she changed." She looked at Willie with a baffled expression on her face. "It doesn't make sense, to kill one and leave the other untouched. Are you sure that Amy Anders is a werewolf too?"

"A lycanthrope," he said. "Yes. Definitely. They were even harder to tell apart as wolves. At least when they were human they dressed differently. Amy liked white lace, frills, that kind of stuff, and Zoe was into leather." There was a cut-glass ashtray in the center of the coffee table filled with Willie's private party mix: aspirin, Allerest, and Tums. He took a handful of pills and swallowed them dry.

"Look, before we go on with this, I want one card on the table," Randi said.

For once he was ahead of her. "If I knew who killed your father, I'd tell you, but I don't, I was in the service, overseas. I vaguely remember something in the *Courier*, but to tell the truth I'd forgotten all about it until you threw it at me last night. What can I tell you?" He shrugged.

"Don't bullshit me, Willie. My father was killed by a werewolf. You're a werewolf. You must know something."

"Hey, try substituting *Jew* or *diabetic* or *bald man* for werewolf in that statement, and see how much sense it makes. I'm not saying you're wrong about your father because you're not, it fits, it all fits, everything from the condition of the body to the empty gun, but even if you buy that much, then you got to ask *which* werewolf."

"How many of you *are* there?" Randi asked incredulously.

"Damned if I know," Willie said. "What do you think, we get together for a lodge meeting every time the moon is full? The pure-bloods, hell, not many, the pack's been getting pretty thin these last few generations. But there's lots of mongrels like me, halfbreeds, quarter-breeds, what have you, the old families had their share of bastards. Some can work the change, some can't. I've heard of a few who change one day and never do manage to change back. And that's just from the old bloodlines, never mind the ones like Joanie."

"You mean Joanie was different?"

Willie gave her a reluctant nod. "You've seen the movies. You get bitten by a werewolf, you turn into a werewolf, that is assuming there's enough of you left to turn into anything except a cadaver." She nodded, and he went on. "Well, that part's true, or partly true, it doesn't happen as often as it once did. Guy gets bit nowadays, he runs to a doctor, gets the wound cleaned and treated with antiseptic, gets his rabies shots and his tetanus shots and his penicillin and fuck-all knows what else, and he's fine. The wonders of modern medicine."

Willie hesitated briefly, looking in her eyes, those lovely eyes, wondering if she'd understand, and finally he plunged ahead. "Joanie was such a good kid, it broke my heart to see her in that chair. One night she told me that the hardest thing of all was realizing that she'd never know what it felt like to make love. She'd been a virgin when they hit that truck. We'd had a few drinks, she was crying, and . . . well, I couldn't take it. I told her what I was and what I could do for her, she didn't believe a word of it, so I had to show her. I bit her leg, she couldn't feel a damned thing down there anyway, I bit her and I held the bite for a long time, worried it around good. Afterwards I nursed her myself. No doctors, no antiseptic, no rabies vaccine. We're talking major league infection here, there was a day or two when her fever was running so high I thought maybe I'd killed her, her leg had turned nearly black, you could see the stuff going up her veins. I got to admit it was pretty gross, I'm in no hurry to try it again, but it worked. The fever broke and Joanie changed."

"You weren't just friends," Randi said with certainty. "You were lovers."

"Yeah," he said. "As wolves. I guess I look sexier in fur. I couldn't even begin to keep up with her, though. Joanie was a pretty active wolf. We're talking almost every night here."

"As a human, she was still crippled," Randi said.

Willie nodded, held up his hand. "See." The burns were still there, and a blood blister had formed on his index finger. "Once or twice the change has saved my life, when my asthma got so bad I thought I was going to suffocate. That kind of thing doesn't cross over, but it's sure as hell waiting for you when you cross back. Sometimes you even get nasty surprises. Catch a bullet as a wolf and it's nothing, a sting and a slap, heals up right away, but you can pay for it when you change into human form, especially if you change too soon and the damn thing gets infected. And silver will burn the shit out of you no matter what form you're in. LBJ was my favorite president, just *loved* them cupro-nickel-sandwich quarters."

Randi stood up. "This is all a little overwhelming. Do you *like*—being a werewolf?"

"A lycanthrope." Willie shrugged. "I don't know, do you like being a woman? It's what I am."

Randi crossed the room and stared out his window at the river. "I'm very confused," she said. "I look at you and you're my friend Willie. I've known you for years. Only you're a werewolf too. I've been telling myself that werewolves don't exist since I was twelve, and now I find out the city is full of them. Only someone or something is killing them, flaying them. Should I care? Why should I care?" She ran a hand through her tangled hair. "We both know that Roy Helander didn't kill those kids. My father knew it too. He kept pressing, and one night he was lured to the stockyards and some kind of animal tore out his throat. Every time I think of that I think maybe I ought to find this werewolf killer and sign up to help him. Then I look at you again." She turned and looked at him. "And damn it, you're *still* my friend."

She looked as though she was going to cry. Willie had never seen her cry and he didn't want to. He hated it when they cried. "Remember when I first offered you a job, and you wouldn't take it, because you thought all collection agents were pricks?"

She nodded.

"Lycanthropes are skinchangers. We turn into wolves. Yeah, we're carnivores, you got it, you don't meet many vegetarians in the pack, but there's meat and there's meat. You won't find nearly as many rats around here as you will in other cities this size. What I'm saying is the skin may change, but what you do is still up to the person inside. So stop thinking about werewolves and werewolf-killers and start thinking about murderers, 'cause that's what we're talking about."

Randi crossed the room and sat back down. "I hate to admit it, but you're making sense."

"I'm good in bed too," Willie said with a grin.

The ghost of a smile crossed her face. "Fuck you."

"Exactly my suggestion. What kind of underwear are you wearing?"

342

"Never mind my underwear," she said. "Do you have any ideas about these murderers? Past *or* present?"

Sometimes Randi had a one track mind, Willie thought; unfortunately, it never seemed to be the track that led under the sheets. "Jonathan told me about an old legend," he said.

"Jonathan?" she said.

"Jonathan Harmon, yeah, that one, old blood and iron, the *Courier*, Blackstone, the pack, the founding family, all of it."

"Wait a minute. He's a were—a lycanthrope?"

Willie nodded. "Yeah, leader of the pack, he—"

Randi leapt ahead of him. "And it's hereditary?"

He saw where she was going. "Yes, but—"

"Steven Harmon is mentally disturbed," Randi interrupted. "His family keeps it out of the papers, but they can't stop the whispering. Violent episodes, strange doctors coming and going at Blackstone, shock treatments. He's some kind of pain freak, isn't he?"

Willie sighed. "Yeah. Ever see his hands? The palms and fingers are covered with silver burns. Once I saw him close his hands around a silver cartwheel and hold it there until smoke started to come out between his fingers. It burned a big round hole right in the center of his palm." He shuddered. "Yeah, Steven's a freak all right, and he's strong enough to rip your arm out of your socket and beat you to death with it, but he didn't kill your father, he couldn't have."

"Says you," she said.

"He didn't kill Joanie or Zoe either. They weren't just murdered, Randi. They were skinned. That's where the legend comes in. The word is *skinchangers*, remember?

343

What if the power was *in* the skin? So you catch a werewolf, flay it, slip into the bloody skin . . . and change."

Randi was staring at him with a sick look on her face. "Does it really work that way?"

"Someone thinks so."

"Who?"

"Someone who's been thinking about werewolves for a long time. Someone's who gone way past obsession into full-fledged psychopathy. Someone who thinks he saw a werewolf once, who thinks werewolves done him wrong, who hates them, wants to hurt them, wants revenge . . . but maybe also, down deep, someone who wants to know what's it like."

"Roy Helander," she said.

"Maybe if we could find this damned secret hideout in the woods, we'd know for sure."

Randi stood up. "I racked my brains for hours. We could poke around a few of the city parks some, but I'm not sanguine on our prospects. No. I want to know more about these legends, and I want to look at Steven with my own eyes. Get your car, Willie. We're going to pay a visit to Blackstone."

He'd been afraid she was going to say something like that. He reached out and grabbed another handful of his party mix. "Oh, Jesus," he said, crunching down on a mouthful of pills. "This isn't the Addams Family, you know. Jonathan is for real."

"So am I," said Randi, and Willie knew the cause was lost.

It was raining again by the time they reached Courier Square. Willie waited in the car while Randi went inside the gunsmith's. Twenty minutes later, when she came back out, she found him snoring behind the wheel. At least he'd had the sense to lock the doors of his mammoth old Cadillac. She tapped on the glass, and he sat right up and stared at her for a moment without recognition. Then he woke up, leaned over, and unlocked the door on the passenger side. Randi slid beside him.

"How'd it go?"

"They don't get much call for silver bullets, but they know someone upstate who does custom work for collectors," Randi said in a disgusted tone of voice.

"You don't sound too happy about it."

"I'm not. You wouldn't believe what they're going to charge me for a box of silver bullets, never mind that it's going to take two weeks. It was going to take a month, but I raised the ante." She looked glumly out the rain-streaked window. A torrent of gray water rushed down the gutter, carrying its flotilla of cigarette butts and scraps of yesterday's newspaper.

"Two weeks?" Willie turned the ignition and put the barge in gear. "Hell, we'll both probably be dead in two weeks. Just as well, the whole idea of silver bullets makes me nervous."

They crossed the square, past the Castle marquee and the Courier Building, and headed up Central, the windshield wipers clicking back and forth rhythmically. Willie hung a left on 13th and headed toward the bluff while Randi took out her father's revolver, opened the cylinder, and checked to see that it was fully loaded. Willie watched her out of the corner of his eye as he drove. "Waste of time," he said. "Guns don't kill werewolves, werewolves kill werewolves."

"Lycanthropes," Randi reminded him.

He grinned and for a moment looked almost like the man she'd shared an office with, a long time ago.

Both of them grew visibly more intense as they drove down 13th, the Caddy's big wheels splashing through the puddles. They were still a block away when she saw the little car crawling down the bluff, white against the dark stone. A moment later, she saw the lights, flashing red-and-blue.

Willie saw them too. He slammed on the brakes, lost traction, and had to steer wildly to avoid slamming into a parked car as he fishtailed. His forehead was beading with sweat when he finally brought the car to a stop, and Randi didn't think it was from the near-collision. "Oh, Jesus," he said, "oh, Jesus, not Harmon too, I don't *believe* it." He began to wheeze, and fumbled in his pocket for an inhaler.

"Wait here, I'll check it out," Randi told him. She got out, turned up the collar of her coat, and walked the rest of the way, to where 13th dead-ended flush against the bluff. The coroner's wagon was parked amidst three police cruisers. Randi arrived at the same time as the cable car. Rogoff was the first one out. Behind him she saw Cooney, the police photographer, and two uniforms carrying a bodybag. It must have gotten pretty crowded on the way down.

"You." Rogoff seemed surprised to see her. Strands of black hair were plastered to his forehead by the rain.

"Me," Randi agreed. The plastic of the bodybag was slick and wet, and the uniforms were having trouble with it. One of them lost his footing as he stepped down, and Randi thought she saw something shift inside the bag. "It doesn't fit the pattern," she said to Rogoff. "The other killings have all been at night."

Rogoff took her by the arm and drew her away, gently but firmly. "You don't want to look at this one, Randi."

There was something in his tone that made her look at him hard. "Why not? It can't be any worse than Zoe Anders, can it? Who's in the bag, Rogoff? The father or the son?"

"Neither one," he said. He glanced back behind them, up toward the top of the bluff, and Randi found herself following his gaze. Nothing was visible of Blackstone but the high wrought-iron fence that surrounded the estate. "This time his luck ran out on him. The dogs got to him first. Cooney says the scent of blood off of . . . of what he was wearing . . . well, it must have driven them wild. They tore him to pieces, Randi." He put his hand on her shoulder, as if to comfort her.

"No," Randi said. She felt numb, dazed.

"Yes," he insisted. "It's over. And believe me, it's not something you want to see."

She backed away from him. They were loading the body in the rear of the coroner's wagon while Sylvia Cooney supervised the operation, smoking her cigar in the rain. Rogoff tried to touch her again, but she whirled away from him, and ran to the wagon. "Hey!" Cooney said.

The body was on the tailgate, half-in and half-out of the wagon. Randi reached for the zipper on the body bag. One of the cops grabbed her arm. She shoved him aside and unzipped the bag. His face was half gone. His right cheek and ear and part of his jaw had been torn away, devoured right down the bone. What features he had left were obscured by blood.

Someone tried to pull her away from the tailgate. She spun and kicked him in the balls, then turned back to the body and grabbed it under the arms and pulled. The inside of the body bag was slick with blood. The corpse slid loose of the plastic sheath like a banana squirting out of its skin and fell into the street. Rain washed down over it, and the runoff in the gutter turned pink, then red. A hand, or part of a hand, fell out of the bag almost like an afterthought. Most of the arm was gone, and Randi could see bones peeking through, and places where huge hunks of flesh had been torn out of his thigh, shoulder, and torso. He was naked, but between his legs was nothing but a raw red wound where his genitalia had been.

Something was fastened around his neck, and knotted beneath his chin. Randi leaned forward to touch it, and drew back when she saw his face. The rain had washed it clean. He had one eye left, a green eye, open and staring. The rain pooled in the socket and ran down his cheek. Roy had grown gaunt to the point of emaciation, with a week's growth of beard, but his long hair was still the same color, the color he'd shared with all his brothers and sisters, that muddy Helander blonde.

Something was knotted under his chin, a long twisted cloak of some kind, it had gotten all tangled when he fell. Randi was trying to straighten it when they caught her by both arms and dragged her away bodily. "No," she said wildly. "What was he wearing? What was he wearing, damn you! I have to see!" No one answered.

Rogoff had her right arm prisoned in a grip that felt like steel. She fought him wildly, kicking and shouting, but he held her until the hysteria had passed, and then held her some more as she leaned against his chest, sobbing.

She didn't quite know when Willie had come up, but suddenly there he was. He took her away from Rogoff and led her back to his Cadillac, and they sat inside, silent, as first the coroner's wagon and then the police cruisers drove off one by one. She was covered with blood. Willie gave her some aspirin from a bottle he kept in his glove compartment. She tried to swallow it, but her throat was raw, and she wound up gagging it back up. "It's all right," he told her, over and over. "It wasn't your father, Randi. Listen to me, please, it *wasn't your father!*"

"It was Roy Helander," Randi said to him at last. "And he was wearing Joanie's skin."

Willie drove her home; she was in no shape to confront Jonathan Harmon or anybody. She'd calmed down, but the hysteria was still there, just under the surface, he could see it in the eyes, hear it in her voice. If that wasn't enough, she kept telling him the same thing, over and over. "It was Roy Helander," she'd say, like he didn't know, "and he was wearing Joanie's skin."

Willie found her keys and helped her upstairs to her apartment. Inside, he made her take a couple of sleeping pills from the all-purpose pharmaceutical in his glove box, then turned down the bed and undressed her. He figured if anything would snap her back to herself, it would be his fingers on the buttons of her blouse, but she just smiled at him, vacant and dreamy, and told him that it was Roy Helander and he was wearing Joanie's skin. The big silver knife jammed through her belt loops gave him pause. He finally unzipped her fly, undid her buckle, and yanked off the jeans, knife and all. She didn't wear panties. He'd always suspected as much.

When Randi was finally in bed asleep, Willie went back to her bathroom and threw up.

Afterward he made himself a gin-and-tonic to wash the taste of vomit out of his mouth, and went and sat alone in her living room in one of her red velvet chairs. He'd had even less sleep than Randi these past few nights, and he felt as though he might drift off at any moment, but he knew somehow that it was important not to. It was Roy Helander and he was wearing Joanie's skin. So it was over, he was safe.

He remembered the way his door shook last night, a solid wood door, and it split like so much cheap panelling. Behind it was something dark and powerful, something that left scars on brass doorknobs and showed up in places it had no right to be. Willie didn't know what had been on the other side of his door, but somehow he didn't think that the gaunt, wasted, half-eaten travesty of a man he'd seen on 13th Street quite fit the bill. He'd believe that his nocturnal visitor had been Roy Helander, with or without Joanie's skin, about the same time he'd believe that the man had been eaten by dogs. *Dogs!* How long did Jonathan expect to get away with that shit? Still, he couldn't blame him, not with Zoe and Joanie dead, and Helander trying to sneak into Blackstone dressed in a human skin.

*. . . there are things that hunt the hunters.*

Willie picked up the phone and dialed Blackstone.

"Hello." The voice was flat, affectless, the voice of someone who cared about nothing and no one, not even himself.

"Hello, Steven," Willie said quietly. He was about to ask for Jonathan when a strange sort of madness took hold of him, and he heard himself say, "Did you watch? Did you see what Jonathan did to him, Steven? Did it get you off?"

The silence on the other end of the line went on for ages. Sometimes Steven Harmon simply forgot how to talk. But not this time. "Jonathan didn't do him. I did. It was easy. I could smell him coming through the woods. He never even saw me. I came around behind him and pinned him down and bit off his ear. He wasn't very strong at all. After a while he changed into a man, and then he was all slippery, but it didn't matter, I—"

Someone took the phone away. "Hello, who is this" Jonathan's voice said from the receiver.

Willie hung up. He could always call back later. Let Jonathan sweat awhile, wondering who it had been on the other end of the line. "After a while he changed into a man," Willie repeated aloud. Steven did it himself. Steven couldn't do it himself. Could he? "Oh Jesus," Willie said.


Somewhere far away, a phone was ringing.

Randi rolled over in her bed. "Joanie's skin," she muttered groggily in low, half-intelligible syllables. She was naked, with the blankets tangled around her. The room was pitch dark. The phone rang again. She sat up, a sheet curled around her neck. The room was cold, and her head pounded. She ripped loose the sheet, threw it aside. Why was she naked? What the hell was going on? The phone rang again and her machine cut in. "This is AAA-Wade Investigations, Randi Wade speaking. I can't talk right now, but you can leave a message at the tone, and I'll get back to you."

Randi reached out and speared the phone just in time for the *beep* to sound in her ear. She winced. "It's me," she said. "I'm here. What time is it? Who's this?"

"Randi, are you all right? It's Uncle Joe." Joe Urquhart's gruff voice was a welcome relief. "Rogoff told me what happened, and I was very concerned about you. I've been trying to reach you for hours."

"Hours?" She looked at the clock. It was past midnight. "I've been asleep. I think." The last she remembered, it had been daylight and she and Willie had been driving down 13th on their way to Blackstone to . . .

*It was Roy Helander and he was wearing Joanie's skin.*

"Randi, what's wrong? You sure you're okay? You sound wretched. Damn it, *say* something."

"I'm here," she said. She pushed hair back out of her eyes. Someone had opened her window, and the air was frigid on her bare skin. "I'm fine," she said. "I just . . . I was asleep. It shook me up, that's all. I'll be fine."

"If you say so." Urquhart sounded dubious.

Willie must have brought her home and put her to bed, she thought. So where was he? She couldn't imagine that he'd just dump her and then take off, that wasn't like Willie.

"Pay attention," Urquhart said gruffly. "Have you heard a word I've said?"

She hadn't. "I'm sorry. I'm just . . . disoriented, that's all. It's been a strange day."

"I need to see you," Urquhart said. His voice had taken on a sudden urgency. "Right away. I've been going over the reports on Roy Helander and his victims. There's something out of place, something disturbing. And the more I look at these case files and Cooney's autopsy report, the more I keep thinking about Frank, about what happened that night." He hesitated. "I don't know how to say this. All these years . . . I only wanted the best for you, but I wasn't . . . wasn't completely honest with you."

"Tell me," she said. Suddenly she was a lot more awake.

"Not over the phone. I need to see you face to face, to show it to you. I'll swing by and get you. Can you be ready in fifteen minutes?"

"Ten," Randi said.

She hung up, hopped out of bed and opened the bedroom door. "Willie?" she called out. There was no answer. "Willie!" she repeated more loudly. Nothing. She turned on the lights, padded barefoot down the hall, expecting to find him snoring away on her sofa. But the living room was empty.

Her hands were sandpaper dry, and when she looked down she saw that they were covered with old blood. Her stomach heaved. She found the clothes she'd been wearing in a heap on the bedroom floor. They were brown and crusty with dried blood as well. Randi started the shower, and stood under the water for a good five minutes, running it so hot that it burned the way that silver fork must have burned in Willie's hand. The blood washed off, the water turning faintly pink as it whirled away and down. She toweled off thoroughly, and found a warm flannel shirt and a fresh pair of jeans. She didn't bother with her hair; the rain would wet it down again soon enough. But she made a point of finding her father's gun and sliding the long silver carving knife through the belt loop of her jeans.

As she bent to pick up the knife, Randi saw the square of white paper on the floor by her end table. She must have knocked it off when she'd reached for the phone.

She picked it up, opened it. It was covered with Willie's familiar scrawl, a page of hurried, dense scribbling. *I got to go, you're in no condition*, it began. *Don't go anywhere or talk to anyone. Roy Helander wasn't sneaking in to kill Harmon, I finally figured it out. The damned Harmon family secret that's no secret at all, I should have twigged, Steven—*

That was as far as she'd gotten when the doorbell rang.

Willie hugged the ground two-thirds of the way up the bluff, the rain coming down around him and his heart pounding in his chest as he clung to the tracks. Somehow the grade didn't seem nearly as steep when you were riding the cable car as it did now. He glanced behind him, and saw 13th Street far below. It made him dizzy. He wouldn't even have gotten this far if it hadn't been for the tracks. Where the slope grew almost vertical, he'd been able to scrabble up from tie to tie, using them like rungs on a ladder. His hands were full of splinters, but it beat trying to crawl up the wet rock, clinging to ferns for dear life.

Of course, he could have changed, and bounded up the tracks in no time at all. But somehow he didn't think that would have been such a good idea. *I could smell him coming*, Steven had said. The human scent was fainter, in a city full of people. He had to hope that Steven and Jonathan were inside the New House, locked up for the night. But if they were out prowling around, at least this way Willie thought he had a ghost of a chance.

He'd rested long enough. He craned his head back, looking up at the high black iron fence that ran along the top of the bluff, trying to measure how much further he had to go. Then he took a good long shot off his inhaler, gritted his teeth, and scrambled for the next tie up.

The windshield wipers swept back and forth almost silently as the long dark car nosed through the night. The windows were tinted a gray so dark it was almost black. Urquhart was in civvies, a red-and-black lumber-jack shirt, dark woolen slacks, and bulky down jacket. His police cap was his only concession to uniform. He stared straight out into the darkness as he drove. "You look terrible," she told him.

"I feel worse." They swept under an overpass and around a long ramp onto the river road. "I feel old, Randi. Like this city. This whole damn city is old and rotten."

"Where are we going?" she asked him. At this hour of night, there was no other traffic on the road. The river was a black emptiness off to their left. Streetlamps swam in haloes of rain to the right as they sailed past block after cold, empty block stretching away toward the bluffs.

"To the pack," Urquhart said. "To where it happened."

The car's heater was pouring out a steady blast of warm air, but suddenly Randi felt deathly cold. Her hand went inside her coat, and closed around the hilt of the knife. The silver felt comfortable and comforting. "All right," she said. She slid the knife out of her belt and put it on the seat between them.

Urquhart glanced over. She watched him carefully. "What's that?" he said.

"Silver," Randi said. "Pick it up."

He looked at her. "What?"

"You heard me," she said. "Pick it up."

He looked at the road, at her face, back out at the road. He made no move to touch the knife.

"I'm not kidding," Randi said. She slid away from him, to the far side of the seat, and braced her back against the door. When Urquhart looked over again, she had the gun out, aimed right between his eyes. "Pick it up," she said very clearly.

The color left his face. He started to say something, but Randi shook her head curtly. Urquhart licked his lips, took his hand off the wheel, and picked up the knife. "There," he said, holding it up awkwardly while he drove with one hand. "I picked it up. Now what am I supposed to do with it?"

Randi slumped back against the seat. "Put it down," she said with relief.

Joe looked at her.


He rested for a long time in the shrubs on top of the bluff, listening to the rain fall around him and dreading what other sounds he might hear. He kept imagining soft footfalls stealing up behind him, and once he thought he heard a low growl somewhere off to his right. He could feel his hackles rise, and until that moment he hadn't even known he *had* hackles, but it was nothing, just his nerves working on him, Willie had always had bad nerves. The night was cold and black and empty.

When he finally had his breath back, Willie began to edge past the New House, keeping to the bushes as much as he could, well away from the windows. There were a few lights on, but no other sign of life. Maybe they'd all gone to bed. He hoped so.

He moved slowly and carefully, trying to be as quiet as possible. He watched where his feet came down, and every few steps he'd stop, look around, listen. He could change in an instant if he heard anyone . . . or any*thing* . . . coming toward him. He didn't know how much good that would do, but maybe, just maybe, it would give him a chance.

His raincoat dragged at him, a water-logged second skin as heavy as lead. His shoes had soaked through, and the leather squished when he moved. Willie pushed away from the house, further back into the trees, until a bend in the road hid the lights from view. Only then, after a careful glance in both directions to make sure nothing was coming, did he dare risk a dash across the road.

Once across he plunged deeper into the woods, moving faster now, a little more heedless. He wondered where Roy Helander had been when Steven had caught him. Somewhere around here, Willie thought, somewhere in this dark primal forest, surrounded by old growth, with centuries of leaves and moss and dead things rotting in the earth beneath his feet.

As he moved away from the bluff and the city, the forest grew denser, until finally the trees pressed so close together that he lost sight of the sky, and the raindrops stopped pounding against his head. It was almost dry here. Overhead, the rain drummed relentlessly against a canopy of leaves. Willie's skin felt clammy, and for a moment he was lost, as if he'd wandered into some terrible cavern far below the earth, a dismal cold place where no light ever shone.

Then he stumbled between two huge, twisted old oaks, and felt air and rain against his face again, and raised his head, and there it was ahead of him, broken windows gaping down like so many blind eyes from walls carved from rock that shone like midnight and drank all light and hope. The tower loomed up to his right, some monstrous erection against the stormclouds, leaning crazily.

Willie stopped breathing, groped for his inhaler, found it, dropped it, picked it up. The mouthpiece was slimy with humus. He cleaned it on his sleeve, shoved it in his mouth, took a hit, two, three, and finally his throat opened up again.

He glanced around, heard only the rain, saw nothing.

He stepped forward toward the tower. Toward Roy Helander's secret refuge.

The big double gate in the high chain-link fence had been padlocked for two years, but it was open tonight, and Urquhart drove straight through. Randi wondered if the gate had been opened for her father as well. She thought maybe it had.

Joe pulled up near one of the loading docks, in the shadow of the old brick slaughterhouse. The building gave them some shelter from the rain, but Randi still trembled in the cold as she climbed out. "Here?" she asked. "This is where you found him?"

Urquhart was staring off into the stockyard. It was a huge area, subdivided into a dozen pens along the railroad siding. There was a maze of chest-high fencing they called the "runs" between the slaughterhouse and the pens, to force the cows into a single line and herd them along inside, where a man in a blood-splattered apron waited with a hammer in his hand. "Here," Joe said, without looking back at her.

There was a long silence. Somewhere far off, Randi thought she heard a faint, wild howl, but maybe that was just the wind and the rain. "Do you believe in ghosts?" she asked Joe.

"Ghosts?" The chief sounded distracted.

She shivered. "It's like . . . I can feel him, Joe. Like he's still here, after all this time, still watching over me."

Joe Urquhart turned toward her. His face was wet with rain, or maybe tears. "I watched over you," he said.

"He asked me to watch over you, and I did, I did my best."

Randi heard a sound somewhere off in the night. She turned her head, frowning, listening. Tires crunched across gravel and she saw headlights outside the fence. Another car coming.

"You and your father, you're a lot alike," Joe said wearily. "Stubborn. Won't listen to nobody. I took good care of you, didn't I take good care of you? I got my own kids, you know, but you never wanted nothing, did you? So why the hell didn't you listen to me?"

By then Randi knew. She wasn't surprised. Somehow she felt as though she'd known for a long time. "There was only one phone call that night," she said. "You were the one who phoned for back-up, not Dad."

Urquhart nodded. He was caught for a moment in the headlights of the on-coming car, and Randi saw the way his jaw trembled as he worked to get out the words. "Look in the glove box," he said.

Randi opened the car door, sat on the edge of the seat, and did as he said. The glove compartment was unlocked. Inside was a bottle of aspirin, a tire pressure gauge, some maps, and a box of cartridges. Randi opened the box and poured some bullets out into her palm. They glimmered pale and cold in the car's faint dome light. She left the box on the seat, climbed out, kicked the door shut. "My silver bullets," she said. "I hadn't expected them quite so soon."

"Those are the ones Frank ordered made up, eighteen years ago," Joe said. "After he was buried, I went by the gunsmith and picked them up. Like I said, you and him, you were a lot alike."

The second car pulled to a stop, pinning her in its high beams. Randi threw a hand across her eyes against the glare. She heard a car door opening and closing.

Urquhart's voice was anguished. "I told you to stay away from this thing, damn it. I *told* you! Don't you understand? They *own* this city!"

"He's right. You should have listened," Rogoff said, as he stepped into the light.

Willie groped his way down the long dark hall with one hand on the wall, placing each foot carefully in front of the last. The stone was so thick that even the sound of the rain did not reach him. There was only the echo of his careful footsteps, and the rush of blood inside his ears. The silence within the Old House was profound and unnerving, and there was something about the walls that bothered him as well. It was cold, but the stones under his fingers were moist and curiously warm to the touch, and Willie was glad for the darkness.

Finally he reached the base of the tower, where shafts of dim light fell across crabbed, narrow stone steps that spiraled up and up and up. Willie began to climb. He counted the steps at first, but somewhere around two hundred he lost the count, and the rest was a grim ordeal that he endured in silence. More than once he thought of changing. He resisted the impulse.

His legs ached from the effort when he reached the top. He sat down on the steps for a moment, his back to a slick stone wall. He was breathing hard, but when he groped for his inhaler, it was gone. He'd probably lost it in the woods. He could feel his lungs constricting in panic, but there was no help for it.

Willie got up.

The room smelled of blood and urine and something else, a scent he did not place, but somehow it made him tremble. There was no roof. Willie realized that the rain had stopped while he'd been inside. He looked up as the clouds parted, and a pale white moon stared down.

And all around other moons shimmered into life, reflected in the tall empty mirrors that lined the chamber. They reflected the sky above and each other, moon after moon after moon, until the room swam in silvered moonlight and reflections of reflections of reflections.

Willie turned around in a slow circle and a dozen other Willies turned with him. The moon-struck mirrors were streaked with dried blood, and above them a ring of cruel iron hooks curved up from the stone walls. A human skin hung from one of them, twisting slowly in some wind he could not feel, and as the moonlight hit it seemed to writhe and change, from woman to wolf to woman, both and neither.

That was when Willie heard the footsteps on the stairs.

"The silver bullets were a bad idea," Rogoff said. "We have a local ordinance here. The police get immediate notice any time someone places an order for custom ammunition. Your father made the same mistake. The pack takes a dim view of silver bullets."

Randi felt strangely relieved. For a moment she'd

been afraid that Willie had betrayed her, that he'd been one of them after all, and that thought had been like poison in her soul. Her fingers were still curled tight around a dozen of the bullets. She glanced down at them, so close and yet so far.

"Even if they're still good, you'll never get them loaded in time," Rogoff said.

"You don't need the bullets," Urquhart told her. "He just wants to talk. They promised me, honey, no one needs to get hurt."

Randi opened her hand. The bullets fell to the ground. She turned to Joe Urquhart. "You were my father's best friend. He said you had more guts than any man he ever knew."

"They don't give you any choice," Urquhart said. "I had kids of my own. They said if Roy Helander took the fall, no more kids would vanish, they promised they'd take care of it, but if we kept pressing, one of my kids would be the next to go. That's how it works in this town. Everything would have been all right, but Frank just wouldn't let it alone."

"We only kill in self-defense," Rogoff said. "There's a sweetness to human flesh, yes, a power that's undeniable, but it's not worth the risk."

"What about the children?" Randi said. "Did you kill them in self-defense too?"

"That was a long time ago," Rogoff said.

Joe stood with his head downcast. He was beaten, Randi saw, and she realized that he'd been beaten for a long time. All those trophies on his walls, but somehow she knew that he had given up hunting forever on the night her father died. "It was his son," Joe muttered quietly, in a voice full of shame. "Steven's never been right in the head, everyone knows that, he was the one who killed the kids, *ate* them. It was horrible, Harmon told me so himself, but he still wasn't going to let us have Steven. He said he'd . . . he'd control Steven's . . . appetites . . . if we closed the case. He was good as his word too, he put Steven on medication, and it stopped, the murders stopped."

She ought to hate Joe Urquhart, she realized, but instead she pitied him. After all this time, he still didn't understand. "Joe, he lied. It was never Steven."

"It was Steven," Joe insisted, "it had to be, he's insane. The rest of them . . . you can do business with them, Randi, listen to me now, you can talk to them."

"Like you did," she said. "Like Barry Schumacher."

Urquhart nodded. "That's right. They're just like us, they got some crazies, but not all of them are bad. You can't blame them for taking care of their own, we do the same thing, don't we? Look at Mike here, he's a good cop."

"A good cop who's going to change into a wolf in a minute or two and tear out my throat," Randi said.

"Randi, honey, listen to me," Urquhart said. "It doesn't have to be like that. You can walk out of here, just say the word. I'll get you onto the force, you can work with us, help us to . . . to keep the peace. Your father's dead, you won't bring him back, and the Helander boy, he deserved what he got, he was *killing* them, skinning them alive, it was self-defense. Steven is sick, he's always been sick—"

Rogoff was watching her from beneath his tangle of black hair. "He still doesn't get it," she said. She turned back to Joe. "Steven is sicker than you think. Something is missing. Too inbred, maybe. Think about it. Anders and Rochmonts, Flambeauxes and Harmons, the four great founding families, all werewolves, marrying each other generation after generation to keep the lines pure, for how many centuries? They kept the lines pure all right. They bred themselves Steven. He didn't kill those children. Roy Helander saw a *wolf* carry off his sister, and Steven can't change into a wolf. He got the blood-lust, he got inhuman strength, he burns at the touch of silver, but that's all. The last of the purebloods *can't work the change!*"

"She's right," Rogoff said quietly.

"Why do you think you never found any remains?" Randi put in. "Steven didn't kill those kids. His father carried them off, up to Blackstone."

"The old man had some crazy idea that if Steven ate enough human flesh, it might fix him, make him whole," Rogoff said.

"It didn't work," Randi said. She took Willie's note out of her pocket, let the pages flutter to the ground. It was all there. She finished reading it before she'd gone down to meet Joe. Frank Wade's little girl was nobody's fool.

"It didn't work," Rogoff echoed, "but by then Jonathan had got the taste. Once you get started, it's hard to stop." He looked at Randi for a long time, as if he were weighing something. Then he began . . .

. . . to change. Sweet cold air filled his lungs, and his muscles and bones ran with fire as the transformation took hold. He'd shrugged out of pants and coat, and he heard the rest of his clothing ripping apart as his body writhed, his flesh ran like hot wax, and he reformed, born anew.

Now he could see and hear and smell. The tower room shimmered with moonlight, every detail clear and sharp as noon, and the night was alive with sound, the wind and the rain and the rustle of bats in the forest around them, and traffic sounds and sirens from the city beyond. He was alive and full of power, and something was coming up the steps. It climbed slowly, untiring, and its smells filled the air. The scent of blood hung all around it, and beneath he sensed an aftershave that masked an unwashed body, sweat and dried semen on its skin, a heavy tang of wood smoke in its hair, and under it all the scent of sickness, sweetly rotten as a grave.

Willie backed all the way across the room, staring at the arched door, the growl rising in his throat. He bared long yellowed teeth, and slaver ran between them.

Steven stopped in the doorway and looked at him. He was naked. The wolf's hot red eyes met his cold blue ones, and it was hard to tell which were more inhuman. For a moment Willie thought that Steven didn't quite comprehend. Until he smiled, and reached for the skin that twisted above him, on an iron hook.

Willie leapt.

He took Steven high in the back and bore him down, with his hand still clutched around Zoe's skin. For a second Willie had a clear shot at his throat, but he hesitated and the moment passed. Steven caught Willie's foreleg in a pale scarred fist, and snapped it in half like a normal man might break a stick. The pain was excruciating. Then Steven was lifting him, flinging him away. He smashed up hard against one of the mirrors, and felt it shatter at the impact. Jagged shards of glass flew like knives, and one of them lanced through his side.

Willie rolled away, the glass spear broke under him, and he whimpered. Across the room, Steven was getting to his feet. He put out a hand to steady himself.

Willie scrambled up. His broken leg was knitting already, though it hurt when he put his weight on it. Glass fragments clawed inside him with every step. He could barely move. Some fucking werewolf he turned out to be.

Steven was adjusting his ghastly cloak, pulling flaps of skin down over his own face. The skin trade, Willie thought giddily, yeah, that was it, and in a moment Steven would use that damn flayed skin to do what he could never manage on his own, he would *change*, and then Willie would be meat.

Willie came at him, jaws gaping, but too slow. Steven's foot pistoned down, caught him hard enough to take his breath away, pinned him to the floor. Willie tried to squirm free, but Steven was too strong. He was bearing down, crushing him. All of a sudden Willie remembered that dog, so many years ago.

Willie bent himself almost double and took a bite out of the back of Steven's calf.

The blood filled his mouth, exploding inside him. Steven reeled back. Willie jumped up, darted forward, bit him again. This time he sank his teeth in good and held, worrying at the flesh. The pounding in his head was thunderous. He was full of power, he could feel it swelling within him. Suddenly he knew that he could tear Steven apart, he could taste the fine sweet flesh close to the bone, could hear the music of his screams, could imagine the way it would feel when he held him in his jaws and shook him like a rag doll and felt the life go out of him in a sudden giddy rush. It swept over him, and Willie bit and bit and bit again, ripping away chunks of meat, drunk on blood.

And then, dimly, he heard Steven screaming, screaming in a high shrill thin voice, a little boy's voice. "No, daddy," he was whining, over and over again. "No, please, don't bite me, daddy, don't bite me any more."

Willie let him go and backed away.

Steven sat on the floor, sobbing. He was bleeding like a sonofabitch. Pieces were missing from thigh, calf, shoulder, and foot. His legs were drenched in blood. Three fingers were gone off his right hand. His cheeks were slimy with gore.

Suddenly Willie was scared.

For a moment he didn't understand. Steven was beaten, he could see that, he could rip out his throat or let him live, it didn't matter, it was over. But something was wrong, something was terribly, sickeningly wrong. It felt as though the temperature had dropped a hundred degrees, and every hair on his body was prickling and standing on end. What the hell was going on? He growled low in his throat and backed away, toward the door, keeping a careful eye on Steven.

Steven giggled. "You'll get it now," he said. "You called it. You got blood on the mirrors. You called it back again."

The room seemed to spin. Moonlight ran from mirror to mirror to mirror, dizzyingly. Or maybe it wasn't moonlight.

Willie looked into the mirrors.

The reflections were gone. Willie, Steven, the moon, all gone. There was blood on the mirrors and they were full of fog, a silvery pale fog that shimmered as it moved.

Something was moving through the fog, sliding from mirror to mirror to mirror, around and around. Something hungry that wanted to get out.

He saw it, lost it, saw it again. It was in front of him, behind him, off to the side. It was a hound, gaunt and terrible; it was a snake, scaled and foul; it was a man, with eyes like pits and knives for its fingers. It wouldn't hold still, every time he looked its shape seemed to change, and each shape was worse than the last, more twisted and obscene. Everything about it was lean and cruel. Its fingers were sharp, so sharp, and he looked at them and felt their caress sliding beneath his skin, tingling along the nerves, pain and blood and fire trailing behind them. It was black, blacker than black, a black that drank all light forever, and it was all shining silver too. It was a nightmare that lived in a funhouse mirror, the thing that hunts the hunters.

He could feel the evil throbbing through the glass.

"Skinner," Steven called.

The surface of the mirrors seemed to ripple and bulge, like a wave cresting on some quicksilver sea. The fog was thinning, Willie realized with sudden terror; he could see it clearer now, and he knew it could see him. And suddenly Willie Flambeaux knew what was happening, knew that when the fog cleared the mirrors wouldn't be mirrors anymore, they'd be doors, *doors*, and the skinner would come . . .

. . . sliding forward, through the ruins of his clothing, slitted eyes glowing like embers from a muzzle black as coal. He was half again as large as Willie had been, his fur thick and black and shaggy, and when he opened his mouth, his teeth gleamed like ivory daggers.

Randi edged backward, along the side of the car. The knife was in her hand, moonlight running off the silver blade, but somehow it didn't seem like very much. The huge black wolf advanced on her, his tongue lolling between his teeth, and she put her back up against the car door and braced herself for his leap.

Joe Urquhart stepped between them.

"No," he said. "Not her too, you owe me, talk to her, give her a chance, I'll make her see how it is."

The wolf growled a warning.

Urquhart stood his ground, and all of a sudden he had his revolver out, and he was holding it in two shaky hands, drawing a bead. "Stop. I mean it. She didn't have time to load the goddamned silver bullets, but I've had eighteen fucking years. I'm the fucking police chief in this fucking city, and you're under arrest."

Randi put her hand on the door handle, eased it open. For a moment the wolf stood frozen, baleful red eyes fixed on Joe, and she thought it was actually going to work. She remembered her father's old Wednesday night poker games; he'd always said Joe, unlike Barry Schumacher, ran one hell of a bluff.

Then the wolf threw back his head and howled, and all the blood went out of her. She knew that sound. She'd heard it in her dreams a thousand times. It was in her blood, that sound, an echo from far off and long ago, when the world had been a forest and humans had run naked in fear before the hunting pack. It echoed off the side of the old slaughterhouse and trembled out over the city, and they must have heard it all over the flats, heard it and glanced outside nervously and checked their locks before they turned up the volumes on their TVs.

Randi opened the door wider and slid one leg inside the car as the wolf leapt.

She heard Urquhart fire, and fire again, and then the wolf slammed into his chest and smashed him back against the car door. Randi was half into the car, but the door swung shut hard, crunching down on her left foot with awful force. She heard a bone break under the impact, and shrieked at the sudden flare of pain. Outside Urquhart fired again, and then he was screaming. There were ripping sounds and more screams and something wet spattered against her ankle.

Her foot was trapped, and the struggle outside slammed her open door against it again and again and again. Each impact was a small explosion as the shattered bones grated together and ripped against raw nerves. Joe was screaming and droplets of blood covered the tinted window like rain. Her head swam, and for a moment Randi thought she'd faint from the pain, but she threw all her weight against the door and moved it just enough and drew her foot inside and when the next impact came it slapped the door shut *hard* and Randi pressed the lock.

She leaned against the wheel and almost threw up. Joe

had stopped screaming, but she could hear the wolf tearing at him, ripping off chunks of flesh. *Once you get started it's hard to stop*, she thought hysterically. She got out the .38, cracked the cylinder with shaking hands, flicked out the shells. Then she was fumbling around on the front seat. She found the box, tipped it over, snatched up a handful of silver.

It was silent outside. Randi stopped, looked up.

He was on the hood of the car.

Willie *changed*.

He was running on instinct now, he didn't know why he did it, he just did. The pain was there waiting for him along with his humanity, as he'd known it would be. It shrieked through him like a gale wind, and sent him whimpering to the floor. He could feel the glass shard under his ribs, dangerously close to a lung, and his left arm bent sickeningly downward at a place it was never meant to bend, and when he tried to move it, he screamed and bit his tongue and felt his mouth fill with blood.

The fog was a pale thin haze now, and the mirror closest to him bulged outward, throbbing like something alive.

Steven sat against the wall, his blue eyes bright and avid, sucking his own blood from the stumps of his fingers. "Changing won't help," he said in that weird flat tone of his. "Skinner don't care. It knows what you are. Once it's called, it's got to have a skin." Willie's vision was blurry with tears, but he saw it again then, in the mirror behind Steven, pushing at the fading fog, pushing, pushing, trying to get through.

He staggered to his feet. Pain roared through his head. He cradled his broken arm against his body, took a step toward the stairs, and felt broken glass grind against his bare feet. He looked down. Pieces of the shattered mirror were everywhere.

Willie's head snapped up. He looked around wildly, dizzy, counting. Six, seven, eight, nine . . . the tenth was broken. Nine then. He threw himself forward, slammed all his body weight into the nearest mirror. It shattered under the impact, disintegrated into a thousand pieces. Willie crunched the biggest shards underfoot, stamped on them until his heels ran wet with blood. He was moving without thought. He caromed around the room, using his own body as a weapon, hearing the sweet tinkling music of breaking glass. The world turned into a red fog of pain, and a thousand little knives sliced at him everywhere, and he wondered, if the skinner came through and got him, whether he'd even be able to tell the difference.

Then he was staggering away from another mirror, and white hot needles were stabbing through his feet with every step, turning into fire as they lanced up his calves. He stumbled and fell, hard. Flying glass had cut his face to ribbons, and the blood ran down into his eyes.

Willie blinked, and wiped the blood away with his good hand. His old raincoat was underneath him, blood-soaked and covered with ground glass and shards of mirror. Steven stood over him, staring down. Behind him was a mirror. Or was it a door?

"You missed one," Steven said flatly.

Something hard was digging into his gut, Willie realized. His hand fumbled around beneath him, slid into the pocket of his raincoat, closed on cold metal.

"Skinner's coming for you now," Steven said.

Willie couldn't see. The blood had filled his eyes again. But he could still feel. He got his fingers through the loops and rolled and brought his hand up fast and hard, with all the strength he had left, and put Mr Scissors right through the meat of Steven's groin.

The last thing he heard was a scream, and the sound of breaking glass.

Calm, Randi thought, *calm*, but the dread that filled her was more than simple fear. Blood matted his jaws, and his eyes stared at her through the windshield, glowing that hideous baleful red. She looked away quickly, tried to chamber a bullet. Her hands shook, and it slid out of her grip, onto the floor on the car. She ignored it, tried again.

The wolf howled, turned, fled. For a moment she lost sight of him. Randi craned her head around, peering nervously out through the darkness. She glanced into the rearview mirror, but it was fogged up, useless. She shivered, as much from cold as from fear. *Where was he?* she thought wildly.

Then she saw him, running toward the car.

Randi looked down, chambered a bullet, and had a second in her fingers when he came flying over the hood and smashed against the glass. Cracks spiderwebbed out from the center of the windshield. The wolf snarled at her. Slaver and blood smeared the glass. Then he hit the glass again. Again. Again. Randi jumped with every impact. The windshield cracked and cracked again, then a big section in the center went milky and opaque.

She had the second bullet in the cylinder. She slid in a third. Her hands were shaking as much from cold as from fear. It was freezing inside the car. She looked out into the darkness through a haze of cracks and blood smears, loaded a fourth bullet, and was closing the cylinder when he hit the windshield again and it all caved in on her.

One moment she had the gun and the next it was gone. The weight was on her chest and the safety glass, broken into a million milky pieces but still clinging together, fell across her face like a shroud. Then it ripped away, and the blood-soaked jaws and hot red eyes were right there in front of her.

The wolf opened his mouth and she was feeling the furnace heat of his breath, smelling the awful carnivore stench.

"You fucker!" she screamed, and almost laughed, because it wasn't much as last words go.

Something sharp and silvery bright came sliding down through the back of his throat.

It went so quickly Randi didn't understand what was happening, no more than he did. Suddenly the bloodlust went out of the dark red eyes, and they were full of pain and shock and finally fear, and she saw more silver knives sliding through his throat before his mouth filled with blood. And then the great black-furred body shuddered, and struggled, as something pulled it back off her, front paws beating a tattoo against the seat. There was a smell like burning hair in the air. When the wolf began to scream, it sounded almost human.

Randi choked back her own pain, slammed her shoulder against the door, and knocked what was left of Joe Urquhart aside. Halfway out the door, she glanced back.

The hand was twisted and cruel, and its fingers were long bright silver razors, pale and cold and sharp as sin. Like five long jointed knives the fingers had sunk through the back of the wolf's neck, and grabbed hold, and pulled, and the blood was coming out between his teeth in great gouts now and his legs were kicking feebly. It yanked at him them, and she heard a sickening wet *crunching* as the thing began to *pull* the wolf through the rearview mirror with inexorable, unimaginable force, to whatever was on the other side. The great black-furred body seemed to waver and shift for a second, and the wolf's face took on an almost human cast.

When his eyes met hers, the red light had gone out of them; there was nothing there but pain and pleading.

*His first name was Mike*, she remembered.

Randi looked down. Her gun was on the floor.

She picked it up, checked the cylinder, closed it, jammed the barrel up against his head, and fired four times.

When she got out of the car and put her weight on her ankle, the pain washed over her in great waves. Randi collapsed to her hands and knees. She was throwing up when she heard the sirens.

". . . some kind of animal," she said.

The detective gave her a long, sour look, and closed his notebook. "That's all you can tell me?" he said. "That Chief Urquhart was killed by some kind of animal?"

Randi wanted to say something sharp, but she was all fucked up on painkillers. They'd had to put two pins in her ankle and it still hurt like hell, and the doctors said she'd have to stay another week. "What do you want me to tell you?" she said weakly. "That's what I saw, some kind of animal. A wolf."

The detective shook his head. "Fine. So the chief was killed by some kind of animal, probably a wolf. So where's Rogoff? His car was there, his blood was all over the inside of the chief's car, so tell me . . . *where the fuck is Rogoff?*"

Randi closed her eyes, and pretended it was the pain. "I don't know," she said.

"I'll be back," the detective said when he left.

She lay with her eyes closed for a moment, thinking maybe she could drift back to sleep, until she heard the door open and close. "He won't be," a soft voice told her. "We'll see to it."

Randi opened her eyes. At the foot of the bed was an old man with long white hair leaning on a gold wolf's head cane. He wore a black suit, a mourning suit, and his hair fell to his shoulders. "My name is Jonathan Harmon," he said.

"I've seen your picture. I know who you are. And what you are." Her voice was hoarse. "A lycanthrope."

"Please," he said. "A werewolf."

"Willie . . . what happened to Willie?"

"Steven is dead," Jonathan Harmon said.

"Good," Randi spat. "Steven and Roy, they were doing it together, Willie said. For the skins. Steven hated the others, because they could work the change and he couldn't. But once your son had his skin, he didn't need Helander anymore, did he?"

"I can't say I will mourn greatly. To be frank, Steven was never the sort of heir I might have wished for." He went to the window, opened the curtains, and looked out. "This was once a great city, you know, a city of blood and iron. Now it's all turned to rust."

"Fuck your city," Randi said. "What about Willie?"

"It was a pity about Zoe, but once the skinner has been summoned, it keeps hunting until it takes a skin, from mirror to mirror to mirror. It knows our scent, but it doesn't like to wander far from its gates. I don't know how your mongrel friend managed to evade it twice, but he did . . . to Zoe's misfortune, and Michael's." He turned and looked at her. "You will not be so lucky. Don't congratulate yourself too vigorously, child. The pack takes care of its own. The doctor who writes your next prescription, the pharmacist who fills it, the boy who delivers it . . . any of them could be one of us. We don't forget our enemies, Miss Wade. Your family would do well to remember that."

"You were the one," she said with a certainty. "In the stockyards, the night my father . . ."

Jonathan nodded curtly. "He was a crack shot, I'll grant him that. He put six bullets in me. My war wounds, I call them. They still show up on x-rays, but my doctors have learned not to be curious."

"I'll kill you," Randi said.

"I think not." He leaned over the bed. "Perhaps I'll come for you myself some night. You ought to see me, Miss Wade. My fur is white now, pale as snow, but the stature, the majesty, the power, those have not left me. Michael was a halfbreed, and your Willie, he was hardly more than a dog. The pureblood is rather more. We are the dire wolves, the nightmares who haunt your racial memories, the dark shapes circling endlessly beyond the light of your fires."

He smiled down at her, then turned and walked away. At the door he paused. "Sleep well," he said.

Randi did not sleep at all, not even when night fell and the nurse came in and turned out the lights, despite all her pleading. She lay there in the dark staring up at the ceiling, feeling more alone than she'd ever been. He was dead, she thought. Willie was dead and she'd better start getting used to the idea. Very softly, alone in the darkness of the private room, she began to cry.

She cried for a long time, for Willie and Joan Sorenson and Joe Urquhart and finally, after all this time, for Frank Wade. She ran out of tears and kept crying, her body shaking with dry sobs. She was still shaking when the door opened softly, and a thin knife of light from the hall cut across the room.

"Who's there?" she said hoarsely. "Answer, or I'll scream."

The door closed quietly. "Ssssh. Quiet, or they'll hear." It was a woman's voice, young, a little scared. "The nurse said I couldn't come in, that it was after visiting hours, but he told me to get to you right away." She moved close to the bed.

Randi turned on her reading light. Her visitor looked

nervously toward the door. She was dark, pretty, no more than twenty, with a spray of freckles across her nose. "I'm Betsy Juddiker," she whispered. "Willie said I was to give you a message, but it's all crazy stuff . . ."

Randi's heart skipped a beat. "Willie . . . tell me! I don't care how crazy it sounds, just tell me."

"He said that he couldn't phone you hisself because the pack might be listening in, that he got hurt bad but he's okay, that he's up north, and he's found this vet who's taking care of him good. I know, it sounds funny, but that's what he said, a vet."

"Go on."

Betsy nodded. "He sounded hurt on the phone, and he said he couldn't . . . couldn't *change* right now, except for a few minutes to call, because he was hurt and the pain was always waiting for him, but to say that the vet had gotten most of the glass out and set his leg and he was going to be fine. And then he said that on the night he'd gone, he'd come by *my* house and left something for you, and I was to find it and bring it here." She opened her purse and rummaged around. "It was in the bushes by the mailbox, my little boy found it." She gave it over.

It was a piece of some broken mirror, Randi saw, a shard as long and slender as her finger. She held it in her hand for a moment, confused and uncertain. The glass was cold to the touch, and it seemed to grow colder as she held it.

"Careful, it's real sharp," Betsy said. "There was one more thing, I don't understand it at all, but Willie said it was important. He said to tell you that there were no mirrors where he was, not a one, but last he'd seen, there were plenty up in Blackstone."

Randi nodded, not quite grasping it, not yet. She ran a finger thoughtfully along the shiny sliver of glass.

"Oh, look," Betsy said. "I told you. Now you've gone and cut yourself."